Praise for John M

"A gripping tale of a Nazi U-boat crew . . . a compelling and stereotype-breaking story. . . . Characters are brought to life, and with the combination of action, war, love, and betrayal, it's hard for any reader not to find something of interest in this World War II drama."

—*Soundings*

"A truly exquisite saga of the human condition in war, told from the point of view of a U-boat crew and their many adversaries. John Mannock delivers heart-stopping action, superb characterizations, richly idiomatic dialogue, beautiful scenic descriptions, amid an absorbing story tapestry woven from raw savagery and noble courage, passion and compassion, irony and poignancy. An unforgettable read, *Iron Coffin* deserves a place beside classics like *Das Boot* and *A Farewell to Arms*."

—Joe Buff, author of *Tidal Rip*

"*Iron Coffin* is *not* your typical WWII submarine novel. Intense, dramatic, and surprising, you'll find yourself rooting for both sides—the captain and crew of a critically damaged U-boat off the coast of Louisiana, and the American salvage diver forced to help them. With this work, Mannock has exposed the human face of war in a battlefield not before explored—the bayous of Cajun country in 1943. An epic page-turner to the very last dive."

—*H. Jay Riker, author of the *Silent Service* series

"John Mannock brings a new twist to an old story. This is a story of men and ships, honor in battle and honorable enemies." —Douglas De Bono, author of *Firewall*

"First-time author Mannock . . . takes the unusual approach of casting the crew of a German U-boat as the book's protagonists. . . . Readers will appreciate this book's unusual perspective and true-to-life characters."

—*Publishers Weekly*

Also by John Mannock

**IRON COFFIN
THE SEN-TOKU RAID**

Published by New American Library

THE WAR MOUNTAINS

JOHN MANNOCK

A SIGNET BOOK

SIGNET
Published by New American Library, a division of
Penguin Group (USA) Inc., 375 Hudson Street,
New York, New York 10014, USA
Penguin Group (Canada), 90 Eglinton Avenue East, Suite 700, Toronto,
Ontario M4P 2Y3, Canada (a division of Pearson Penguin Canada Inc.)
Penguin Books Ltd., 80 Strand, London WC2R 0RL, England
Penguin Ireland, 25 St. Stephen's Green, Dublin 2,
Ireland (a division of Penguin Books Ltd.)
Penguin Group (Australia), 250 Camberwell Road, Camberwell, Victoria 3124,
Australia (a division of Pearson Australia Group Pty. Ltd.)
Penguin Books India Pvt. Ltd., 11 Community Centre, Panchsheel Park,
New Delhi - 110 017, India
Penguin Group (NZ), cnr Airborne and Rosedale Roads, Albany,
Auckland 1310, New Zealand (a division of Pearson New Zealand Ltd.)
Penguin Books (South Africa) (Pty.) Ltd., 24 Sturdee Avenue,
Rosebank, Johannesburg 2196, South Africa

Penguin Books Ltd., Registered Offices:
80 Strand, London WC2R 0RL, England

First published by Signet, an imprint of New American Library,
a division of Penguin Group (USA) Inc.

First Printing, March 2006
10 9 8 7 6 5 4 3 2 1

Copyright © McKinnaMedia, Inc., 2006
All rights reserved

Ⓟ REGISTERED TRADEMARK—MARCA REGISTRADA

Printed in the United States of America

Without limiting the rights under copyright reserved above, no part of this
publication may be reproduced, stored in or introduced into a retrieval system, or transmitted, in any form, or by any means (electronic, mechanical,
photocopying, recording, or otherwise), without the prior written permission
of both the copyright owner and the above publisher of this book.

PUBLISHER'S NOTE
This is a work of fiction. Names, characters, places, and incidents either are
the product of the author's imagination or are used fictitiously, and any resemblance to actual persons, living or dead, business establishments, events, or
locales is entirely coincidental.
   The publisher does not have any control over and does not assume any
responsibility for author or third-party Web sites or their content.

If you purchased this book without a cover, you should be aware that this
book is stolen property. It was reported as "unsold and destroyed" to the
publisher and neither the author nor the publisher has received any payment
for this "stripped book."

The scanning, uploading, and distribution of this book via the Internet or via
any other means without the permission of the publisher is illegal and punish-
able by law. Please purchase only authorized electronic editions, and do not
participate in or encourage electronic piracy of copyrighted materials. Your
support of the author's rights is appreciated.

The War Mountains is dedicated to my father, A. J. McKinna, of Alida, Saskatchewan—professional baseball player, World War II combat flier, renowned neuro-ophthalmologist and surgeon, professor emeritus of medicine, Fellow of the Wilmer Institute at Johns Hopkins—who passed on suddenly in January of 2003. In addition to his many professional accomplishments, he was a beloved husband, father, brother, teacher, and friend.

I know you're not gone, Dad—just gone on ahead. Leading the way for the rest of us, as usual.

—J. M.

Author's Note

This novel is set aginst the backdrop of World War II and is based upon historical fact. Utmost care has been taken in executing the necessary research regarding the weapons, vehicles, and field equipment of sixty-plus years ago, but alas, nobody's perfect. Therefore, as usual, for any and all technical inaccuracies, intentional or otherwise, I claim Sanctuary in the Cathedral of Fiction.

—J. M.

Acknowledgments

Many thanks to my longstanding literary agent,
and one of the best in the business,
Jimmy Vines,

and

my excellent editor at NAL,
Mark Chait.

Also

special thanks to my father-in-law,
Master Sergeant Richard E. Durrance, USMC (ret.),
for editorial advice on military content.

And of course

all my love and gratitude to my wife,
Teresa, for whom all my books are written.

Contents

PART ONE

PART TWO

Part One

"*The enemy of my enemy is my friend.*"

—Arab proverb

"*What's past is prologue.*"

—William Shakespeare

Prescript

I put my youngest grandson on the bus this morning. He trembled slightly as he mounted the boarding steps and my hand slipped from his shoulder, but he was a brave boy and gave no other indication of his trepidation. At the tender age of eleven, who would not tremble at the prospect of embarking upon an unfamiliar journey? He smiled at me through the window as the bus pulled away, and to give him courage I smiled back.

I sit now beneath the awning of a streetside café, in the shade where the sun cannot leach away what little strength remains in my eighty-six-year-old body. It is burden enough to carry the permanent pain of old wounds. The coffee is good; hot, black, and sweet. Likewise the tobacco in my cigarette. It is Turkish and roughly cut. Out of long habit I have rolled the cigarette myself. The smoke is dark, heavy, and with each inhalation produces the customary pleasing ache deep in my chest.

The bus is long gone, and the street is full of people. People hurrying here and there to complete their business before the morning sun reaches its full, burning height. No one notices an old man sitting alone at a shaded table in a streetside café, sipping coffee and smoking.

Waiting.

3

Prologue

There had always been tales of unholy things that lurked in the dark alpine forests of central Yugoslavia. Tales of werewolves and trolls, of vampires and witches, of goblins and dwarves and strange forest people with eyes in their shoulders that let them peer at you sideways. Ancient things that were aligned with the old gods and the devil, and were kept at bay after nightfall by locked doors and well-stoked fireplaces and the power of the Eastern Orthodox priest in his church in the center of the village.

The girl was fifteen years old and long past believing in spooks and spirits and monsters, as did young children and many of the old people. The great forest of the Majevica Mountains had always been a place of solace and refuge to her, not a wilderness to be feared. Most country folk were superstitious and silly, she had long since decided, and she did not wish to be either of those things. When she was older, she would live in one of the grand cities like Belgrade or Bucharest, where people were educated and notions of fell creatures never entered their heads.

That was why she was so completely unprepared, as she carried a pail of milk from the barn to her grandfather's house one cold autumn afternoon, to see monsters burst from the forest edge, down the slope from the village, and begin to charge up the incline.

They were huge and black and hideous and they climbed the steep slope between the trees and the first houses with terrifying speed, churning up clods of dirt and shale and grass and snow. They roared and snarled as they came loping upward, belching black fumes. The girl screamed and dropped the milk and ran for the house.

The small band of Partisans—perhaps thirty—had been using the village as a temporary base for nearly a week; an out-of-the-way sanctuary from which to scout the common border areas between Serbia, Bosnia, and Croatia. Experienced guerillas, they were accustomed to having enemies all around. But this time, despite all their precautions, they were taken completely off guard.

The Partisan commander was the first man to throw open a window in one of the exposed houses and prop a captured machine gun up on its sill. His eyes grew wide as he focused on the two gigantic German tanks that were literally *speeding* up a forty-degree incline toward him, the long barrels of their main turret cannons bouncing like obscene antennae as they lunged over the rough terrain.

"Impossible," he whispered. Then, at the top of his voice: *"Fire, comrades, fire!"*

As if by way of contradiction, the cannon of the nearest tank belched smoke and flame. The huge shell crashed into the house occupied by the Partisan commander and exploded, obliterating the tiny dwelling and its occupants. In the house next door, huddled with her grandmother and grandfather, the girl who had dropped the milk pail screamed. The three Partisans firing submachine guns from the corner window pulled back with shouts of panic and scrambled toward the front door. At the opposite end of the room, the girl and her grandmother and grandfather held each other more tightly and prayed.

The massive black hull of the second Nazi tank smashed through the side of the house at high speed. There was an awful, shattering impact; a horrendous cacophony of bursting masonry, splintering timber, and roaring machinery; a blur of churning, crushing steel treads. And glaring out from the side of the tank's immense turret, the black war cross and diabolical death's-head emblem of the SS. The three Partisans shrieked as, just beyond the ruined house, the tank ran them down.

The two tanks thundered down the little village's single road, veering left and right in order to smash through house after house, firing their cannons and machine guns indiscriminately. The population of the village, terrorized, driven from their homes, fled before the tanks like sheep before wolves. Some dashed for the forest, but most followed the remaining Partisan soldiers to the village square and into the Eastern Orthodox church—a white-painted wooden structure with a single steeple—that stood at its center. The few who tried to flee through the square and down the westward road leading out the far side of the village encountered six German half-tracks loaded with SS troops. The troopers disembarked and began to advance in a tight skirmish line, firing relentlessly into frantic men, women, and children.

The giant tanks wheeled in tandem, crushing dead and half-dead bodies, and clanked to a halt side by side, facing the front door of the church. The SS troops continued their sweep through the village from its western end, killing every living thing in their path. Several dozen SS gathered behind the tanks, eyeing the church and waiting.

The fifteen-year-old milkmaid, whose name was Magda, had fled, at the urging of her grandmother and grandfather, down the same slope the tanks had ascended only minutes before. She reached the cover of the trees just as SS troops entered the ruined house where her grandmother and grandfather still crouched, holding each other. There was a long burst of machine-gun fire. Magda shrieked, pressing her hands to her ears, and half blinded by tears and terror, fled deeper into the gloom-filled alpine forest.

Three of the surviving Partisans were in the belfry of the steeple with sniper rifles. They knew they were about to die, had long expected to, and so were resigned rather than afraid. There was fear only where there was hope.

"Those are Tiger tanks of some kind," one of the Partisans muttered as he changed clips in his rifle. He gazed down into the square below. "How did they charge up the slope like that? Any other tank would have toppled over backward or skidded out."

"Yes, it would be nice to know exactly what new type of infernal German machine is killing us," one of his companions—an educated, acerbic type—said. He glanced down past the stock of his rifle, which was trained on the SS troops crouching behind the tanks. "Oh, perfect. Now here's the damned priest."

The doors of the church opened and the priest came out. He was gray haired, with a long beard, and wore a white cassock trimmed with gold. A short gold cape was draped over his shoulders, and he held a Bible clutched to his chest with one hand. The other hand he raised slowly, palm out, as he stared from beneath fierce, bushy eyebrows at the tanks and soldiers.

"This is a holy place!" he shouted in Serbo-Croatian. His voice was the deep, commanding instrument of an experienced orator. "A house of God. Those within its walls are granted sanctuary, protected by Almighty God!"

A tall SS officer in a peaked cap stepped out from behind one of the idling tanks, leveled a rifle borrowed from one of his men, and shot the priest through the chest. As the cleric pitched forward down the steps of his church, the officer returned the rifle and picked up an intercom phone handset from a metal box on the side of the tank.

"Destroy the church," he said into the mouthpiece. He hung the phone back on its cradle, closed the door of the box, and turned to face his men. "Kill everyone left alive once the tanks are done, and burn the wreckage. Remember: you are *Handschar* of the SS! These are Serbs—Christian infidels who have murdered your kinsmen by the thousands! Hiding with them are atheistic Communist Partisans who would kill you for believing in any god at all! Now is your chance to be rid of an entire nest of these murderous brigands for good!"

A ragged cheer went up from the SS troops; some brandished their weapons overhead. The officer grinned and turned back to the church.

"Good-bye, Herr Sturmbannfuehrer," the acerbic Partisan in the church steeple said, and squeezed the trigger. His rifle cracked.

The bullet hit the death's-head insignia on the front of the grinning Nazi major's peaked cap and blew off the back of his head in a red mist. In the same instant, the cannons of both Tiger tanks blasted point-blank at the church. The hulking war machines bucked on their chassis with the recoil. The church disintegrated in a whirl of shattered planking and timber. The steeple collapsed on itself in a cloud of smoke, dust, and flying detritus.

The tanks kept pouring cannon shells and machine-gun fire into the ruins of the church for a full five minutes. When they were done, the SS troops moved in and with torches and gasoline set fire to the heaps of wood, rubble, and bodies.

The afternoon wore on, and as evening drew near, two of the troopers wandered out to the half-demolished house where the milkmaid Magda and her grandmother and grandfather had lived. The brutal work of soldiering done for the day, the two SS men took a few minutes for personal concerns. Setting down their weapons and removing the field-gray fezzes they wore, both extracted small mats from their packs and unrolled them on patches of clean, dry ground.

Then, like the good Muslims they were, the two troopers of the SS Division Handschar knelt on their mats and began to pray toward the east.

Chapter One

"Permit me to quote from your letter of January 20, 1941," Adolph Hitler remarked, his dark gaze fixed on the face of the Muslim cleric occupying the fine leather armchair on the opposite side of his office desk. "Written a mere three years ago. Addressed to me personally."

Haj Amin al-Husseini, the exiled Grand Mufti of Jerusalem, recrossed his legs beneath his black robe and nodded pleasantly, meeting the Fuehrer's stare with the neutral calm of the seasoned politician. "Please," he said, motioning gracefully with his right hand.

On either side of him, seated in matching armchairs like the remaining two opposing points of a four-direction compass, SS chief Heinrich Himmler and Abwehr head Wilhelm Canaris stirred slightly. Rivals in the Nazi hierarchy, the two men detested each other. In the presence of the Fuehrer, neither showed it.

Hitler cleared his throat, held up a single page, and began to read:

" 'Your Excellence! England, that bitter and cunning enemy to the true freedom of the Arab nation, has never ceased to forge fetters in which to enslave and subjugate the Arab peoples—either in the name of a deceitful League of Nations or by the expression of perfidious and hypocritical humanitarian feelings, but with the actual aim of effecting her imperialist machinations, which are camouflaged by so-called principles of democracy and of deceitful internationalism.

" 'With regard to Palestine: His Excellency is well aware of the problem faced by this country, which has suffered greatly from the deceitful actions of the English. They have attempted to place an additional obstacle before the unity and independence of the Arab states by abandoning Palestine to world Jewry, this dangerous enemy whose secret weapons—finance, corruption, and intrigue—have traditionally been aligned with British bayonets. For twenty years, we have confronted these various forces face-to-face. Full of unvanquished faith, the Arabs of Palestine fought with the most elementary means. The Palestinian problem united all of the Arab states in a mutual hatred of the English and Jews. If mutual hatred is a prerequisite for national unity, it can be said that the problem of Palestine hastened this unity. From an international point of view the Jews owe allegiance to England in the hope that after her victory she will be disposed to help them realize their dreams in Palestine and in the neighboring Arab countries. Any aid to be extended by the Axis to the Arabs in their war against Zionist aspirations will, therefore, cause the Jews to lose heart. The Jews of America especially, seeing their dream of a Zionist homeland in Palestine shattered to pieces, will be so discouraged that they will cease to support Britain with such enthusiasm and will reconsider their position before the catastrophe.' "

Hitler paused to sip from a glass of water, eyeing the mufti as he did so, and continued:

" 'Your Excellency, the warm sympathy felt by the Arab peoples toward Nazi Germany and the Axis is an established fact. No propaganda can refute this truth. The Arab peoples are ready to serve our common enemies their just deserts, and to take their place enthusiastically alongside the Axis in order to fulfill their part in bringing about the well-deserved defeat of the Anglo-Jewish coalition.

" 'Your Excellency! Arab nationalism is greatly indebted to you for raising the Palestinian question in your impressive speeches on a number of occasions. I wish to reiterate my gratefulness to His Excellency and to assure him that the Arab peoples feel friendship, sympathy, and a great admiration for His Excellence, the great Fuehrer, and the courageous German people.

" 'I close with wishes for long life and happiness for His Excellency, and for a shining victory and prosperity for the great German people and for the Axis in the near future.' "[1]

Hitler laid the paper down on the desktop. "Most eloquent," he said, gazing at al-Husseini again. "Not to mention verbose. I take it you still stand by these lofty sentiments, Haj Amin."

The white-turbaned cleric responded with a placid nod. "Of course, Your Excellency. One does not abandon the righteous course simply because the path temporarily becomes rocky. Difficult or not, the road of virtue is still the correct road."

Odd, Canaris thought, that an Arab-Muslim leader from Palestine, born in Jerusalem, would have such a Caucasian—even Aryan—appearance. Haj Amin al-Husseini's eyes were a pale gray-green, his neatly trimmed beard reddish blond. His complexion was not particularly dark. His nose was large and straight, dominating his face, but his chin was weak, receding, and his mouth had no set to it—only a pulpy softness that suggested either intellectual smugness or a surfeit of inner tranquility.

Or maybe both. Canaris's shrewd eyes flickered over the mufti from head to toe once more. Haj Amin al-Husseini, although he was certainly no fool, had at least one tedious mannerism that seemed to be congenital in political leaders whose authority was religion based: when answering straightforward questions he tended toward the cryptic, decorating his replies with theological platitudes or mundane parables. Canaris had observed the same affectation in a rogues' gallery of popes, cardinals, archbishops, abbots, ministers, rabbis, imams, and other assorted denominational riffraff, and it bored him to no end. Not because he had anything against so-called spiritual leaders, particularly—they had their place in the food chain—but because on a personal level it smacked of one-upmanship; the spiking of a reply with a mini lecture that inferred the respondent had special access to higher knowledge.

"Indeed, my Fuehrer," Himmler contributed, "Haj Amin has been instrumental not just in the formation of the SS Division Handschar, but in numerous other mobilization projects involving Muslim peoples in the disputed territories of the Third Reich—"

"All of which have come to naught," Canaris cut in dryly. He waved a hand as the bald, pudgy Reichsfuehrer-SS turned to stare, buglike, at him through his pince-nez. Very few people dared interrupt Heinrich Himmler in the middle of a sentence. "The proposal that Arab-Muslim intelligence and army units under Haj Amin be created and deployed to help secure Italian and German conquests in North Africa—abandoned in early 1943. Attempts by Haj Amin to inspire the Muslim leaders of Tunisia, Morocco, and Libya to join the fight against the—what was the phrase? 'American-Jewish-English aggression'— completely without result."

"My Fuehrer," Himmler countered, displaying the

chilling absence of emotion that was his trademark, "no one could have foreseen that the Italians—with whom the mufti was working at the time—would give up the ghost so easily, first in Africa, and then in their own homeland.[2] Admiral Canaris is conveniently forgetting Haj Amin's many successful contributions to the sacred goals of the Third Reich. As I have just stated, he was responsible for inspiring numerous Bosnians, Croatians, and even Palestinians to join our exclusively Muslim SS Division Handschar—which even as we speak is achieving considerable success in Yugoslavia against the communist Tito's Partisan vermin."

Canaris rubbed his upper lip. The mufti was sitting with his eyes on the wall just above Hitler's head, the very picture of placid benevolence, listening to Himmler further laud his efforts on behalf of the Handschar division. Haj Amin looked very pleased with himself. But pudgy Heinrich the malignant superbureaucrat, the admiral knew, was in reality not singing the mufti's praises as much as his own. The all-Muslim SS Division Handschar—"Scimitar"—was a pet project of Himmler's, a logical extension of his bizarre racial theories and ongoing fascination with supposed historical Aryan connections to the Islamic peoples of Yugoslavia, Turkey, Persia, and Arabia.

In early 1941, with the state of Yugoslavia distintegrating into a snake pit of internecine rivalries even as the SS and Wehrmacht armored divisions of the Third Reich smashed southward to overrun the country, the Muslims of the newly repartitioned territories of Croatia, Serbia, Montenegro, and Bosnia and Herzegovina had found themselves subjected to genocidal attacks from militant Roman Catholic and Eastern Orthodox forces—their former Yugoslav countrymen exacting a blood toll for ancient ethnic and religious hatreds. Murdered by the thousands, Yugoslavia's Muslims had seen less of a threat in the invading Germans than in their own erstwhile fellow citizens.

Recognizing in their desperate situation an opportu-

nity, Himmler had proposed the formation of the SS
Division Handschar—conveniently loosening his rigid
Teutonic racial qualifications for entry into the SS—
and with the help of Haj Amin al-Husseini's recruitment efforts had filled its ranks with twenty thousand
Muslim volunteers and willing conscripts, primarily
from war-torn Bosnia. The premise was that after
fighting under German command to destroy the
threatening elements within the former Yugoslavia—
Serbian patriots, Croatian rebels, and Tito's Partisans,
among others—the Muslims would be permitted to
live in safety and stability in their own state within
the Greater German Reich. As a side benefit, the
complete elimination of Yugoslavia's Jews, whom no
one—Serb, Croat, Catholic, Byzantine, Muslim, or
modern atheist—wanted anything to do with, could be
accomplished.

Canaris's subtle gaze drifted to Hitler. The great
Fuehrer, savior of Germany, was not looking well
these days. After the debacle of Operation Barbarossa—
the failed invasion of Russia—the Nazi regime's string
of exhilarating conquests had turned into a series of
costly defeats, and the war situation at present was
deteriorating on nearly every front. Hitler's face was
deeply lined, troubled, and he had developed a nervous tic in the muscle of his right cheek. In earlier
days, he had been engaging, spontaneous, positive.
Now he was paranoid and borderline delusional, given
to fits of rage and bouts of black depression. And yet
he still held power, still operated with a megalomania-
cal cunning and personal omniscience that kept his
best generals, despite their better judgment, subservi-
ent to his will. An amateur tactician at best, Hitler's
impractical strategies routinely took precedence over
the carefully considered plans of the most competent
military professionals in the Third Reich. It was an
unworkable situation that would lead Germany to disaster. *God help us,* Canaris thought, *if our sins are*

not so great already that whatever god may be listening has decided to wash his hands of us altogether.

Himmler was still talking. "Just recently, my Fuehrer, Haj Amin played a key role in preventing the emigration—by that I mean *escape*—to Palestine of over four thousand dangerous Bulgarian Jews. He did so by counseling our good soldier Eichmann, in charge of their disposition, to ship them to concentration camps instead. In so doing, he provided direct support for our goal of a Final Solution to the Jewish problem in Europe."

That was more than Canaris could bear. "The dangerous Bulgarian Jews you speak of," he stated coldly, "were four thousand children, most of them orphans, who were about to vacate Europe permanently by fleeing to Palestine via Turkey and Syria. It would have made good operational sense for Eichmann simply to let this particular crop of noncombatant Jews remove themselves from Reich-controlled territory— he is all but overwhelmed by the sheer enormity of the task of eliminating every Jew in Europe—but Haj Amin, who as we all know can be very convincing, had other priorities."

The Grand Mufti turned his head slowly to look at Canaris for the first time, then blinked and smiled. "SS Obersturmbannfuehrer Adolph Eichmann is a personal friend," he said mildly. "I am more than pleased to be able to offer him my humble advice on issues of mutual interest."

"The Jewish children and their adult handlers were about to cut and run," Canaris persisted. "Not having to transport them to the camps would have freed up several trains for more pressing military uses. But Haj Amin convinced Eichmann to keep the Jews in Europe, not simply let them remove themselves from the picture. Why? Because he is more concerned with keeping fleeing Jews out of Palestine, where they could one day outnumber the Arabs and compete for political dominance, than he is with truly aiding the Third Reich in its difficult task of cleansing Europe of its Jewish infestation. To the extent that he helps us, he does so out of self-interest."

Hitler actually smiled. "Self-interest is the engine that drives politics," he said, waving a dismissive hand. "I don't have to remind an intriguer as experienced as yourself, Admiral, of that fact."

The elegant Canaris came close to scowling. "It is also the engine that drives treachery, my Fuehrer. And there is a very fine line between the two."

You should know, Himmler thought in silent retort. *No one walks it more brazenly than you.* But the Reichsfuehrer-SS said nothing and kept his expression impassive. As wily as Canaris—the aging master spy and head of Abwehr, or German military intelligence[3]— was, he seemed unconscious of the fact he was fast losing favor with Hitler, a consequence of both his own questionable intrigues and the Fuehrer's increasing suspicion of those who did not treat him with absolute deference. The halcyon days when the white-haired fox of the Abwehr could spar with the Fuehrer in conference were long gone. Now the admiral's familiarity and directness of speech were driving a wedge between him and his supreme leader, and he could not see it. All he, Himmler, head of the Black Order of the SS, had to do was stand quietly by, the embodiment of Nazi loyalty, and let Canaris dig his own grave, word by word. His inevitable downfall would leave the Abwehr rudderless, and the SD and Gestapo—the intelligence and security entities of the SS—perfectly positioned to fill the power vaccuum.

"You seem inordinately concerned with the fate of a few thousand Jews," Himmler observed, his steel-blue eyes narrowing behind his pince-nez.

"I am concerned when vital military assets such as trains are not utilized to optimum advantage!" Canaris retorted, letting an edge creep into his measured tones. He glanced at the mufti. "I am concerned when a 'friend' of the Reich, who draws substantial pay from both the German Foreign Office and the SS, *and* enjoys state-provided luxury accommodation and personal security here in Berlin, uses his influence to advance his own agenda to the detriment of his host nation."

Al-Husseini held up his hand again, patiently shaking his head. "I really must protest, Admiral Canaris."

"One would almost think you'd developed a soft spot for that particular swarm of Jewish brats," Himmler commented. "Good heavens, considering how many we've already managed to eliminate, why bother?"

Canaris's smile was steely. "I am far too old to let you put your words in my mouth, Herr Reichsfuehrer. And I stand by my analysis: these particular Jews should have been allowed to emigrate out of Europe, in order to reduce the load on our severely overtaxed supply lines and infrastructure."

Himmler snorted. "Preposterous."

Hitler's fist slammed into his desktop, bringing the exchange to an abrupt halt.

"Shall we dispense with this bickering?" he growled. His dark, sunken eyes shifted from man to man, finally coming to rest on the Grand Mufti. "Haj Amin: you are not here to answer to any charges. You are a representative of the Arab people as a whole, a valued ally, and an honored guest of the Third Reich."

Al-Husseini smiled and nodded, spreading his hands. "Thank you, Your Excellency."

"You will excuse the momentarily lively debate between Reichsfuehrer Himmler and Admiral Canaris," Hitler went on. "As heads of coexisting but separate intelligence organizations, they are understandably occasional competitors. A healthy thing—as long as both are striving for the same goal: the ultimate triumph of National Socialist Germany over its enemies." His gaze shifted and lingered on Canaris for a long moment.

"As an ally and admirer, I could not agree more, Your Excellency," Haj Amin responded. "I—"

"Good," Hitler continued, "because a problem has developed that you are in a unique position to remedy. In prior conference, Admiral Canaris has raised the issue of a decline in the morale of Reichsfuehrer Himmler's much-vaunted Handschar division. If you would elaborate, please, Admiral."

The white-haired Abwehr chief smoothly picked up the narrative. "Reliable intelligence coming to me from front-line Wehrmacht infantry and armored units in Yugoslavia, fighting alongside the SS Division Handschar, indicates a slow but steady stream of desertions by the Muslim rank and file. Some are joining Tito's Partisans—occasionally switching sides in the middle of a battle!—while others are simply forming independent bandit groups and making for the mountains of their Bosnian homeland. Apparently they have forgotten the oath of allegiance they swore to the Fuehrer and to Germany upon completion of their training."

Himmler shifted irritably in his chair. "It is essential to point out that overall the performance of the Muslim SS Division Handschar has been and continues to be outstanding. In less than a month, the division has driven the Partisans southward back across the Sava River and into the foothills of the Majevica Mountains."

"Nevertheless," Canaris continued, "the steady stream of desertions is indicative of serious internal problems within Handschar. A cancer of unreliability—"

"A slight morale issue," Himmler interrupted, "which can be addressed most effectively by—"

"Unreliability that cannot be considered acceptable in any German unit," the admiral reinterrupted, "much less a front-line combat division!"

"This is absolutely intolerable—" Himmler fumed, adjusting his pince-nez.

"*Verdammt,* enough!" Hitler's outburst was punctuated by a second crash of his fist on the desktop. There was a long pause, during which the Fuehrer drew breath and stretched his arms out at full length, palms down on the expanse of polished marble in front of him. When he spoke again, his voice had regained a measure of its familiar composure. "Come now, gentlemen, you must get along. I really cannot do without either of you." He turned to the mufti. "You can see, Haj Amin, the pressures that times such as these force upon even the oldest of colleagues. Reichsfuehrer Himmler is quite rightly protective of the reputation of his new SS Division Handschar, and is justified in his assertion that it deserves full credit for its recent—and ongoing—victories against the Partisans in Yugoslavia. Admiral Canaris, on the other hand, is quite rightly concerned with the problem of potentially traitorous or subversive elements that may linger within this otherwise effective combat division."

Hitler raised a conciliatory hand and gestured first at Himmler, then at Canaris. "Both the Reichsfuehrer and the admiral want the same thing, although they are pursuing it from different angles: the consolidation of morale within SS Division Handschar in order to guarantee the unit's continued effective deployment in Yugoslavia. This, my dear Haj Amin, is where you come in."

Al-Husseini smiled beneficently. "Of course I would be honored by the opportunity to assist the Reich in any way I can."

"Yes," Hitler said, "of course you would. Particularly since you were instrumental in organizing Handschar's internal officer corps of imams charged with the spiritual leadership of the Muslim rank and file. I need not remind you that an SS division which permits the incorporation of company-grade religious authority alongside its standard military command structure represents a considerable concession to our Muslim allies. A considerable sensitivity on the part of the Third Reich to the spiritual needs of the Muslim soldier."

Oh yes, Canaris thought fleetingly, *if there's one thing we're known for in the Third Reich, it's our sensitivity.* He shot a glance at Himmler. The Reichsfuehrer-SS was sitting in silence with his hands folded in his lap, regarding Hitler with the diffident attentiveness of a grade-school math teacher. It was truly remarkable, Canaris reflected for the thousandth time, that a man so plain, so banal in appearance, could be the repository of so much dark, sociopathic power. Heinrich Himmler would happily murder the world if in so doing he could realize his vision of absolute Aryan racial supremacy. A vision of blond Teutonic warriors and maidens frolicking in a Wagnerian paradise—a paradise free of squat, dark, inferior races such as Jews, Slavs, and Mongols.

And there he sat: squat, plump, balding, with a chin that receded even more than al-Husseini's. Like Hitler, the antithesis of the Aryan superman he so adored.

For a split second, Canaris was overwhelmed by desperation. Such moments of internal panic, unfortunately, were becoming increasingly frequent. *How did things come to this?* he anguished in silent turmoil. *Why did we who should have known better follow these malevolent fanatics so far down the road to ruin?*

Haj Amin al-Husseini spoke carefully, addressing Hitler: "The SS Division Handschar is indeed a magnificent testament to the Third Reich's willingness to partner itself with brethren races. The Muslims of Yugoslavia, in return, are at this very moment proving their fealty by shedding their blood under the banners of the swastika and death's-head. The soldiers of the Islamic world are honored by the opportunity to serve in the great Nazi war machine—a machine which will ultimately be victorious in the global conflict currently underway.

"Of course," the mufti went on, "it bears mentioning that the combat utilization of twenty thousand Muslims by the Waffen-SS in Yugoslavia *relieves*, to a not-inconsiderable degree, the military recruitment pressure on the German male population. The Third Reich can no longer fight a multifront war using only its purely Teutonic native sons; the manpower requirements are too great. In this regard, Germany truly needs the continued cooperation of the Muslim peoples, if it wants to keep its armies fighting at full strength."

Ah, Canaris thought, *there it is.* The thinly veiled threat. The allusion to withdrawal of support.

"With regard to the morale of the Muslim rank and file within Handschar: is it not true that the morale of soldiers is largely dependent upon the quality of their leadership? While the bulk of the division is made up of Muslims, including the imam officer corps, the ranking officers are all German. Is it not possible that a certain amount of miscommunication between German officers and their Muslim soldiers is responsible for the alienation of some individuals? After all, as we have found in the past, there are some barriers of language and culture that can be difficult to overcome completely." A faint smile developed on al-Husseini's thin lips. "Perhaps the entire division should be placed under the command of Muslim officers, to avoid . . . misunderstandings."

You went too far there, my friend, Canaris thought.

Hitler's face twisted into a dark scowl. "The SS Division Handschar," he stated, "will remain exclusively under the authority of German SS officers. This is the only way the Reich can maintain the integrity of its military command structure. The imams within Handschar are charged with the duty of maintaining the spiritual health and morale of the Muslim recruits. If there is a problem of communication between the German officers and their men, that is the responsibility of the imams. That is what they are there for." He paused and leveled on al-Husseini the penetrating stare that had transfixed millions the world over. "My conclusion is that the imams have lost focus, and are neglecting to minister adequately to the unique spiritual and motivational needs of the troops under their care. The German SS officers in command of Handschar are making sound operational decisions according to German military doctrine. The division is winning in Yugoslavia. Therefore, this hemorrhaging of personnel cannot be due to disenchantment with Handschar's leadership. Rather the imams—your imams, Haj Amin—have permitted the concentration of the men upon their sworn duty to fight for the Third Reich to wander. You must put this right." Hitler glanced at Himmler. "Herr Reichsfuehrer?"

Himmler looked down fussily at his hands, which he was twisting together in his lap. "It has been decided that you, Haj Amin, should undertake a tour of SS Division Handschar in the field in Yugoslavia, for the twin purposes of inspiring the rank and file and conducting a series of lectures directed at the imam corps."

"In these lectures," Hitler said, "you will use all of your spiritual and political authority, all of your famed powers of persuasion and inspiration, to revitalize the imams' approach to maintaining the combat morale of the Muslim troops—by which I mean a prompt and aggressive reaffirmation of these soldiers' sworn commitment to fight loyally for the Third Reich until its operational goals are achieved."

The Grand Mufti's placid smile was somewhat tighter. "In the field? Your Excellence, while I have every confidence in the combat capabilities of SS Division Handschar, I respectfully remind you that the situation in Yugoslavia is rather . . . fluid. The Partisans are guerillas, and guerilla warfare is by its very nature unconventional—not to mention unpredictable. No field position can be considered entirely secure. Were I to undertake a front-line tour, I would be placing myself at considerable risk. I am nearly fifty years of age, and while I served as an officer in the Turkish Ottoman Army during the Great War, my capacity for dodging bullets has long since deserted me." Al-Husseini licked his lips briefly. "Not that I am concerned for my own safety on a personal level," he continued, "but I must think of my position, my responsibilities as the premier international representative of the Arab-Muslim world. It is my duty to consider my own security—for who will speak for my people if something should happen to me?"

"I have a feeling someone would step up," Canaris commented, deadpan. "And as for dodging bullets during the last war, I doubt if you often found it necessary while serving as a supply officer with the Forty-seventh Turkish Brigade in the Black Sea area, stationed as you were many miles from the front."

Al-Husseini glanced at the head of Abwehr in barely concealed annoyance, at the same time chiding himself internally. It was dangerous to embellish the truth about one's personal history in the presence of Admiral Wilhelm Canaris. The wily old intelligence chief had files on everyone.

"Your security, of course, will be the responsibility of the SS," Himmler declared. "In addition to your own personal bodyguard, you will have a hand-picked escort drawn from the ranks of both the Waffen-SS and the Gestapo. True professionals, whom I myself will select."

"As to the risk involved," Hitler said, sitting back in his chair and folding his arms across his chest, "I remind you that you are under considerable risk right here in Berlin. The British Secret Service and the Jewish Agency in Cairo have each had several cracks at you during the past two years, and they are unlikely to stop trying. It is entirely due to the vigilance of the intelligence and security services of Third Reich that you have not been assassinated already." The Fuehrer paused. "Of course, we are only too glad to be able to extend such protection to our valued allies. . . . Those who continue to cooperate and work with us as we strive toward our ultimate victory."

Al-Husseini, Canaris noted, was not slow to take Hitler's unspoken meaning. But the Palestinian was reluctant to appear unsettled by the inference that his protection might be removed. Straightening in his armchair, he adopted an air of affronted dignity.

"Your Excellency," the mufti said, speaking with deliberate precision, "I reiterate: I must consider the risks involved in venturing into the contested regions of Yugoslavia, for my life is not my own but an instrument to be used—and preserved—for the benefit of my people. I am not at liberty to leave the Arab-Muslim world, at this pivotal point in history, suddenly bereft of its most capable advocate."

"That would be you," Canaris remarked.

Al-Husseini shifted in his seat. "Of course. It is a fact. And therefore, while I would be willing to evaluate the possibility of conducting a series of lectures for the imams of SS Division Handschar in some secure, occupied location such as Prague, for example, or Budapest, I must reject the notion of traveling into the front-line areas of Yugoslavia. Particularly since there *are* no front lines to speak of—only a generalized and continually shifting combat zone characterized by interminable hit-and-run engagements and the occasional large-scale battle."

The mufti folded his hands in his lap and looked at Hitler looking at him. The Fuehrer's eyes seemed to have sunk even farther into their dark sockets.

"Perhaps," Himmler said uneasily, "an accommodation could be reached. The Serbian city of Belgrade is currently under occupation, and is quite secure. It is much closer to Handschar's area of operations. It would be a simple matter to arrange for the division imams to rotate into Belgrade to meet with Haj Amin—"

"Belgrade is a suitable place from which to *start* a motivational tour," Hitler stated, "but all personnel of SS Division Handschar will remain on duty in the field. Their uninterrupted presence in the foothills and higher elevations of the Majevica Mountains, in pursuit of Tito and his Partisans, is absolutely critical to the success of our military initiative to secure Greater Yugoslavia, once and for all, for the Reich." He glowered at the mufti again, then glanced at a small wooden clock on the corner of his desk. "It is late, gentlemen. We will adjourn for the evening. Haj Amin: I am certain that, upon reflection, you will see the vital necessity of this proposed tour of SS Division Handschar. I am confident that you will reconsider your position."

"I do not think so, Your Excellency," al-Husseini replied. "As I have pointed out, my life does not belong to me but to—"

"Your people," Hitler finished. "Yes, I know." He rose to his feet behind his desk. "And as *I* have just pointed out, I am confident that over the next several days you will reflect and reconsider." The Fuehrer clasped his hands behind his back and gave both Himmler and Canaris a cursory nod. "Gentlemen."

He turned on his heel, and as he stalked across the room toward a side door, Himmler got hurriedly to his feet, came to attention, and snapped off a straight-arm Nazi salute. "Heil Hitler!"

Canaris, moving more slowly, merely stood up. He did not salute or speak. When the oaken door closed behind the exiting Fuehrer, he collected his briefcase, donned his old naval cap, and turned to al-Husseini, who was still sitting languidly in his armchair, swathed in his cleric's robes.

"Good evening," he said. He raised his eyes and caught Himmler glaring impotently at him. "Herr Reichsfuehrer."

Without waiting for or even expecting a reply, Admiral Wilhelm Canaris wheeled and departed Adolph Hitler's Reichs Chancellery office through its double main doors.

*   *   *

The old master spy walked briskly through the magnificent main gallery of the Chancellery building, his heels clicking on its polished marble flooring. Designed by Nazi architect Albert Speer, the long hall, like its parent edifice, was a study in strength and elegance—vaultlike spaciousness defined by marble, gilt, and stone. Berlin's high temple of National Socialism. For all Canaris noticed its splendor, he might have been walking through an abandoned coal mine.

As usual in the wake of an important meeting, his mind was awhirl with fresh data: new orders, technical details, personal impressions. And his razor-sharp intellect, out of lifelong habit, was automatically replaying, sorting, analyzing, and evaluating this new material. Storing it in a vast mental archive of potentially useful information—information that was his greatest weapon.

The trouble was, since about 1940—or quite possibly much earlier—Admiral Wilhelm Canaris's conflicts with his own conscience, starting with a deep-seated moral despair about his current position and that of the German nation as a whole, inevitably intruded upon the straightforward intellectual exercise of getting his facts organized. Simple facts no longer, they were nuggets of ever more discouraging information tainted by the dark phantoms of his own worsening depression. He was acutely aware of the problem but could do nothing about it. Objective analysis and subjective worry had become inseparable.

Himmler: a ghoul. A soulless *bourgeois* with a pathological need to elevate himself at any cost; to define for himself a place in history based upon race supremacy and murder. A *chicken farmer*, for the love of God. And one currently simmering with outrage at Canaris's meddling in the affairs of the SS Division Handschar, at his manuevering of Haj Amin al-Husseini into conflict with Hitler.

As usual, the Reichsfuehrer-SS, arguably the second most powerful man in Nazi Germany and a lethal adversary, would bear watching. Even the head of Abwehr could not assume total immunity from Himmler's vindictive orchestrations. Fortunately—and despite his worry Canaris came close to smiling at the thought—he had a rather damning file on Pudgy Heinrich the Chicken Farmer. Just as he'd had on SS Obergruppenfuehrer Reinhard Heydrich, the one-time SD intelligence chief, race supremacist, and murderer of Jews whose dirty little secret was that he himself had Jewish blood—not to mention homosexual predilections. That had been a useful file. But useful no longer, however. In May 1942, Heydrich had been assassinated near Prague by Czech resistance fighters.

Canaris paused beneath a huge red wall tapestry bearing the Nazi swastika, and lit a cigarette to calm his nerves. The habit provided little comfort these days, but it was better than nothing. Smoke drifted up through the still air of the great hall, lingering in front of the crooked cross. The admiral drew deeply, trying to relax even as his mind continued to work.

Haj Amin al-Husseini was a garden-variety political opportunist. While he enjoyed a certain undeniable stature in the Arab-Muslim world, his position as spokesman was by no means as official or exclusive as he liked to claim. Canaris had looked into it. The product of a well-positioned Palestinian family that could demonstrate verifiable blood ties to the Prophet Muhammed, al-Husseini had, through astute political handling by powerful Arab friends and relatives, been appointed Grand Mufti—or religious leader—of Jerusalem in 1921 by the High Commissioner of British Palestine, at the tender age of twenty-six. Since that heady day nearly a quarter of a century ago, he had added many layers to his public persona: rabid Arab-Palestinian nationalist, equally rabid anti-Zionist and anti-Semite, fomenter of abortive revolts against British rule in both Palestine and Iraq—for which the British had summarily exiled him from his homeland—and now aider and abetter, for his own ulterior purposes, of the marauding Nazi regime. He was on record as saying that when the Germans finally reached the Middle East, they should allow the Arabs to "solve the Jewish problem in Palestine and the other Arab states in accordance with the interests of the Arabs, by the same methods which were used to solve this problem in the Axis countries."[4]

Canaris exhaled smoke, confident that he had recalled the quote exactly. This Amin al-Husseini, spiritual leader though he might be, was really nothing more than a classic, wandering agent provocateur—a political orphan combing the international landscape for allies. A manipulator in search of an advantage that would return him to power.

What made him so dangerous, and what had not been lost on Reichsfuehrer-SS Heinrich Himmler when he had first enlisted al-Husseini's help in forming the SS Division Handschar, was that the high-profile mufti was the most likely conduit through which the world's 350 million Muslims could be brought into the Nazi fold as cocombatants against the British, Americans, and other Allied nations. The success or failure of Handschar as a fighting unit was the test case by which the Islamic world would judge the expedience of throwing in its lot, militarily, with Nazi Germany. Not to mention the prudence of continuing to follow the lead of Haj Amin al-Husseini.

A massive influx of Muslim manpower into the Wehrmacht and Waffen-SS would mean a perpetuation of the Nazi regime. An indefinite extension of the Nazi Party's stranglehold on political and military power in Germany and throughout Europe. And a prolonging of the most destructive war in history.

Canaris crushed the smoldering butt of the cigarette beneath his shoe and drew a long breath. God, the things he had to do, to say, in order to maintain his position within the glorious Third Reich—to keep the gangsters at bay and the wolves from his throat. Sprinkle his conversation with appalling phrases like "Jewish infestation." Show no concern for untold masses of murdered men, women, and children—only for the logistical problems associated with their transport and handling. Take occasional food and drink with creatures like Heinrich Himmler, Joseph Goebbels, Martin Bormann, and that fat, discredited ass Hermann Göring without becoming nauseous and throwing up on the spot.

The worst of it was that he couldn't stay and he couldn't go. As head of Abwehr he was forced to issue atrocious, immoral orders on a regular basis—but at the same time he was in a position to frustrate some of the worst excesses of the Nazi regime. How many Jews had he saved from the concentration camps by sending them on supposed spying missions to Allied countries, knowing full well they would never return? He'd lost count. How much vital information had he disseminated to the Allies, taking on for himself—at dreadful risk—the role of double, triple, *quadruple* agent? Enough to fill a small library.

Canaris walked toward the main doors of the Reichs Chancellery, continuing to brood. As he approached, a black-uniformed SS trooper, resplendent in silver gorget, polished black helmet, and bright red swastika armband, gave the straight-arm salute and opened the door.

Absently the admiral flipped his hand up as he walked out into the light evening rain that was wetting down the cobblestones and pavement of the Willemstrasse. As the door closed behind him, he could not suppress a short, bitter laugh. How innately hypocritical, he mused, that out of reflex he would return the signature Nazi salute in kind. Despite his high position within Hitler's regime, he had never even joined the Nazi Party.

No, he could not stay and he could not go. The pressure of trying to dismantle the Nazi power base from within—before his beloved Germany was subjected to total ruin—was slowly killing him; he often felt less than one short breath away from a fatal heart attack. But he could not simply abandon his powerful position and disappear. As cold and ruthless as he often had to be in order to fulfill his role as Germany's greatest spymaster, whoever came after him would certainly be a diehard Nazi—and a hundred times worse.

He put another cigarette between his lips and lit it, shielding the flame from the misty rain with cupped hands. *You are a walking contradiction, Canaris,* he told himself. *A damned enigma. And quite possibly damned to hell.*

But at least, he thought as he began to make his way along the Willemstrasse, *you're going to have plenty of company.*

Exactly one hour later, in a dilapidated apartment on one of central Berlin's seediest side streets, an old man with an unkempt mop of shaggy gray hair and an equally unkempt handlebar mustache sat hunched in a simple wooden chair, an ancient woolen overcoat pulled around him, listening intently to the muted sounds—broken phrases in English, French, and German—that seemed to be coming from a large radiator beneath the room's single window. Heavy blackout curtains covered the window's narrow panes of grimy glass, permitting not even the meager light from the lone candle perched on the sill to escape into the street. Britain's Royal Air Force had not yet turned its devastating night-bombing capability against Berlin—the high-flying Lancasters were concentrating on industrial centers like Hamburg and Dresden—but it would not be long now.

The old man leaned forward, his head almost on his knees, and reached in between the pipes of the radiator with two fingers, adjusting something. The droning, monotone sounds became imperceptibly louder. German technology had not yet come up with a way to jam the BBC's continuous flooding of the European airwaves with Allied radio programming—including the hourly recitation of encoded messages intended for the resistance fighters and special agents who were operating everywhere on the embattled continent.

"And now"—the dulcet tones of the British announcer seemed incongruous with the desperate wartime atmosphere into which they were being broadcast—"a message for our friends within Germany itself: *Mary had a little lamb, its fleece was white as snow. Mary had a little lamb, its fleece was white as snow.*"

Pause.

"Jack has a brand new car. Jack has a brand new car."

Pause.

"The black lyre plays a solo nocturne. The black lyre plays a solo nocturne."

The old man started violently, nearly losing his seat on the chair.

"Next messages to come in one hour. And now let's listen to the swinging sounds of Benny Goodman and his orchestra as they perform their marvelous number 'Stompin' at the Savoy'. . . ."

The old man reached between the pipes of the radiator and turned off the hidden radio. Then he heaved himself up out of the wooden chair, gathering his bulky, threadbare overcoat around him, and headed for the door of the apartment.

From the spacious rear seat of the Daimler touring car, Haj Amin al-Husseini took a moment to examine the partial reflection of the driver's face in the windshield rearview mirror. The helmeted SS trooper behind the wheel did not once look away from the road, though an increased stillness in his already rigid expression suggested that he was well aware of the mufti's perusal. The Daimler cruised around a sharp turn, rocking gently on its soft suspension, and the driver's youthful Teutonic features—immaculately pale and hard planed—disappeared from the mirror.

Al-Husseini looked briefly out through the rain-slicked bulletproof glass of the left rear side window, then glanced at the two Germans sitting opposite him in the luxury passenger compartment. His plainclothes Gestapo bodyguards—a young Hauptsturmfuehrer named Julius Neurath and a lesser rank identified only as Grohl—continued to study the upholstery of the car's floor and roof liner, respectively, looking humorless, professional, and bored.

Neurath was a stereotype: a slender, blond mixture of effeminacy, toughness, and arrogance that was the very definition of the Nazi *Übermensch*, or superman. Grohl, on the other hand, was a neckless, swarthy beast of a man who was wider across the shoulders than three Neuraths put together. The backs of his huge hands were covered in black hair, and his lower jaw was immense—a massive, squared-off mandible that made the rest of his features appear far too small for his face. Both Gestapo men wore suits, knee-length overcoats, and wide-brimmed fedoras, the hats soaked with rain and pulled low over the brow.

Al-Husseini shifted uncomfortably. You never knew with Europeans. He had seen many Englishmen and Jews who looked just like these two. Plants and traitors were everywhere—even, he did not doubt for a moment, within the ranks of the dreaded Gestapo. That was why he never traveled anywhere without being accompanied by Mustapha Snagi.

He looked sidelong at the fourth man in the passenger compartment, who was sitting next to him on the forward-facing bench seat. Mustapha Snagi appeared to be dozing, arms crossed and chin on his chest. Haj Amin al-Husseini knew otherwise.

His personal manservant and bodyguard never seemed to sleep at all—only slip into a kind of conscious trance that apparently sufficed to refresh and rejuvenate him. Snagi—a Macedonian Muslim with numerous relatives in Palestine—was al-Husseini's constant shadow, sworn to protect him with his life. Jowly and black bearded, of middle height and medium build, the twenty-five-year-old manservant was altogether unremarkable in appearance—an effect that was amplified by his ill-fitting gray suit and the water-stained brown rain cape that he wore around his shoulders like a large, dirty blanket. The grubby ensemble was topped off by a purple fez, tassel dangling, that was nestled on top of his generous head of dark curls.

Mustapha Snagi smacked his lips in his apparent doze, and al-Husseini saw Neurath's pale eyes shift onto the rival bodyguard in distaste. Grohl did likewise, looking like a bad-tempered ogre. The mufti smiled faintly. The two Gestapo men had little use for Snagi, who never spoke to them, and who exhibited behavior they did not understand—such as bedding down on the outer doorstep of any room in which his master happened to be quartered for the evening. It was quite clear that they regarded him as some kind of subhuman, dismissable curiosity—a misperception arising from the fact that they had never seen Mustapha Snagi in action.

The front and rear seats of the touring car were separated by a sliding glass partition, which was open. Neurath twisted his head sideways and spoke over his shoulder impatiently to the driver: "What's taking so long tonight, Beckmann? Road repair?"

The SS trooper's helmet bobbed in response. "*Jawohl,* Herr Hauptsturmfuehrer. Crews are out replacing damaged cobbles. Several of the streets along our usual route are blocked off. I've had to take two detours already."

Agitated, Neurath tapped nicotine-stained fingers on the sleeve of his coat. "How much farther to the hotel?" Al-Husseini did not permit smoking in the close confines of the Daimler, and it had been nearly half an hour since Neurath's last cigarette.

"If I can take the next left, only two more miles, Herr Hauptsturmfuehrer," Beckmann replied. "Perhaps five minutes."

"Hurry it up, man."

"*Jawohl,* Herr Hauptsturmfuehrer."

Mustapha Snagi raised his swarthy head and opened his eyes as the touring car swayed through a left-hand turn and accelerated. He and Grohl stared at each other across the passenger compartment for a long moment. Snagi finally terminated the pointless confrontation by setting his chin back on his chest and closing his eyes again.

The Daimler bounced elegantly over a set of streetcar rails and began a wide turn to the right. A large black edifice, seven stories tall, appeared in the rain-streaked windshield. The building's numerous windows emitted no light, but the main entrance was illuminated by the soft glow of two curbside pedestal lamps. A canopy-style awning extended from the entrance to the street, providing some rain protection for anyone arriving or departing by car.

"The Hotel Jürgenplatz, Herr Hauptsturmfuehrer," Beckmann said.

"About time," Neurath muttered. He sat up and began to peer intently out the windows of the Daimler, examining the darkened street. "All clear on your side, Grohl?"

The oversized Gestapo agent took a moment to answer. "*Ja,*" he grunted.

Neurath nodded. "All right, then." He leaned forward, opened the rear door, and stepped out onto the curb. Even as he reached for his cigarette case, his eyes were automatically scanning the immediate surroundings. In the arch of the hotel's main entrance, at the top of a short flight of marble steps, a liveried doorman was standing. Neurath caught his eye, recognized him. It was the usual weeknight attendant—one who correctly knew not to approach a guarded dignitary's car without first being beckoned.

Neurath bent his head to light his cigarette as Grohl began to exit the Daimler. As a result the wide brim of his fedora prevented him from seeing the silent bicyclist come gliding down the street out of the darkness. By the time Neurath straightened, inhaling deeply, the rider was beside the car's front bumper.

Several things happened simultaneously. Mustapha Snagi threw himself on top of al-Husseini, forcing him down onto the rear seat and covering his master's body with his own. Hauptsturmfuehrer Julius Neurath bit his cigarette in two and clawed inside his left lapel for his shoulder-holstered Walther P-38 automatic pistol. Agent Grohl, moving with uncanny speed for so large a man, twisted out of the Daimler, banged his head on the door frame, and dropped to one knee on the curb. And the old man on the bicycle, shaggy gray hair and bulky overcoat flying, bent low and with one hand bowled a spherical object about the size of a grapefruit under the car.

"Get—" Neurath screamed. It was as far as he got.

A fiery explosion kicked the rear end of the Daimler four feet into the air. All of the vehicle's tires and bulletproof windows blew out in the same instant. The curbside pedestal lamps flanking the hotel entrance shattered like twin prisms of ice.

Only the two inches of steel armor plate lining the underside of the specially built limousine saved Snagi and al-Husseini from being cremated or killed by concussion. That same armor plate redirected the main force of the blast out laterally from beneath the Daimler, catching the kneeling Grohl and throwing him back into Neurath. Grohl's misfortune was Neurath's salvation. The slender Hauptsturmfuehrer landed hard on his back on the lower stairs of the hotel entrance, the shrapnel-riddled body of his much larger companion on top of him. Incredibly, Neurath was unhit.

But he was winded and dazed, his vision blurred and his ears ringing. Gasping for breath, he shoved

Grohl's limp, torn body to one side and staggered to his feet. Off balance, disoriented, he steadied himself against the stone railing of the hotel stairs and got his Walther out of its shoulder holster just as Snagi and al-Husseini lurched out of the twisted, burning Daimler. Snagi had one arm around his master, supporting him, as the pair stumbled toward the hotel entrance. A second or two later, Beckmann forced open his jammed front door and reeled out onto the sidewalk, minus his helmet. His close-cropped blond hair was smoking, and the right side of his face was black.

"Inside!" Neurath yelled, waving the mufti and his bodyguard past with his pistol. A sudden billow of acrid smoke stung his eyes, and when it cleared, he saw the old man approaching at the run. . . . Pulling something from beneath his flapping overcoat . . .

Neurath jerked up his Walther. The old man raised his own pistol, aiming at al-Husseini from less than fifteen feet away. Neurath pulled the trigger of his weapon. The usually reliable P-38 jammed.

The old man fired four times in rapid succession—*crackcrackcrackcrack!* On the top step of the hotel stairs, Mustapha Snagi interposed his body between al-Husseini and the would-be assassin. One slug went wide. The other three hit Snagi in the back as he drove his master forward through the glass doors of the entrance and into the Hotel Jürgenplatz's main lobby.

Cursing, Neurath dropped the jammed Walther and dove on top of Grohl, groping for the dead agent's weapon. As he did so, Beckmann opened fire with his own sidearm, from a kneeling position beside the wrecked Daimler. One of his flurry of shots struck the old man high in the right shoulder, spinning him around.

Deftly the old man switched his pistol to his left hand, snapped off two quick rounds at Beckmann—

which missed but sent the driver sprawling—and
sprinted off down the darkened street.

"Get him!" Neurath shrieked, apoplectic. *"With
me, Beckmann!"*

Jerking up Grohl's Walther, he fired several shots
at the dodging, ducking assailant and took off in hot
pursuit, with Beckmann on his heels.

Neurath was young and fast on his feet, so it came
as something of a surprise to him that he did not
appear to be closing the distance on the old man after
nearly a full minute of flat-out running. Beckmann, fit
and approximately the same age as he, was twenty
yards behind and laboring to keep up. But the old
man was able—somehow—to match Neurath's best
pace.

The Gestapo agent cursed, frustration and fury
boosting his already soaring adrenaline level, and
willed his legs to move faster. Three sets of rapidly
pounding footfalls, interspersed by ragged gasps,
echoed through the empty, blacked-out streets. The
crack of a pistol split the night as Beckmann tried
another shot. But no lights flickered on in darkened
windows, no doors opened to reveal the curious. In
Berlin, as in all of the Third Reich, no one dared draw
attention to themselves when the Gestapo were on
the hunt.

The old man, some forty yards ahead, was approaching another intersection. Instinct told Neurath
that his quarry was about to make a sharp right
around the corner of an upcoming bank and continue
on down the crossing street. Halting abruptly, he
raised his Walther in both hands, took steady aim,
paused his breathing, and fired.

He thought he saw the old man stagger slightly as
he cut around the corner of the bank and out of sight.
A hit! Neurath felt a surge of vicious jubilation. He
half turned as Beckmann caught up and passed him
on his left shoulder.

"I got him!" Neurath panted, breaking into a run again. "The swine won't be able to move so fast with a bullet in his—"

The old man reappeared suddenly around the corner of the building, firing rapidly from a distance of less than twenty feet. Beckmann, slightly in the lead, went down with a cry. Neurath dove into the gutter behind a parked Volkswagen truck. Several slugs punched into the vehicle's side panel. Neurath rolled away, getting a face full of backed-up sewer water. As he scrambled around the street side of the truck, he could hear Beckmann yelling incoherently and returning fire.

He reached the driver's door, threw his arm up on the hood of the truck, and emptied his Walther at the corner of the bank. Granite chips and dust flew. But when the percussive echoes of his rapid-fire volley faded away, the old man was nowhere to be seen.

Beckmann staggered to his feet, grimacing, and leaned heavily on the hood of the truck, changing clips in his pistol. Blood was soaking the left shoulder of his uniform where a bullet had clipped the top of his trapezius muscle.

Neurath ejected the spent clip from his Walther and slapped home another. "Come on, man!" he shouted, vaulting past the trunk's front bumper and onto the sidewalk. "Get after the bastard!" He did not bother to inquire whether or not Beckmann could.

The Gestapo agent skirted wide around the corner, pistol raised, in case the old man was still there. He was not. He was at the far end of the block, running diagonally through the center of the next intersection. He was moving less quickly than before, and there was an odd jink in his stride.

You're mine, Neurath thought exultantly. He glanced at the wet sidewalk in front of him as he dashed toward the end of the block. There it was. A sporadic trail of blood, mixing with the rainwater and running in slow, dark rivulets off the edge of the curb. A *lot* of blood.

The animal was badly wounded. Very soon now, it would go to ground. Neurath's mouth flattened into a sliver of a smile. This was his favorite part of the hunt—overtaking and cornering the game—because it was the most dangerous. The thrill was almost sexual.

The old man was running down the right sidewalk of the next street, skirting garbage cans and trying to keep low. Neurath sprinted off the curb and out into the intersection, keeping his eyes fixed on the fugitive. There were many narrow alleys on this street, and instinct again told him that the old man, no longer able to escape his pursuers by flight, would try to duck into one of them and hide.

As he reached the center of the intersection he heard a shout. Glancing over his shoulder, he saw a knot of black-uniformed SS troopers—security guards from the small contingent stationed inside the Hotel Jürgenplatz—advancing down the crossing street from the opposite direction. The trooper in the lead brought up a Schmeisser machine pistol and yelled at Neurath to halt.

"Nicht schiessen!" the agent bellowed, slowing and throwing up his arms. "Don't shoot! I'm Gestapo, idiot!" He gestured frantically over his shoulder. "The terrorist is getting away, damn you!"

The SS Rottenfuehrer at the head of the security squad heard *Don't shoot, idiot,* and *Damn you,* and was about to cut down the suspect in the trench coat—who was still moving away at a half-run in defiance of the order to halt—with a burst from his machine pistol when the SS-uniformed Beckmann stumbled into view. At the last second, the Rottenfuehrer reconsidered and held his fire. Then as the two figures in the intersection turned and sprinted off down the street together, he barked a command for his three comrades to follow, and broke into a run himself.

In the exchange with the Rottenfuehrer, Neurath
had lost sight of the old man. Cursing, he dodged
between two parked cars and up onto the sidewalk.
Beckmann stayed on the street, running parallel to
him. Desperately Neurath scanned the doorways and
closed-up shop fronts as they flashed by, searching for
some sign of where the old man had gone.

"Watch the alleys!" he shouted to Beckmann. "He
might have gone down—"

The crash of an overturning garbage can reverberated out of the alley they were just passing. Neurath
leaped to the side of the nearest building and flattened
himself against its rough brick, his Walther up and
ready. On the sidewalk at the front of the alley, a
large smear of blood glistened darkly.

Beckmann took up position on the opposite wall,
breathing hard. Neurath caught his eye, held up his
open palm, then leaned forward and peered cautiously
into the alley.

A flurry of shots exploded out of the black void,
chipping brick next to Neurath's face and sending him
recoiling back. Beckmann swore aloud and without
exposing his head shoved his pistol around the corner
of the building and emptied it blindly into the darkness. Recovering, Neurath did the same. More crashing of garbage cans.

At that moment, the SS Rottenfuehrer and his
three troopers arrived on the scene. Without needing
Neurath's shouted prompting, the four soldiers
spread across the entrance to the alley and opened
up with their machine pistols, saturating the narrow
passageway with fire. The shattering volley lasted
nearly fifteen seconds, until each of the four automatic weapons had exhausted its magazine. Then
there was silence.

Reloading hurriedly, the SS guards looked into the
empty blackness of the alley, then at each other. At
the walls flanking the entrance, Neurath and Beckmann crouched, waiting. Still no one spoke.

There was a sound like a piece of pipe rolling across the floor of a garage.

A smooth gray sphere, about the size of a grapefruit, rolled slowly out of the alley and onto the sidewalk. The Rottenfuehrer stared quizzically at the benign-looking object.

"Vas ist?" he muttered.

Neurath and Beckmann threw themselves back, clawing for cover, just before the custom-made rolling bomb exploded. The blast knocked the SS security guards off their feet—killing the Rottenfuehrer, mangling the arm of a second man, and stunning the remaining two.

In the aftermath of the explosion, the old man burst out of the alley—a staggering, stumbling apparition wreathed in swirls of dirty smoke. He was doubled over, one arm clamped across his stomach, his right leg dragging. His gun hand was up, swinging, as he tried desperately to fire in every direction at once.

Neurath rolled into the partial shelter of a shop doorway as several of the old man's wild shots ricocheted off the sidewalk near his feet. Beckmann was on his hands and knees, groping for his dropped pistol, when a random slug drilled through his jackboot and smashed his right ankle. He belly flopped onto the pavement with a howl.

The old man made it nearly halfway across the street when the two unscathed SS troopers opened up on him simultaneously with their burp guns. The crossfire caught him in the upper body, hammered him upright, and for a moment seemed to hold him there—a shaking, demoniac figure with flying hair and disintegrating overcoat—before propelling him backward and depositing him in crumpled heap in the gutter on the far side of the street.

Neurath rose to his feet and ran toward the downed assassin, brandishing his Walther at arm's length. He slowed as he approached the body, keeping his pistol aimed at the shaggy gray head, and gave it a vicious kick. There was no reaction.

"Ach!" Neurath spat. "Dead." He lowered the pistol in disgust and looked at one of the two SS troopers. "What can a dead man tell me? Eh?" He looked back at the corpse. "Not a damn thing." On impulse, he jerked up his Walther and fired three quick shots into the body. The two SS troopers glanced uncertainly at each other.

On the far sidewalk, Beckmann had ceased to howl and was now merely groaning, rolling from side to side on his back and clutching his shattered ankle with both hands. Neurath regarded him dispassionately for a few seconds.

"Go help my driver," he told the nearest trooper, his tone making it clear that Beckmann's agony was little more than an irritant to him, and turned back to the bullet-riddled body in the gutter.

The dead assassin was lying with his torso twisted sideways, his face turned into the curb and partly concealed. Neurath stooped down, seized the tangle of gray hair, and yanked. The body flopped over and the mop of hair came away in his hand.

Neurath blinked. But for its gray handlebar mustache, the face staring up at the starless night sky bore no marks of age. Neurath tossed the blood-soaked gray wig aside, took hold of the mustache, and pulled. It too came away easily.

The old man was not old but young—younger than he. His short hair was very dark, as were his sightless eyes and the sparse patches of stubble on his chin. He would have had trouble growing a full beard. His features were square and clean, ruggedly handsome, but with a hint of scar tissue around the brows and a slight flattening of the bridge of the nose, suggesting that at one time he might have been a boxer.

"Of course," Neurath muttered. "Of course . . ." He reached into his trench coat, withdrew a black-ivory pocket knife, and pressed a button on the handle. A five-inch stiletto blade snicked into view.

Squatting on his haunches, the Gestapo Hauptsturmfuehrer jerked open the dead man's bullet-torn overcoat, slid the knife blade under the thin leather belt securing his cheap, baggy trousers, and slashed upward. The belt parted. Another slash, and the trouser material was opened from waist to crotch.

Roughly, Neurath yanked down the corpse's trousers and undershorts, exposing the genitals. Then he sat back on his heels and nodded with grim satisfaction.

"Ah, there, you see?" he declared triumphantly, without glancing back at the SS trooper hovering near his shoulder. "Circumcised. A filthy Jew." In a sudden fit of viciousness he slashed a few times at the dead man's groin, got to his feet, snapped shut the switchblade, and put it back into his pocket. "No matter how many of these brutes we manage to exterminate, there are always a few more running around, stirring up trouble." Neurath paused to withdraw a cigarette from his case and light it. "But we'll weed them all out eventually. Do you know why?"

"No, sir," the SS trooper said quickly.

"Because we can always readily identify them," Neurath said, sounding both amused and disgusted. "Their own repulsive traditions betray them. They all cut their cocks like that." He glanced down at the desecrated body of the young man as if regarding roadkill. "Can you imagine? What a barbaric culture."

He let out a short, harsh laugh, turned on his heel, and walked away, trailing cigarette smoke. Headlights began to cast moving shadows over the walls of the surrounding buildings as several armored personnel carriers converged on the scene, engines roaring. A military ambulance pulled up beside Beckmann, who was still lying on the sidewalk. The first personnel carrier shuddered to a halt in the middle of the street, disgorging helmeted SS troops like a cascade of black-carapaced beetles.

The soldier to whom Neurath had spoken was still standing beside the assassin's body when his comrade, who had been aiding Beckmann, rejoined him two minutes later.

"What about the driver?" the first trooper asked.

The second trooper shrugged. "Hit in the ankle. Smashed to bits, it looks like. And damned painful, too. But the meat wagon boys have him now." He looked down at the dead man in the gutter. "So. A Jew. Well, we really took care of him, didn't we?" He patted the machine pistol slung around his neck and grinned.

The first trooper swallowed. "I suppose."

"What's the matter with you?" his comrade demanded. "You look pale."

Other soldiers were beginning to mill around the body. The first trooper glanced furtively over his shoulder and rubbed his fingers across his upper lip.

"You know, Horst," he muttered, his voice very low, "I'm circumcised myself. The doctor my mother took me to when I was a baby thought it was a good thing. A matter of medical hygiene."

The second trooper looked shocked. "Really?"

"Yes, really."

The second trooper stared at the first for a long moment. "How did you pass the physical to get into the SS?"

"I lied. I said it was corrective surgery for an infection. The way the doctor did it, you see, it's not that obvious. And my Aryan heritage is indisputable. The SS medical officers believed me."

The trooper named Horst shook his head. Ten feet away, several other SS soldiers began to drag off the assassin's limp body. Beside the nearest personnel carrier, Gestapo Hauptsturmfuehrer Julius Neurath was watching the proceedings with a baleful eye, smoking.

"Well, for God's sake, Willi," Horst whispered to his friend, "keep your mouth shut about it."

The orderly tiptoed up to the huge four-poster bed, laid a hand on the hunched shoulder beneath the satin coverlet, and shook gently. It was just after four thirty a.m.

"My Fuehrer," the orderly said, keeping his voice low. "My Fuehrer."

"*Mmphnng . . .*" Adolph Hitler came groggily out of his drug-induced slumber. The orderly waited. The insomnia that had plagued the Fuehrer for decades could now only be overcome by a nightly injection of sedative.

Hitler sat up, looking bedraggled and dyspeptic, and leaned back on the pillows that his orderly hurriedly rearranged against the headboard. "What is it?" he demanded, smoothing his lank forelock sideways with one hand. His toothbrush mustache twitched in irritation.

The orderly produced a telephone, cord trailing. "Admiral Canaris, my Fuehrer. He insisted it was most urgent."

Hitler smacked his dry lips and grunted. "Isn't it always, Kirchbaum?" He held out his hand. "Give it to me."

Kirchbaum relinquished the phone and departed, pulling the bedchamber doors closed behind him. Hitler rubbed his swollen, black-circled eyes.

"Obviously you have something pressing to tell me, my dear Canaris," he grumbled into the receiver.

"Good morning, my Fuehrer," Canaris replied, his voice sounding tinny and far-off. "My apologies for disturbing you this early, but there has been an interesting development, and I thought that you should be informed of it without delay."

"Go on."

"Last night," Canaris said, "the Grand Mufti was

the target of another assassination attempt. It took place at approximately eleven o'clock, outside the main entrance of the Hotel Jürgenplatz."

"Good heavens."

"Indeed, my Fuehrer. A lone operative—Jewish, apparently—who rolled a small bomb under the mufti's car and then pressed the attack with a handgun."

"How shocking," Hitler remarked. "In the very heart of Berlin. Was the mufti injured?"

"No," Canaris replied. "Through the courageous actions of his security detail he was able to escape into the lobby of the hotel. But his personal bodyguard—the Macedonian named Snagi—took three bullets in the back."

"Dead?"

"No, my Fuehrer," the admiral continued. "Oddly enough, the man was wearing a very fine vest of chain mail under his clothing—a virtual museum piece. The kind of lightweight body armor Saladin's horsemen would have worn into battle against the Crusaders a thousand years ago in the Holy Land." Canaris paused. "The bullets penetrated, but only superficially. He'll recover."

Hitler grunted. "How interesting. Any other casualties?"

"One of the mufti's Gestapo bodyguards, Grohl, was killed by the explosion of the bomb. The assassin fled. In the ensuing chase, the SS driver, Beckmann, was shot in the shoulder and ankle. An SS Rottenfuehrer who had been assigned to the hotel was killed by a second bomb, and one of his squad injured. But the assassin was eventually dispatched by Gestapo Hauptsturmfuehrer Neurath, agent in charge of the mufti's security detail—according to his own oral report on the incident."

"Mmm."

"Interestingly enough, preliminary investigation indicates that the bombs used by this Jewish operative were of the same compact, rolling design utilized by

Czech resistance fighters to assassinate Obergruppenfuehrer Heydrich back in 1942."

"You mean Czech terrorists," Hitler said.

"Of course, my Fuehrer."

"In other words," Hitler went on, "the bombs were
of British origin."

"Exactly," Canaris confirmed. "Built by the British
Secret Service. Supplied by the British Secret Service.
For all we know, the British Secret Service parachuted
the Jewish agent into Germany, just as they parachuted the Czech resistance commandos—er, *terrorists*—
into the outskirts of Prague to ambush Heydrich."

"The British, the British," Hitler muttered. "They
are the great bogeymen of the civilized world, are they
not? Working their intrigues everywhere, always, with
their confounded fingers in every pie. A nation of
warrior-pirates. If only they would join us, instead of
fighting against us. United—true Anglo and true
Saxon—we would be unstoppable."

"Unlikely, my Fuehrer," Canaris said. "But, as you
say, they are the great bogeymen—particularly as far
as our friend Haj Amin al-Husseini is concerned."

Hitler sat up straighter in bed. "Ah. He is aware
that it was a Jew, backed by the British, that nearly
got him last night?"

Canaris did not chuckle, but his tone lightened.
"Yes, my Fuehrer. I myself made him acutely aware
of that fact when I debriefed him only two hours ago."

"Elaborate please, my dear Canaris."

"He was somewhat . . . distraught, shall we say.
Shaken. While I sympathized, I took the opportunity
to point out to him that here was a brutal reminder
of the fact that he is a prime target of one of the most
relentless secret service organizations in the world—
and that it would be tragic indeed if by his own refusal
to work in harmony with his host nation, that nation
were forced to deem it impractical to continue to provide him with the personal security he so obviously
requires."

There was a long pause.

"And what was his response?" Hitler inquired.

Canaris let a beat pass for effect.

"He informs me that he has had a change of heart, and that he would be only too glad to undertake the proposed inspirational tour of the SS Division Handschar in the field in Yugoslavia—at the Fuehrer's earliest convenience."

Chapter Two

"They missed him," the British general said. "The Jewish Agency. Their operative botched it. And got himself killed into the bargain."

The broad bulldog face behind the immense Victorian desk worked for a moment, producing reams of smoke from a foot-long Havana cigar. It took several seconds for the slowly rotating ceiling fan to clear the fog. The eyes that met the general's were small and quick, leprechaun sharp and diamond bright.

"What happened?" Winston Churchill demanded.

General Sir Stewart Graham Menzies—chief of Britain's primary secret service, MI-6—shook his head. "Our information—very spur-of-the-moment, mind you—was that the mufti would be entering his new residence at the Hotel Jürgenplatz last night, accompanied by only his personal bodyguard—no Gestapo." Menzies paused. "That did not turn out to be the case. The usual contingent was with him: two agents and an SS driver."

"Damnation," Churchill growled. He plucked the

cigar out of his mouth and exhaled a long cloud of smoke. "The JA's operative didn't think to back off and wait for another opportunity once he saw that al-Husseini was sporting full security?"

"Unfortunately not, Prime Minister," Menzies replied. "You know how these Jewish agents are—just like the Poles and the Czechs. Their enthusiasm for mixing it up with the Nazis knows no bounds. I imagine the poor devil just couldn't restrain himself."

Churchill harrumphed, shifting in his chair and crossing his legs beneath the red satin day robe he preferred to wear before noon. "Not to split hairs," he grumbled, bringing the cigar to his lips again, "but the mufti isn't a Nazi. Not strictly speaking, anyway."

A grim smile creased the general's face. "A distinction which is lost upon our Hebrew friends, I'm afraid. Association is as good as affiliation, to their way of thinking. And who can blame them?"

"Certainly not I," the prime minister said. He puffed thoughtfully on his cigar. "It's just a damned shame to lose an agent who was so well placed. The follow-up information out of Berlin is interesting, but good Lord, his handlers in Cairo had him living within a stone's throw of the Reichs Chancellery."

"Yes, well," Menzies sighed, "*c'est la vie*, as de Gaulle would say."

Churchill scowled. "Please don't put me in mind of that pompous bloody *crapaud* right now, Sir Stewart." Cigar smoke billowed furiously. "Constantly maneuvering at cross purposes under our very noses to ensure that he, and only he, will run France when this is all over. Creating conflicts at every turn."

"Mmm," Menzies replied, nodding in agreement. "He's pursuing his own agenda; there's no doubt about that."

Churchill stalked around his desk and poured a splash of brandy from a crystal decanter into a large snifter. "I was speaking to Roosevelt just yesterday," he growled. "Do you know he actually recommended that I have British troops place de Gaulle under arrest and hold him in exile?"

Menzies's canny eyes widened momentarily and he smiled. "What did you tell him?"

Churchill swirled his brandy and took a sip. "I told Franklin we call de Gaulle Joan of Arc, and we're looking for some bishops to burn him."

A brief guffaw escaped the general's lips. "My word," he chuckled.

"Frustration manifesting itself in my renowned wit," Churchill went on acidly. "Obviously we can't arrest him without alienating all the Free French, and we're not about to do away with him on the sly. So we'll just have to put up with the bugger."

"Rest assured, Prime Minister," Menzies said, "for the immediate future, we'll be able to keep him at least partly under our thumb."

"Fine, fine." Churchill drained the snifter and set it down on the desk. "Now, look: have you talked to Gubbins over at SOE about this latest Yugoslavian project?"

"I have," Menzies said. "I spoke to Sir Colin yesterday. Special Operations Executive[1] confirms that Operation Handschar is a go. Personnel selected, trained, and equipped. Schedule set. The Yanks anted up with a couple of OSS agents who have been fully integrated into the team. Former Jedburgh candidates—very tough fellows."[2]

"Good," Churchill said. "With the SOE and the OSS both operating in Yugoslavia, we can't afford to risk putting Uncle Sam's nose out of joint by executing a dazzler like this without inviting the Americans in on it. Not when we're finally starting to work together effectively in the Balkans. Of course," he added ruefully, "if the whole bloody undertaking turns into a royal cock-up, they might be glad if we'd left them out of it."

"Too late," Menzies said. "They're in."

"Hmph." Churchill chewed on his cigar, circumnavigated the desk once in silence, and sat down in the leather armchair behind it. When he looked up at the chief of MI-6 again, his eyes had the enthusiastic glint of the thoroughly stimulated gamester. "All right," he said. "Now to our concept of killing two birds with one stone. You're certain the standard protocol of not informing the majority of the team of the mission's true objective has been maintained?"

"According to General Gubbins," Menzies replied, "absolutely. Only the team leader and the other necessary principal know the real goal. The other team members have been purposely kept in the dark so that if they are captured, they cannot be forced to give up information crucial to the success of the mission."

"Excellent," Churchill said, rubbing his palms together. He was enjoying himself—the supreme strategist in love with strategizing. "Two birds with one stone . . . and now maybe even three." He gazed off into the distance for a moment, then refocused on Menzies. "In light of the information that's just come out of Berlin regarding this particular deceased Jewish Agency operative *and* the newly stated intentions of the glorious Grand Mufti of Jerusalem, I want you, Sir Stewart, to take the following instructions to General Gubbins at SOE. . . ."

The young man was of medium height and athletic build, with dark, close-cropped hair, tan complexion, and a belligerent set to his jaw. Not unlike several million other highly motivated, highly trained, highly aggressive twenty-something-year-old males presently roaming England and Europe, General Sir Colin McVean Gubbins thought. He continued to watch as the young soldier in the khaki uniform and black beret strode to within the regulation three paces of his superior's desk, came to attention, and saluted smartly.

"Sergeant David Weiss reporting as ordered, sir!" he rapped out.

Gubbins touched his brow. "At ease, Sergeant." He

sat back in his swivel chair as Weiss widened his stance and clasped his hands behind his back. The warm sunlight of an uncharacteristically clear London day flooded into the office through the single large window, the blackout curtains of which had been drawn back.

The SOE chief gazed down at the personnel profile on his desk, stroking his neatly trimmed mustache, and then up at the young NCO before him. Jerusalem born, American educated, combat experience with the British Expeditionary Force in France all the way up to the Dunkirk evacuation, currently a member of the Jewish Brigade, on tap for special operations duty. The general continued to look him over, head to toe. Weiss's eyes dropped to meet his briefly, then resettled on the hand-painted portrait of an Elizabethan noble on the wall above Gubbins's head.

"Do you know who that is?" Gubbins asked mildly.

Weiss hesitated, then cleared his throat. "I'll guess Drake, sir."

"Not a bad guess." Gubbins smiled. "You have the correct era. That is Sir Francis Walsingham, the spymaster of Queen Elizabeth the First. He founded the British intelligence service—what is now MI-6—in order to deal with the threat of the Spanish Armada."

Weiss nodded slowly, trying to think of something appropriate to say. "Er . . . did it work, sir?"

Gubbins continued to stroke his mustache and appraise Weiss. "You might say that. Most of the invading armada ended up burning to ashes in the middle of the English Channel, thanks to Walsingham's advance warning and a subsequent encounter with a fleet of British fireships." He pointed a finger to the right. "Perhaps you recognize that other gentleman."

Weiss looked at the wall to his left. Another portrait hung above a set of steel-gray filing cabinets. "That's Benjamin Franklin, sir," he said. "The famous American diplomat and scientist."

"Correct," Gubbins responded. "Now, Walsingham

decorates my office because even though he is the founder of what is essentially a rival secret service as well as an allied branch of government, I admire his skill and effectiveness. But what about Franklin?"

Weiss shifted his weight from foot to foot, unsure of where all this was going. "Well, from what I understand, he was a very admirable and capable person, sir." He paused to lick his lips. "Uh . . . an inventor . . . a—a publisher . . . the discoverer of electricity . . ."

Gubbins let him struggle on to the point of failure, as if Weiss were a schoolboy singled out to recite a lesson for which he hadn't prepared. It was a tactic the general used often—the immediate maneuvering of a person into an exchange in which they were forced to play catch-up with him. Rank notwithstanding, it conditioned that person to accept the role of He Who Would Be Told, rather than He Who Would Do The Telling. Gubbins, like most effective leaders, believed in the establishment of authority on an unconscious as well as a conscious level—particularly when dealing with the independent, often headstrong young individuals who staffed his cadre of field agents.

"You are correct, Weiss," Gubbins remarked, gazing across the room at the portrait of the cherub-faced older man with the long white hair, bemused expression, and wise, fathomless eyes. "Franklin was all of those things. A scientist, inventor, publisher, administrator, celebrity diplomat—one of the most famous men of his age." The general looked at Weiss again. "He was also one of the greatest spies who ever lived. Before he ever got around to being one of the Founding Fathers of the United States of America, he was a founder of the Secret Committee of Correspondence— the secret service of the original Thirteen Colonies. He helped to run guns, influence and bribe world leaders, establish a spy network in Europe, and originate codes and cyphers—all the while hiding in plain sight as one of the most visible guest celebrities in France. Truly remarkable."

Weiss shook his head. "I had no idea Benjamin Franklin was a spy, sir," he said.

"Which, of course, is definitive proof of how good he was at it," Gubbins remarked. "Great spies are never known as such. At least not in their lifetimes. Franklin's been dead for one hundred and fifty years, and people still think of him as the charmingly rustic colonial physicist out flying his kite in a thunderstorm—not as America's first spymaster."

"Yes, sir," Weiss said. He waited, fixing his gaze on Walsingham again.

"We all have role models in life," Gubbins went on. "These two men from the past are a couple of mine." He paused, studying the young sergeant from beneath salt-and-pepper brows. "You see, Weiss, in addition to being brilliant and idealistic, they were also cunning and realistic. They wished for a perfect world—as they defined it—but in the absence of that were quite capable of doing what was necessary for the greater good of their respective countries—capable, in other words, of doing the dirty work."

Weiss looked down from Walsingham's portrait. "Ruthless, sir?"

Gubbins smiled. "Yes. That would be another way of putting it. The fact is, Weiss, in their business—our business—the willingness to indulge in lies, deception, manipulation, duplicity, and betrayal in the name of the greater good is a heroic quality. Frankly, not everyone is capable of it. You understand that, don't you?"

"Yes, sir," Weiss answered. "The end justifies the means."

Gubbins lifted an eyebrow. "Precisely. And of course, anyone—*anyone*—in our business can find himself in the position of having to use lies or manipulation, even with respect to allies, to achieve an immediate goal. To serve the higher motive. Some people object to this, Weiss. What's your personal opinion? Could you do it if you had to?"

Conversely, the general thought, *anyone in our business can also find himself in the position of having been lied to or manipulated.*

"I could, General," Weiss replied. "I believe that if it's necessary to deceive someone—even an ally—in order to accomplish a mission, then it has to be done."

"Excellent," Gubbins said. Then he added almost casually, "Could you respect the higher motive, even if it was done to you?"

The general watched as instantly Weiss's guard went up. The young sergeant hesitated, then cleared his throat before answering. "If it was a higher motive I believed in, sir, then yes. If I could see the necessity." He met Gubbins's gaze directly and held it. "I beg your pardon, General, but are you trying to give me a warning?"

The head of SOE chuckled and rocked back in his chair. "Oh, heavens, no, Weiss. Nothing like that. This is merely a theoretical discussion. You see, my boy, we have to flesh out a special operations team scheduled to drop into Yugoslavia four days from now—a key member has suddenly taken ill—and I'm thinking of replacing him with you. You have the necessary qualifications, which we'll go into in a minute, but my primary concern is that you understand that in taking part in a mission in Yugoslavia, you will be entering one of the most confusing, internally divided, treachery-filled combat theaters of this entire global war. In order to accomplish its mission, your team will not only have to liaison with Tito's Partisans, but navigate safely past a host of rival groups—Chetniks, Ustashe, and the like—who are all battling each other for future control of the country even as they fight, and in some cases collaborate with, the occupying Nazis.

"There is essentially a vicious civil war going on in

Yugoslavia," Gubbins continued, "in tandem with an equally vicious war against the Nazi invaders. A more dangerous, backstabbing situation you will not find anywhere." He smiled. "Hence my fatherly little lecture about the need to nurture an appreciation for the tactics of duplicity and manipulation. You're about to jump into a place where you can trust no one—not even if he presents himself as a friend. Do you follow?"

Weiss nodded, relaxing somewhat. "Yes, sir. I do."

Gubbins stroked his mustache. "Good. And of course, I could simply order you to report to the team. But like all SOE endeavors, this is exceptionally hazardous duty. On key missions, I prefer to offer my men the courtesy of declaring themselves." The general paused, his shrewd gaze very steady. "So, Sergeant Weiss, knowing no more than the little I've already told you: are you up to this?"

Weiss blinked at the portrait of Walsingham, then spoke: "May I ask one question, sir?"

"Go ahead."

"Will I have the opportunity to kill Germans on this mission?"

Gubbins smiled again slowly. "Most definitely, Sergeant."

Weiss smiled in return. "Then yes, sir. I am up to it. . . . Most definitely."

"Good," Gubbins said. "By the way, have you ever hunted gamecock?"

"Sir?"

"Gamecock," the general repeated. "The wild fowl of the moors. Have you ever had an opportunity to hunt them in the field?"

Weiss cleared his throat, taken off guard again. "Well, yes sir, I have, actually. With an officer acquaintance of mine whose family owns a country estate up near the Scottish border."

"Wily little buggers, aren't they? Evasive."

"Yes, sir."

"Did you enjoy hunting them?"

"Yes, sir. Very much."

"And how did you do?"

"I believe we knocked down several dozen between the two of us in one afternoon, sir." Weiss's brow furrowed and he looked directly at his superior. "I beg your pardon, sir, but why are you asking me this? It seems an odd question."

Gubbins waved a hand. "Oh, it's just something Prime Minister Churchill mentioned. He saw you on the SOE range the other day, was impressed with your marksmanship and said you had the look of a hunter." The general smiled enigmatically. "He just wondered in passing if you'd ever tried your hand at gamecock."

Later that day, precisely at tea time, SOE head General Sir Colin McVean Gubbins was sitting comfortably in a velvet-and-mahogany armchair in the parlor of the prime minister's official residence at 10 Downing Street. To his right was MI-6 head General Sir Stewart Graham Menzies, on his second residence visit of the day, studiously adding milk to his bone china cup of Darjeeling. To his left, in front of the parlor's tall bay window, Winston Churchill was pacing quietly back and forth, hands clasped behind his back, smoking. Gubbins was reminded of an old, restless lion.

On the richly upholstered davenport next to Menzies sat two American officers. One was Gubbins's U.S. counterpart—Colonel Joseph Haskell, head of SO, or Special Operations. The other was a handsome, silver-haired man in his midfifties who exuded the confident, aggressive air of the successful Wall Street lawyer he was. General William "Wild Bill" Donovan had been many other things in his spectacularly active life: thrice-wounded World War I veteran, Medal of Honor winner, international businessman and gatherer of intelligence, New York State gubernatorial candidate, confidante of presidents from Wilson through

Roosevelt, and now, by executive order, founder and head of the Office of Strategic Services—the OSS, parent organization of Haskell's SO.

There was a sixth man in the room—a tall, slender civilian in his early sixties with a full head of snow-white hair, an immaculately tailored suit, and the distinguished air of a retired bank director. He sat somewhat apart from the others, legs crossed with his intertwined fingers resting on one knee. He appeared to be examining the weave of the expensive Persian rug that covered the parlor floor.

"Where the hell are they?" Churchill grumbled. He pulled a pocket watch from his waistcoat and consulted it. "I'm five minutes fast, but they should have been at the front door by now."

As if on cue, a dull chime sounded through the residence, followed by a low muttering of voices from the entrance foyer. Shortly thereafter a uniformed aide entered the parlor and came to attention.

"Major Merritt and Captain Throckmorton are here, Mr. Prime Minister," he said.

"Ah, good." Churchill slipped the watch back into his waistcoat and beckoned with his cigar. "Thank you, Hopkins. Send them right in."

"Sir."

As the aide departed, Churchill sat down in the thronelike armchair that dominated the room, and recut the dead end of his cigar. "A faulty roll, this," he growled to no one in particular. "Poor draw. You'd think at the price of these things the bloody Cuban who made it would have taken a little pride in his work."

Donovan smiled. "How often do you get a bad Cohiba, Mr. Prime Minister?" he asked.

Churchill chuckled as he stuck a wooden match and put it to the cigar's newly trimmed end. "Well, General," he replied, "admittedly not often." His sharp eyes, amused, flicked up to meet Donovan's. "Not so long ago I was grateful when a Cohiba of any description made it past the Atlantic U-boat packs and into England. I must be a bit testy today. Perhaps I'm feeling my age."

Donovan's smooth attorney's manners slipped effortlessly into gear. "Not so, Mr. Prime Minister," he said. "You remain your usual charming and imperturbable self, I assure you."

Churchill grinned past his cigar. "It's easy to see why you did so well on Wall Street, General."

Donovan shrugged good-naturedly.

The aide returned and ushered two officers in British uniform into the room. The first, who wore the rank insignia of major, was a well-proportioned six-footer with the lean look of an athlete. He removed his peaked cap and tucked it under his arm in one motion, revealing close-cropped auburn hair. His clean-shaven face seemed permanently tanned and windburned, as if he had spent his entire life out of doors in harsh weather, and exhibited that quality peculiar to the seasoned combat soldier of looking both young and old at the same time—a physical age of approximately thirty in combination with a much greater age of experience.

He locked his heels together and saluted. "Major Walter Merritt and Captain Duncan Throckmorton reporting as ordered, sir."

The second man, a rather weedy-looking individual of perhaps thirty-five with a gaunt, deeply lined face, limp blond hair, and an air of upper-class dissipation about him, also came to attention and saluted, much more casually. To Donovan, the contrast in personal styles between the two officers was striking. Merritt exuded the quiet, controlled lethality of the trained commando—a kind of stillness that suggested great physical competence. Throckmorton, on the other hand, seemed an absolute HQ attaché/Officers Club type—one of the species of high-born, aging rich kids that tended to cruise through the war kowtowing to, shuffling paper for, and occasionally dining out with rear-echelon brass, courtesy of parental connections. The command centers of Washington and London were choked with them: the sons of senators, of Members of Parliament, of judges and millionaires and dukes and lords, most of them using the war as an opportunity for career advancement even as they sidestepped the brutal reality of having to face enemy fire. Donovan felt nothing but disdain for them.

But even though Throckmorton's carriage and demeanor had put him in mind of such creatures, Donovan had learned to reserve judgement until a man had revealed his character unequivocally. So he filed away his first impression and waited to find out more.

Churchill nodded in response to Merritt's salute and address, settled back in his chair, and looked over at Gubbins. Sir Colin rose to his feet, returned the salute, and pointed toward a vacant couch.

"Please sit down, gentlemen," he said. He resumed his seat, as Merritt and Throckmorton complied.

"The reason you are here," Gubbins continued, "is to provide our American allies General Donovan and Colonel Haskell an opportunity to have a look at the officers who will be leading Operation Handschar—the least we can do, considering they have supplied two top-quality U.S. combat specialists to flesh out the team."

Throckmorton crossed his legs elegantly and made a languid gesture with his hand. "Actually, sir," he said, "the mission leader is Major Merritt here. I'm simply along for the ride. . . . More or less."

Once again, Donovan was irritated. There was an effete ennui in the way Throckmorton spoke, in the way he crossed his legs and moved his hand. And the first words out of his mouth were an unsolicited contradiction of his commanding officer. But to Gubbins it appeared to be water off a duck's back. He did not seem perturbed in the slightest. In fact, when the SOE head spoke again, Donovan found his tone surprisingly gentle, almost paternalistic.

"Now, now, Duncan—it's not necessary to sell yourself short. It's true that Walt is the tactical leader, but you know how crucial you are to the success of this operation."

Throckmorton regarded the ceiling idly. "I suppose. Mind if I smoke?"

Donovan glanced sidelong at Haskell. The color was rising to the SO colonel's cheeks. Donovan felt an indignant flush begin to sting his own face. But the two American commanders remained silent.

Gubbins nodded good-naturedly and waved his hand. "Absolutely, Duncan, go ahead. You too, Walt."

Merritt shifted his weight on the couch. "Thank you, sir. I don't smoke."

"Ah, that's right. Of course you don't."

Donovan continued to regard Throckmorton with distaste as the slender captain extracted a cigarette from a gold case and lit it with a jeweled Dunhill lighter.

"Major Merritt does not indulge in tobacco," General Gubbins remarked, "a legacy from his days as an Olympic athlete."

"Indeed?" A former athlete himself, Donovan was immediately interested. "Which Olympics, Major Merritt?"

"Munich, back in 'thirty-six, sir."

"What event?"

"The hundred-yard dash, General." Merritt gave a wry smile. "I didn't win. I was beaten in the semifinals by several other sprinters—most notably an American Negro named Jesse Owens."

"Ah yes," Donovan said. "the famous Mr. Owens. What an embarassment he turned out to be for the so-called Master Race, eh?"

Merritt looked at Haskell, then back at Donovan. "Not just for the Germans, sir." The wry smile again. "He made me look like I was standing still."

"Major Merritt has since gone on to even greater

things," Gubbins interjected, "such as organizing a last-minute counterattack to cover the evacuation of the British Expeditionary Force at Dunkirk back in 'forty. After that little escapade, we at SOE, who occasionally manage to recognize a good thing when we see it, plucked the major for special operations duty. In the past three and a half years, he has led various commando raids in Norway, France, and Italy. But his true area of expertise is Yugoslavia. So far, we have parachuted Major Merritt and his supporting personnel into that country . . . how many times is it now, Walt?"

"Six, sir," Merritt answered. "Five by parachute into the mountains, once by gunboat to the coast of Montenegro." He looked at Donovan. "Short-term operations, General, with specific targets: bridges, dams, railways. My great advantage in Yugoslavia is that I speak Serbo-Croatian fluently, along with several related dialects. My mother's maiden name is Petrović. She was born in Sarajevo."

Donovan nodded. "Useful, Major, without a doubt." His piercing blue eyes shifted to Throckmorton, who was lounging and smoking. "And you, Captain. Are you also fluent in Serbo-Croatian?"

Throckmorton picked his cigarette from between his lips with a bored flourish. "I'd say competent rather than fluent. Unlike Major Merritt, I didn't learn the language at my mother's knee." He paused to draw on his cigarette again, and took his time about it.

Donovan felt his molars set together, the heat rise to his cheeks. Throckmorton had a rare gift for getting on a man's nerves. . . . *His* nerves, anyway. He cleared his throat. "And so? How did you learn it?"

"I picked up Serbo-Croatian while yachting in the twenties and thirties with various and sundry uncles who kept boats in Trieste and enjoyed cruising the Dalmatian Coast."

The bored, petulant way Throckmorton drew out the word "yaww-ting" nearly caused Donovan to blow a main fuse. But with the possible exception of Haskell, no one in the parlor was aware of it.

"I would imagine that yachting in the Adriatic these days is somewhat limited," Donovan commented tightly.

"Yaas," Throckmorton responded. "Quite."

"As a matter of fact," Menzies put in, "Sir Colin and I had discussed the option of inserting Major Merritt's team into Yugoslavia by submarine, possibly in the vicinity of the Croatian port city of Zara. But that would have required too much overland travel through hostile territory to reach the mission target, which is in the Majevica Mountains of the interior. So no yachting, so to speak. We're going with parachute insertion."

"Another railway bridge, I understand?" Haskell said.

"Not just any railway bridge," Gubbins replied. He handed the American colonel two identical eight-by-ten photographs. Haskell passed one to Donovan, who put on a pair of steel-rimmed glasses to study it.

"This is the Zpoda Skyway Bridge," Gubbins continued, "one of the highest multiarch, brick-and-steel constructions in the world. And high in this case does not refer just to the bridge itself, but where it is located: at an altitude of nearly seven thousand feet on the upper rim of the Zpoda Gorge.

"The Germans—notably the SS Division Handschar—have pushed Tito's Partisans far back into the Majevica Mountains and are managing to maintain a more or less consistent line of advance that runs from gorge to peak to gorge across the northern third of this range. There is one rail line supplying the advance, and it runs across the Zpoda Skyway.

"Now then, most of this railway lies in the flat country of the Sava River plain. As it ascends through the foothills of the Majevicas and up to the Zpoda Gorge, it runs through numerous tunnels connected by narrow, well-supported rock beds and embankments. Naturally Marshall Tito and his Partisans, who are at present in a rather hellish mountain-warfare situation, would very much like to have this rail line cut. . . . Permanently, if possible."

Donovan grunted and removed his glasses. "The obvious solution," he said, "is to send bombers to destroy it."

"We tried that," Menzies responded, "twice. Lancasters and then Halifaxes out of Bari, in southern Italy. It didn't work."

"Why not?" Haskell demanded. "Did they miss the mark both times?"

Menzies glanced at Gubbins, who cleared his throat and answered. "No. They hit the line in several places. But there are some problems. First of all, we've learned that if we bomb the railway in the flatland area of the Sava River plain, the Germans have the capacity to repair it virtually overnight. On such accessible terrain, they can reconstruct five miles of blown track in ten hours.

"The higher a rail line climbs up into a mountain range, the more difficult it is to repair—normally. But the abundance of tunnels in the Majevicas provides shelter from aerial attack over much of the train route. In addition, the Germans have stationed heavy-duty plow engines and repair cars inside the tunnels at regular intervals, so that if a bomb blast brings down rubble on an exposed section of line, it can be cleared—and if necessary reconstructed—in short order.

"But the Zpoda Skyway Bridge . . . that's another story. It's such an inaccessible and complex structure that if we were able to destroy it, there would be no way the Germans could replace it. The mountain supply route would be dead-ended at its highest, most inconvenient point—directly behind the main line of advance. The German thrust would begin to starve."

"Once again," Donovan said, "why not bombers?"

Gubbins stroked his mustache and shook his head.

"Take another look at that photograph, General. The bridge links two tunnel entrances that face each other on opposite sides of the gorge. It sweeps around in a quarter-mile-long curve, hugging the sheer cliff just beneath the gorge's uppermost rim. Do you see that thick, shelflike cap of rock that overhangs the bridge along its entire length between the two tunnels? That's the problem.

"The Royal Air Force can't get its bombs on the bridge because they keep hitting the overhang, which our engineers inform us is no less than one hundred and fifty feet of solid granite. We can't get a vertically falling bomb to travel horizontally enough to slip under the overhang and hit the bases of the support arches where they tie into the cliff, much less the track itself."

Donovan scratched his chin. "How about using Mosquito fighter-bombers to fly straight up the gorge from north to south? Pull up hard at the last minute and try to lob their bombs under that rock shelf?"

"The Germans have installed antiaircraft gun positions on the ridgetops along the entire length of the gorge. In addition, there are antiaircraft gun cars located on side tracks in nearly every tunnel. These too can be rolled out in the event of an aerial attack. Pilots flying up the gorge in the manner you suggest to try to bomb or rocket the supports would be running a suicide gauntlet." Gubbins gave a grim smile. "Not that we wouldn't try it if we thought such an approach had a ghost of a chance of succeeding. We've used similar tactics in fjords in Norway. But in this instance our best planners put the likelihood of success at nil, and the projected losses at one hundred percent."

"Rather unpromising," Donovan remarked.

"Yes, rather."

There was a long pause as Gubbins poured himself a cup of tea from the silver service on the tray next to his chair. He glanced at Churchill as he set the teapot down; the prime minister shook his head silently and continued to puff on his cigar. Donovan and Haskell reexamined the photographs they had been given.

"So that's why you requested a couple of specialists from the Tenth Mountain Division," Donovan said finally. "You need skilled climbers, men who know rope work, to help place charges on the supporting arches of that bridge."

"Correct," Gubbins replied. "Men who can keep up with Walt Merritt here, who also happens to be an expert mountaineer." He sipped tea. "But this operation has not one but two interesting elements—both of which we feel you and Colonel Haskell should be made aware of."

"Elements of an extremely . . . *delicate* nature," Churchill grunted. It was the first time he had said anything since Merritt and Throckmorton had entered the parlor.

Gubbins looked at the prime minister and nodded. "Extremely delicate," he reiterated.

He set his teacup down on the service tray, glanced at Churchill again, then gestured across the room in the direction of the elegant, white-haired gentleman who had been sitting in complete silence off to the side throughout the meeting. "General Donovan, Colonel Haskell, allow me to introduce an old and dear friend of the prime minister's, Mr. Martin Judson. Mr. Judson is a renowned British industrialist and economic expert with a large number of prewar ties to the European continent. Some of these ties have proven to be . . . useful.

"Mr. Judson, with Major Merritt's assistance, would you please elucidate for our esteemed American colleagues on the 'elements of a delicate nature' to which the prime minister has just referred?"

It was well after dark by the time Donovan and Haskell exited 10 Downing Street and climbed into their waiting military staff car. As the vehicle pulled away from the prime minister's residence, Haskell puffed his cheeks and blew out a long breath.

"What do you think, General?" he asked.

Donovan shook his head. "Damnedest multiobjective operation I've ever heard of. Churchill was right: two birds with one stone."

"If they can pull it off," Haskell said dubiously.

The general was silent for a moment. Then he rubbed his chin and folded his arms. "Look," he said, "the whole thing's a high-wire stunt—literally. But if they can succeed in executing even half of it, it'll be worth it. Either one of those two objectives is worth achieving."

Haskell grunted. "Even if they all get killed in the process?"

Donovan turned and looked at his Special Operations chief in feigned surprise. "Well, of course, Joe. Even if they all get killed. Business as usual. As you're so fond of pointing out, this is war, not checkers."

Chapter Three

Every rivet in the shuddering fuselage of the Halifax seemed on the verge of vibrating loose. *Not unlike my teeth,* Merritt thought, shifting his weight on his small metal seat and rebracing his feet. The Royal Air Force heavy bomber continued to batter its way through the turbulent night air above the coastal mountains of Montenegro, its four Rolls-Royce Merlin engines driving it onward to the northeast. . . . Ever deeper into the rugged interior of war-torn Yugoslavia.

Not for the first time, Merritt found himself longing for a window, a port of some kind—anything through which he could catch a glimpse of the sky, the stars, the moon, or the horizon. Every one of his five previous jumps into Yugoslavia had been from a Halifax bomber, and this particular design of warplane afforded viewing capability only to aircrew for whom it was essential—pilot and copilot, nose and turret gunners. Parachutists huddled amidships in the darkened fuselage above the empty bomb bay did not need to

see where they were going. Or what might be coming
at them.

The Halifax heaved upward in a sudden vortex of
turbulence. Merritt felt his stomach bottom out, his
spine compress. In the floor of the modified bomb bay,
the four-foot circular wooden hatch that covered the
joe hole rattled violently against its retaining clips,
buffeted by the irregular slipstream.

"Jeezus H. Christ!" a voice shouted from the opposite side of the fuselage. "Think that sky jockey's tryin'
to hit every patch of bad air in the goddamn Balkan
Peninsula?" It was Bristow, one of the two Americans
plucked by OSS from the Tenth Mountain Division.
He was a big, brawny Texan with a wide Scots-Irish
face, a ready smile, and a dry, laconic wit. Beside him,
dwarfed by comparison and all but smothered by the
equipment he was wearing, sat the other American, a
feisty little New Yorker of Italian extraction named
D'Amato. The two—sergeants both—were best
friends, and for their own amusement kept up a habit-
ual banter consisting largely of routine back-and-forth
insults interspersed with disgusted observations about
military life and the war in general. It would have
been easy, upon first listen, to dismiss them as frivo-
lous or negative, but Merritt had observed them carefully during SOE mission training in Scotland, while
en route to Allied-controlled southern Italy via North
Africa, and in the few days before the team's final
departure from the Adriatic port of Bari, and concluded that Bristow and D'Amato, despite their irrev-
erent mannerisms, were indeed professional soldiers,
highly competent and disciplined. Disciplined enough,
in fact, to have picked up basic Serbo-Croatian language skills in a matter of weeks. Merritt—well traveled, down-to-earth, and personally devoid of the
Anglocentric puffery that characterized much of the
British officer class—had found that he liked them
both immensely.

The Halifax heaved and bucked again, then settled

down. Merritt's eyes shifted to the two bulky, helmeted figures sitting just aft of Bristow and D'Amato. Sergeants Hurst and Stirling were British Regular Army—experienced commandos with demolition and mountaineering training. Each of them had accompanied Merritt on one previous mission: Hurst to Norway; Stirling to France. They were good men, resourceful and reliable.

Next to Stirling sat the late addition to the team, Weiss. He appeared to be asleep, his helmet tipped forward over his eyes, his arms folded on top of his reserve chute. He was something of an unknown quantity to the other men. Merritt watched him for a moment.

A wet cough sounded in Merritt's ear above the roar of the engines. He glanced to his left as Throckmorton, sitting beside him, wiped his lips with a handkerchief. The slender captain was calmly reading a Serbo-Croatian grammar book, a pencil flashlight stuck in the webbing of his jump helmet. The two men's eyes met.

Merritt leaned in close. "How are you, Duncan?" he called.

Throckmorton nodded. "Just ducky, thanks. You?"

"All right." Merritt glanced at the illuminated dial of his wristwatch. "Should be only another few minutes to the drop zone."

Throckmorton shrugged and smiled. "Fine. Have the butler notify me when it's time to go." He went back to reading his grammar text.

Merritt gave a short laugh and sat back. He noted without concern that, as expected, his mouth had become quite dry. The tension was building now, as it always did just before a night jump. So many things could go wrong. Parachutes could fail to open or get hung up on the rear undercarriage of the plane. Even with deployed canopies, jumpers could be swept into cliffs or gorges, or killed on impact with the ground— particularly in rough terrain in the dark. And as mission commander he worried not just about himself, but about every man on his team.

And as usual he countered the looming worry by reminding himself that every member of the team was a skilled, experienced combat parachutist equipped with the best British and American gear available, that everything from static lines to reserve chutes to boot soles had been checked and rechecked a half-dozen times, and that if by some chance anything crucial had been overlooked, it was too damned late to fret about it now.

An RAF flight sergeant waddled past in the darkness, clad against the bitter chill in heavy insulated coveralls and trailing a long safety tether from a full-body harness. He grinned at Merritt, stepped down into the bomb bay, and bent over a large aluminum canister the approximate size and shape of three fifty-gallon oil drums laid end to end. Working quickly, he shucked his heavy gloves and ran his hands over the elongate parachute pack strapped to the canister's midpoint. Then he pulled out a length of the cargo chute's static line, leaned over, and hooked the end to a heavy steel ring bolted to the port side of the fuselage.[1] As he did so, a small red light mounted on the forward bulkhead of the bomb bay compartment came on, bathing the six jumpers and the flight sergeant in a dull crimson glow.

The sergeant turned to Merritt, on the starboard side of the aircraft, redonning his fleece-lined gloves, and stepped partly up out of the bomb bay.

"Got signal fires up ahead, Major. Pilot's going to overfly the drop zone once, confirm that it's the Partisans down there and not the bleedin' Nazis by exchanging the correct series of identification flashes." The sergeant's cockney accent was all but indecipherable over the roar of the engines. "Once that's done, we'll come around for another pass, and I'll slide your gear canister out the bleedin' joe hole. Third time around, it's your turn." He grinned again. "All seven o' you, quick like."

Merritt nodded. "I'll lead off, followed by Captain Throckmorton here."

"Yes, sir," the sergeant said, touching his eyebrow.

The bomber began to bank steeply. The RAF sergeant braced a leg against the side of the bomb bay and waited. The aircraft canted to nearly forty-five degrees, maintained that attitude for the better part of a minute, then eased back down onto level flight. As Merritt and his team members resettled themselves, the sergeant bent down and released the clips on the joe hole cover. He pulled the circular wooden lid aside, revealing the open mouth of a four-foot-diameter metal tube, three feet deep, that extended below the belly of the Halifax. Merritt leaned forward and peered down, on the off chance that he might catch a glimpse of a signal fire. There was nothing at the lower end of the tube but a frigid black void of rushing air.

The sergeant heaved one end of the big cargo canister over the joe hole, then stepped around to its opposite end and waited, looking up at the red light in the forward bulkhead. The plane's engines throttled back, changing in pitch. Merritt felt his ears pop as the Halifax sank through the air, losing altitude. The red light winked off and was instantly replaced by a flashing green. The sergeant seized the canister, tilted it up against his shoulder with a curse, and slid the eight-foot-long package out through the joe hole in one practiced motion. There was a faint *whap* beneath the bomber as the cargo chute opened, and then a light battering sound as the deployed static line, now detached from the parachute, began to beat a tattoo on the underside of the fuselage in the slipstream.

"Clear and gone!" The sergeant grinned and gave Merritt the thumbs-up. "Your turn now, sir," he called. "Come on down and have a seat. The captain, too." On the forward bulkhead, the flashing green light switched back to red.

Merritt and Throckmorton clambered down into the bomb bay and sat next to each other on the forward edge of the joe hole, legs dangling, facing aft. The RAF sergeant motioned for Bristow and D'Amato to sit in similar fashion on either side of the two British officers. As they moved into position he tended to all four static lines, ensuring that they were lying fair and there would be no risk of entanglement.

Along the port side of the fuselage, Hurst, Stirling, and Weiss shuffled forward until they were occupying the metal seats nearest the joe hole. As Bristow and then D'Amato followed Merritt and Throckmorton out, the last three would step down into the bomb bay in sequence, as per their training, and make their respective exits.

The Halifax began to bank again. Once more, the RAF sergeant turned sideways and braced a leg. Merritt, Throckmorton, Bristow, and D'Amato leaned back from the gaping joe hole and found secure handholds. The bomber rose steeply onto its port wingtip, repeating the pattern of its first circuit. The four big Merlin engines roared in angry chorus as they powered the heavy warplane around.

Another gale of turbulence rattled the fuselage. The aircraft settled back down to level. Again, the engines dropped in pitch as the pilot throttled back. Merritt felt the seat of his pants nearly leave the floor of the bomb bay as the Halifax lost altitude.

The RAF sergeant half turned and knelt on one knee on the opposite side of the joe hole, facing forward. His broad Cockney face, serious now, was bathed in the eerie glow of the red light directly behind Merritt.

"When I point at you, you go," he shouted to everyone. "In sequence. Got it?"

"We've got it," Merritt confirmed. He placed his gloved palms on the floor of the bomb bay, fingers and thumbs over the edge of the joe hole, eyeing the sergeant. Just below his dangling boots, the black slipstream shrieked and howled past the underbelly of the plane. Unconsciously he licked his lips. His mouth was very dry.

The seconds dragged by. Merritt stared at the red-tinged flight sergeant. The sergeant stared at the red light behind Merritt's head.

The color of the sergeant's face changed from red to green. As the fleece-lined glove came down to point at him, Major Walter Merritt leaned forward and for the sixth time in his life dropped through the joe hole of a Halifax bomber into the night skies over Yugoslavia.

"I can hear it coming around again," Haak said, his breath condensing into frosty plumes. "A Halifax, for certain."

"No lights, of course, sir," Langwolt muttered at his side.

"Of course."

Haak stopped searching the sky long enough to glance across the open, semiwooded slope where four evenly spaced signal fires were casting faint orange glimmers across the new-fallen snow. The silhouettes of his men moved back and forth in front of the leaping flames.

"I want those fires kept bright," Haak said, tipping his head back and resuming his upward gaze.

The windblast hit Merritt with such freezing force that it literally snatched the breath from his lungs. Gasping, he tumbled downward in pitch-blackness, buffeted by invisible fists of air, straining to maintain the proper compact body position.

WHAP.

The opening of the parachute canopy jarred him from neck to tailbone, the straps of his body harness momentarily cinching garotte tight. He felt himself bounce in the chute risers and swing wildly, a corkscrewing human pendulum. . . .

And then the chaotic motion subsided and he was swaying gently in his harness, suspended like a life-sized marionette at the end of twenty-eight invisible strings, drifting through a vast black void of bone-chilling cold. The throaty roar of the Halifax's engines seemed very far off now. He looked up. Just below the lower edge of his deployed canopy he could see four faint blue dots set close in a horizontal line—heat glow from the bomber's engine exhausts—receding in the darkness.

He looked down. The mountainous terrain below his dangling boots was broken, gloomy, and forbidding. There appeared to be no level ground, only a jigsaw puzzle of crooked, twisting shadows, snow-covered slopes, and dense clusters of spirelike evergreen trees. Every other shadow looked like a jagged ridge or bottomless crevasse. A sudden gust of wind hit him, taking his breath away and rocking him in the parachute risers. The whirl of frigid air felt like a white-hot blade against his cheek.

He twisted in his harness, looking over his left shoulder and down. *There.* Two signal fires, flickering like tiny oases of orange warmth in the desolate landscape. The only visible orientation points. Merritt tugged on his risers, trying to slip the chute sideways to the left.

The humped outlines of ridges, arêtes, and peaks, looming snow blanketed and tree bearded like the sleeping winter giants of Norse myth, rose dramatically around him as he sank out of the night sky. He craned his neck and looked upward, trying to catch a glimpse of his comrades' parachutes, but could see nothing. He looked down again.

He was heading for a dense black tangle of trees, and it was coming up very quickly. To the right, a pale expanse of snow gleamed dully in the ambient starlight. Merritt yanked on his risers, got his boots together, flexed his knees. . . .

He brushed past the drooping branches of an evergreen, slipping sideways fast, and hit the slope in an explosion of snow. The chute dragged him through the drifts like an unwilling plow for another fifteen feet before finally collapsing. He was down.

Rolling over, he hit the release buckle of his parachute harness and shucked it. Then he scrambled to his knees, blinking snow out of his eyes, and freed up the Sten submachine gun strapped across his chest. Several dark figures were running toward him, laboring across the slope through thigh-deep drifts. Behind them, through the trees, flickered the orange flames of a signal fire.

Merritt swung the Sten up and fell forward onto his stomach. The nearest figure was less than twenty yards away, floundering toward him through the snow with greatcoat flapping and rifle at high port. Identifying details were impossible to make out. Merritt leveled his weapon at the charging form and shouted, *"Živio Tito!"*

"Long live Tito." The prearranged challenge, spoken in Serbo-Croatian. Second by elapsing second, Merritt waited for the correct reply. His finger tightened on the trigger of the Sten.

The greatcoated figure stopped thrashing toward him and raised the rifle above its head with both hands. *"Smrt Fašismu!"* came the hoarse cry. *"Smrt Fašismu!"*

"Death to Fascists." Correct. Merritt let out a long breath and eased his grip on the submachine gun. As he rose to his knees and sat back on his haunches, the man in the greatcoat lowered his arms and bulled forward through the deep snow. Beneath an immense fur hat, Merritt could make out the pale curve of a broad grin.

"Hello, British, hello!" The man stopped about a

yard in front of Merritt, beaming downward through
a bushy black beard that would have done justice to
a Cossack. He had to be at least six and a half feet
tall. . . . Perhaps more. "Jolly good to see you, comrade! Eh, wot?" He nodded at his own fractured English and bent over to clap Merritt on the shoulder.
It was like being hit by a ten-pound maul.

"Greetings to you, comrade," Merritt replied, opting for Serbo-Croatian. He got to his feet and brushed
snow off his heavy battle jacket. "I take it you're
with Cernović."

"If I wasn't," the giant answered happily, "you'd
be dead."

"Look out below, goddamit!"

The yell was in West Texas American twang, and a
heartbeat later Bristow came swinging by, narrowly
missing the big Partisan. He hit the snow with a muffled curse about ten feet behind Merritt and was
dragged downslope another fifty by a gust of wind that
kept his parachute inflated at an oblique angle. Two
other Partisans floundered after him, shouting encour-
agement.

Merritt watched with concern, then broke into an
unconscious smile as the big Texan somersaulted to
his feet, still swearing, and collapsed the canopy with
a powerful yank on one of the risers. A hundred yards
away, near the stand of trees through which the closest
signal fire could be seen, D'Amato's compact form hit
the snow, feet together, under a quietly descending
parachute. It was a perfect landing, without wind in-
terference, but the little sergeant had touched down
on a particularly deep drift. He plunged through the
clean white surface and disappeared completely. His
camouflage-patterned canopy settled over over the
entry hole like a shroud.

Merritt began to stride through the snow toward
D'Amato, sinking thigh deep with every step. He
paused as the collapsed canopy began to heave and
billow. A few seconds later, the long blade of a jump

knife poked through the camo silk and slashed length-
wise. D'Amato emerged from the slit, shedding snow,
and began to cut away the suspension lines of his
chute, which had become tangled around his head
and shoulders.

Merritt turned back to Bristow. The big Texan was
wading through the snow toward him, flanked by the
two Partisans who had pursued him down the slope.
Being considerably shorter than the American, both
were struggling to keep up, even as they maintained
a constant stream of congratulations in some obscure
Serbo-Croatian dialect.

Merritt looked skyward, checking for more parachutes.

Throckmorton, second through the joe hole, after
Merritt, had been blown by a random gust of wind
past the drop zone demarcated by the obvious signal
fires and along a precipitous ridge of ice-covered rock.
At first he'd thought he would be able to land in the
snow at the far end of the clearing before being carried into the cliff face, but the same icy zephyr that
had pushed him past the DZ had updrafted at the last
minute, briefly interrupting his descent. The short
delay had been enough to waft him like a helpless kite
into the jagged wall of black rock.

He'd hit hard about eighty feet above the snowdrifts
at the base of the cliff—an impact violent enough to
knock the wind out of him. His canopy had collapsed,
snagged, torn, snagged again, and then hung fast on
an outcropping of rock approximately twenty-five feet
above his head.

Currently Captain Duncan Throckmorton was trying to keep very still in his harness, even as he
searched for a way out of his predicament. Every few
seconds the overstrained silk of the parachute would
give way a little more with an ominous tearing sound.

Most unpleasant.

*   *   *

Sergeants Hurst and Stirling had exited the Halifax almost on top of one another. Hard-earned experience had taught them that the best way to avoid wide dispersal on a combat drop was to leave the plane simultaneously. Now they were descending under deployed canopies barely fifty feet apart, Stirling perhaps ten feet higher than Hurst. The close jump grouping would put them on the ground together, at the same time, where each could watch the other's back. For the professional British soldier, the fighting war had started in 1939. They'd been watching each other's backs for a long time now.

"There, Hurstie!" Stirling called out, his voice hoarse in the freezing air. "Two signal fires, just over that bleedin' ridge. Slip left, mate!"

"Left it is," Hurst shouted back, pulling on his risers. Facing the wrong direction, he could just barely see one of the fires, glimmering through the black trees below, out of the corner of his eye.

A gust of wind hit the two commandos, lofting them over the knife-edged ridge. Now Hurst could see not one but three signal fires, spaced several hundred yards apart in a series of small, snow-covered clearings that interrupted the dark mat of evergreen trees. Close to the nearest fire, the silhouettes of men were clearly visible against the pale luminosity of open ground. They were moving in a ragged group to meet the two parachutists at their likely landing point in the middle of the clearing.

The same gust that had lifted Hurst and Stirling past the ridge had also moved them farther apart. Hurst was the first to touch down, sinking to his hips in deep snow. Just overhead, he caught a glimpse of Stirling being wafted sideways toward the trees at the edge of the clearing. Then his parachute canopy came down over his head and the view was lost.

Swinging his arms, he swept the camouflage-patterned silk off his head and shoulders, kicked free of the clinging snow, and struggled to a kneeling position. He looked up the gentle slope of the clearing toward the signal fire. Coming toward him, spread out in a skirmish line and plunging forward through the snow, were at least twelve to fifteen dark figures, all armed. There were more behind.

At least the bloody Partisans were where they were supposed to be. Hurst brushed snow off the back of his neck and put a hand on the reassuring grip of his Sten. Force of habit.

"Živio Tito!" he shouted. Again, just to be sure they'd heard: *"Živio Tito!"*

The dark figures continued to advance, but no one gave the countersign. Hurst felt the well-conditioned hackles at the back of his neck begin to rise. . . . Or maybe it was just the confounded snow melting under his collar. The pilot of the Halifax had exchanged the proper flash signals with the Partisans on the ground, or the team wouldn't have gotten the green light to jump. Wouldn't do to start off the mission by machine-gunning a baker's dozen of the friendly resistance for want of a short verbal response.

Bloody foreigners. Hurst raised his free hand and tried again. *"Živio* perishin' *Tito,* damn your eyes! What the hell d'you lot think a countersign's for?"

The lead figure—a tall man in bulky winter mountain gear—halted, raised his arm, and leveled a pistol at Hurst. The others pressed forward, beginning to fan out around the British commando.

"Get your hands above your head, tommie!" SS-Obersturmfuehrer Rolf Langwolt barked in perfect English. *"Schnell!* You have no chance—"

Hurst's was the instinctive reaction of a true warrior. He threw himself sideways in the snow, jerking up his Sten gun, and opened fire.

Langwolt staggered back, firing his Luger as Hurst's first two rounds slammed into his shoulder and collarbone. Desperately the British sergeant fanned the compact machine gun to the left, across the line of ducking soldiers less than thirty feet away, twisting his body in the snow as he did so. The enemy troopers were so taken off guard by the reaction of the out-flanked man they'd expected to capture without a fight that for a brief moment they couldn't return fire. Hurst continued to swing the long, continuous burst through the infantrymen to his left. . . . Hitting some, driving the others onto their faces.

But there were half a dozen more on his right. . . .

Stirling was on his belly in the snow at the edge of the clearing, squinting through the rear battle sight of a No. 4 Mark 1 Enfield sniper rifle. The weapon was minus its telescopic sight, which was stowed deep in the commando sergeant's jump duffel to protect it from landing shock. Stirling had little need of it now—the squad of enemy soldiers virtually on top of Hurst was less than fifty yards away. A second skirmish line was bypassing Hurst's position and advancing toward him, barely a hundred yards distant.

Stirling blinked icy sweat out of his eyes, settled the battle sight on a dark hump just beyond Hurst, and fired. The .303 slug found its mark; the hump jerked and sagged into the snow. It took the veteran commando sniper less than a second to work the Enfield's bolt, eject the spent shell, chamber a fresh round, locate another target, and fire again. And again. And again.

The dark figures ringing Hurst had finally opened up, some with machine pistols. Little slivery lines of fire were converging on the half-surrounded sergeant like spokes to the hub of some hellish wheel. Stirling realized with a sudden numb rush that his old friend was no longer moving.

"Hurstie!" he yelled once, then rolled over and over in the deep snow, gained his feet, and plunged head-long into the black trees at the edge of the clearing, bullets hissing and snapping through the pine needles all around him.

*   *   *

SS-Hauptsturmfuehrer Ulrich Haak was standing beside the prostrate body of the bleeding, grimacing Langwolt, gesturing in angry frustration with his drawn Luger. He took a quick step to the side as a medic ran up and dropped to one knee to tend to the wounded Obersturmfuehrer.

"Alive, you idiots!" he bellowed at his scattered men, who were in hot pursuit of Stirling. He glanced over in annoyance at the huddled, bullet-riddled corpse of Sergeant Hurst. *"I want at least one of these cursed jumpers alive, do you understand?"*

"They'll . . . they'll get him, sir," Langwolt grunted. He winced as the medic applied pressure bandages to the twin wounds in his right shoulder. "The snow's too deep for him to move fast."

"Maybe they will—the Muslim turds. Unless he makes it over the ridge and finds the Partisans first. And he might; paratroopers are always elite soldiers— look at this one." He gestured again at Hurst's body. "A brave death, eh? It's enough to make me wish I hadn't transferred out of the airborne infantry myself. I'm getting particular about the company I keep." Haak peered down at his second-in-command. "How bad, Rolf?"

Langwolt grunted again. "Bad enough, sir. But I think I can walk in a few minutes."

Haak pulled a silver cigarette case from his pocket, opened it, and offered it to his wounded second-in-command. "Take a couple, Rolf, to calm your nerves. The last of my custom hoard from Munich."

Langwolt accepted with a grateful nod. "Thank you, sir."

"The wound in the top of the shoulder is just a graze," the medic offered, "but the other bullet went right through near the collarbone front to back. The clavicle may be broken, sir." He looked up askance at Haak, the commander's offhand remarks about Muslims—of which he was one—burning in his ears.

Haak repositioned his forage cap on his close-cropped blond head, pulling the brim down over his brows almost to the bridge of his aquiline nose. "Get back to the half-tracks," he ordered. "Try to follow along the base of this ridge; see if you can find a way through. We'll rendezvous in that vicinity in forty minutes." He started forward. "After we kill or capture the jumper, we may be able to intercept some of the Partisans he and his companion were trying to coordinate with."

"There may have been other jumpers," Langwolt said, struggling to his feet with the aid of the medic. "They may have hit the Partisans' landing zone instead of our decoy."

"Possible," Haak commented over his shoulder, "or maybe they're just wandering around in the woods, lost." He began to high-step through the snow in the tracks of his infantrymen, toward the trees through which Stirling had fled. "With any luck we'll run into a few of them, too."

"I am Anton Cernović," the goateed, huskily built Partisan commander had said to Merritt in accented English, extending his hand as he approached. The words were barely out of his mouth when the muted rattle of Hurst's Sten gun echoed out of the woods to the left. Instinctively the little knot of parachutists and Partisans had dropped into a collective crouch, eyes scanning the darkness for signs of attackers.

"Major Walter Merritt, Commander Cernović," Merritt reciprocated in a low voice. "British Special Operations Executive." He shifted his own Sten gun to one knee, continuing to search the tree line. "These are Sergeants Cole Bristow and Frank D'Amato, American mountain warfare specialists on loan to SOE for this mission."

The din of machine gun fire increased, punctuated by the flat crack of rifle shots. Reverberating through the snowy crags and sentinel trees along with the clamor of the furious firefight were the sounds of men yelling.

"I'm short four of my men, Commander," Merritt stated tersely, his breath rolling out in clouds of condensation. "And obviously one or more of them has run into a German patrol, from the sound of those Schmeisser machine pistols."

Cernović didn't hesitate. Standing up, he waved a gloved hand at the Partisans scattered across the slope on either side of him. "Lost parachutists!" he shouted in Serbo-Croatian. "Move out and engage the Fascists! *Try not to kill any parachutists, comrades!*"

Bristow glanced at D'Amato, then Merritt. "Try?"

Cernović heard him, gave a rueful smile and a shrug. "The best we can do, my friend," he said, switching back to English, "under the circumstances."

"Jeezus," Bristow growled, hefting the .45-caliber Thompson submachine gun that was his weapon of choice.

The Partisan infantry was disappearing into the woods in a ragged skirmish line, led by the black-bearded giant who had first made contact with Merritt. The sounds of an ongoing firefight had stopped now, replaced with those of men shouting to each other and the occasional lone rifle shot. Each rifle report was answered with a brief clattering of fire from multiple Schmeisser machine pistols.

Merritt cocked his head, listening. "Enfield sniper rifle," he said. "That's Stirling. He's on the run, and they're hunting him." He rose to his feet and started forward. "Let's go."

Cernović grunted an order over his shoulder to the three Partisans who'd remained with him, and moved up alongside Merritt. Bristow and D'Amato spread out on the British major's opposite side, cradling their weapons and trudging through the thigh-deep snow.

Again, a lone rifle shot cracked through the trees above the mournful whine of the alpine wind.

*   *   *

Sergeant Colin Stirling was running for his life. *Fire and evade. Fire and evade.* The familiar phrase pulsed through his brain like a mantra. But it was hard to evade when you were plowing through snow up to your belt and leaving a trail as plain as a drainage ditch for your pursuers to follow.

Stirling floundered up a forty-five-degree slope toward the base of an immense black crag that jutted out of the mountainside like the bow of a ship. He might be able to move faster among the rocks beneath the overhang, where the snow was not as deep. His breath was coming in agonizing gasps, the thin, frigid air lancing his lungs like a chestful of razor blades.

His head was spinning from lack of oxygen. He had to stop—get his wind back. With a final effort he plowed upward through the crest of a snowdrift and staggered behind a massive boulder at the base of the cliff. Vision blurring, steam rising off his sweat-slick face, he sagged to his haunches with his back to the rock, momentarily done in.

The shouts of his pursuers resonated off the black crag that towered into the night sky above him. They were very close, working their way up the slope. Following his trail.

Stirling gathered his strength, pushed himself erect, and brought his rifle to bear around the back side of the boulder. There were five dark figures laboring up the slope toward him, machine pistols slung across chests. They were less than thirty yards away. Stirling centered the Enfield's battle sight on the middle figure and fired.

It was an easy shot for a marksman of Stirling's caliber, despite his dizziness and blurred vision. The slug hit the enemy soldier square in the chest and knocked him backward down the snowy slope. The other four dove left and right and opened up with their Schmeissers.

The barrage of bullets drove Stirling back down behind the rock in a flurry of granite splinters. Desperately he rolled to the opposite side of the boulder and swung his rifle around, preparing to shoot from a prone position. Unrelenting machine-gun fire continued to hammer into the rock all around him. Stirling knew what the Germans had in mind: two of them would keep him pinned down with a base of fire, while the remaining two would rush his position. He had to return fire. There was nowhere to run.

Abruptly the machine-gun fire ceased. Stirling rolled out on his elbows, trying to expose himself as little as possible. Over the barrel of his rifle he was just in time to see the dark shape of an enemy soldier, legs pumping, burst through the snowdrift directly in front of him. He was so close that Stirling could make out the pale gleam of gritted teeth in a swarthy face beneath a death's-head fez.

The British sergeant fired. The enemy soldier stopped as if he'd run into a wall and fell backward with a strangled cry, dropping his machine pistol. Stirling rolled toward the opposite side of the boulder, working the Enfield's bolt as he did so. Just above him, there came the scraping sound of boot soles on rock. . . .

With the speed born of desperation, Stirling rammed the bolt home and swung the rifle around, adrenaline pumping through his body like an electric charge. . . .

It was too late. The second enemy soldier had made it around the boulder and was standing over him, his Schmeisser already brought to bear.

Everything went into slow motion.

Stirling locked eyes with the SS trooper through the Schmeisser's ring sight.

Damn, he thought, waiting for the burst.

The enemy soldier's head snapped over onto his right shoulder. At the same time, Stirling heard an odd, sharp *pop*.

Like a marionette with its strings suddenly cut, the

SS trooper folded up and crumpled facedown into the snow.

The death's-head fez he wore somehow remained on his head. In the top of it, near the tassel attachment, was a small hole. Stirling blinked. Blood began to spread out around the enemy soldier's head, a dark stain on the pristine pallor of the snow.

Bewildered, Stirling glanced around. Then, his eye catching nothing, he rolled to one knee and shouldered his rifle once again. There were at least two more enemy soldiers on the slope, and they'd be coming next.

Stirling raised his head and shoulders above the boulder, sighting down the Enfield. The two remaining SS troopers were standing thigh deep in the snow, aiming their machine pistols . . . *straight upward.*

Stirling fired. The .303 slug smacked into the forehead of the soldier on the left, sending his fez flying end over end and his limp body toppling backward down the slope. The last enemy soldier jerked down his Schmeisser and trained it on the British sergeant.

Stirling hunched back down behind the boulder, working the Enfield's bolt. In his haste, his boot slipped on a patch of ice. He lost his balance and fell onto one arm, partially exposing himself beyond the edge of the covering rock.

As the SS trooper squeezed the trigger of his machine pistol, Sergeant David Weiss stepped out from behind a pine tree some twenty feet farther along the slope and killed him on his feet with a two-second burst from his Sten gun. The Schmeisser slugs hammered harmlessly into the snow as the dead man fell.

Stirling regained his balance and, crouching behind the boulder, waved at Weiss. The younger sergeant waved back and began to climb rapidly across the snow-packed slope toward him. As Weiss neared the base of the crag, Stirling spotted first one dim human form, then another and another, appearing through

the trees from around the contour of the incline.
Alarmed, he threw up his rifle and sighted on the
lead figure.

"Quick, Weiss!" he hissed. "Get in here!"

Weiss lunged through the top of the snowdrift that
abutted Stirling's boulder and ducked down beside
him. "What is it?" he asked, breathing hard.

"Don't know. Maybe more Huns." Stirling's brow
furrowed as he concentrated on the new arrivals. "But
they're coming from the opposite direction, and
they're not all wearing the same winter gear. Mismatched clothing, no real uniforms. Mismatched
weapons, too."

Weiss peered cautiously over the top of the boulder.
"Sounds like Partisans."

Stirling watched in silence for another few seconds,
then lowered his rifle. "It is."

The two British commandos stood up as the skirmish line of Partisans advanced across the slope like
a sparse, ragged wave. The lead figures had only just
disappeared into the dark trees through which Stirling
had fled when there was an outbreak of machine-gun
and rifle fire, accompanied by frantic shouts in both
German and Serbo-Croatian. Instinctively Stirling and
Weiss hunched back behind the boulder.

"I guess they found more of the Nazis who were
chasing you," Weiss said. He glanced over at the body
of the dead enemy soldier with the hole in the top of
his fez. The pool of dark blood around the man's head
was a yard in diameter and already frozen solid.
"Looks like SS, by that death's-head symbol on the
fez. . . . But I don't see any SS runes on the collar or
anywhere else. Strange."

"The man is a Muslim trooper of the SS Division
Handschar," said Anton Cernović, approaching with
practiced stealth along the base of the crag. Following
him were Merritt, Bristow, D'Amato, and three very
tough-looking Partisan infantrymen. Startled, Weiss

and Stirling spun around and brought their weapons up, but upon recognizing Merritt lowered them immediately.

Cernović halted and regarded the body with casual disinterest. "As a non-Aryan," he continued, "he is not permitted to wear the actual runic symbol of the SS. Only German officers within Handschar may do so, on the left pocket of their battle tunics." He pointed. "You see the insignia on the collar? The arm holding a scimitar in combination with a Nazi swastika? That is the official emblem of the Handschar division."

The Partisan commander glanced up as another heavy outburst of small-arms fire echoed through the dark trees below and to the right. Then he shrugged, fished beneath his coat, withdrew a crumpled hand-rolled cigarette, and stuck it between his lips. One of the Partisans stepped forward with a match, and Cernović turned his head sideways to take the light.

"This man was a dangerous fighter," he remarked, exhaling smoke. "You did well to kill him and his companions. They are members of a Jagdkommando unit within Handschar."

Weiss shifted his Sten in his arms. "What exactly is a Jagdkommando unit?"

"A hunter-killer group," Cernović replied, "varying from platoon to company strength. The Jagdkommando are sent out into the hills on tracked vehicles and on foot, heavily armed, with orders to hunt down and kill every Partisan they can find. So naturally"—he smiled swarthily around his cigarette like an evil gypsy—"when we get an opportunity to kill *them*, we do so with considerable relish."

"Commander Cernović has just told me that the Jagdkommando have recently taken up the habit of stalking Partisan drop zones and then quietly setting up duplicate signal fires nearby—perhaps just over the next ridge," Merritt said. "Jumpers can get confused, head for the wrong lights. Apparently that's what just happened to some of us. By the way," he added, "good to see you alive, Weiss. And you, too, Stirling."

"Thank you, sir," the two sergeants replied in unison.

Merritt turned to Cernović as yet another burst of gunfire chattered through the trees, none too distant. "What's your assessment of the situation, Commander? Is there a whole company of SS Jagdkommando out there? If so, you're badly outnumbered."

The Partisan commander shook his head, exhaling smoke. "We had reports of only two platoon-strength hunter-killer groups operating in this area in the past three days. No other deployments from the main forces of Handschar. Even if the two groups have linked up, that's still only eighty or so men and perhaps four or five half-tracks. I have ninety-two men, Major." The swarthy smile again. "Even odds, more or less."

Merritt nodded and looked at Stirling. "Where's Hurst?"

The commando sergeant cleared his throat before replying. "Dead, sir. Shot it out with the buggers when they tried to take him alive."

"I'm sorry, Stirling. He was a good man."

"Yes, sir. That he was. And a good friend."

Merritt blew out a long, frosty breath. "So that leaves Throckmorton. Have either of you seen him?"

Stirling and Weiss shook their heads. "Afraid not, sir," Stirling said. "Frankly, I haven't had time to look. Been running for my life since I touched down. And if it weren't for Weiss here taking out these two troopers for me"—he pointed down at the corpses on the slope and at the body of the enemy soldier with the holed fez—"I'd have been as dead as poor Hurstie." He paused, then glanced at Weiss. "Can't think how you managed to shoot *up* and still hit this one bastard in the top of the head, though. . . ."

Weiss blinked. "The only man I killed was lower down on the slope," he said. "I never shot up in this direction."

"You didn't?" Stirling looked confused. "Then who—"

"I say, there." The voice, clear but at the same time strangely distant, seemed to come out of the rock face itself. "Perhaps you chaps would care to lend a gentleman a hand, now that the excitement's died down somewhat."

The little knot of men glanced around, momentarily baffled. Then Merritt looked up. Eighty feet overhead, suspended against the cliff in the torn remnants of his parachute, was Throckmorton. As the rest of the party stepped back and stared upward, the slender British captain waved the Webley pistol he held in his right hand and gave a wry smile.

"Tallyho," he remarked, his tone as dry as the alpine air.

Abruptly Merritt grinned. "What the hell are you doing up there, Duncan?" he called.

"Just hanging about," came the reply. "Taking in the scenery."

Stirling cleared his throat. "You mean to say you've been up there the whole time? Watching the SS hunt me to the base of this cliff?"

"Well, I couldn't see you until you actually got here, Sergeant," Throckmorton said. "And since you brought company with you, I thought it might be wiser just to hang here like a wallflower and not attract any attention. That is," he added, "until it became expedient—for *your* sake—to drop a round into the top of that fellow's head." He waved the pistol again and smiled. "Unfortunately his remaining two comrades then noticed me. A bad moment, that—looking down into those machine pistols. But you and Weiss took care of them, so all's well that ends well, eh?"

"You might have said something a little sooner, Duncan," Merritt said. "Let us know you were up there."

"Well, you were having such a pleasant conversation," Throckmorton replied, managing somehow to look mildly bored with it all despite his precarious position, "I didn't want to interrupt."

"Jeezus," Bristow muttered to D'Amato under his breath. "What a pisscutter this guy is."

Merritt put a hand on Cernović's shoulder. "Commander. We need the mountaineering gear in the equipment cylinder that was dropped before we jumped—at least one rucksack with a full length of rope. Did you receive it?"

"Yes," Cernović answered. "That was one supply container that did not end up in the hands of the Germans." He clapped his gloved hands together and pointed back along the cliff base. "Vlado! Boris! The equipment, back up in the clearing! One rucksack and a long rope, quickly!"

Two of the three Partisans took off through the rocks at a fast trot. Cernović grunted, inhaled the dregs of his cigarette, and flicked the butt into the snow. "They'll be back in ten minutes," he mused. "Now if we only had—"

"People coming through the trees down there, Major," D'Amato said, swinging up his Thompson. "Heading up the slope."

Merritt peered down over the snowdrift. A dozen or so armed guerillas were plodding up the incline toward the base of the crag. In the lead was the giant Partisan with the black beard.

"Friendlies, Sergeant," Merritt said. "Easy, now."

"That big bastard in front don't look so friendly," D'Amato muttered, lowering his machine gun. "Didn't I see him back on the drop zone?"

Cernović let out a short, guttural laugh and raised a hand to the oncoming Partisans. "That is Bozidar Yagovac," he said. "Known to all simply as Bozi. One of my senior lieutenants, and my best combat leader. A force of nature, you might say."

"Damn, I believe it," Bristow commented. "He's a big 'un, alright."

"He is . . . useful," Cernović said.

Merritt watched for a moment as the Partisans—most of them a full head shorter than Yagovac and one much shorter than that—continued to trudge up the slope. Then he looked back up at Throckmorton.

"How are you, Duncan?" he called.

"A trifle chilled, thanks," Throckmorton answered. "I can't really move, you see. When I do, the chute I'm hanging from has a nasty habit of ripping."

"Right, stay still," Merritt said. "We're coming up with a rope in just a few minutes."

"Ah, splendid. I'll just relax here, then."

There was a sudden sound of fabric tearing, clearly audible to everyone at the base of the cliff.

"Oops," Throckmorton said.

Merritt's mouth tightened into a hard line as he stared up. "Where the devil is that climbing gear, Commander? My man's about to fall."

"Christ, it'll take another fifteen minutes to get up to him once we have it," Bristow growled, "driving pitons all the way. This cliff's sheer and damn near smooth."

Merritt continued to stare up helplessly. "Bloody hell."

Cernović, standing off to one side, turned to Yagovac as the giant Partisan clambered over the top of the snowdrift, followed by his ragtag soldiers. "Report, Bozi," the commander said, digging in his coat for another cigarette.

"One large platoon of Jagdkommando, Comrade Commander," Yagovac rumbled, brushing snow off his greatcoat. "About fifty men total. Plus two half-tracks with MG-42 machine guns mounted. But they couldn't use them." The giant grinned through his beard. "They couldn't maneuver. The terrain was too uneven and the snow too deep. We kept to the slopes, swept around both flanks and killed maybe a third of them as they retreated toward their vehicles." He chortled happily, rubbed his hands together, and looked back at the little band of ragged, grimy fighters behind him. "Maybe half of them, eh?" There was a general cackling of satisfied agreement from the soldiers, along with the metallic clanking of weapons being adjusted. The steamy vapors of evaporating sweat and condensing breath rose into the night air.

"Is that Comrade Kozo back there?" Cernović demanded, squinting as he lit his cigarette.

"Yes, Comrade Commander," Yagovac said. "With three fresh kills tonight, no less."

"Excellent, excellent," Cernović declared. "Come here, Kozo. I have a job for you."

A Partisan fighter who barely came up to Yagovac's greatcoat lapel appeared from the rear of the motley pack and shuffled forward, carrying—like many of the men—a captured Schmeisser machine pistol. The soldier's head was covered with an immense fur hat, earflaps tied down. A scarf protected his face, leaving only a small slit for the eyes. Layers of bulky winter clothing, all of it dirty and threadbare, provided insulation from neck to knees. The soldier's lower legs and boots were wrapped with long strips of cloth, making his feet appear huge. He waddled to a halt in front of Cernović, exhaling condensation through his frost-rimed face scarf.

"Ah, here comes a rope," Cernović said, glancing back along the cliff trail. Vlado and Boris had reappeared and were hurrying through the rocks toward the group. "Kozo, I want you to climb up there and secure a line to the parachutist so we can lower him to the ground. Quickly, I think. His parachute seems to be on the verge of giving way."

The small Partisan nodded, unslung and handed off his machine pistol, and began to undo the buttons of his thick combat jacket.

Merritt looked up at Throckmorton dangling on the sheer cliff, over at the undressing Partisan, and finally at Cernović. "Ah, Commander," he said, "you don't need to put one of your people at risk. We're quite capable of handling this ourselves."

Cernović chuckled and drew on his cigarette. "Of course you are, Major. But not as quickly as Comrade Kozo, I promise you."

Merritt was about to reply when the harsh sound of tearing silk came from above once more.

"Blast," Throckmorton said.

"Stay still, Duncan!" Merritt shouted. "Someone's coming up with a rope right now!" He stepped back and regarded Cernović. "All right, Commander. If your man's as fast as you say, the job's his."

"I'm sure Comrade Kozo appreciates your confidence," Cernović said, looking amused.

Merritt frowned slightly, puzzled at the Partisan commander's odd, secretive grin.

"Ah. Ready now, Sylvia?" Cernović inquired, looking past Merritt's shoulder.

The furrow in Merritt's brow deepened, and he turned around.

The short, stocky Partisan in the thick layers of winter clothing was gone. In his place was a lithe, pale-skinned young woman of perhaps twenty-two. She was clad in tight, high-cut shorts, a snug-fitting man's sleeveless undershirt, and the immense fur hat the Partisan soldier had worn. On her feet were what appeared to be black ballet slippers.

Merritt gaped. So did Bristow, D'Amato, Stirling, and Weiss. The loitering Partisans chuckled among themselves.

The young woman stood with her shoulders back, firm breasts pressing against the grimy fabric of the undershirt, her arms loose by her sides. Her legs were slender but well muscled—dancer's legs—and she stood with the unconscious poise of a ballerina. Her face was fine featured, pixieish, with sharp, high cheekbones and slanted, vaguely oriental eyes. Her mouth was small and full lipped, slightly downturned

at the corners, and her pointed chin jutted forward
aggressively—a function of her high-held head and
what seemed to be a permanently set jaw. The biting
cold appeared to have no effect on her whatsoever.

Cobra-eyed was the phrase that leapt to Merritt's
mind. The young woman's eyes were hooded, the lids
heavy and half closed. They lent her a dangerous
rather than doeish aspect.

"Allow me to introduce you to Comrade Sylvia
Kozo, Major Merritt," Cernović said. "Our climbing
specialist."

Merritt nodded, still somewhat dumbfounded.
"Charmed, Miss."

Unsmiling, the young woman ignored him, stepped
forward, and extended a hand toward the Partisan
named Vlado. "Rope," she said.

The soldier tossed her the end of a long, finely
braided mountaineering line. Working quickly, she
knotted a bowline into it, slipped the loop diagonally
over her shoulder, and walked to the base of the cliff.

"Slack," she said to Vlado. With that, she kicked
snow off her black slippers, reached up, found all-but-
invisible fingerholds in the sheer rock face, and began
to climb.

Chapter Four

"**G**oddamn," Bristow muttered. "What's holdin' her on there? That little gal must have suction cups for fingers."

"Or magnets," D'Amato said. He craned his neck farther back and scratched the stubble on his chin. "Or maybe claws, from the look on her face. Hell, Cole—think she ever *smiles*?"

"Don't look like it," the Texan concluded.

The young woman named Sylvia Kozo was already forty feet off the ground and moving steadily upward with the agility of a spider monkey. It was mesmerizing to watch her climb; her movements had a rhythmic economy, in combination with tremendous flexibility and considerable strength, and resembled nothing so much as a vertical, slow-motion dance. It would have been an impressive display of skill on a warm summer's day on dry, clean rock, never mind in the dead of a Balkan winter, *at night*, on a cliff face booby-trapped with innumerable ice patches.

"That's quite incredible," Merritt said, standing beside Cernović and gazing upward. "She's an amazing athlete."

"Yes, she is," Cernović replied. "In fact, she's one of the best professional athletes in Eastern Europe. A circus acrobat of considerable renown."

Merritt raised an eyebrow. "Really?"

"Oh yes. From a family of acrobats. The Flying Kozos. A star act in the Moscow, Vienna, Budapest, and Berlin circuses. Surely you've heard of them?"

"Unfortunately not. Perhaps they didn't get the attention they deserved in Britain."

"No doubt." Cernović puffed on his ubiquitous cigarette. "Anyway, Sylvia was the eldest daughter, and the family's star flier. The first woman to execute a triple aerial somersault to a catch without a net."

Merritt whistled through his teeth. "I'm impressed."

"All the more impressive when you consider she did it in 1937, when she was only fifteen. As she got older and more . . . fully formed, shall we say . . . she found it more difficult to execute high-speed aerials—to improve on what she'd already accomplished. Plus she wanted to develop her own identity separate from that of her famous family—Sylvia is a very independent-minded young woman, you see. So she began to promote herself as the Great Sylvia, Conqueror of Buildings. There was no man-made structure she could not climb using only her hands and feet, she claimed. And then she proceeded to prove it, climbing cathedrals, castles, and towers all over Europe—at least until this war unpleasantness developed."

"A remarkable story," Merritt said. "And now she fights with the Partisans."

Cernović exhaled smoke into the night air, watching idly as the young woman maneuvered to within fifteen feet of the dangling Throckmorton. "Yes, she does," he said. "Her entire family, with the exception of one younger brother, was killed by Stuka dive bombers in the German attack on Belgrade back in 'forty-one. It changed her dramatically, as similar experiences have changed so many of us over the past several years."

Merritt nodded. "Tragic. And her brother?"

"Murdered by SS troops a month later. Shot in a ditch along with fifteen other civilians because someone threw red paint at an SS commander in a passing tank."

"Not that it matters," Merritt said bitterly, "but he probably didn't even have anything to do with it."

"A fairly accurate assumption, I'd say. He was only eight years old."

Merritt looked at Cernović, met his eyes. The Partisan commander's mouth tightened into a grim smile. "Sylvia enjoys killing SS," he said.

Eighty feet up the cliff, Sylvia Kozo was just drawing abreast of Throckmorton. "Hello, my dear," he said in English, intrigued.

Sylvia glanced sideways at him through her hooded lids and climbed on past, trailing the long mountaineering rope behind her.

"Nice to have met you," Throckmorton called, as a slender ankle and black slipper moved upward past his head. The icy granite jutting into his back was considerably warmer than the pale sprite that had just manifested itself on the rock, he decided.

Carefully he craned his neck and looked up. The young woman was already at the small horn of rock that had snagged his chute. One black-slippered toe was balanced on some indiscernable irregularity in the cliff face; the opposite leg was drawn up so that the knee was hooked over the rock horn. The woman was leaning back, hips in, holding herself in place with only her legs. With both hands thus freed she was rapidly sorting through the tangle of loose parachute lines.

In less than a minute she had knotted two of the lines into a double loop around the rock horn and passed her trailing rope through it. Tying the end loosely around her waist, she then down-climbed to within arm's length of Throckmorton, pulling the rope with her.

"Hello again, my dear," Throckmorton said pleasantly. "Captain Duncan Throckmorton at your service."

Sprawled against the rock face, hanging on by two toes and one hand, Sylvia responded by pulling the rope from around her own waist and jamming the end roughly through Throckmorton's harness belt above his groin, making him flinch.

"I *say!*" he wheezed.

One-handed, the young woman threw a locking hitch into the mountaineering rope, yanked it tight, then leaned away from Throckmorton to take the strain off her toes and supporting hand.

"Well, I'll try once more," Throckmorton said, this time in Serbo-Croatian. "Captain Duncan Throckmorton, madam, at your service."

Sylvia turned her head slowly and regarded him without expression from beneath her heavy lids. "I understood you the first time, Captain," she said in accented but fluent English. Repositioning her hands and feet on the rock, she leaned down and withdrew Throckmorton's jump knife from its leg sheath.

"Did you, now?" Throckmorton replied, arching an eyebrow. "I would have thought a courteous hello would have warranted a courteous acknowledgement."

Sylvia's hooded eyes closed a fraction farther. "Perhaps you haven't noticed. I've been busy saving your life."

"Actually I had, my dear—"

"Of course, you couldn't possibly know how weary I am of being subjected to smug English aristocrats with greasy manners and ulterior motives, who routinely drop into my country to play at war for a few weeks at a time—as if war were nothing more than an exotic sporting event to be rehashed over brandy and cigars at some posh, private London club upon their heroic return."

Throckmorton was silent for a moment, his expression pleasant but immobile. "And here was me," he said, "thinking that you were merely rude."

Sylvia reached out and with one swipe of the jump knife slashed through both parachute risers supporting Throckmorton. The British captain dropped like a stone for twenty feet before bouncing painfully to a halt in his harness as, far below, Vlado and Boris threw their combined weight against the lower end of the mountaineering rope.

It took the better part of three hours to reach the Partisan encampment, trudging down a series of steep, snow-clogged switchback trails in single file beneath silent, snow-laden evergreen trees, coaxing along the dozen or so cranky, obstinate mules that carried most of the field supplies and ammunition. The succession of gullies and small gorges that had to be traversed, in particular, seemed endless—down one side and up the other, again and again, to the point of exhaustion. Only two-thirds of the original Partisan force was returning; Cernović had sent the giant Yagovac and thirty men to harass the shot-up Jagdkommando unit all the way back to the main body of Handschar.

"Home, for the moment," Cernović said, stepping off the trail to a small overlook between two immense slabs of rock. "Such as it is."

Merritt moved up beside him. The dim light of pre-dawn was just beginning to filter through the trees. One hundred and fifty feet below was yet another heavily forested, snow-blanketed gorge, its sides so steep that a man could not descend into it without local trail knowledge or the aid of a rope. It was not unlike the last ten gorges the small guerilla column had negotiated, but scattered on the floor of this one were several dozen log lean-tos, their roofs covered with snow and certainly all but invisible from the air.

Here and there in front of these rudimentary shelters, a small pennant of smoke from a carefully concealed fire twisted up into the still air of early morning, dissipating before clearing the tops of the trees.

"The Soujak Mine," Cernović said, pointing. Through the still haze Merritt could make out a dark opening in the far side of the gorge, a fracture in the rock. "An abandoned copper dig." The Partisan commander smiled thinly. "Now one of many Majerica Mountain bolt-holes used by the underfed but undaunted Second Proletarian Brigade of the glorious Partisan Army of Yugoslavia."

Merritt matched Cernović's rueful smile with one of his own. "Do I detect a touch of cynicism, Commander?"

"What you detect, Major Merritt," Cernović answered, "is *weariness*."

The two men turned away from the overlook and stepped back onto the trail. Stirling was just passing by, trudging along in the single-file track behind a mangy, uncooperative pack mule that was practically being dragged through the snow by a cursing Partisan. The veteran commando sergeant appeared very tired—heavy footed and with head down—and his lean face had a haunted look to it. He was whistling tunelessly under his breath.

Merritt touched his shoulder. "All right, Sergeant?"

Stirling glanced up and nodded. "Yes, sir. Never better."

"Good. Not far now."

"Yes, sir."

Stirling resumed both his slogging pace and quiet, unmelodic whistling. Merritt watched him for a moment, then looked back up the trail at the thin, ragged parade of exhausted Partisans. About fifty yards back he caught sight of Throckmorton.

"Coming, Major?" Cernović inquired, falling in behind a soldier bearing a captured MG-42 machine gun across his shoulders.

"I'll be right along, Commander," Merritt replied.
"I want to speak with Captain Throckmorton."

"Certainly. Watch your step as you make your
way down."

"We will."

Merritt leaned back against a tree trunk as the soldiers, looking like a procession of tattered specters in
the wan gray light of early morning, continued to file
past at a slow shuffle. Throckmorton was clearly having difficulty, staggering through the snow with his
breath coming in great billows of condensation. Merritt stepped in beside him as he drew abreast, and got
an arm under his.

"Steady, Duncan," he muttered. "We're there. No
need to hurry."

"Blood . . . bloody good . . . thing," Throckmorton
gasped. "Bloody air's . . . too . . . bloody thin . . . up
here." He coughed violently, turned his head, and spat
into the snow.

The Partisan just ahead of them turned and peered
back at Throckmorton, then at the dark spot where
the phlegm had landed. Merritt gave him a hard look.
The soldier shook his head slightly, turned back
around, and continued on down the trail.

Merritt pulled Throckmorton off to one side. "Let's
just rest here for a minute," he said.

"Bloody . . . fine with . . . me," Throckmorton wheezed,
bending over and bracing his hands on his knees.

The ragtag soldiers continued to trudge past, the
dry snow crunching and squeaking under their boots.
No one spoke, and very few of them even bothered
to glance up at the two Englishmen. All those who
did wore the same expression: a hollow-cheeked,
sunken-eyed mask of strain, resolve, and bone-deep
fatigue.

A Partisan wearing a filthy greatcoat and an immense fur Cossack-style hat, his Mauser rifle slung
across his back with a piece of rope, staggered past,

panting. The next man in line was Weiss. He nodded
to Merritt and stepped off the trail.

"Hard going, sir," he said, wiping a glove across his
frost-rimed nose and mouth. "Need help?" He looked
pointedly at Throckmorton, who was still bent over
with his back heaving.

"We'll be all right in a minute," Merritt said.

Weiss pulled off his gloves and blew into his cupped
hands. "God, it's cold up here." Merritt nodded silently, his eyes roving through the trees. Weiss blew
into his hands again, then cleared his throat. "You
know, Captain Throckmorton," he said, "that was a
fairly spectacular shot—putting a pistol round into the
top of that SS trooper's head while you were dangling
eighty feet in the air."

Throckmorton nodded from his bent-over position. "At
night, too, don't forget." His wind seemed to be returning.

"Of course. At night."

Merritt stopped scanning the trees and turned to
Weiss. "Captain Throckmorton is a former Olympian,
like myself. In fact, that's how we first met back in
1936. British Olympic team."

Weiss smiled and began to put his gloves back on.
"Ah. That explains a lot. Don't tell me: target pistol
shooter."

"Silver medalist," Merritt confirmed, "and second
only by a hair."

"Quite an accomplishment," Weiss said. "Who won
the gold?"

Throckmorton stood up, put his hands on his hips,
and tipped his head back, concentrating on his breathing. "Some Nazi sod," he remarked. "One of those
damnable Von-something-or-others. Personally I think
he was using doctored ammunition—flatter shooting,
you see. Of course, I couldn't prove it, and the German judges buried my protest, curse them."

Merritt smiled faintly behind Throckmorton's left
shoulder. His old friend was feeling better.

"But I got my own back that evening at a reception at the British ambassador's residence. Von Whatsit showed up in SS evening tails, with his gold medal draped around his neck and some slinky baroness clinging to his arm—her upper works spilling half out of her gown beneath her fox stole, I might add."

Sensing Throckmorton's rhythm, Weiss filled in dutifully, "And what did you do, Captain?"

Throckmorton's fine right nostril curved upward. "I cut the bugger dead on the entrance carpet in front of everyone, impugned his honor to the upscale riffraff for the next two hours, then concluded the evening by spiriting away his jiggly Junker harlot and rogering her red in the face until dawn. A quite deliciously nasty piece she was, too."

Weiss burst out laughing. "You have a poet's turn of phrase, Captain."

"He's famous for it," Merritt said. He clapped a gloved hand onto Throckmorton's shoulder. "Shall we go now, Duncan? We want to be down in that encampment before it gets too light."

The slender captain nodded. "Might as well," he said, stepping onto the trail. "There's no sign of the bloody limousine I ordered."

Bozidar Yagovac and his thirty Partisan guerillas had dogged and harassed the retreating Jagdkommando unit for nearly six miles through the rugged alpine forest when the three Fieseler Storches floated in over the trees in the cold silver gleam of dawn. Light, low-level reconnaissance aircraft with fabric skins and small single engines, they would have appeared as innocuous as the American Piper Cub they resembled were it not for the pair of MG-42 machine guns each had clamped to either side of the fuselage just ahead of the wing struts—vertically mounted, muzzles pointing straight down. They drifted ahead like great dark-green bats, side by side, heading directly into the wind with engines throttled back so

hat their forward motion was almost impossibly slow.
But not too slow to overtake tired men floundering in
deep snow.

"*Disperse, comrades!*" Yagovac bellowed right and
left into the trees. "*Hunter-Storches! Disperse and find
cover! And fire at the bastards when you can!*"

He threw up his Schmeisser and let loose a long
burst at the nearest Storch as it hovered toward him
at treetop level. Then he turned and began to struggle
through the snow toward the trunk of a huge pine
tree. Crouching behind it was Vlado, the Partisan in-
fantryman who, along with Boris, had manned the
rope Sylvia had taken up the cliff to the snagged British officer Throckmorton. He was gazing up at the
black-crossed Storch like a rat caught in the paralyzing
stare of a viper.

"*Fire if you're going to stay there!*" Yagovac
shouted, churning his way forward. "*Try to knock the
bastards down before they open up on us!*"

Vlado started as if stung, looked uncertainly at Yagovac, then sprang to his feet and floundered off beneath the overhanging pine boughs. The giant Partisan
cursed eloquently in four dialects and made it to the
base of the tree just as the trio of Storches moved
directly overhead and opened up.

The vertically mounted machine guns on each plane
spat twin cones of fire downward at fifteen hundred
rounds per minute, chopping the forest below into a
maelstrom of pine needles, wood splinters, and ex-
ploding snow. The chaotic line of death advanced
steadily through the trees as the planes came on, maintaining their high volume of fire.

Partisan fighters were flushed from their places of
concealment as the moveable killing zone swept
toward them; vertical tree trunks provided cover from
horizontal fire, not a continuous barrage coming
straight down out of the sky. As the first panicked
soldiers tried to flee clumsily through the deep drifts,
the advancing wall of fire overtook them. Screams

echoed through the trees above the relentless mechanical snarling of the aerial machine guns, floundering men became contorting silhouettes within a blizzard of whipped-up snow, and then the wall passed, leaving ruined foliage and dead shapes in its wake.

"Crūmgržkt!" gnashed Yagovac, which was a curse so ancient, pagan, and blasphemous that any person who dared utter it in the presence of an Eastern Orthodox priest was sure to receive a week's hard penance on the spot. He stared in helpless fury at the dozen or so slaughtered men who lay like torn scarecrows in the stained snow.

Abruptly the Storches stopped firing. Having overflown the main concentration of Partisans, they revved their engines and banked off in opposite directions, two to the north and one to the south.

Yagovac staggered to his feet. *"Move, comrades!"* he roared. *"They're coming around for another pass! Everyone split up, disperse! Make your own way back to the mine, and make sure the planes don't follow you! Disperse, curse you, disperse!"*

He turned, and there was Vlado again, behind the next tree, staring at him with the same erratic look in his eyes.

"Well, don't just stand there, idiot!" Yagovac growled, striding past. "Follow me!"

The interior of the Soujak Mine was cold and damp, but palpably less frigid than the little hidden valley outside. Kerosene lanterns hung here and there on rough walls hacked long ago by pickax and hammer from the ore-rich rock of the mountain, providing a flickering orange light. Oily smoke hovered in the stagnant air, which was also permeated by the reek of human sweat; the aroma of horse meat, paprika, and garlic stewing in cook pots; the tang of fresh blood; and the sickening stench of putrefying flesh. The severely wounded were lying shoulder to shoulder along the walls of the main passageway, some of them with advanced gas gangrene.

Merritt, Throckmorton, Bristow, D'Amato, and Weiss were sitting in a shallow, lantern-lit alcove in the rock—alternately smoking, eating bowls of horse-meat stew, and checking through the containers of explosives and mountaineering equipment piled around them. Stirling sat slightly apart from the rest, on the floor of the alcove with his back against the rock wall, head down, slowly sipping from a tin mug of broth that he held in both hands.

"What's wrong with him?"

Merritt looked up from the detonator he was inspecting to see Sylvia Kozo, clad now in shapeless wool trousers and a moth-eaten, too-large British Army turtleneck sweater, standing over him with a bucket of stew in one hand and the other on her cocked hip. She was looking down her small nose at him from beneath her heavy lids, fairly exuding aggression, challenge, and no small measure of calculated hostility. A reasonable defensive posture for a beautiful twenty-three-year-old woman accustomed to acclaim and privilege who now found herself the sole survivor of a murdered family and an active combatant in a world gone mad, Merritt decided.

He smiled carefully and looked back down at the detonator in his hand. "Sergeant Stirling lost a friend last night," he said.

Sylvia frowned across the alcove at Stirling, considered a moment, then gave a brief snort and shifted her weight to her opposite hip. "Losing friends is an occupational hazard around here," she remarked, scowling. "It hardly makes him unique." As Merritt sat in silence, reflecting that her comment merited no response, she plucked the ladle from her bucket and slopped a fresh serving of stew into the bowl by his side with a wet, messy sound—*flotch*.

"There," she declared, lifting her chin and turning

on her heel, "have some gourmet Serbian horse." She
glared down at Throckmorton as she stalked past.
"You won't find any Savoy Grill crown roast in the
Soujak Mine."

"My, you're a sour one," Throckmorton drawled,
recrossing his legs atop a munitions crate as he
lounged back against the cave wall. He contemplated
his fingernails for a moment. "Tell me, my little Gor-
gon: has any man ever gazed into your lovely eyes
without being turned to stone?"

Sylvia rounded on him. "Listen, you English
bast—"

"That's enough, Comrade Kozo!" The barked command came from farther down the passageway. A
stocky figure in an unbuttoned officer's coat, mis-
shapen peaked cap, jodhpurs, and battered black riding boots emerged from the lantern-lit dimness.
Beneath the cap, a striking, highly chiseled Slavic face
smiled wearily. "Go to your bed, Sylvia. Don't terror-
ize our English and American friends any more tonight. You might make them leave, and they've only
just arrived."

"Huh!" Sylvia looked like a pouting twelve-year-
old for a second or two, then lowered her head slightly
and stepped out of the alcove. "Yes, Comrade Marshall Tito," she muttered, and moved off down the
passageway.

All the men got hurriedly to their feet. *Marshall
Tito*. Aka Josip Broz, leader of the Yugoslav Communist Partisans. The warlord who along with his hard-
scrabble army was the one wild card in the Balkans
that kept the Nazis from subduing the entire region.
Winston Churchill's favorite thorn in the side of the
Third Reich, whose relentless hit-and-run military operations forced the ongoing commitment of German
manpower, machinery, and munitions that could otherwise have been utilized on the Eastern and Western Fronts.

Tito was not particularly tall, but broad shouldered

nd strong looking along peasant lines. His tanned,
eamed face supported a square, set jaw and a pair of
tartlingly pale blue eyes that had the quality, as such
yes often do, of seeming to look right through whom-
ver they fixed upon. Then, once again, he smiled, and
t was an engaging, charismatic smile.

"Please come this way, Major Merritt," he said,
eckoning. "Your men, too."

Chapter Five

"What happened to your former partner? Grohl, wasn't it?"

Gestapo Hauptsturmfuehrer Julius Neurath continued to gaze out the window of the luxury train car as the lights of Zagreb flickered past. His arrogantly handsome features pinched as he drew on his cigarette. Then he plucked it from his lips and blew a thin stream of smoke at the plate glass.

"He was killed by a terrorist a short time ago in Berlin," he said. "A Jew who was trying to assassinate the Grand Mufti with a hand bomb." Neurath raised the cigarette to his mouth again with a black-gloved hand. "Grohl was too slow and clumsy. The fool didn't get out of the way in time and caught the full force of the blast." As usual, his brief recounting of the incident omitted the fact that Grohl's body had stopped the shrapnel that almost certainly would have resulted in his own demise.

The black-uniformed SS Hauptsturmfuehrer who had posed the question settled back in his coach seat

and swirled the red wine in his glass. "Unfortunate.
You were nearby?"

"We had arrived at the Hotel Jürgenplatz in the
same staff car."

"And yet you emerged unscathed, while the other
two bodyguards with you—your partner and the SS
driver—were killed and quite severely wounded, respectively." The SS man, a rugged-looking Bavarian
with dark hair and complexion named Matthias Juttner, smiled thinly and sipped his wine, leaving a silence that resounded with innuendo.

Neurath turned slowly and regarded him with a pale
stare. The armored train—engine, coal car, SS bunk
car, antiaircraft-gun car, private coach, and caboose—
clattered and shook over a level crossing. Juttner
raised his glass carefully to prevent the wine from
being spilled by vibration.

"If you know about Grohl and Beckmann," Neurath said, "then obviously you've been briefed on the
assassination attempt or read my official report. You
know I was there in the thick of it, so what the devil
are you implying?"

Juttner smiled again and held his glass up to the
dim light of the overhead chandelier, examining the
wine's color. "I'm inquiring, not implying," he replied.
"I merely find it interesting that the two men with
whom you were formerly partnered both found themselves either suddenly dead or mangled beyond repair,
while you sustained not a single scratch." He blinked
pleasantly up at Neurath. "After all, *I'm* your new
partner in this al-Husseini security assignment."

Neurath stared down—unpleasantly. "I was
knocked flat on my back by the bomb blast," he said.
"The device went off beneath the car and Grohl was
in the wrong place at the wrong time. Beckmann was
protected from the major force of the explosion by
the car's armor plate, and was only singed. He assisted
me in running down the assassin, but in so doing lost
his composure and became hysterical, indulging in a

series of ill-advised heroics. This resulted in his being shot several times. His own fault."

Juttner finished his wine and set the glass down on the coach-seat service table. "You won't find me so obligingly eager to step into the path of every bullet that comes our way, Hauptsturmfuehrer Neurath," he said.

"I think I've absorbed enough of your insulting ruminations for one night, Juttner," Neurath declared. "I'm retiring to my berth. And by the way, you'd do well to remember that *I'm* the senior man on this security detail."

"By virtue of duration only," Juttner riposted seamlessly. "Not by rank."

Neurath turned a shade paler than his usual bone white. "Good night, Hauptsturmfuehrer."

"Good night, Hauptsturmfuehrer."

As Neurath stalked, simmering, down the length of the passenger compartment toward the door of his berth, Juttner lit a thin black cigar with a gold lighter, propped one gleaming jackboot up on the service table, and gazed contentedly out at the thinning lights of the outskirts of Zagreb. Why the city would not be under blackout, what with Allied planes flying random bombing and reconnaissance sorties over northern Croatia, he could not imagine. At the other end of the coach, Neurath's door closed with a notable bang.

Juttner chuckled and blew a smoke ring at Zagreb. Never before had he found himself on assignment with a fellow officer of equivalent rank who had proven to be so instantly contemptible. The man was, without a doubt, a borderline sociopath.

There was a sustained thumping from within Neurath's quarters.

Juttner drew again on his cigar. The train trip from Berlin to Belgrade was a long one. It was mildly diverting—if too easy by half—to push his new counterpart's buttons, and if Neurath woke the Grand

Mufti with his exhibition of temper and caught hell
for it, the evening would be complete.

In a side chamber of the Soujak Mine, Tito, Cerović, Merritt, and Throckmorton, with occasional
input from Stirling, Bristow, D'Amato, and Weiss,
were still working out the final details of the proposed
assault on the Zpoda Skyway Bridge. They had been
talking and poring over topographic maps by lantern
light for nearly three hours. Tito, in particular, seemed
tireless—completely absorbed by the minutest of details, concerned about the most improbable chance
of failure.

Periodically this or that Partisan lieutenant would
appear at the chamber entrance and interrupt briefly
to inform Tito and Cernović that several more members
bers of Bozidar Yagovac's guerilla unit had returned.
Tito would nod, exchange glances with Cernović, and
ask to be kept up to date until all the men were ac-
counted for.

Finally Tito pushed his battered peaked cap back
on his head—an oddly American gesture, Merritt
thought—and stepped back from the wooden table
that held the last topo map.

"That's it," he said. "I can think of nothing else."
He rubbed his eye with a knuckle, looking quite tired
for the first time. "A daring plan, Major Merritt. And
very, very risky."

"Name me one thing that isn't these days, sir," Merritt returned.

Tito gave rueful smile. "I can't."

"With this bridge gone," Merritt continued, "the
German advance through the Majevica Mountains will
starve. The Partisans will be able to roam these passes
at will; fight, fall back, regroup, and redeploy. You'll
have breathing room, Marshall."

"*Lebensraum,*" Cernović put in, quoting the infa-
mous Hitlerian term that meant "living room." He
smiled slyly and lit another cigarette.

"Ha," Throckmorton said, nodding. "*Lebensraum—*
I like that. Back at the bastards, eh?"

Cernović grinned openly and exhaled smoke. "Back
at the bastards, Captain."

"So all that is left to do," Tito said, "is assign you
your guides and supporting infantry."

"The smaller the group, the better," Merritt said,
"as we discussed. This is not an operation that will
succeed by force of numbers. The fewer men involved,
the greater the chance of remaining undetected."

"In that case," Tito replied, "you'll be delighted to
hear that I've decided I can spare only two of my
remaining people to participate in this admirable
fool's errand with you—both of them guides."

Merritt looked at Throckmorton. "Only two?"

"And only one is a man."

Throckmorton rolled his eyes and turned away.
Merritt hesitated, then cleared his throat. "You don't
mean—"

Tito raised a hand, and suddenly the ruthless commander, the iron man of Yugoslavia, was very much
in evidence. "Yes, I do. Comrade Kusić—you know
him as Vlado—will lead you through the German lines
and to the base of the Zpoda precipice via a rarely
used hunter's footpath known as Zlostup. Of all my
people, he is the most familiar with this part of the
mountains. He confirmed only three days ago that
Zlostup remains open and useable, despite rock slides
and heavy snowfall."

"What's Zlostup mean?" Bristow interjected on
impulse.

Tito's expression relaxed slightly. " 'Bad Step' "

"Sounds great," Bristow grumbled.

"Don't it, though?" This from D'Amato, at Bristow's shoulder.

"It's called Zlostup," Cernović filled in, "because if
you take a bad step, you fall somewhere around three
thousand feet, give or take a bounce or two. The trail
is about two feet wide, sheer drop on one side, sheer

rock wall on the other. It's a thousand years old—probably more—and not well-known. Certainly not by the Nazis."

Merritt looked at Tito. "You were saying something about a second guide."

"That will be Comrade Kozo. I have decided that she will lead you up the cliff face to the bridge supports in the final climb."

"Oh, for Christ's sake," Throckmorton drawled, folding his arms.

"Duncan," Merritt said, his voice hard. He turned back to Tito. "It's not necessary for the girl to be put at risk, Marshall. We have mountaineering specialists on hand to do this: myself, Sergeants Bristow and D'Amato, Sergeant Stirling—"

"She will go," Tito declared, straightening his cap. "The venture has a far greater chance of success with a climber of her skills picking the best way up the rock for you." He gave Merritt a steady look. "There are not many things I can do to improve your odds, Major, but insisting that you use Sylvia is one."

Merritt clamped his lips together in exasperation. "Marshall—"

"I said, I insist. The discussion is closed."

Merritt glanced over at Throckmorton, who was slowly shaking his head, and at that moment the ratty blanket that served as the door to the conference chamber was pushed aside and one of the Partisan lieutenants appeared. "Comrade Marshall. Vlado has returned. He insists on reporting to you personally."

Tito waved a hand. "Send him in. I have a job for him, anyway."

"Immediately, Comrade Marshall."

The man withdrew, letting the blanket fall back into place. Tito silently accepted a cigarette and a light from Cernović, reexamined the topo map briefly, and sat down in the collapsible wooden armchair behind the table. His gaze—stony rather than warm now—roved over the Allied soldiers parked against the walls

of the little chamber. Merritt had been warned that
Tito, like many a great leader, could be mercurial,
moody. Here, he reflected, was hard evidence of the
fact. *Proceed carefully.*

There was a stirring out in the main passageway;
voices raised, some of them in apparent dismay. The
men took notice, shifting in place as they smoked and
waited. . . . And then the blanket-curtain was pulled
back and the Partisan named Vlado stepped into the
chamber. He was disheveled and bareheaded, his lank
black hair and scraggly beard moist and steaming with
perspiration. His olive drab forage coat and pants—
British military cast-offs—were still caked with damp
snow, as were his cloth-wrapped winter boots. A Mauser rifle hung from a sling over his left shoulder. His
expression was that of a man stricken.

"Ah, Vlado," Tito said. "You turn up at last."

"Any more with you?" Cernović inquired quickly.

Vlado settled his weight back on his heels, let out
a sigh of sheer exhaustion, and shook his lank head.
"No," he muttered. "No more. No . . . more."

Bristow held out a lit Camel. "Here you go, friend."

Vlado half turned, accepted the smoke with a grateful nod. "Thank you. I haven't had a decent cigarette
for months."

Cernović glanced at Tito. "Vlado. Where's—"

"Lieutenant Yagovac is dead," Vlado blurted. He
put the cigarette to his lips with a shaking hand. "Bozi
is dead." He exhaled a long stream of smoke at the
floor.

Cernović blinked, the cynical good humor that usually dominated his face replaced for once by an expression of blank shock. "What? Bozi dead? You're
sure?" When Vlado didn't respond, merely kept staring at the floor and smoking, Cernović cursed fluently
and added, "How?"

Vlado looked up, his eyes red and wet. "Hunter-
Storches, three of them. They caught us in deep snow
as we were maneuvering for one more attack on the

Jagdkommando unit. We didn't hear them coming because they flew up out of the next valley and came in
low over the nearest ridge at treetop level."

"I heard about the Storches from some of the others
who got back before you," Cernović said. "I know at
least a dozen were killed before you could disperse.
What happened to Bozi?"

"He was killed in the Storches' first pass, Comrade
Commander," Vlado said through gritted teeth.
"Damn them to hell. He was trying to get the men to
take cover, and took none himself."

"That sounds like Bozi," Cernović muttered.
"Downward-firing machine guns?"

"Yes, Comrade Commander. The usual."

Cernović said something incredibly foul under his
breath, reached out a hand, and put it on Vlado's
shoulder. "All right, Vlado, all right. No point in
dwelling on it. Take a seat and rest for a moment."

As the exhausted Partisan shuffled over to an unoc-
cupied chair and slumped down into it, Cernović
turned to Tito. "A bitter loss, Comrade Marshall. I
cannot replace a combat leader like Bozidar Yagovac.
He was one of a kind."

Tito nodded, gazing at Vlado sitting in his chair with
head bowed. The marshall's expression was a curious
blend of sympathy and pragmatic fatalism. "How
many irreplaceable men have we lost to date, Comrade Commander? And yet we go on. Those who remain step into the breach, become irreplaceable
themselves." Cernović nodded silently, and Tito directed his next comment at Vlado: "You must eat,
Comrade. Eat and then sleep. I have another task for
you. . . . For you and Sylvia." He turned toward the
blanket-curtain. "Marko!" he called. "Come here!"
The blanket swung aside and a youthful Partisan stuck
his head into the chamber. "Send Comrade Kozo to
me," Tito ordered, "and tell her to bring a bowl of
stew when she comes."

*   *   *

A veritable pall of cigar smoke hung in the air of the prime minister's study at Number 10 Downing Street. Generals Sir Stewart Graham Menzies and Sir Colin McVean Gubbins stood by silently, waiting. Churchill puffed on his Montecristo with the steady rhythm of an automated bellows, examining the document on the desk before him through a pair of half-lenses perched on the end of his pug nose. He was reading the material for the third time. Finally the prime minister sat back with a grunt in his leather chair, plucked off his reading glasses, and tossed them onto the desk.

"Are we sure about this?" he asked Menzies. "King Tigers?"

"Not just King Tiger tanks, Mr. Prime Minister," Menzies replied swiftly, "but a specially modified version. The Black Lyre was most specific."

"Modified how?" The cigar tip glowed red. Smoke billowed like fumes from Vulcan's forge.

"Heavy-duty transmissions," Menzies said. "More reliable steering hydraulics. Fuel capacity and travel range increased at least twenty-five percent. Even larger diesel engines. Special extra-wide treads with multiple steel teeth on every section to improve traction. Maximum elevation angle on the eighty-eight-millimeter main gun increased by more than forty percent."

"The Black Lyre claims that a small unit of these special King Tigers was field-tested recently on the Croatian-Serbian border by the SS, and performed well beyond expectations," Gubbins went on. "Supposedly the tank can climb a rock-strewn forty-five-degree slope at fifteen miles per hour. Trees up to eighteen inches in diameter don't stop it; it just pushes them over."

"The Huns have customized a Tiger tank for mountain fighting," Churchill said.

"There's no other logical conclusion, Mr. Prime Minister, given this vehicle's capabilities." Gubbins looked briefly at Menzies, who nodded in confirmation. "The increased elevation arc of the main gun is to allow the tank to fire upward at a steep angle—say, from the bottom of a deep, narrow gorge to the high ridges on either side."

"I see," Churchill growled around his cigar. "The Tigers are deployed into the valleys of the Majevicas, sweeping them clean as high up the slopes as possible. Tito's Partisans are forced up onto the ridges and mountaintops, where there's little shelter or water, and plenty of extreme cold. There the Tigers can pound them with their high-elevating eighty-eights and the Luftwaffe can bomb them from the air."

"That seems to be the intent, Mr. Prime Minister." Menzies unfolded a small map and placed it on Churchill's desk. "The train—it's huge—left Germany seven days ago. Eight engines pulling it. It's less than thirty-six hours from the deployment point in Yugoslavia as we speak."

Churchill, in the act of redonning his reading glasses, lowered them and peered up at the MI-6 chief. "How many King Tigers are on those flatcars again?"

Menzies cleared his throat. "Forty-eight, according to the Black Lyre."

"Good God. An SS tank force of that size could knock Tito and his Partisans out of the war permanently. Can we scramble our available Mosquitos or B-26s to bomb that train? Perhaps a flight of Typhoons or Thunderbolts to rocket it?"

"Several problems there, Mr. Prime Minister, including availability of aircraft on such short notice for a mission of this range, the time factor—we're already out of it, basically—and the precision required to make such a mission a success. We're dealing with a moving target. In addition, the Black Lyre informs us that the Luftwaffe has committed to a staggered series of covering flights by fighter aircraft all along the route, for the purpose of engaging any Allied aircraft intent on attacking the train."

"Bloody hell," Churchill muttered. "We'll try a last-minute interception mission, anyway. Typhoons or Thunderbolts, like I said. Something that can deal with Luftwaffe fighter cover as well as hit the train."

"I doubt if there's time, Mr. Prime Minister," Menzies said, "but we'll have a go at it."

"A second train behind this one carries supporting vehicles—fuel-hauling half-tracks and trucks," Gubbins added. "That sort of thing."

Churchill bent over the map. "And what, according to the Black Lyre, is the tank train's destination? The deployment point?"

Menzies set a finger on a red X in the map's center. "Right here, sir. Mount Zpoda, at the far end of the Zpoda Skyway Bridge."

Chapter
Six

The young Partisan named Marko was one of four
skilled radio operators attached to Tito's immediate
support staff, fluent in Morse and a variety of complex
code ciphers. He was also adept at disassembling and
tinkering with the bulky, temperamental military field
sets provided to the Partisans by the British and
Americans. After sleeping through most of the daylight hours since the last of Bozi Yagovac's guerillas
had returned to the Soujak Mine, it was now his turn
on radio watch—generally a long, boring shift of six
hours or more—and he intended to pass the time by
rewiring one of the British backpack radios, a battered, aging beast of a unit he'd nicknamed The Ogre.

Working on The Ogre also helped take his mind off
the knowledge that one of the gas-gangrene cases
lying against the wall of the mine's main passage, just
a few yards down from his radio alcove, had died an
hour earlier—and that the gas-gangrene case had been
Georgi, his best friend from childhood. Georgi, young
and crazy-brave, had been machine-gunned in the hips

during an ambush several weeks back, and had suf
fered greatly—and in silence—since then. Mercifully
he had slipped into unconsciousness two days ago, and
now the gangrene had finally taken him.

Marko set the blade of his screwdriver into the slot
of the radio cowl's first retaining screw and began to
twist. It was best not to think about Georgi.

Abruptly a rapid-fire series of nonsensical Morse
dits erupted from the speaker of the primary head
quarters radio set, signaling the imminent arrival of a
coherent message. Marko dropped the screwdriver
slid over behind the big radio, clapped a pair of head
phones over his ears, and seized a pencil and notepad
The flurry of meaningless tones gave way, after a brief
pause, to a smooth flow of sequenced dits and dahs
urgent but controlled. His brow furrowed in concen
tration, Marko began to write rapidly on the pad.

When the transmission was completed he ripped the
page off the notepad, ditched his headphones, and
hurried out of the radio alcove into the main passage
way. The rocky floor of the mine was littered with
sleeping bodies, and he inadvertently kicked a few as
he hastened along, drawing muffled curses and threats
He scarcely heard them. His heart was pounding in
his ears much too loudly for that.

Tito was lying on his cot, reading, when Marko
pushed aside the blanket-curtain and entered the commanders' alcove. On the far side of the little recess
Cernović was stretched out on a second cot, snoring
Marko nodded respectfully as he approached, then
held out the notepaper as Tito pulled off his reading
glasses and looked up.

"Intelligence communication from the British, Comrade Marshall," the young Partisan said. "Extremely
urgent."

Tito hoisted himself up against his pillow and took
the paper. "Thank you, Marko. I'll call if I need you."

The boy nodded again and backed out of the alcove
letting the blanket-curtain fall to behind him.

Tito replaced his glasses and scanned the message. His expression began to darken. He swept the rough blanket off and swung his legs to the floor. "King Tigers," he muttered under his breath. "Forty-eight specially modified King Tigers."

Abruptly he got to his feet and crossed the alcove in two quick strides. "Anton," he said, touching Cernović on the shoulder. "Wake up."

The Partisan commander jerked in midsnore and rolled to a sitting position before he was even half awake, the Luger he always slept with brandished in his right hand. Tito quickly stepped sideways; Cernović blinked the sleep out of his eyes, got his bearings, and let his gun hand sag between his legs.

"One day, Anton," Tito remarked, "you're going to come up shooting, and that will be the end of Josip Broz."

Cernović smiled wearily and rubbed the side of his face. "But not this day, Comrade Marshall."

Tito stepped over to the table and consulted the map spread out on top of it. "We've just received some extremely alarming news from British intelligence. A train loaded with King Tiger tanks specially modified for mountain warfare is barely two days away from the Zpoda Skyway Bridge. If those tanks make it across the divide at Mount Zpoda and are deployed into the rest of the Majevicas against us, we could be decimated."

"Wha-what?" Cernović hoisted himself to his feet and stumbled over to the table. "Damn it, I'm so tired I can hardly think. King Tigers, you say? But Comrade Marshall, aren't those open-country tanks? The Nazis use them out on the steppes where they have plenty of running room."

"Specially modified for mountain warfare," Tito repeated. "Here, I'll show you approximately where the train carrying them is right now." He set a finger on the map. "This is the best guess. You see? We have very little time."

Cernović blinked some more, focusing. "But this
perfect. Merritt is on his way to blow that bridge ¿
we speak."

"The plan was for him to take all the time h
needed to mine the bridge without being discovered.
Tito said. "Since he doesn't realize time is sudden!
of the essence, he may take up to three or four day
to set his explosives. He has no radio, so he can
know about the approach of the train."

"It could steam across the bridge and offload i
Tigers on the crest of Mount Zpoda while Merritt an
his people stood there watching it," Cernović muse
"powerless to do anything to prevent it because the
charges weren't yet placed or wired." He straightene
and looked at Tito. "We have to send a messenge
after them; tell Merritt that the bridge must be blow
before the train arrives."

"No," Tito said. "We must go one better. If Merri
blows the bridge before the train arrives, the Naz
still have their forty-eight King Tigers." He smile
suddenly, and it was a hard, ruthless smile. "We hav
an opportunity not just to destroy the Zpoda Skywa
Bridge as a primary supply route, but to deny th
enemy the use of nearly fifty battle tanks.

"We must tell Merritt to blow the bridge while th
train is on it, and send the King Tigers to the bottor
of the Zpoda Gorge."

Cernović nodded. "I'll choose someone to sen
after Merritt and his people. They only have a fou
hour head start. If these estimated times for the train
arrival are accurate—"

The blanket-curtain suddenly whipped back, revea
ing Marko's flushed, tense face. "Comrade Marshall,
he hissed. *"Fallschirmjager!"*

The late-afternoon sun was drawing long shadow
through the snowbound alpine forest when Merri
paused at the crest of the steep ravine that his team–

omplete with three fully laden pack mules—had just ̣raversed. About ten paces ahead of him, Vlado, in ̣he lead, forged onward through the knee-deep snow, ̣ooking like a tireless, tattered mummy in his thread-̣are military coat, dirty scarves, and ragged leggings. ̣Merritt scanned the nearby trees and terrain, then ̣ield up a hand as Bristow and D'Amato, next in file ̣ehind him, approached, leading one of the mules.

"Hold up a minute," he said quietly. He turned ̣ack toward Vlado, who was still slogging his way ̣long the ravine crest. "Vlado! Wait." The Partisan ̣uide halted, turned, and looked back, exhaling con-̣ensation. Merritt pointed. "These trees are freshly ̣carred by heavy gunfire. And there are two bodies in ̣he snow over there. Partisan bodies."

Vlado shrugged and looked out across the gully. ̣ʼhe wind had stopped blowing and the forest was ̣uite still now, almost cathedral-like. In the utter si-̣ence and bone-chilling cold, Vlado's voice, a husky ̣nurmur, carried with stark clarity to the ears of every ̣eam member. "This is where the Hunter-Storches ̣aught us as we were about to launch our final attack ̣n the Jagdkommando unit, Major. This is where we ̣ook our casualties."

Merritt nodded. "And this is the quickest way to ̣ʼlostup?"

"Yes, Major," Vlado replied. "It happens to be. A ̣oincidence."

"All right." Merritt looked back down the way they ̣ad come. Throckmorton was struggling up the route ̣ext. Behind him were Stirling and Sylvia, each with ̣ hand on opposite sides of the second pack mule's ̣alter. Weiss was bringing up the rear, leading the ̣hird mule. "Everyone keep following Vlado. I'm ̣;oing to move out on our flank for a few minutes."

"What for, Major?" Vlado asked. "They're all dead, ̣nd the Germans are gone."

"Just taking a look," Merritt replied. "Maybe I'll

find Yagovac's body. And as a matter of fact, I thin
I'll take Sergeant Bristow and Sergeant D'Amat
with me."

"What for?" Vlado repeated. There was an edge o
exasperation in his voice.

"Security," Merritt replied curtly. "Lead on, Com
rade." He nodded to Bristow and D'Amato, steppe
sideways out of Vlado's tracks, and began to move a
a divergent angle toward the bodies under the trees.

"Major, you could easily get lost in here," Vlado
persisted, and in his tone Merritt heard the same qual
ity of deceit that had struck him wrong when Vlad
reported the death of Bozidar Yagovac to Tito an
Cernović in the Soujak Mine.

He shifted his Sten gun from his shoulder to th
crook of his arm and continued across the ravine crest
Bristow and D'Amato pacing him to either side
"We'll be fine," he called out to Vlado. "We'll swee
back in and rejoin you in about twenty minutes."

"But—"

"Lead on, Comrade. That's an order."

Vlado stared for a moment, looked back helplessl
at Throckmorton, then shook his head and began t
slog forward again. As the rest of the team and th
small mule train resumed their pace, Merritt and th
two American sergeants waded off through the snov
and began to push their way through the sagging lowe
limbs of the evergreen trees.

It was several minutes before they arrived at th
two corpses Merritt had spotted from the trail. Botl
bodies were facedown and badly shredded. Bristov
knelt down, resting his Thompson submachine gun o
one knee, and pulled the rigid body of the first deac
Partisan over.

All three men, battle hardened though they were
felt a jolt of revulsion at the sight of the corpse's face
The young Partisan—not more than seventeen, al
though it was hard to tell—had been shot multipl
times in the shoulders and head. The frontal part o

the skull, the forehead and temples, was gone back to the crown. In the void above the brows was a nauseating mass of black-red blood, white bone splinters, and brain tissue. Slugs traveling down from directly above had blown away the boy's lower jaw and exploded one eye out of its socket. The other stared up horrifically like a dull white marble, the pupil and iris occluded. The upper lip was peeled back from the remaining teeth in an an awful grimace, frozen in place by the subzero temperatures.

"Ugh, Jeezus," Bristow grunted, averting his eyes momentarily. "Just a damn kid, too."

"Ain't they all these days?" D'Amato remarked. He surveyed the nearby trees and hefted his Thompson. "Fuckin' Krauts."

Merritt studied the two corpses. "Both literally hammered from directly overhead by heavy machine-gun fire. Ugly and effective."

"I'll say," D'Amato commented.

Merritt nodded at Bristow. "Turn him back over, Sergeant."

As Bristow rolled the dead boy facedown again, Merritt peered through the trees to the left, which were the most heavily bullet scarred. "Do you both have a fair recollection of what Bozidar Yagovac looked like? The big man with the black beard. We all met him on the drop zone and again at the base of the cliff."

Bristow and D'Amato exchanged glances. "Hell, yeah, Major," Bristow said. "Would we forget runnin' into an upright grizzly bear?"

"Right." Merritt let a smile flicker across his face. "I want his body found. Fan out about thirty feet on either side of me. We'll sweep across this little ridge, following the shot-up trees. As big a man as he was, he shouldn't be hard to pick out."

"Got somethin' on your mind, Major?" Bristow asked, moving off.

Merritt began to stride forward. "Just checking a hunch," he replied, "as you Americans say."

D'Amato started to move out to Merritt's right, then halted, cocking his head. Bristow glanced back at him, saw him standing there, and paused himself. "Major."

At the big sergeant's word Merritt looked back and halted. Bristow watched D'Amato for several seconds, then said quietly, "Frank. What's up, *amigo*?"

D'Amato cocked his head the other way, listening. "You hear 'em?"

"No, what?" Bristow lifted the earflap of the head muffler he was wearing. Merritt did the same with the lower edge of his wool balaclava.

There was a faint mechanical drone, just barely audible, humming through the sentinel trees.

"Planes," D'Amato said. "More than one, I think. A long way off."

"Flying high enough for the sound to carry," Merritt added. "If they were moving through the valleys below the peaks and ridges, doing search-and-destroy missions like those Storches, we wouldn't hear them."

"Bombers, maybe?" Bristow suggested. "Kraut reconnaissance . . . or maybe our own?"

Merritt listened a moment longer, then pulled the edge of his balaclava back down over his ear. "Maybe," he said, and set off through the snow once more. "Let's go."

SS Hauptsturmfuehrer Ulrich Haak had been the first man out the door of the lead plane as the big Junkers 52 trimotor transport, loaded with seventeen heavily armed Muslim Fallschirmjager,[1] led twenty of its kind over the hidden gorge concealing the Soujak Mine. Now, dangling in his parachute with the frigid air stinging his face and the ragged black tops of snow-laden evergreen trees jutting up toward him, looming ever nearer as he descended, he took a few seconds to look up and note with satisfaction the multiple sticks of jumpers trailing out of the remaining transport aircraft, the white blots of their canopies blooming like sudden flowers in the late-afternoon sky. It had taken an unbelievable amount of paperwork and petitioning of superiors over the past several months to gain both permission and means to parachute-train nearly two hundred volunteers from the Jagdkommando units of the SS Division Handschar, but now here they were, descending upon the abhorred Partisan foe with the element of surprise completely in their favor. It wasn't like Crete,[2] Haak lamented fleetingly, but it was a bona fide airborne assault. *Today, he thought, we get results. We make some real progress against these damned subhuman Slavic Communists.*

The drop was going perfectly. He was coming down onto the very edge of the southern ridge overlooking the gorge. Time to get ready.

One of his most recent acquisitions had been a marvelous new personal weapon called a Sturmgewehr.[3] Basically a submachine gun like the more common Schmeisser, it was elongated, more accurate, and had a curved, high-capacity ammunition clip. It fired well on the range, and Haak had seen to it that every one of his new Muslim Fallschirmjager was equipped with a Sturmgewehr of his own.

Haak was low enough now to make out a lone Partisan running awkwardly through the snow along the top of the ridge. As he watched, the figure fell, losing its hat. Long, dark hair spilled out over the shoulders of a tattered, olive drab winter coat.

The Partisan rolled, staring up at Haak with an expression of hatred and terror. It was a woman. She scrambled to one knee, her mouth working in what the Hauptsturmfuehrer supposed were curses or prayers or both, and swung up her rifle, taking aim.

Haak cut her down with a long burst from his Sturmgewehr. She screamed as she died, shuddering under the impact of the bullets, which he found oddly satisfying. Then, with the delicacy of a descending angel, he made a perfect landing in the thigh-deep snow between two immense evergreens.

All around him, his Muslim Fallschirmjager began
to drift down through the trees, seeding the southern
rim of the Soujak Gorge and half enveloping the Partisan forces bivouacked near the mine entrance.

On the opposite rim of the gorge, Fallschirmjager
precision dropped slightly farther to the north were
descending under a long row of swaying canopies to
close the trap.

Cernović was at the entrance of the mine, gesturing
furiously to those nearby and eyeing the numerous
parachutes floating down on either rim of the gorge,
while behind him men and women fled out across the
snow and into the trees, some supporting staggering
wounded. The stutter of automatic weapons fire
began, and several hundred yards off to Cernović's
right, to the south, a grenade flung from the gorge rim
exploded with an upheaval of powdery whiteness and
a muffled *whumpff.*

"Head down the valley, comrades!" the Partisan
commander bellowed. *"Don't let them link up and cut
us off! Shoot your way out!"*

A pair of Partisans bearing a stretcher between
them stumbled past. Cernović took one look at the
ashen face of the blanket-wrapped casualty lying upon
the crude bier and seized the trailing soldier by the
arm. "Leave him!" he shouted. "He's a dead man.
Save yourselves!"

"He's our brother, Comrade Commander," the
older of the two Partisans panted, lank black hair falling across his swarthy face. "We are the last three of
our mother's nine sons."

"I don't need to lose two more men on top of this
one!" Cernović barked. He waved his Luger at the
man on the stretcher. "He won't last the night. You
know that. And there's no time to argue!"

The two stretcher bearers set their burden down in
the snow and looked at each other with anguished

faces. "Go, Jakob," the older brother muttered. "I'll do it." The younger man hesitated, then stumbled toward the trees as his brother drew his sidearm.

The older brother pulled off his scarf, knelt down, whispered something in the dying man's ear, and kissed him on the forehead. Cernović looked away.

The pistol cracked.

When Cernović looked back, the older brother was gone. His scarf was draped over the face of the man on the stretcher. The last few Partisans were disappearing into the trees and snowdrifts, firing upward to either side as they fled pell-mell down the gorge to the east.

The angry chatter of a Sturmgewehr on the southern rim, much closer to the mine entrance now, sent snow skiffing up between Cernović and the corpse on the stretcher. Out of sheer defiance, the Partisan commander stood his ground, raised his pistol, and emptied it at the white-clad figures now moving rapidly toward him along the upper lip of the gorge. Then he hunched low and dashed back into the mouth of the Soujak Mine.

The main passageway was nearly empty. Along the walls were crumpled blankets and bedding where the wounded had lain. Here and there a few of them still lay, their bodies covered head to toe by the lice-ridden blankets that were their death shrouds. Too badly injured to be moved, they had been killed by friends or relatives. All knew the kind of mercy Partisan wounded would receive from the SS if captured.

Cernović ran past alcoves and recesses still flickering with the eerie light of cooking fires, the perpetual haze of smoke in the poorly ventilated mine stinging his eyes. In the dimness ahead, Tito was just emerging from the commanders' alcove, a leather document satchel under one arm and a Walther pistol in his free hand. Clustered around and ushering him along the passageway were a half-dozen soldiers of his bodyguard and support staff, including the young radio operator, Marko. Two of the Partisans carried guttering oil lanterns.

"Is everyone out?" Tito shouted to Cernović as he approached.

"All but the dead," Cernović responded. "The main body is attempting to break out through the eastern end of the gorge under subcommanders Lesković and Ribar." He paused, panting heavily. "There are paratroopers above the mine on both sides, starting to work their way down." He glanced at Marko. "Everything ready?"

"Yes, Comrade Commander," the young Partisan replied, bent under the weight of the large field radio strapped to his back.

"Good," Cernović said. "We—"

Two sharp, cracking explosions shook the rock walls and foul air of the passageway. Dust sifted down from overhead shoring timbers and boiled into the mine from the direction of the entrance. Several of the men instinctively clapped their hands over their ears as the double concussion hit them.

"Grenades!" Cernović shouted. "They're coming! Deeper into the mine, quickly!"

The little knot of men, propelling Tito along in their midst, retreated several dozen yards to where the passageway took a sudden turn to the left. Cernović paused, hissed at the two trailing bodyguards, and took cover behind the edge of the rock wall, glaring back the way he had come, with the barrel of his pistol pressed up against his cheekbone. The two Partisans, each armed with a Schmeisser, found shallow firing niches on opposite sides of the passageway.

The first thing German to appear at the far end of the dim corridor was a brace of potato-masher hand grenades, tumbling end over end along the rocky floor. Cernović and his two men shrank back and opened their mouths to protect their ears. The grenades went off simultaneously with a single tremendous bang that nearly knocked the Partisans to their knees. Shrapnel chipped shards of rock from the walls from ceiling to floor.

Hard on the heels of the blast, two Fallschirmjager clad in white winter camouflage smocks and gray field fezzes leapt into view, Sturmgewehrs trained ahead. Cernović and his two comrades opened fire. One of the paratroopers was hammered back against the mine wall and slumped down dead. The other was hit but managed to lurch back behind the curve of the passageway and out of the line of fire.

"Fall back!" Cernović whispered hoarsely, and waited until the two Partisan submachine gunners had taken a few running steps after Tito and the rest of the bodyguard before pulling back himself and following.

"I told you we would trap a few in this rat hole!" Haak declared triumphantly, kneeling on the floor of the passageway with one of his Scharfuehrers as white-clad Fallschirmjager streamed past him deeper into the mine. He grinned, his breath forming clouds of condensation. "We may have some commanders backed up into a corner. Perhaps even Tito himself!"

"*Jawohl*, Herr Haupsturmfuehrer," the Scharfuehrer replied. "We'll root them out."

Haak got to his feet, still grinning, and shifted his assault rifle in his arms. "Just kill them," he said. "These are Slavs, Schmidt—human rats—and this is extermination duty. Leave one or two pests alive out of a nest and the next thing you know they've multiplied back up to plague proportions all over again. Don't complicate my day with prisoners."

The Scharfuehrer nodded but lifted an eyebrow. "Not even Tito sir, if he's here?"

Haak spat on the floor of the passageway. "Especially not Tito. He's the head rat."

Chapter Seven

"Over here, Major!"

Merritt paused his steady trudge through the snowdrifts and peered under an overhanging pine bough in Bristow's direction. The big American sergeant was standing between an angled slab of rock and the trunk of an immense evergreen tree, waving. There was a large black shape in the snow at his feet. Merritt and D'Amato moved to join him.

Bristow gestured with a cigarette and then stuck it between his lips. "I believe that's him, sir. Yagovich-or-whatever." There was a metallic *snick* as he thumbed open his Zippo lighter.

"Yago*vac*." Merritt stooped down. Bozidar Yago-vac was lying flat on his back, his sightless eyes staring up at the sky between the treetops. Frost had rimed his bushy beard so that it appeared as gray-white as his skin. The giant Partisan's overcoat was unbuttoned and open, as was his threadbare woolen underjacket. Merritt probed Yagovac's pockets gently, gazed at the corpse for a moment or two, then sat back on his haunches and began to survey the surrounding area.

"Some more bodies down in that hollow and along that rise," Bristow said matter-of-factly. He blew a stream of smoke. "Most of 'em partly covered up by new snow. Tracks are still visible, but gettin' filled in, too." He shook his head. "I counted fourteen dead just in that area. Them Storches really tore these boys up. They've all got the same head-and-shoulders wounds."

"The trees are really shot to shit over there, too, Major," D'Amato added. "Chopped into splinters. Not like right here."

Merritt nodded slowly and got to his feet. "That's absolutely correct, Sergeant," he said. "Not like right here." He gazed down at Yagovac's body again, then off into the woods. "Interesting. You can still see three sets of tracks in the snow. Yagovac's, obviously, plus those of two others."

"Vlado and another Partisan, I guess," D'Amato muttered, "probably checking on Bozo here when he got hit—although I'm damned if I can see where. There ain't a mark on him."

Merritt's wry smile reappeared. "*Bozi*, Sergeant."

"Yeah, right, Bozi."

"There are foot tracks all over the place, Major," Bristow said. "They were runnin' every which way, tryin' to lose the planes and get back to the mine."

"Right," Merritt replied. "That's why it's rather strange that one set of tracks takes off to the east, in the direction of the Soujak Mine, with long, running strides, while this set"—he pointed with a gloved finger—"approaches at what looks like a slow, careful walking pace from the direction of the German forces at Mount Zpoda. . . . And returns the same way."

D'Amato frowned. "Kraut? Maybe a scout from a reconnaissance patrol. You know, checking up on the Storches' handiwork."

"Mmm." Merritt's eyes flickered over the tracks,

the blue-white snow, the evergreen boughs drooping nearby. All at once, he took a step to one side and plucked out something caught in the needles of a waist-high pine branch.

"Whatcha got there, Major?" Bristow asked.

Merritt held the item up between his thumb and forefinger. "Cigarette butt. Black paper, small gold-colored filter with the name Richterhaus imprinted on it."

"Filter?" Bristow remarked, looking incredulous. "Who smokes cigarettes with filters? A broad, maybe." He drew heavily on his unfiltered Camel.

"Richter-*who*?" D'Amato inquired.

"Richterhaus," Merritt repeated. He rolled the butt in his fingers. "Translation: 'House of Richter.' A very high-end tobacconist from Munich. That's gold foil around the filter. This is a custom-made cigarette, and very expensive."

"No shit," D'Amato commented. "Some Kraut tossed it for sure, I guess."

"Probably an officer," Merritt said, "and since he had time to smoke, he was in no hurry, evidently." He put the butt in his pocket and gestured at Yagovac's body. "Would you mind turning him over, Sergeant?"

"Yessir." Bristow bent over, his Camel clamped between his lips, and with D'Amato's aid rolled the heavy corpse over. The entire back of Yagovac's coat was encrusted with frozen blood, as was the snow beneath his body. There was a single small hole in the center of the dead man's back, directly between the shoulder blades.

Merritt considered the mortal remains of Bozidar Yagovac for another long moment. Then his mouth tightened and he nodded to Bristow and D'Amato.

"All right," he said. "Let's go."

"Fire!" Cernović yelled.

The pursuing Fallschirmjager flung themselves left

and right as the two Yugoslav infantrymen covering
Tito's retreat opened up with their burp guns. Slugs
whined and caromed off the passageway walls in a
flurry of rock chips and dust. The chattering of Partisan Schmeissers and SS Sturmgewehrs was earsplitting
in the close confines of the mine.

The German officers and their Muslim shock troops
were finding the pursuit more difficult. They had long
since penetrated past the existing light sources—
cooking fires and random lanterns—near the mine entrance, and were now probing down the passageway
with battery-powered flashlights and lamps. The Partisans, who had the twin advantages of knowing the
mine's primary and secondary tunnels *and* being able
to stop and wait for their oncoming enemy, lost no
opportunity to shield their lanterns and set a mini ambush at every appropriate turn in the passageway.
They simply waited for the enemy lights to appear.

"Fall back!" Cernović hissed as the firing died away.
Farther up the passageway, a Partisan kneeling with
a lantern unmuffled it slightly to illuminate the rear
guard's withdrawal. From the direction of the Fallschirmjager came the sound of moans and shouting.

"We're nearly to the fork!" Tito exclaimed. "Left
or right?"

"Left to the cascade, Comrade Marshall," Marko
said quickly. "The right branch is a dead end after
another hundred yards."

"Are the ropes still in place?" Tito asked as the
little band of men hustled along the barely lit tunnel.
There was a nervous quaver in his voice, Marko
thought—probably more due to the unavoidable gym-
nastics ahead than the killers behind. It was common
knowledge that Tito did not like heights.

"The ropes are there, Comrade Marshall," Cernović
panted, catching up with the rear guard. "Marko, the
box is ready?"

"Yes, Comrade Commander," the young Partisan
replied. He shifted the radio pack on his back. "This

damned thing is heavy—I call it The Ogre, it's so ugly and awkward. And I'd like to ditch it."

"No." Cernović put a hand on his shoulder as they hurried along. "We have a critical use for it beyond establishing contact with the main body of our forces again. We must get a message to Major Merritt and his team within the next half-day, and with all these cursed SS on top of us we aren't going to be able to send a runner after him."

There was a mind-numbing *BANG* as a grenade went off in the tunnel behind them, barely two turns back. The Partisans clapped their hands to their ears, grimacing in pain.

"Bu . . . but, Comrade Commander," Marko said, as the ringing in his ears died away, "the British major doesn't have a radio."

"Correct," Cernović said. "But Quisp does. We'll radio a message to him, request that he rendezvous with Merritt somewhere on Zlostup. He knows the territory and how to avoid the Germans."

Marko shook his head in the dim light. "Very well, Comrade Commander. But—Theobald Quisp? Begging your pardon, but isn't he somewhat—ah—unpredictable, sir? I mean . . . the one time I saw him . . ."

Cernović coughed forcefully and spat a wad of plegm into the darkness as he trotted along. "Unpredictable, yes. Unreliable, no. There's a difference, Comrade." He glanced over his shoulder at the sound of more shouting from the pursuing SS. "Quisp is a classic English eccentric, but he will get our message to Merritt if asked. Anyway, he's our only option right now. And any later will be *too* late."

"Yes, Comrade Commander," Marko said.

"Alright. I'll give you the message after we make the cascade descent. Go on ahead with Marshall Tito and the others. Hurry."

As the young radioman nodded and trotted on at the rear of Tito's bodyguard, Cernović dropped back behind an outcropping of rock. Just for a moment, here in the darkness where no one could see, his face took on a look of utter exhaustion and all but unbearable sadness. Then, as quickly as it had come, the haunted expression ebbed away, replaced by the familiar rogue-Gypsy grin.

"*Hsst!* Stefan! Boris! Take cover there and there! We'll bloody these damned SS noses one more time before we shut the door for good, eh? Get ready. . . ."

Stirling let go of the pack mule's halter and turned to Sylvia. "Can you handle this animal alone for a few minutes, ma'am?"

Sylvia shot him a hooded-eyed glance that said *Probably better than you*, refocused on the terrain ahead, and kept walking. Stirling grunted, shrugged, and set off at a trot to catch up to Throckmorton, who was struggling along in deep snow with the mule Bristow and D'Amato had turned over to him. Heavily laden and with an uncertain hand on its halter, the mule was becoming uncooperative.

"Miserable beast," Throckmorton grumbled, tugging on the animal's halter as Stirling approached. "Will you move, you stinking nag?"

"Having a little trouble, sir?" Stirling inquired, puffing out condensation. He shifted his Enfield rifle by its shoulder strap and took hold of the opposite side of the mule's halter.

"A battle of wills, Sergeant," Throckmorton said, looking pale and depleted. He coughed hard, turned, and spat wetly. "Damnation."

Stirling watched him, his brows furrowing slightly. "You don't look well, sir. Perhaps you should ride for a while. Save your strength."

"What?" Throckmorton looked aghast. "You're not actually suggesting I should climb up and *straddle* one of these greasy pseudoequines, are you?"

Stirling couldn't help smiling. Sick though he was, Throckmorton's sardonic humor and dry delivery were

as incisive as ever. The man was the walking embodi
ment of the legendary Stiff Upper Lip. "Well, I gues
not, sir," Stirling said.

"Good," Throckmorton rejoined, "because there
isn't enough bug powder in the Allied arsenal to de
louse me if I *was* to mount one of the foul creatures."
He leaned back, tugging on the mule's halter, while
the animal sat farther back on its haunches and dug
in its forehooves. "Come on, *come on*, curse you!"

Sylvia plodded up, leading her mule without diffi
culty. She went past Stirling and Throckmorton about
fifteen feet, then tied off her animal's short lead to a
hanging branch and retraced her steps.

"Come to help, have you?" Throckmorton ob
served. "Or perhaps to gloat?"

"Gloating at the incompetent is a sign of low char
acter," Sylvia told him, "a vicious amusement mos
often indulged in by members of the English gentry
in my experience." She moved past Stirling to the
stubborn pack mule's hindquarters.

"By God, you are a pleasant female," Throckmor
ton drawled. "Do I really offend you that much?"

Sylvia glanced sideways at him as she rummaged in
one of the pouches attached to her ammunition belt
"You bore me," she said. "English aristocrats look
down their long noses at everyone else in the world
simply because they're not English. They also feel free
to make denigrating remarks about people who don't
share their peculiar pomposities. Get this through you
head, Englishman: you won't find me a willing target
of your so-called wit."

Throckmorton blinked languidly. "I'm just trying to
get along, my dear. . . . Not make enemies."

Sylvia held up a small metal stick about the size of
a threepenny nail. "This is a pencil flare," she said
"Phosphorus."

With a quick jerk she broke it in half. There was a
sharp *snap*, and a white-hot ball of light began to sizzle
in her gloved hand. The uncooperative mule jerked

its head around, eyes wide with alarm. Sylvia touched the flare to the back of the animal's rump, just beneath the tail.

With a squalling bray, the mule lunged forward, sending Stirling and Throckmorton stumbling back. Throckmorton lost his balance and sat down heavily in the snow. The smell of burned hair mixed with the tang of phosphorus smoke in the still alpine air.

Sylvia stalked after the mule, holding the hissing flare by her side. "Instead of trying to get along," she remarked as she bypassed Throckmorton, "try getting out of the way."

Stirling crossed the churned snow of the mule track and extended a hand to Throckmorton. "Here, sir," he said.

Throckmorton clasped the hand and got to his feet, brushing snow off the seat of his pants. "Thank you, Sergeant." He gazed after Sylvia Kozo as she prodded the suddenly energetic mule up the trail. "I guess we should take the animal she tied off to the tree," he commented.

Stirling smiled. "Bit of a harpy, isn't she?"

Throckmorton extracted a cigarette from inside his coat. "I like her," he said, "even if she doesn't particularly care for me. She has *verve*." He offered a second cigarette to Stirling. "Let's have a smoke and wait for Weiss to catch up, eh? He's dropped a little too far behind, I think."

He nodded down the slope of the ridge they'd been following. Several hundred yards back, the young Jewish sergeant was coaxing his mule through a series of deep drifts. It was slow going; the heavily laden animal had developed a noticeable limp.

"Is that mule going to bear up, Weiss?" Stirling called.

Weiss looked up as he and the mule floundered out of the last drift. "We may have to spread some of its load between the other two animals," he shouted back, breathless. "It gashed its left rear leg on a chunk of ice about half a mile back. It was bleeding a fair bit until I wrapped it." He patted the mule, which was steaming with sweat and exhaling twin torrents of vapor out its nostrils. "The leg's still giving it a lot of trouble."

"Fetch the brute up here," Throckmorton called, smoking idly. "We'll rearrange the ordnance and comestibles more to its liking. Maybe give it a lovely warm Epsom salts bath, too, don't you know."

Stirling chuckled again. "You're a card, sir, begging your pardon for sayin' so. Is there anything you don't see the humor in?"

"No, Sergeant," Throckmorton declared, exhaling smoke, "because in my opinion, life itself is one great protracted farce—and I don't wish to be the sort of dullard who isn't in on the joke."

A sharp whistle cut the late-afternoon air. Throckmorton and Stirling looked up to see Merritt, Bristow and D'Amato emerging from the dense forest on the left-hand side of the upper ridge, some three hundred yards ahead. Vlado, far in the lead on the main trail, raised a hand as they approached.

Merritt and the two American sergeants stalked across the sloping, snow-covered clearing that lay between them and the trail, working their way down. Vlado waited, watching them, his face devoid of expression. Snow disturbed by their passage slid in mini avalanches off to the right, into the deep ravine that bordered the main trail; some of the snow formed balls and ran down the incline with ever increasing speed, leaving little bluish tracks across the clear white expanse before tumbling out into empty space.

"Did you find him?" Vlado asked as Merritt drew near.

Merritt regarded the gaunt Partisan with a level gaze. "No," he said. "We found a few more corpses but they were partially covered with new snow. Yagovac's body must be completely covered." He paused as Bristow and D'Amato moved up on either side of him, submachine guns casually at the ready. Bristow dug inside his combat jacket for a cigarette and lit it; D'Amato was chewing gum. Both men were silent, and both of them were looking steadily at Vlado.

Merritt shook his head and let air whistle out between his teeth. "Those Storches made a real mess in there. Shot the poor devils to hell." He half glanced over his shoulder at Bristow. "Didn't they, Cole?"

Slowly, Bristow removed the cigarette from his mouth. The even, unsmiling gaze he had locked on Vlado never flickered. "A real mess, sir."

"Wouldn't you say so, Frank?" Merritt added.

The tough little Italian-American sergeant nodded, working on his gum. "Yessir. A real mess." He, too, continued to look at Vlado, his expression neutral, ambiguous.

"It must have been bad for you," Merritt said to Vlado, his tone leavened with a note of sympathy.

The Partisan's eyes shifted from Merritt to Bristow to D'Amato and back to Merritt again. "It was. It was terrible. A bloodbath. As you saw."

Merritt nodded. "Yes, well, we did see. You're lucky you made it out, Vlado." He reached over and clapped the Partisan gently on the upper arm. "A little farther, and we'll bivouac for the night. Get a few hours' sleep, eh?"

Vlado looked uncertain for a split second, then indicated the trail behind him with a slight jerk of the head. "It looks like we have a lame mule to tend to, Major."

"Ah yes. Weiss's. I see it limping down there. We may have to redistribute its load."

"I think so," Vlado agreed. "Well, I'll lend a hand." He started off through the snow as Sylvia trudged up, leading her own mule.

"Oh, by the way," Merritt said, "before you go— are you absolutely sure that Yagovac was killed in the

Storch attack? I mean, there's no chance the Germans
captured him, is there? Not a hope that he may still
be alive?"

Vlado shook his head absently. "No. The Storches
machine-gunned him from overhead, just like all the
others. I saw it happen."

"Ah." Merritt paused, examining the snow at his
feet. "Hit in the head and upper body, I suppose.
Fatal wounds."

"That's right," Vlado said. "His head was nearly
blown from his shoulders. It was terrible, Major. I'll
never forget it."

He turned away and continued back down the trail
toward Throckmorton, Stirling, Weiss, and the two remaining mules, unaware of the cold stares being directed at him by Merritt, Bristow, and D'Amato.

The extreme end of the Soujak Mine's main passageway terminated at a natural fault in the rock of
the copper mountain's heart—a huge subterranean
flaw in the form of a yawning vertical fissure some
twenty feet wide and several hundred feet from top
to bottom. Beside the small ledge onto which the
passageway led, a large horizontal crack in the sheer
rock face functioned as a natural outlet for alpine
groundwater—a cascade that tumbled into the
lightless void in summer and froze solid in winter. It
was out onto this motionless waterfall of ice, poorly
illuminated by weak oil lamps, that Tito now swung,
rappelling awkwardly down into the darkness on a single thin rope with two younger, more agile Partisans
on either side of him, on ropes of their own, to
steady him.

"The rest of you hook up to the other ropes!" Cernović barked to the half-dozen men still lingering on
the edge of the precipice. "Get going after the Comrade Marshall, assist and cover him at the bottom.
Go!"

He turned back to the mouth of the passageway as

the gunfire reverberating out of it doubled in ferocity. Fifty feet in, at the last turn, his four best close-combat submachine gunners were holding the oncoming Fallschirmjager at bay—barely. Just inside the passageway, Marko was bent over a small black box about half the size of a carton of cigarettes, tightening wire ends onto its two brass terminals.

Yet another German grenade exploded with a bone-rattling *BANG*. The concussion hurt Cernović's eyes and sinuses. A scream shrilled out of the darkness above the cacophony of small-arms fire, to be followed by a cry of despair in Serbo-Croatian.

"Hurry up!" Cernović shouted to Marko, and ran into the passageway with his Luger held out in front of him. He was nearly to the rear guard's position when a second explosion—this one filling the mine with white-hot light—threw him against the rock wall, all but blinded. *Flash grenade*, he thought frantically. . . .

The Fallschirmjager came around the corner hard on the heels of the blast, firing, while the defenders' vision was momentarily compromised. Cernović threw his pistol up and fired back, blinking and rubbing his tearing eyes. He could see the silhouettes of his men, backlit by a wall of dancing German flashlights, staggering and falling as they were driven from cover and shot down.

The Luger clicked on an empty chamber and he spun and dashed back down the passageway toward the cascade ledge, still half blinded. Marko was waiting, crouched on the right just outside the exit. Cernović lunged out of the passageway and off to the left side of the ledge as a fusillade of Sturmgewehr fire sprayed out of the darkness behind him.

"Blow it!" he screamed, collapsing against the fissure wall.

Marko twisted the trigger of the electric detonation box. For an interminable second, nothing happened. . . .

Then, with a roar that shook the very bones of the mountain, the twenty-five twelve-pound bricks of high-grade plastic explosive that the Partisans had planted along the ceiling of the final two hundred yards of the Soujak Mine exploded, directly over the heads of the lead Fallschirmjager.

A tremendous gout of dust and shattered rock blasted out of the passageway and into the empty air of the vertical cavern. Cernović was certain he caught a blurred glimpse of a disembodied leg and boot wind-milling past as he huddled against the fissure wall with his hands clasped over his ears.

Then the paltry ledge on which he and Marko were crouching broke in two. The right-hand side support-ing the younger Partisan sagged but stayed in place. The left-hand side under Cernović crumbled and fell into the abyss.

As the rock beneath his feet dropped away, Cer-nović twisted his body and made a desperate lunge for the half-dozen ropes dangling beside the frozen waterfall. He managed to wrap his fingers around two of them. As he slammed backward into the column of ice, the crude steel spike anchoring one of the ropes to the rock pulled out.

The other rope held. Gasping, the wind knocked out of him, the Partisan commander summoned his last reserves of strength and, kicking, managed to get the rope half wound around one leg. It was enough to brake him as he slid downward, the coarse fibers of the rope burning between his trembling fingers.

Still, Cernović had the presence of mind to think of Marko. He stared up at the remains of the ledge as he descended, half out of control, into the gloom. The underpinnings of the little shelf of rock were crum-bling, disintegrating, even as he watched. . . .

"Marko!" he yelled. *"The ropes, boy! Jump. Jump!"*

The young Partisan took two running steps and leapt. He would have made it if not for the bulky pack adio on his back. The extra weight of The Ogre was imply too much. Cernović saw Marko soar, spread-agled, through the air above him, saw him get a hand n one of the ropes, and for an elated second thought e would hang on. . . .

Then the rope slipped from his grasp and his body ame hurtling down, inverting with the weight of the adio as it fell.

"Noooooooooo!" Cernović heard himself scream. He ade a frantic grab for Marko as he tumbled past, ut it was futile. The cold metal of the radio scraped is clutching fingers—and then the boy was gone. one without uttering a sound.

Two seconds later there was an awful, muted *splat* rom the darkness below.

Cernović let out an anguished groan and pressed is face to the rope, teeth clenched and eyes tightly hut. For a moment he hung there, dangling in space, queezing the rope as if by so doing he could embed is helpless grief and fury in its strands.

Then the brief surge of strength left him and his ands relaxed once more, and he resumed his perilous lide down the rope to the bottom of the frozen aterfall.

Twenty minutes later, SS Hauptsturmfuehrer Ulrich Iaak and the handful of Muslim Fallschirmjager who ad survived the blast staggered out of the mouth of le Soujak Mine and into the white purity of the nowbound gorge, blackened from head to toe by rock ust, and coughing as if to spew up their lungs iecemeal.

Haak and Scharfuehrer Schmidt collapsed to their nees, clutched up handfuls of snow, and pressed them o their stinging eyes and faces. All around them men ere doing the same, spitting and hacking as they tried o soothe their streaming eyes.

"I . . . I never thought . . . we'd find our way . . . out f there, Herr Hauptsturmfuehrer," Schmidt croaked,

wheezing. He looked slowly over his shoulder. "*Mei*
Gott. Only seven . . . maybe eight . . . made it out . .
besides us."

Haak blew his nose between his thumb and forefir
ger and wiped the sleeve of his combat jacket acros
his upper lip. With his red, puffy eyes, sweaty, dir
caked face, and phlegm-covered chin, he looked lik
the survivor of a poison-gas attack, Schmidt though
The Scharfuehrer had no doubt that he looked a
bad himself.

"We went in . . . with an assault team . . . of twenty
five," Haak panted, his condensing breath wreathin
his head. "If it cost eighteen dead . . . to be rid c
Tito . . . then it was worth the price."

"You're . . . you're sure . . . he was there, Her
Haupsturmfuehrer?" Schmidt asked.

"I caught . . . a glimpse of him . . . just after w
stormed the mine entrance," Haak replied. "The ligh
was on his face . . . as he looked back at us." H
wind was returning. "I know it was him; that face
unmistakeable. The head rat of the Slavic Commu
nists, damn him."

Schmidt looked back at the mine entrance, whic
was still discharging a thin haze of dust and smoke
"So . . . you feel he's dead, sir?"

Haak nodded. "Dead or soon to be. Either way
he's not coming out of that hole again, that's fc
certain."

"Perhaps there is another way out," Schmidt saic
"A back door?"

"No." Haak shook his head. "That miserable min
penetrated right into the heart of the mountain. Th
far side of it is a solid vertical rock face overlookin
yet another cursed gorge, complete with waterfall–
we reconnoitred it as we flew in for the drop. Th
miners wouldn't have dug the main shaft clear to th
opposite side of the mountain only to have it open ou
onto an unusable cliff. Too much work for no reason.

Schmidt got painfully to his feet. "Suppose ther

re side tunnels leading back to this opening," he suggested. "Maybe the Partisans knew there was a way
to collapse the main passageway on top of us and then
bypass the blockage—get back to the main entrance
and escape."

"Possible," Haak said, "although I think the bas-
ards committed suicide when they saw we had them
rapped—tried to take us with them. But we're not
going to take any chances. We're going to set charges
in the mine entrance and bring the whole thing down
on itself. If any Slavs *do* happen to be alive in there,
they can wander around in the dark until they go mad
and kill each other or simply starve to death." He
removed his cigarette case from inside his jacket,
opened it, and extracted a black paper cigarette with
a gold foil filter. "Either or," he said, "it doesn't mat-
er to me."

A nearby object caught Haak's eye. It was a dead
body on a stretcher with a hand-knit scarf draped over
ts face. The Hauptsturmfuehrer scowled, cleared his
hroat, and spat forcefully on the corpse. Then he
icked his lips.

Schmidt held out a wooden match, popped it into
lame with his thumbnail.

"Ah, thank you, Schmidt," Haak said, bending to
he light and drawing. He offered the open case.
"Here. Have one yourself."

"Thank *you*, Herr Haupsturmfuehrer," the Schar-
uehrer replied. "Richterhaus, eh? Very fine, sir."

Haak smiled and gazed into the empty black en-
rance of the Soujak Mine. "Nothing but the best,"
he said.

"Smashed to pieces," Cernović muttered angrily,
hrowing down a fragment of the radio that had plum-
neted along with Marko to the bottom of the water-
all chasm. He and the other Partisans, including Tito,
were sitting on boulders about twenty feet back from
a narrow cleft in the rock through which a cold, ebbing

daylight penetrated. He blinked and turned to look a the wrapped-up body lying among the rocks at the foot of the frozen cascade, then put his head in hi hands and stared at the ground between his feet. *I'm the one who told him he had to carry that damned beast of a radio. . . .*

"Since the Nazis can no longer pursue us through the mine," Tito said, "we'll wait here for nightfall be fore making our exit. We should be able to rejoin ou main force by dawn. Commanders Lesković and Riba have certainly broken out by now and will make fo the Ugljevik Pass to regain a terrain advantage ove any pursuing Fallschirmjager or Jagdkommando units." The marshall paused and looked over at Cer nović. "Anton."

Cernović did not answer.

"Anton," Tito said again.

Wearily the Partisan commander raised his head from his hands. "What?"

Tito's handsome face hardened, but he restrained himself, and when he spoke it was without anger "Anton. The boy is dead. He was a good soldier and died well. And that's the end of it."

Cernović turned his head and regarded the shrouded body lying among the rocks again. Then he looked the other way, toward the daylight filtering in through the cleft in the rock, and cleared his throat "I know, Comrade Marshall," he said quietly.

"Of course you do," Tito returned. He folded hi arms. "We have no radio, Anton. We must get ou message regarding the King Tiger train to Merrit before tomorrow is done, or he will not know to ac celerate his schedule for mining the Zpoda Skyway Bridge." He gestured at the handful of Partisans sit ting nearby. "None of these men know the way to Zlostup. They are from Slovenia in the north, and are not familiar with the hidden pathways of the Majevicas."

Cernović passed a hand over his brow, pushing aside his unruly black hair.

"That leaves you," Tito said.

There was a long silence. Then Cernović sat up, looked about him, and sighed. Slowly the rakish Gypsy grin, albeit subdued, spread across his face once more.

"I'll move out of the cavern ahead of the rest of you," he said, "just after the sun drops behind the mountain."

Chapter Eight

"Keep it tight, Sid. You, too, Peter."

RAF squadron leader Alan Stuart adjusted his throat mike and glanced back past his port and starboard wingtips to check the proximity of the other two Typhoons. The big fighters, heavy with underwing rockets and drop tanks, were spaced perfectly in the close triangle formation, as Stuart had known they would be. Flight Officers Cox and MacLeish were two of his best, if a bit young. He continued to scan the ground rushing by barely three hundred feet below, praying all the while that he wouldn't lead the small attack flight into some barely visible radio tower the Germans had erected. The dim light of evening was fading rapidly into darkness, he didn't know the terrain of north-central Yugoslavia all that well, and there was no telling what the damned Nazis might have stuck in their path. In addition, if they didn't encounter the tank-carrying train in question pretty soon, it would be too dark to maintain visual contact with the railway tracks and the mission would be a scrub.

"Are we even sure this is the right train line?" Cox asked, his voice crackling in Stuart's earphones.

"My drop tanks are nearly empty," MacLeish chimed in. "Are we good for fuel, sir? I don't fancy ditching in the Adriatic and swimming the last fifty miles back to Bari."

Stuart chewed his lip in irritation. "No, I'm not sure this is the right bloody train line," he growled. "And yes, we're good for bloody fuel. For another ten minutes, that is—at which time we'll have to break off and head for home, anyway, because it'll be too dark to see the bloody ground." He paused momentarily. "Anyone have any more bloody questions?"

"No, sir," Cox radioed.

"No, sir," MacLeish echoed.

"Bloody good, then. Keep it quiet and keep it tight."

The two flying officers let out deep breaths and glanced across the intervening fifty feet of airspace at each other. They could still make out each other's faces through the Plexiglas of their fighters' cockpit canopies, although daylight was waning to a fiery golden glow as the sun began to sink behind the purple hills to the west.

Stuart was about to give up and order the flight homeward when he saw first the black, billowing smoke and then the engine of a train coming around a low hill some six miles ahead. He checked his fuel. His drop tanks were empty, like MacLeish's and probably Cox's, and this far into Yugoslavia the Typhoons' regular tankage would get them back across the Adriatic Sea to southern Italy only if their big Napier Sabre engines were mechanically benevolent enough to run on dregs and fumes. It was a toss-up, yea or nay.

"Right," Stuart said, holding his throat mike against his larynx, "let go drop tanks and attack the train coming into view ahead of us. Two passes, line formation. Behind me, Sid, then you, Peter. Two rockets only on the first pass. Then one strafing run and head for home. Everyone clear?"

"Clear, sir," Cox replied. He throttled back slightly to move his Typhoon in behind Stuart's.

"Clear," MacLeish said, letting his aircraft drop back several hundred yards. "Sir, do you think that's the right train?"

"Lis—" Stuart began.

"It doesn't look like the right train to me. It's too short."

"MacLe—"

"And where's the Luftwaffe air cover that's supposed to be following the tank train? We haven't seen a Hun fighter all day."

Suddenly Squadron Leader Alan Stuart—frustrated, tired, scared, and heartily sick of war—became very annoyed with Flying Officer Peter MacLeish. Racing in at four hundred miles an hour barely a stone's throw from the ground to attack a heavily armored military train with inadequate daylight and scant fuel to get home was hardly the appropriate moment for petulance.

"Listen," Stuart barked, "it's a bloody train. We're out of time and we're out of daylight, and it's *here*, so it's the one we're bloody attacking. Otherwise this whole bloody exercise is a wasted trip."

"Yes, sir," MacLeish radioed.

He still sounds petulant, Stuart thought irritably, as he steadied his Typhoon on the onrushing locomotive and thumbed the launch triggers of his rockets.

"More tea, Your Excellency?" Matthias Juttner inquired, lifting the silver-and-glass flask off the white linen cloth that covered the luxury coach's main dining table. The ice cubes in the crystal water glasses rattled slightly as the train swayed around a gradual bend in the track.

"Yes, I believe I will," Amin al-Husseini replied. "A pleasant finish to a rather superb rack of lamb."

Juttner smiled as he leaned forward in his chair and refilled the grand mufti's tea glass. "It was quite adequate, wasn't it? For a train meal, anyway." He continued to smile as he turned to Julius Neurath, who was the third diner at the table. "Hauptsturmfuehrer Neurath? Tea?"

The pale Gestapo officer directed a flat stare at Juttner. "No, thank you."

Juttner shrugged, imperturbable, and topped up his own glass. "I hope you're not off your food, Hauptsturmfuehrer. You look somewhat moribund. Perhaps the garlic, eh?"

"I'm fine," Neurath said.

"I'm so glad," Juttner responded. "I was becoming concerned about your rather alarming . . . *translucency* of complexion."

Neurath paled even more, the muscles along his jaw working in suppressed rage, as al-Husseini snapped his fingers in the air. "Snagi! My tonic, please." The mufti always concluded dinner with a cocktail of natural digestive aids—juices, herbs, and spices.

Mustapha Snagi, moving carefully due to the pain of his recent gunshot wounds, appeared at the door of the private car's small galley. "At once, Your Excellency."

He turned to go, and at that instant two tremendous explosions went off on either side of the train, rocking it on the tracks. The panes of several windows on both sides of the coach blew inward, spraying the luxurious interior with glass.

"Aaaagh!" al-Husseini cried, throwing his arms up in front of his face.

Juttner and Neurath staggered up off their chairs and made for the front of the car. Snagi came through the door of the galley, followed by a terrorized chef and his assistant, and lunged for al-Husseini. The Macedonian bodyguard collected the mufti in his arms and swept him to the floor next to a large purple velvet divan, partially covering him with his own body.

Juttner and Neurath burst through the coach's front door and onto the small forward-end platform. They were just in time to see the smoke trails of two rockets suddenly streak the sky mere yards overhead, accompanied by a whining *whoosh*, and hear the dual impacts as the projectiles struck somewhere just behind the train. Two seconds later there came the deafening roar of a powerful engine as an RAF Typhoon, the distinctive air scoop beneath its propeller hub gaping like the black mouth of some airborne shark, overflew the train, heading in the opposite direction.

"Why don't those fools on the antiaircraft car open fire?" Neurath yelled, craning his neck to watch as the two Typhoons began to bank around over the undulating countryside, setting up for another pass.

Juttner, holding on to the handrail of the shaking, swaying end platform, opened his mouth to reply—and two more rockets shrieked in. One exploded on the hillside to the left of the train. The other hit the cab of the locomotive, just behind the boiler. There was a blast that made all five cars in tow—coal car, bunk car for the bodyguard detachment of SS, armored antiaircraft gun car, al-Husseini's private coach, and caboose—dance on their metal wheels. Scorching clouds of fire, smoke, and steam began to stream back along the entire length of the train. Incredibly the locomotive did not derail, nor did it lose power. Juttner leapt to the left side of the end platform, where he could look up the inside of the curve they were negotiating and see the whole train from the engine back.

The cab of the locomotive was a twisted tangle of blackened steel, with orange flame, black smoke, and white steam gusting out of it. The coal car had caught fire, adding to the smoke and flame licking back over the SS bunk car and the antiaircraft gun car immediately behind it. Juttner grimaced and coughed as oily fumes whipped into his face—and then there was another earsplitting din as a third Typhoon roared down the length of the train less than seventy-five feet overhead.

"The engine's had it!" Juttner shouted to Neurath. "It's only a matter of time before it dies or blows up! And the coal car's burning!" He watched as whipping sheets of flame from the coaler drove back SS troopers who had appeared on the forward-end platform of the bunk car, trying to beat out hot spots with jackets and blankets. "The bunk car's catching fire, too!"

The SS gunners on the two rotating 40-millimeter antiaircraft cannon finally opened up, sending red streams of tracer shells scudding after the three British fighters that were banking low and fast across the purple-and-gold evening sky. The guns fired with a rapid, distinctive sound of their own, their multiple barrels punching in and out with every recoil:

Pom pom pom pom pom . . .

"I don't bloody believe it!" Squadron Leader Stuart fumed over the radio. "Six rockets fired and only *one* hit?" Possibly the worst of it was that his own two rockets had been the first to miss. "Forget strafing. Fire the rest of your rockets on this next pass, and, gentlemen, I want that bloody train *knocked off the bloody track! Clear?*"

"Roger that, Squadron Leader," Cox acknowledged.

"Maybe you'll get a hit yourself this time, sir," Mac-Leish remarked dryly. He had to say it; it was impossible for him not to. Flying Officer Peter MacLeish was nineteen years old, a tank-busting Typhoon ace three times over, flushed with his own power and apparent immortality, and had not lived long enough to learn that there are many occasions in life when a man, regardless of what he thinks, should resist the urge to sound clever, and keep his mouth shut.

"You're bloody going on report for that, Mac-Leish!" Stuart shouted, enraged that the young flier's insolence was consuming even a fraction of his mental energy in the middle of an attack. By God, he'd never heard of such a thing. He refocused out the port side of his cockpit canopy on the damaged train as his fighter swept ahead. . . . Around . . .

To starboard, the Messerschmitt 109s came corkscrewing in out of the fiery glare of the setting sun, wing guns blazing. The three Typhoon pilots were caught off guard by the German fighters, concentrating as they were on the ground target to their left.

Cox never had a chance. The first 20-millimeter cannon shells from the lead Messerschmitt tore through the exposed underbelly of his banking fighter and into its primary fuel tanks. Seconds later, the Typhoon exploded in a ball of flame.

Cannon shells from the second Messerschmitt shattered the cockpit canopy of the lead Typhoon, decapitating Squadron Leader Alan Stuart. His relatively undamaged aircraft rolled over, dove straight into the ground, and blew up.

Peter MacLeish's nineteen-year-old reflexes saved him. As German cannon shells hammered into the fuselage of his fighter, puncturing the cockpit wall and shredding the thigh muscles of his right leg, he yanked back on the stick, throttled up, and stood his Typhoon on its tail. Rolling over and through the attacking 109s, missing a midair collision by inches and pure luck, he muscled the plane upright, dove for the deck, and fled at maximum speed into what was left of the setting sun. The Messerschmitts buzzed around in his wake like angry hornets, and four of the attacking flight of eight broke off to give chase.

One of the peculiarities of the Typhoon—and what made it such an effective ground-attack aircraft—was that despite its limitations as a dogfighter and high-altitude interceptor, it was extremely fast at low altitudes, even with its heavy armament. To the surprise of many wartime designers, including its own, the Hawker Typhoon had proven to be faster at ground level than the highly revered Supermarine Spitfire. Faster than the much-vaunted Focke-Wulf 190. And considerably faster than the Messerschmitt 109.

Flying Officer Peter MacLeish would nurse his shot-up Typhoon all the way back across the Adriatic Sea to Bari in southern Italy, racked with the pain of his mangled thigh and dizzy from loss of blood—the sole survivor of the rushed, ill-fated ground-attack mission against the King Tiger train. He would crash-land and live to grow older, wiser, and humbler . . . at the cost of his right leg.

The rail line just over a mile past the bend where the Typhoons had rocketed the Grand Mufti's private train was a beehive of activity. Night had fallen, the temperature had dropped even farther below freezing, and all around the critically damaged locomotive—now sitting motionless on the tracks, with its crumpled superstructure smoking and ruptured boiler steaming—German troops were coming and going, waving lanterns and flashlights, shouting orders and directions to each other. The scene had a surreal, Dantesque quality to it: all shadows and angles and harsh light, interspersed with hissing vapors and the clanking throb of heavy machinery. A hundred yards behind the ruined locomotive, crawling forward along the sloped side of the rail bed like a giant bug, was a King Tiger tank.

The King Tiger train, its numerous tank-bearing flatcars, gun cars, and engines stretching well back around the hillside bend where several of the Typhoon rockets had struck, was stopped dead behind the mufti's damaged and now immoveable train. A slender, middle-aged SS officer in a peaked cap and greatcoat was stalking along the gravel bed beside the mufti's shrapnel-pocked private car, the lantern light glinting off his steel-rimmed glasses. Walking with him were two of his own aides, Haj Amin al-Husseini, Gestapo

Hauptsturmfuehrer Julius Neurath, and SS Hauptsturmfuehrer Matthias Juttner. Snagi trailed along several
paces behind his master.

"But Standartenfuehrer Kronstadt," Neurath was
saying, "one of your train's eight locomotives *must* be
reassigned to the Grand Mufti's train. It is absolutely
imperative that a dignitary of his stature be provided
safe conduct to Belgrade without delay."

"No," the SS colonel replied, "it is absolutely imperative that my forty-eight King Tigers be transported to their deployment point in the Majevica
Mountains without delay. And this heap of scrap
metal"—he waved a black-gloved hand at the steaming hulk that had been the mufti's locomotive—"is
preventing that from happening."

Amin al-Husseini, looking cold and annoyed in his
expensive town coat, stepped aside and reboarded his
private car. As usual, Mustapha Snagi followed him.

"The Grand Mufti is a special guest of the Reich,"
Neurath pressed on, "a key associate and ally of the
Fuehrer himself. If he was to become a fatality due
to your—"

Standartenfuehrer Kronstadt stopped in his tracks
and turned to face Neurath directly. "It was only by
the merest of chances that the British Typhoons at-
tacked your train instead of mine; I was barely twenty
miles behind you. And if my preassigned fighter cover
had not spotted the attack on your train and inter-
vened so effectively, you and your companions, including His Excellency the Grand Mufti of Jerusalem,
would in all likelihood be dead. Now, having saved
your lives once tonight, I have no intention of lingering here, shuffling engines back and forth, while the
British and Americans send out more search-and-
destroy missions. And I will not decrease the hauling
capacity of my train, which must negotiate a number
of steep inclines in the Majevicas, by sacrificing one
of my locomotives just so the mufti can branch off
this line and head directly to Belgrade for his own

convenience. There is a military priority here, Hauptsturmfuehrer Neurath, and the delivery of my Tiger tanks to the battle front takes precedence over the chauffeuring of your temporarily marooned dignitary to his next luxury hotel."

Kronstadt, a supremely no-nonsense individual, had leaned in until his hard, seamed face was now less than six inches from Neurath's. The intelligent eyes behind the steel-rimmed lenses were as cold and steady as chips of ice. "We will proceed thusly: the King Tiger now approaching will topple your damaged locomotive off the track. My train will then move forward to couple to your caboose and remaining cars, and push them ahead of us all the way to the Zpoda Skyway Bridge. I will not stop and expose myself to further air or saboteur attack. The mufti and you can then disembark at the fortified bridge chalet, which is garrisoned by soldiers of the very SS Division Handschar he has come to Yugoslavia to speak to—according to you—prior to my train's final transit across the bridge itself to the crest of Mount Zpoda.

"Frankly, I don't see why His Excellency is so adamant that he be routed to Belgrade when he must then promptly travel on to the very location to which we are now headed. From his standpoint it's six of one, half a dozen of the other.

"And that is how it will be, Hauptsturmfuehrer Neurath. I suggest you inform your distinguished guest of the unavoidable change in itinerary."

Neurath's thin mouth twitched. "I will put a detailed account of your unwillingness to accommodate the grand mufti into my report to Reichsfuehrer Himmler," he said.

"Do that," Standartenfuehrer Kronstadt replied, turning on his boot heel. "I'm a combat officer, not a travel agent." He waved a gloved hand in the air, ignoring Neurath entirely. "Move that Tiger into position, Obersturmfuehrer!"

Behind Neurath, Hauptsturmfuehrer Matthias Juttner smiled to himself, placed a thin black cigar between his lips, and stepped farther down the gravel embankment as the crawling King Tiger approached.

Chapter Nine

Černović had been alternating between a fast walk and a double-time trot all night. Now dawn's silver light was bringing the cold gleam of a new day to the silent trees and black crags and snow-packed slopes of the high mountain country just east of the Zpoda Gorge. Fortunately after ducking out of the Soujak Mine's hidden rear exit the previous evening, he had been able to evade the Fallschirmjager still patrolling the forests above the mine and pick up Merritt's trail without difficulty. Following along in the trodden-down snow of the mule track had been relatively easy, and he'd been able to make good time.

Now his beard and mustache were caked with ice from the freezing condensation of his own breath, his fingers and toes were numb, his thighs and calves ached, his lungs were raw from panting in the dry, bitter air, and he desperately wanted a cigarette. Even more desperately he wanted to stop and rest. But Merritt and his companions were still somewhere ahead,

so he hugged the Mauser carbine he had borrowe
from one of his men more tightly between his folde
arms, put his head down, and soldiered on.

The terrain had become incredibly rugged and dra
matic. The ridgelines he was following were knif
edged with steep inclines on both sides—one wron
step could send him tumbling down a snow-covere
seventy-degree slope with no hope of stopping beyon
crashing into the trees hundreds of feet below. An
yet, as hazardous as the ridge trail was, he knew it wa
nothing compared to the real "Bad Step"—Zlostup—
which lay only a few miles ahead.

Cernović quickened his pace to a trot as the trai
sloped gently downward for a few hundred yards be
fore resuming its upward course, winding through on
of the small thickets of stunted evergreens that wer
becoming less frequent as he gained altitude. Movin
into the trees always gave him a sense of comfort; h
did not like being so exposed on the open ridges. Th
towering peaks and chasms of the high mountain
were spectacular, awe-inspiring—but a man could b
spotted from a long way off in such country.

The sun shot its first pale rays over the crags t
the east just as he reached the center of the copse
illuminating a perfect little sheltered hollow in th
trees through which the trail passed. As tired as h
was, the temptation to stop was overwhelming. Plus
Cernović realized, he was becoming badly dehydrated
which was dangerous. He had been trying to eat snov
while traveling through the night, but it was no
enough to compensate for the moisture loss of sweat
ing under his winter clothes and panting in the ari
mountain atmosphere. He needed to stop, make a
small, smokeless fire, melt snow in the rusty tin ca
he kept as a field cup, have a real drink of perhaps a
quart or more of warm water, eat some of the suga
cubes he carried in his shirt pocket, smoke one of hi
two remaining cigarettes, and rest for ten or fifteer
minutes. Then he could catch up to Merritt.

He sighed, leaned his Mauser carbine up against a convenient boulder, and began to gather low deadwood from the nearby trees. There was plenty available, and it was dry. Obviously no mountain travelers had camped in this particular copse for some time.

He had just gotten the fire going and was filling up his tin can with snow when a stick broke behind him with a sharp *crack*.

He dropped the can and spun, clawing in his coat pocket for his Luger.

"Yoo-hoo, Cerny!" cooed the gaunt, red-bearded man squatting on the boulder against which Cernović had propped his carbine. His eyes, vividly blue in the clear morning light, fixed on the Partisan commander's with the intensity of electromagnets. He grinned, showing a mouthful of long, yellow teeth, and tossed the two halves of the stick he had just broken onto the snow. "A touch jumpy are we, my boy? Yes, a touch jumpy I think."

Cernović lowered his pistol with an exasperated sigh and rubbed his eyes with his thumb and forefinger. "Quisp."

"The very same, I do confess it!" the piratical apparition on the boulder exclaimed, bouncing on his heels. "Do I not? Yes, I do!"

God, Cernović thought. He turned back to the fire and retrieved his dropped meltwater can. "You took me off guard, Professor," he said, refilling the tin with snow.

"And that is a worrisome thing, old bean. Shouldn't happen."

Quisp hopped down off the boulder, walked across the intervening ten feet, and squatted on his haunches on the opposite side of the fire, facing Cernović. The Partisan commander hadn't seen the Englishman for nearly two months, and so examined him with some interest as he held his can of snow over the flames by its wire bail.

Theobald Fenton Quisp, PhD, was one of those

scrawny, red-haired Scots-Irish hybrids who, by virtue
of their jittery temperament and unnaturally bright
eyes, tend to look perpetually crazed. He could not
keep still even when squatting in one place: his hands,
eyes, mouth, facial muscles—all the muscles in his
body, in fact—were in constant motion, shifting, flexing, wandering. It made Cernović tired just to look at
him, not to mention slightly irritable; Quisp's congenital restlessness had a catching quality.

　　The Englishman was starting to look more than a
little worn, Cernović decided, as if advancing middle
age and the strain of living alone in the mountains,
constantly hunted by the SS and their collaborators,
were catching up to him. There wasn't an ounce of
fat on his stringy body, but the lines in his face had
multiplied and deepened and there was a considerable
amount of gray in his unkempt red beard. Cernović
wondered how much longer he would be able to keep
up his self-declared one-man war of surveillance, sabotage, and general harassment against the Nazi occupi-
ers. His presence and activities in Yugoslavia were not
sanctioned by the British military—or any military, for
that matter. He was a complete independent; a lone
wolf. Or perhaps a lone lunatic. Everyone fighting the
Nazi war machine was glad to have Theobald Quisp
running around the mountains, gathering intelligence
and occasionally blowing something up, but no one
was quite sure what he was apt to do from one moment to the next. He would cooperate with requests
from the British and Partisan militaries, but he would
not take orders and he would not agree to being evac-
uated from Yugoslavia, although the British had offered to extract him several times.

　　An improbable person, this eccentric Englishman,
this professor of archaeology who had written several
prewar textbooks on the ancient Greeks, Macedo-
nians, and Thracians, Cernović thought as he warmed
the meltwater in his tin can. This foreign-born guerilla
adventurer who was both strangely reliable—loyal

even—undeniably brave, and disconcertingly unpredictable all at the same time.

The Partisan commander lifted the can from the
tiny fire and gingerly sipped the steaming water. It
was not the last time, he was certain, he would think
so about Theobald Quisp.

"Are you thirsty, Professor?" he asked, holding out
the can. "We can melt all the snow we need."

"No, thankee," Quisp replied, bouncing. He unslung the Schmeisser machine pistol he was carrying
from his shoulder and set it across his knees. Then he
pulled off his tattered gloves, cupped his hands in
front of his mouth, and blew into them. "Rather
balmy up here today, my boy, don't you think? Yes,
balmy. Balmy's the word."

Cernović sipped more hot water and crunched one
of his sugar cubes between his teeth. "I think it's
damned cold. I'm half frozen to death."

Quisp clucked his tongue and slapped his knee.
"Circulation, my lad. Circulation is the key. The blood
must rush—*rush*, I tell you—around the body, building
up and maintaining heat through friction as well as
metabolic combustion. One must develop this capacity
with a program of internal cleansing, vigorous exercise, and brisk massage. Absolutely essential to good
health, what?"

Cernović smiled involuntarily behind the rim of his
meltwater can, remembering the disbelief and conster-
nation on Marko's face the day Cernović and the
young radio operator had rendezvoused with Quisp at
one of his temporary camps, at his request, to change
out a faulty transmitter in a field set. The Englishman
had been striding in circles around his lean-to, stark
naked but for his combat boots, raking his fish-belly-
white skin from neck to ankle with two stiff-bristled
brushes, one in each hand. His scrawny torso, but-
tocks, and thighs were livid with red splotches from
the vicious self-flagellation, and he was singing some
appalling Gaelic folk song in a lusty baritone as he

whaled away at himself. He did not so much as blink when Cernović and Marko walked up, and, in fact, asked if they would care to join him in his daily routine. Marko, Cernović recalled, had looked ready to flee for his life.

"I don't doubt it works for you, Professor," Cernović said, "but I think I'll stick to long walks and staying clear of stray bullets to keep myself healthy." He coughed, finished his water, and put a battered cigarette between his lips.

Quisp watched him intently as he lit the smoke with a twig from the fire. "And that is another thing, my boy: the abomination of habitually ingesting toxic gases through one of the body's most vital organs, the lungs. Far be it from me to lecture you on how best to maintain the temple of your material being—yes, far be it." He looked off to one side and up, raising a finger. "However, the harmful effects of this habit have long been recognized, and to support the point I shall now quote from the famous essay 'A Counterblaste to Tobacco.' To wit: it is 'a custom loathesome to the eye, hateful to the nose, harmful to the brain, dangerous to the lungs, and in the black stinking fume thereof, nearest resembling the horrible Stygian smoke of the Pit that is bottomless.' End quote."

"You're ruining my cigarette, Professor," Cernović said, exhaling. "And how do I know you didn't just make that up?"

Quisp jumped to his feet. "You don't, my lad, you don't! Not unless you are familiar with the insightful writings of the worthy King James the First of England, who penned those trenchant words in the year 1604! By the Leaping Lord Harry, didn't he just? Yes, he did!" Quisp executed a bizarre theatrical flourish with one hand and, bowing, squatted back down.

"Good for him," Cernović grunted, inhaling contentedly.

Quisp clucked his tongue again and wagged a finger.

I see what you're thinking, old fellow. You're thinking, *Quisp considers me a lost cause, a fellow human condemned to the slow degradation of health and vitality by means of autotoxification!* But you are wrong—wrong, I tell you! I shall never give up on you, Cerny. I shall save you from your own compulsive indulgences in the long run, have no doubt!"

Cernović blew out another long stream of smoke. "I'd much rather you saved me from the Nazis, the Ustashe, the Chetniks, and the Handschar Muslims, if it's all the same to you."

"Speaking of the Nazis," Quisp said, changing gears, "aren't you wondering why I've dropped in on you here atop this godforsaken rock pile?"

"Yes. It had crossed my mind." Cernović knew from long experience that one had to allow the loquacious Englishman all the time he needed to get to the point. Prodding him for specific information before he was ready to give it only prolonged the waiting process.

Quisp grinned conspiratorially. "Tito asked me to. I received a radio communication from him just before midnight last night. The witching hour—oooooh!" He bugged his eyes and waggled his fingers at Cernović.

The Partisan commander smiled again. "You're quite insane, you know, Professor," he remarked. "Of course, you're well aware of that fact, aren't you?" The question was rhetorical.

"Naturally," Quisp replied. "Attempting to remain sane in an insane situation such as total global war would quickly make one crazy. Far better to adopt a complementary approach to said situation and truly accept it, thereby sacrificing one's sanity but retaining one's wits."

Cernović nodded patiently. "That makes perfect sense to me. Now, there was a radio communication from Comrade Marshall Tito?"

Quisp fluttered his hand. "You forced me into a digression, there, Cerny—shame on you. Yes, as I said,

I did receive a message from the Tito's camp. Som
new information has come to light since you departe
the Soujak Mine, and I was asked to pass it on to yo
and this countryman of mine—Merritt, isn't it?—wh
is even now stealing his way along Zlostup toward th
Zpoda Skyway Bridge.''

"How far ahead are they?" Cernović asked.

"Approximately seven miles," Quisp told him. "
spotted them from across the gorge early this mornin
as I was hastening to meet you. We'll soon catch u
to them—Zlostup is badly iced and snowed in. The
won't be moving very quickly with three mules, wi
they? No they won't, my boy!''

"And the specifics of the Comrade Marshall's mes
sage?'' Cernović continued.

"There is, apparently, a military train bearing
large cargo of King Tiger tanks headed in this direc
tion. That you know, and that is what you must relat
to Major Merritt. What you do not know is that yes
terday afternoon a small private train immediately i
front of it was rocketed by British Typhoons, blockin
the tracks. It took most of the night to clear away th
wreckage, repair some sprung rails, and get the tan
train underway again. That amounted to a twelve-hou
delay. Merritt and his demolition team have gaine
half a day's grace to get the Zpoda Skyway Bridg
mined.''

Cernović nodded. "That's good news. That extra
twelve hours may make all the difference.''

Quisp bounced on his haunches. "Indeed, indeed
But there is more. Marshall Tito additionally relate
that the Soujak Mine units of the Second Proletaria
Brigade have broken through encircling Nazi Fall
schirmjager and Jagdkommando forces and success
fully executed a strategic redeployment into th
Ugljevik Plateau region via the Ugljevik Pass.''

"Strategic redeployment?" Cernović echoed, raisin
an eyebrow. "That sounds suspiciously like retreat.''

Quisp tsk-tsked. "My boy, as a high-ranking office

the Partisan Army of Yugoslavia, you should be
uite inured by now to the blatant euphemisms of the
ommunist ethos. Of course it means retreat. They
n for their lives, shooting wildly, and barely escaped
nnihilation, from what I can gather. Commander
ibar was killed. Only Lesković and, of course, Tito
imself remain."

Cernović cast his eyes down at the ground for a
oment, then flicked his cigarette butt into the dying
re. "I am sorry to hear about Comrade Ribar," he
id. "He was a good man. His father, one of the
arty's founders, will be heartbroken."

"Yes, it is unfortunate," Quisp agreed. "But Dr.
ibar is a strong individual. I happen to know him. He
ill persevere."[1] The Englishman got to his feet. "Per-
aps we should do the same and press on, Cerny, my
d, and talk further as we go. Shouldn't we? Yes, I
ink we should."

Cernović, still dwelling on the thought that yet an-
ther close friend had been killed, looked up at Quisp.
Professor," he said with a tired smile, "why is it that
ou always finish your statements with a question
hich you then immediately answer yourself?"

Quisp looked incredulous as he slung his Schmeisser
ver his shoulder. "Good heavens," he replied, "I'm
uite sure I don't know what you're talking about. I
on't do that, do I? Of course I don't!

"Now, come along, my boy. Up and at 'em, eh?
here is more to tell and miles in which to tell it, ha-
a! The good marshall spoke of a possible diversion-
ry attack on the far side of Mount Zpoda just prior
the arrival of the tank train, and of a certain
amecock—of all things—an individual whose updated
ovements may be of particular interest to Major
lerritt, for some reason. . . ."

Chapter Ten

Merritt walked carefully to the break in the narrow footpath, knelt in the snow with his Sten gun in the crook of his arm, and peered down. Veteran mountaineer and parachutist though he was, the vast empty space that yawned beneath him took his breath away. The drop to the bottom of this section of the Zpoda Gorge had to be every bit of two thousand feet—give or take a bounce or two, as Cernović had so colorfully put it.

He stood up, stepped back, and surveyed the towering cliff face that formed the left-hand side of the ancient trail known as Zlostup. The rock was mostly bare, with few cracks, crevices, or protrusions. Not much ice, which was good, but not much to hold on to or drive a piton into, either. Forty horizontal feet away, the narrow trail resumed its snaking, precarious route up and along the southern wall of the gorge. In between was a complete void—a gap where the footpath had once been but now simply did not exist. In

as as if a giant ax had hacked out a ten-meter section
f solid rock with one swipe.

"Avalanche," Merritt said to his seven companions,
ho were gathering behind him. "It swept away the
ail cleanly for forty feet or more. There's not so
uch as a toehold left of it." He looked at Vlado. "I
ought you told Tito and Cernović that Zlostup was
ill passable."

The lean Partisan brushed a stray lock of dark hair
ut of his eyes and avoided Merritt's gaze. "It was,
1ajor, but that was nearly five days ago. The ava-
inche must have happened since then."

"It doesn't look that recent to me," Merritt said.
And I've seen a few."

Vlado shrugged. "Rock slides are a daily occurrence
1 these mountains, Comrade Major. I tell you this
ust have happened only a day or two ago, because
1e path was intact when I used it during an
1telligence-gathering patrol just before your para-
hute drop."

Merritt turned to face him. "You go out alone on
:connaissance patrols, Vlado? Close to the German
ositions?"

"Close enough," the Partisan said. "We need a con-
ant flow of information in order to stay one step
head of the enemy. I and some of the others scout
lone because we've learned that one man has less
hance of being discovered than two or three."

"I'd say the enemy was one step ahead of you the
ther day," Bristow commented, leaning against the
ock wall with his arms folded on top of his Thomp-
on, gazing at Vlado. "Yagovac and his boys walked
ght into a shootin' gallery."

"And the Krauts had our drop zone staked out
retty good the other night, too," D'Amato added.
Decoy fires and SS troops layin' low right next to
1e DZ, all set for us to come floatin' down outta the
ky like a flock of dumb pigeons."

Vlado swallowed, feeling the hard eyes of the

American sergeants on him. "The Germans and the Muslim collaborators in the Handschar division ar very effective opponents," he said. "They routinel try to interrupt Allied air drops with decoy fires an Jagdkommando patrols. Sometimes they are in th right place at the right time. It's a matter of chance. He looked directly at Bristow. "And *I* was fightin alongside Bozidar Yagovac the morning he and man of my other comrades were killed, Sergeant."

"Yeah, sure," Bristow growled. "I forgot."

There was an awkward silence. Vlado hung his hea and put his hands in his pockets and sling his rif over one shoulder, looking sullen. Merritt looked hir up and down, then turned and examined the rock fac immediately above the missing section of trail. Mo: of it was featureless, but there were a few finger-widt cracks, and about fifty feet above the opposite trunc; tion of the path, a wedge-shaped chunk of granite tha stood out about five feet from the cliff proper like giant knuckle.

Merritt stood there for a few minutes, considerin; The day was clear and fairly still, but high on the star crags above Zlostup, the wind coursed through clef and crevices with an eerie, rising moan. Finally h turned and faced his companions.

"Obviously we can climb and piton our way acros the gap," he said, "and set up a Tyrolean traverse[1] t get all the equipment across. The problem is th mules. We can't mine the bridge without all the climb ing gear and explosives, and we can't carry it all with out the mules."

Vlado shuffled his rag-wrapped boots in the snov "We're turning back then, Major?"

"Not just yet." Merritt pointed up at the knuckl of granite sticking out of the sheer wall above the fa end of the trail. "We have ropes and blocks. If w can secure a block-and-tackle arrangement to that out cropping, we can rig slings for the mules, support thei weight, and pull them across the gap with tag line after we unload and transfer the equipment. Then we load the animals up again and proceed to the objective."

"You'll never get a mule to step off the edge of that cliff," Vlado said immediately. "When it sees the drop and decides it doesn't want to go, all eight of us won't be able to push it off, either."

"That's why we'll blindfold them," Merritt responded. "Three or four of us on the other side will hoist them off their hooves one at a time and they'll be across before they know what's happening." He looked pointedly at Vlado. The Partisan guide opened his mouth as if to argue, but then thought better of it.

Throckmorton sauntered up. "More aerobatics?" he asked.

"A little climbing and rigging," Merritt replied, "and a lot of unloading and hauling, I'm afraid." He smiled. "It's the only way, Duncan, as you can see."

The slender British captain stepped past his friend and cast a languid glance down into the gorge. "Yaas," he drawled, "it appears to be. Bloody substantial drop, that."

"Substantial's the word," Merritt said. "Where's Sylvia?"

"Loitering in the rear of the procession with her mule—whose company she seems to prefer to ours."

Merritt nodded and walked back down the trail, sidestepping between the rock wall and the first two mules, followed by Bristow. D'Amato, with Stirling and Weiss by his side, continued his casual observation of Vlado.

Sylvia Kozo was seated on a small boulder, smoking, beside the third mule. She looked up as Merritt drew near, regarding him from under her heavy lids.

"Miss Kozo," Merritt said, "perhaps I could prevail upon you to undertake a little climbing for us."

Sylvia nodded silently, the smoke from the cigarette cupped in her hand trickling up through her fingers.

"I need you to establish a line across that gap, then

climb to that protruding rock up there and secure a
block and tackle to it," Merritt went on. He glanced
over his shoulder as Bristow moved up behind him.
"Do you think you can do it?"

Sylvia blinked slowly at him. "I know I can do it."
She drew on the cigarette, holding it shielded in her
palm between her thumb and forefinger.

Merritt nodded. "It'd save us time and effort. Any
one of my men with mountaineering skills can pound
a line of pitons across to the far side—and up to the
overhead rock, as well—but you can certainly cover
the same distance much faster. . . . If you're sure that
face is climbable."

"Anything is climbable," Sylvia said, getting to her
feet. "It just depends upon who's doing the climbing."
She drew once more on the cigarette, flicked it aside,
and slipped past Merritt and Bristow, heading for the
front of the little column. "Get your ropes and blocks
ready, Major."

Merritt did not reply. He and Bristow were looking
at the same thing: the black paper cigarette with the
gold filter that lay smoldering on the hard crust of the
snowpack. The British major and American sergeant
met each other's eyes, and then Merritt took two
paces forward and crushed the butt down into the
snow with the sole of his boot.

"Watch her," he said quietly to Bristow as he
moved past the second mule, following Sylvia Kozo
back toward the head of the column.

Cernović and Quisp had been walking for nearly
two hours and had just moved onto the lowest stretch
of Zlostup. Quisp had been doing most of the talking,
and had covered everything from the disasterous military consequences of having four dozen King Tigers
deployed into the valleys of the Majevicas to the geol-
ogy of the rock in the surrounding cliff faces. Cernović
had listened patiently as he walked, at times lapsing
deeply into thoughts of his own. Now, with the empty

chasm of the Zpoda Gorge dropping away on the right side of the ever narrowing trail, he interrupted Quisp's latest irrelevant digression—a stream-of-consciousness lecture on the dietary benefits of wild garlic—with a more pertinent concern.

"Something's been bothering me," he said. "How did the German command in the Majevicas know exactly where to drop their Fallschirmjager? How did they know to ring the gorge and to storm the Soujak Mine itself? It was as if they were certain Tito and his staff would be inside."

Quisp, striding along at Cernović's shoulder, shrugged his shoulders. "Intelligence, my boy. The Germans are sticklers for up-to-date intelligence. God knows there are enough low-level reconnaissance flights buzzing the peaks and gorges these days."

"They should not have known about the Soujak Mine," Cernović insisted. "Weather has been too poor for effective air-to-ground surveillance, the mine and its gorge are well concealed and located well back from the main German line of advance, and we have been meticulous about security."

"Not meticulous enough, apparently," Quisp said, "unless, of course, they simply got very, very lucky. Followed a random trail in the snow, perhaps . . . or caught sight of the smoke from a cooking fire."

"No," Cernović said. "We have been too careful about those things. And the weather has almost continuously covered for us."

Quisp looked over at him. "Well, then, Cerny, perchance you have a rat in the hold. A rotten apple in the barrel. A Judas amongst the disciples, eh? Yes. Yes, I think that metaphor is the most apropos. A Judas, my boy—a Judas with a fist full of silver."

Cernović frowned but did not reply immediately. "I've been thinking the same thing," he said finally. "We have Yugoslavs of every stripe in the Partisan Army: Serbians, Croatians, Montenegrins, Bosnians, and Slovenians. We have Roman Catholics, Eastern

Othodox, Muslims, Jews, and Gypsys. All that is re
quired for entry into the Proletarian Brigades is the
willingness to discard old nationalistic and religious
loyalties and to swear to fight for a united Yugoslavia
under the even hand of the Communist authority as
personified by Comrade Marshall Tito.

"It is equally easy to leave. Fighters join all the
time, and a certain percentage of them promptly desert. We usually shoot the few we catch, just to guard
our backs, but obviously a significant number evade
us and make their way to our enemies. The thing
is, only inner-circle commanders and their trusted
lieutenants know specific details about parachute
drops, unit maneuvers in force, and command-post
locations. We have been encountering improbably
well-positioned SS Handschar patrols again and again
for more than six weeks now, and taking significant
casualties. It is starting to look as though it is not
by accident."

"Well, Cerny," Quisp stated, "the easiest thing for
a man to do is change his mind."

"It is," Cernović acknowledged. He stepped over a
snow-covered tree trunk that lay across the trail. "The
question is: which man?"

"Or woman," Quisp said. "Tito and the lesser pa-
shas in the Central Committee keep plenty of those
loitering around, too, don't they? Oh yes they do, my
lad. Yes they do."

Cernović looked at the Englishman, perplexed. It
was a possibility he hadn't considered.

"There are many women in the Partisan Army," he
said quietly. "Nearly all of them fight and die as
bravely as any man."

"But the women who tend to circulate near Tito
and his inner circle," Quisp persisted, "are they not
for the most part a gaggle of vicious harridans? You
yourself have seen it—not so much out here in the
front-line command posts, but in the safer environs of
vanguard headquarters locations. The predatory fe-

nales gather. Each hates the other; all are manuever-
ng for influence and position. And someone always
as to lose. How many competitors for Tito's af-
ections has that vile-tempered wife of his—Zdenka—
ttacked, harangued, humiliated, and ultimately driven
ff? Eh? Do you think it possible that some of these
efeated sirens harbor resentment toward Tito, his
ife, his other loves, or the Partisan Army in
eneral?"

Quisp rolled his eyes and addressed the heavens.
Oh, it is possible, my boy, it is possible! Remember:
Hell hath no fury like a woman scorned!' William
Congreve, as I recall."

Cernović's mind was racing now as he trudged
hrough the snow, rife with images of the women he'd
een hovering near the great, charismatic Marshall
Tito—flirting, laughing, fawning, sparring, testing,
uestioning. There had been so many, starting with
he ferocious Zdenka. . . .

" 'Frailty, thy name is woman!' " Quisp recited in
ull theatrical voice, his boots crunching through the
ew snow. "The Bard himself—William Shake-
peare."

Cernović barely heard him, immersed as he was in
is own thoughts. There had been Tanya, the former
pera singer with the raven hair and the slow, side-
ong glance. . . .

" 'All wickedness is but little to the wickedness of
a woman!' Ecclesiastes, that one, my dear boy."

There had been Mileva, the gushing, full-bodied
blond farm girl who was also a superb personal secre-
ary and therefore a major threat and irritant to the
domineering, paranoid Zdenka. . . .

" '*Quippe minuti, semper et infirmi est animi exigu-
que voluptas ultio. Continuo sic collige, quod vindicta
nemo magis gaudet quam femina!*' How's your Latin,
old bean?" Quisp glanced quickly over at Cernović as
he strode along beside him.

There had been Zora, the beautiful, husky-voiced

young widow of one of Tito's personal bodyguards
who had seen an opportunity to mitigate the loss of
her husband by assuming his place just behind the
Comrade Marshall's shoulder. . . . And eventually by
charming her way into Tito's bed. Trading up, as it
were . . .

"Not good, I see. Very well, I shall translate: 'Indeed, it is always a paltry, feeble, tiny mind that takes
pleasure in revenge. You can deduce it without further
evidence than this, that no one delights more in ven-
geance than a woman.' That quote comes from Juve-
nal, Cerny, my lad—d'ye see? Of course you do."

Cernović looked at Quisp briefly, having heard his
nickname and little else.

And there had been Sylvia, pouting prettily at Tito
like a spoiled, favored child when he'd gently chas-
tened her away from the British and American paratroopers only two nights ago in the Soujak Mine. . . .

"I still don't see how she does that," Bristow
grunted to D'Amato, looking up at the almost featureless rock face above the gap in the trail.

"Neither do I, Cole." D'Amato was punishing the
gum again, cracking it between his molars.

Forty-five feet above the far side of the avalanche-
ruined section of Zlostup, Sylvia Kozo, stripped once
again to abbreviated black shorts, rubber-soled slippers, gray-white men's undershirt, rabbit-fur hat, and
little else, was moving up the vertical cliff like a fly
marching up a pane of glass. Dangling from a short
line knotted beltlike around her waist was the upper
block of a three-fall block and tackle, the multiple
lengths of rope reeved through it snaking and twisting
down behind her. Merritt stood on the trail's end at
the far side of the break, tending the ropes with Weiss
standing by. On the single horizontal traverse line Sylvia had secured across the gap before beginning the
climb with the block and tackle, Stirling was now dangling, hooked on by carabiner and working his way

cross the sickening chasm hand over hand, as Merritt nd Weiss had done before him.

"All right, Sergeant?" Merritt called.

"Fine, sir," Stirling puffed, kicking off the cliff face s he pulled himself along. A few shards of rock broke ee under his boots and tumbled slowly into the byss.

Throckmorton was sitting on one of the crates of igh explosive that had been offloaded from the ules, watching Sylvia's progress with interest. He lit fresh cigarette, and Vlado stepped back out of reflex.

"Captain," he said, "do you see what you're sitng on?"

Throckmorton nodded. "Yaas. Explosives."

"Er . . . the cigarette . . ."

The slender officer shrugged. "There's no danger. he stuff is completely inert unless you set off a detoator in it or hit it with a tracer round. The latest oncoction, Comrade. We could even break off a hunk of it, light it with a match, and cook our dinner ver it as it burns—in perfect safety."

Vlado looked dubious. "No."

"Oh yes. It needs both heat and impact to make it o off with the traditional bang. You could probably re that rifle into it without result. Now, a tracer or ncendiary round—that would be another story."

D'Amato cracked his gum again and craned his eck back, shielding his eyes from the sun with a hand o his forehead. "She's almost there. Just a few more eet and she can start runnin' line around that hunk f stone to secure the block."

"I wish she'd drive a piton or two," Bristow said. 'Run a safety rope through them so we could catch er if she slips." He gestured with his Camel at the aping void before them. "Awful damn long way to all."

"She won't fall," Throckmorton remarked. "She's n artist immersed in her element when she's on the ock. She believes she can't fall, that the possibility

does not exist, and she certainly isn't going to unde
mine that certainty by attaching a safety rope to he
self. You see?"

D'Amato grinned. "You know, Captain, in the U.!
military there's something called a catch-22. You kno
what that is?"

"No, I'm afraid I don't."

Bristow gave a snort of laughter, nodding, and dre
on his cigarette.

D'Amato grinned again and went on: "It's a claus
in army regulations that says a soldier's request to b
relieved from combat duty can only be accepted
he's mentally unfit to fight. But it goes on to say tha
any soldier with the sense to ask to be excused fron
something as god-awful as war is obviously nc
crazy—so he has to stay and fight. Get it?"

Throckmorton gazed at D'Amato for a few second
then smiled broadly. "That's exquisite, Sergeant. Sim
ply exquisite. And I thought only the European mil
taries were sufficiently evolved to come up with
regulation that feeds off itself like a snake eating i
own tail."

"Hell, Captain," Bristow said, "the U.S. military
evolvin' faster than a snowball meltin' in the Lared
sun. Pretty soon them boys with the shiny brass bu
tons and the scrambled egg on their caps'll have u
all so locked up in regulations, the only thing we'll b
good for is marchin' around in circles."

"Anyway," D'Amato said, "it's kinda like what yo
were sayin' about this little Partisan gal. Same inside
out logic, you know? She don't believe she'll fall, s
she won't, so a safety rope ain't necessary. But if sh
does the smart thing and puts a rope on, it means sh
don't believe she can't fall—so she just might."

"Now I'm gettin' confused," Bristow grumbled.

Throckmorton chuckled again. "I follow you, Ser
geant. You're right. It's the same thing as catch-22, a
you call it." He shook his head. "Catch-22. That'

ruly beautiful. Someone ought to write a book about it."

D'Amato shrugged and looked back up at Sylvia. "Maybe someday someone will."

The lithe young woman had hung the heavy wooden block with its trailing lines on a knob of rock for the moment, and was now scrambling around the main granite knuckle like a spider, running several loops of rope around the entire outcropping. She appeared to be adhering with her fingers, toes, elbows, and knees to the smooth cliff face by magnetism or magic; there was little or nothing to hold on to. And yet there was never a slip, never a hitch in the smooth rhythm of her movements.

When she had draped a total of three loops of rope around the outcropping, she climbed up on top of it and squatted down on her heels for a moment, resting. She looked like a pale, svelte gargoyle, Throckmorton thought, crouched there on her frigid rampart of barren rock. . . . As though she might suddenly spread batlike wings, push off, and soar out into the empty air of the Zpoda Gorge.

"She sits there too long, she's gonna freeze her tits off," Bristow muttered.

As if she'd heard him, Sylvia gripped the front edge of the outcropping and swung down. Holding on by one hand, with the toes of her slippers planted against the cliff, she pulled the suspended wooden block over to the loops she'd just run and placed its supporting hook over all three ropes. Then she secured the mouth of the hook with a few wraps of twine.

"That's it," Bristow said. "She's got it. Let's get the first mule ready."

Stirling was standing beside Merritt and Weiss on the far side of the gap, removing the rope harness and carabiner he'd used to suspend himself from the traverse line. When he'd shed the climbing gear, Merritt handed him the slack block-and-tackle ropes and

together they pulled the falls tight. Up at the top
block, Sylvia deftly wrapped a leg around the rope
and transferred her full weight to them. Then, with
Merritt, Stirling, and Weiss keeping the block-and-
tackle arrangement taut, she slid down fifty feet to
the footpath.

Merritt caught her as she reached the end of the
falls so she wouldn't break an ankle finding her footing. She couldn't have weighed much more than a
hundred pounds, and as he supported her with one
arm around her waist, he was aware that her slippered
feet barely extended past his knees. Her face was level
with his, and as she drew back and regarded him from
beneath her hooded lids, he braced himself for the
slap or blow he suddenly felt sure was coming.

Instead Sylvia crossed her arms, leaned her elbows
on his chest, and looked down her nose at him with
an expression bordering on amusement. "You may put
me down now, Major," she said.

Merritt blinked. "Of course. Ah, watch your footing
on these broken rocks." He lowered her carefully to
the ground. "We brought your clothes over while you
were setting the block and tackle. Better get into them
before you freeze." He pointed at the bundle lying on
a a flat boulder nearby.

With the upright poise of a dancer, Sylvia swiveled
toward the clothing, then looked slowly back over her
shoulder at Merritt and smiled. "Thank you," she said.

Merritt nodded, the corner of his mouth tightening
upward. "You're welcome." As Sylvia began to collect
her winter clothes, he caught Stirling's eye and indicated with a jerk of his head that the girl was still to
be watched closely.

Then he turned to face the rest of the party, waiting
with the mules and equipment on the opposite side of
the gap. "Duncan!" he called. "You come across and
help us on this side. Sergeant Bristow, Sergeant D'A-
mato! Pull this block over and hook it up to the harness of that first mule." He picked up the lower block

of the hoisting arrangement and rapidly tied it onto a secondary line that had been strung below the main traverse rope. As D'Amato pulled the block across, suspended on its three falls from the granite outcropping overhead, Merritt fed out his end of the secondary line while Stirling paid out slack to the block and tackle.

Throckmorton clipped a carabiner from his rope harness onto the traverse line, let it take his weight, and began to make his way hand over hand across the dizzying void while behind him D'Amato, Bristow, and Vlado blindfolded the first mule and maneuvered it into position. The animal was skittish, well aware of the drop and not wanting to move while deprived of its sight. Finally the three men got it to the edge of the pathway and secured the lifting block to its body harness at a point just behind the shoulders. Bristow tied a holdback line to the lifting block and coiled the slack into the snow at his feet.

Opposite them, Throckmorton clambered up beside Merritt, gasping for air. "Next time pack me a pair of wings, old fellow," he cracked.

Merritt smiled and steadied him with a hand on his shoulder. "Get your breath, Duncan. When you're ready we're going to need your weight on this block and tackle."

"I suppose we have to lift the filthy beast at least a foot or two off its hooves, eh?" Throckmorton coughed wetly, turned his head, and spat. "All right, more damnable blue-collar labor. Let's get about it, then."

He stepped in between Stirling and Weiss and seized the main hoisting line of the block and tackle with both hands. The two other men did likewise, and with Merritt at the front of the hauling contingent they took up all the remaining slack in the system. Stirling looked over his shoulder quickly as Sylvia moved up behind him and gripped the rope, as well.

"Ready?" Merritt called. Bristow, standing beside

the mule with a hand on its halter, gave the thumbs
up. "All right, then," he continued. "As we take it
weight, push it off the edge!"

"And mind the beast doesn't kick your teeth in a
it goes," Throckmorton added. "It has no gratitude
you know."

"All right," Merritt said, setting his feet. "One, twc
three—*pull!*"

The block-and-tackle falls snapped tight and th
mule was jerked a foot in the air. D'Amato and Vlad
barely had time to push before the animal was off th
end of the footpath and swinging along the cliff face
bucking and kicking in its harness. Its hind hoove
clapped into the rock, sending shards spinning into th
abyss. Bristow leaned back, attempting to control th
mule's swing by putting some tension on the holdbacl
line as it ran through his gloved fingers.

Merritt, Weiss, Throckmorton, Stirling, and Sylvi;
dug in their heels as the animal swung forward
scraping along the sheer granite wall. As the bloc
and tackle went completely vertical, the mule's kickin;
forehooves clattered against broken rock at the fa
side of the gap. Merritt stepped up, seized the animal'
halter, and yanked backward with all his might as th
remaining four lifters threw their combined bod
weight against the rope. Its fore and hind legs workin;
like pistons, the mule clawed its way up onto the trai
bucked and shied several times, and then stood still
trembling and snorting and steaming.

Sylvia stepped forward, removed the animal's blind
fold, and began to talk to it in a low voice, holdin;
its halter and rubbing its nose and jaw. Merritt discon
nected the lifting block and holdback line, helped he
lead the mule along the trail for a few yards, the
returned to address the men on the opposite side o
the gap again.

"That's one," he called. "So far, so good, gentle
men. Pull the block back and let's have another."

Bristow waved and began to haul in on the hold

back line. "Damnedest thing I ever seen," he said to D'Amato. "A flyin' mule. Lead that next critter on up here, Frank, and make sure its blindfold's on real good."

"We ain't got a lotta horses in the Bronx, ya know," D'Amato told him, moving to the head of the next mule. "Used to be plenty when my folks came over from the old country back in 'oh-five, pullin' milk carts and meat wagons and the like. Nowadays it's all cars and trucks." The little sergeant cracked his gum. "Less shit to sweep up."

"You don't say," Bristow remarked, grabbing the hoisting block and pulling some slack. "That's real interestin'. And by the way, that ain't a horse you got here, city boy. It's a mule."

"I know it's a goddamn mule," D'Amato shot back, stepping carefully between the animal and the edge of the dropoff. "Who can tell the difference? Looks like a horse to me. Stinks like one, too."

"Just bring it up here, willya?"

"I ain't kiddin', Cole. Damn animal stinks worse'n—"

Vlado struck D'Amato across the face with the butt of his Mauser rifle. The American sergeant reeled back, clutching at thin air. His boot crunched on broken rock and ice at the edge of the trail and then he toppled backward off the precipice with a cry of despair. From the far side of the gap, Merritt and his companions watched stunned as D'Amato's body dropped into empty space, turning slowly over before disappearing from view.

"Frank!" Bristow yelled, dropping the block and reaching for the .45 automatic holstered at his side.

Vlado brought the Mauser down and fired from the hip at point-blank range as Bristow was twisting out of the way. The bullet tore through the breast of the big sergeant's combat jacket, cutting a furrow in his pectoral muscle. Like D'Amato, Bristow took a bad backward step. He lost his balance and fell off the

end of the path, partly against the cliff face. Unlike
D'Amato, his clawing hands found purchase and he
managed to arrest his fall after sliding down only a
couple of feet. He got the toe of one boot into a small
niche, braced himself against the rock, and looked up
to see Vlado just above him on the path, swinging
down the barrel of his rifle. The Partisan guide's eyes
were as black and hollow as the muzzle opening
pointed at Bristow's head.

Stirling fired across the gap from a kneeling position, having dropped to one knee to snatch up his
Enfield sniper rifle. The hurriedly aimed .303 slug
smashed through the knuckles of Vlado's right hand
and into the teak stock of his Mauser in a small spray
of blood, bone, and wood splinters. With a howl, the
Partisan dropped his rifle and staggered back from the
edge of the path, bending nearly double to clutch his
wounded hand to his midriff.

Stirling racked another cartridge into the breech of
his Enfield and fired again. The slug missed the lurch-
ing Vlado by an inch and passed between the legs of
the second mule. With a backward sneer, the turncoat
Partisan began to bull his way past the shying pack
animals toward the last bend in the trail.

"Kill him, Stirling!" Merritt shouted, brandishing his
Sten but powerless to use it for fear of hitting Bristow
or the mules. "Don't let him get around the corner!"

The British sergeant rose to his feet, working the
bolt of his rifle, and took aim. At that moment Bristow, who had been trying to get his .45 out of its
holster one-handed, lost his grip and slid down another five feet before catching himself. Stirling's eye
flickered onto him, and that second of distraction was
enough time for Vlado to get past the last mule and
stumble out of sight around the bend.

Throckmorton fired his revolver once, more out of
frustration than anything else; the slug chipped the
rock impotently where the Partisan's head had been
two seconds earlier.

"Watch the girl!" Merritt barked to Weiss. "Keep her here!"

As Sylvia gave him a startled glare, he slung his Sten over his shoulder, grabbed the traverse line, and began to scramble hand over hand across the gap toward Bristow. The big sergeant was losing his grip, his arms and legs shaking with the strain of bracing himself in the vertical corner formed by the foundation rock of the trail and the cliff wall.

Merritt covered the ten-plus meters of empty air in as many seconds and clambered up onto the trail. Dropping to his stomach with his head over the edge, he tossed a loop of holdback line down to Bristow.

"Grab this!" he panted.

Bristow seized the rope with one hand just as his boot toe slipped out of its precarious niche. He swung for a second or two, legs bicycling, then got his other hand on the rope as Merritt gritted his teeth and bore the downward strain of his entire 250-odd pounds. Snow disturbed by Merritt's exertions fell in small clumps past Bristow, tumbling with interminable slowness into the gaping chasm beneath his dangling boots.

And then Throckmorton was there beside and slightly above Bristow, breathing hard, hanging from a six-foot length of rope knotted around his waist and clipped by carabiner onto the traverse line. Finding toeholds for his boots, he seized the American sergeant by the coat collar and hoisted.

"Come on, old fellow," he grunted, "can't have you hanging about all day long, you know."

Using their combined strength, Throckmorton and Merritt managed to help Bristow get his elbows up over the edge of the path. Then with one last effort, the sergeant heaved himself up onto the trail and rolled over on his back in the snow, gasping.

Merritt had snatched up his Sten and was just getting to his feet when a little cascade of rock flakes fell on him from above. He raised an arm to protect his head and face and peered up. Sylvia Kozo, clad in

baggy fatigue pants, slippers, stained men's undershirt
and fur hat was scrambling across the vertical wall
some seventy feet overhead, heading toward what
looked like a long shelf of rock that led to a crevice
some thirty feet above her. Her Schmeisser machine
pistol was slung across her back.

Merritt swore under his breath and shot a glance
back across the gap. *"Weiss!"* he yelled. Then he
pulled back the bolt of his Sten and raised it high,
sighting in on Sylvia Kozo's fast-moving form. With a
single burst he could stop at least one potential traitor
from escaping and informing the Germans of the sabotage mission; the girl was still a good five seconds from
the lip of the shelf.

Throckmorton and Bristow were barging past the
mules in pursuit of Vlado. As Bristow hustled along,
grimacing with the pain of the flesh wound in his chest,
he glanced back at Merritt.

"What are you waitin' for?" he rasped. "Shoot
the bitch!"

Merritt's finger tightened on the Sten's trigger—but
he didn't fire. He wasn't sure. And then Sylvia was
up and over the lip of the rock shelf. Merritt saw the
fur hat and pale shoulders moving laterally as she ran
toward the crevice, and then she was gone.

"What the hell, Major!" Bristow shouted angrily,
moving out after Throckmorton.

Merritt didn't bother answering. On the far side of
the gap, Stirling was helping a dazed Weiss to his feet.
Even across the forty-foot distance, Merritt could see
the bloody gash on his temple where Sylvia had
struck him.

"Stirling!" he yelled, "take care of Weiss and secure
the mules!"

Then he tucked his Sten into the crook of his arm
and ran down Zlostup after Bristow and Throckmorton.

Chapter
Eleven

"I'm telling you, those shots we heard weren't that far off," Cernović said, holding his carbine at the ready as he stalked along the footpath. "I'm not denying that sound travels amazingly well in the these gorges, especially in winter, but I'm sure it wasn't hunters shooting for the pot in the forest down below."

"All I'm saying, my boy," Quisp replied, "is that we didn't hear a single machine gun. Merritt's people, according to you, are carrying Stens, Thompsons, and Schmeissers as well as rifles. The Germans have no end of Schmeissers, in addition to Mausers. If they were involved in some kind of firefight up ahead on Zlostup, wouldn't you think we'd be hearing automatic weapons? Yes, you would, old bean. Yes, indeed."

Cernović broke into a trot, his eyes searching the rocky, snow-covered terrain ahead. "I hope you're right, Professor," he panted. "I don't—"

He halted abruptly and jerked up his carbine as Vlado came stumbling at the run around the next

bend in the path, clutching his bloodied right hand
to his stomach. The wounded Partisan did not notice
Cernović and Quisp right away; when he did, he
balked sideways like a frightened animal and threw a
desperate glance over his shoulder.

"Vlado," Cernović called out, lowering the carbine
and raising a hand, "what's wrong?"

The lanky Partisan hesitated, looking at Cernović
and Quisp and then back up the trail again. Then he
seemed to make up his mind and ran forward, his face
deathly pale, his dark hair flopping over his forehead.

"Comrade Commander!" he gasped. "Jagdkom
mando patrol, coming down the path after me! They
are only minutes behind!" He staggered up to Cer
nović, apparently on his last legs. "I'm wounded
sir. . . . Shot in the hand . . ."

"Take cover, Quisp!" Cernović hissed, grabbing
Vlado by the shoulders and hustling him into the lee
of a nearby boulder. The Englishman was already be
hind a slab of granite on the opposite side of the trail
sighting in on the next bend with his machine pistol.

"Where's Merritt?" Cernović asked, bringing his
carbine up to the firing position on top of the boulder.
"What happened?"

"Dead, Comrade Commander," Vlado panted. His
eyes were wild as he stared from Cernović to Quisp
and back up the trail. "They . . . he . . . the Jagdkom
mando were coming down Zlostup from direction o
Mount Zpoda and ambushed us. I-I think all the oth
ers are dead. Either that or they . . . they may still be
fighting. I was separated from the group and shot.
only just got away, Comrade Commander. There—
there was nothing I could do."

"How many are after you?" Quisp demanded from
across the path.

"May-maybe eight," Vlado stammered. "Maybe more."

Quisp looked at him, frowning. "An ambush, eh?
How long ago?"

Vlado threw up his good hand, wincing in pain and

exasperation. "How long ago? Only a few minutes . . . perhaps ten? How do I know? I've been running for my life!"

Quisp continued to stare at him. "Why haven't we heard any machine-gun fire? Or any sustained firing at all, for that matter? Eh?"

Vlado's face twisted. "You—"

"A pretty quiet ambush, my lad, if you ask me." Quisp's fierce, arching brows knitted together. "Something isn't right. . . . Rotten in Denmark . . ."

"Look out!" Vlado screamed, yanking a small pistol from his pocket with his good hand and wildly throwing his arm up over the top of the boulder. He loosed off four shots in rapid succession—*powpowpowpow!*—at the bend in the trail, the weapon jumping in his fingers.

From behind the rock formation around which the footpath curved came an immediate answering burst of machine-gun fire: *brrrrrrrrrraaaaap!* Vlado recoiled with a sharp cry, spinning back from the boulder and flopping into the snow. Cernović and Quisp ducked as slugs zipped and cracked around them, chipping up ice and granite fragments. Then, as one, they returned fire, Cernović with his Mauser carbine and Quisp with his Schmeisser.

Bristow jerked back with a curse, cordite smoke curling out of the muzzle of his Thompson, as bullets hammered into the rock at the bend in the trail. Merritt, just catching up, hunched down beside him. Throckmorton—long bypassed by the two fitter men—was several hundred yards behind on the descending footpath, still out of sight.

"He must've run into a Kraut patrol!" Bristow rasped, breathing hard. "Goddammit, Major—this mission's been snakebit right from the git-go!"

Merritt put a hand on Bristow's shoulder and peered cautiously down the path. "How many, do you think?"

The American shrugged. "Volume of fire ain't much. I dunno—maybe five or six guys. Maybe less."

Merritt thought a moment. "Alright—we're going to find out, Sergeant." He pointed left and right. "We've got broken ground on either side of the trail here to move on. I'll go this way and you go that. Stay low—we'll draw fire and see if we can spot how many shooters and where."

"Well, let's give 'em a volley to get their heads down," Bristow grunted, checking his Thompson, "before we go runnin' out into their sights like a pair of jackrabbits."

Merritt nodded, his thin smile flickering across his face. "Absolutely." He glanced over his shoulder as Throckmorton came puffing down the trail, slipping and sliding on the loose rock and snow. "Duncan! Stay low!"

Throckmorton collapsed to his haunches next to Bristow, wheezing. His face was the color of soggy newsprint. "Good . . . *Lord!*" was all he could say.

"Are you alright?" Merritt asked. Throckmorton nodded, licking spittle off his lips. "Fine. Listen: there are a handful of Germans up on that rise where the trail runs between the granite slab and the big boulder. We want to find out how many and where they are. Sergeant Bristow and I are going to flank out left and right to draw their fire. Try to spot them, will you? Maybe pop off a few shots while we're running, just to keep them from getting too ambitious." He clapped Throckmorton on the shoulder.

The badly winded captain managed a grin. "Ri-righty-o, old chap." He pulled his Webley revolver from its holster, checked the cylinder, and set it on the rock just above his head. Then he hefted his Sten and looked at Merritt. "A burst or two for luck as you leave, I take it?"

"Correct," Merritt said. "Ready, Sergeant?" Bristow nodded, turning to the right, setting his feet under him. "All right, then." Merritt crouched, preparing to sprint left. "Fire on my command. . . . And . . . *fire!*"

Together, Merritt, Throckmorton, and Bristow brought their weapons to bear over and around the rock and opened up. There was a tremendous blast of combined automatic fire from the two Stens and the Thompson—and then Merritt and Bristow were sprinting left and right, respectively, hunched low and moving fast with the peculiar skittering run of the trained soldier. Throckmorton finished the clip in his Sten, grabbed his Webley, and began to crack off individual shots at the granite slab and boulder.

There was no return fire at all.

Throckmorton cocked the pistol and rested its butt on the rock, the barrel pointing skyward. Keeping low, he glanced left and right. Thirty feet away, Merritt was lying in the snow behind a little rise, crawling for a better vantage point. Bristow was kneeling behind another large boulder, his Thompson at his shoulder and pointed down the trail. Both men were unscathed.

Throckmorton ran his eyes over the assumed enemy position. He could see nothing. On impulse, he brought the pistol level and squeezed off a shot. Chips flew off the granite slab, but again, there was no return fire or movement.

Then a voice, clear and incredulous, sang out in impeccable English:

"I say, do my eyes deceive me, or was that a ruddy *Yank* that just cavorted out on our left flank?"

Cernović leaned over cautiously and peered up the footpath from behind his boulder as Quisp's shrill voice died away. "It's Cernović!" he shouted. "Who's there?"

"What the bloody hell—" came the furious reply from across the rocks. "It's Merritt! *Merritt!*"

"What?" Cernović blinked across the trail at Quisp and stuck his head up over the boulder. Off to his

right, some twenty yards away, Major Walter Merritt
was just getting to his feet from behind a small rise.

With a curse, Cernović swung around to confront
Vlado.

"What the hell are you playing at, you—" he
began, enraged.

But Vlado was gone.

Bewildered, Cernović searched the terrain behind
him. It was several seconds before he was able to pick
out Vlado's fleeing form among the broken rock, scrub
brush, and drifted snow. The Partisan guide was a
good three hundred yards away; a dark, elusive shape
moving fast over the rough ground.

"I'd say the bugger's turned," Quisp remarked, ob-
serving Vlado's headlong flight. "There's your Judas
Cerny—one of 'em, anyway."

"I don't believe it," Cernović muttered, staring.
"Not Vlado."

"Believe it!" Merritt panted, rushing past him. "He
killed Sergeant D'Amato and took a shot at Sergeant
Bristow. Come on! We have to stop him before he
reaches the Germans!"

"What about that damn girl?" Bristow shouted,
charging down the path between Quisp and Cernović.
"She's up in those crags somewhere to our right!"

Merritt ran onto the trail just ahead of the big
American. "She has to come this way to get out of
the gorge," he replied breathlessly, "according to the
topo map. Otherwise she'd have to climb across an
entire high-altitude snowfield, and she doesn't have
the clothing to do that. No coat, remember? And if
she just stays hidden up there she'll freeze. We'll see
her again soon, I'm sure."

"I'm glad somebody's sure about something," Bristow growled, pounding along behind Merritt.

Vlado was fast on his feet for an undernourished
man enduring the pain of a nasty hand wound. The
knowledge that the comrades he had just betrayed—

and had, in fact, been betraying for many weeks—would not hesitate to execute him on the spot if they caught him was a powerful incentive to keep moving. The thought of being confronted by Cernović, in particular, gave him a sick feeling in the pit of his stomach; the Partisan commander, normally a man of even temperament and compassion despite his hardness, had been known to shoot confirmed traitors in the kneecaps before dispatching them.

There were few ways to get off the lower reaches of Zlostup beyond descending near-vertical slopes on one side or climbing truly vertical cliffs on the other—but just ahead was one of them: a rare thicket of low, dense evergreen trees with a single thin side trail snaking through it and up toward the high crags that lined the gorge all the way to Mount Zpoda. The trail was known only to a few scouts who had spent considerable time on Zlostup, and its divergence from the main path was not obvious. A good place to hide. Vlado glanced over his shoulder as he ran the last fifteen feet into the trees; his pursuers, not more than a few hundred yards behind, were out of sight for the moment. Perfect.

After he let Cernović and the others pass by, he could make his way on up the side trail to the base of the crags, and then climb the long, rough route to the Zpoda snowfields. A day to get across that high alpine desert of snow and rock, and he would reach the German lines. Reach SS Hauptsturmfuehrer Ulrich Haak.

The trek would be hard, but Vlado Kusić was used to hard things. So used to them, in fact, that he had woken up one morning—sick and exhausted from yet another late-night running battle with the SS Division Handschar—to find that he had forgotten how to feel anything at all. Period. The futility of his situation had finally come home to him.

That had been nearly two months ago, and soon after he had made contact in the field with the German officer Haak. After years of suffering for everyone around him—especially the little tyrants (for that is what they were) in the Communist Central Committee—Vlado Kusić had decided to do something for Vlado Kusić. Life was pitifully, brutally, *terrifyingly* short. . . . As he had seen time and time again. Even without a bullet or explosion or disease to snuff it out in its early prime.

He hunkered down in the snow behind a thick cluster of pine boughs. The main trail was icy in this area, for a stretch of a mile at least. Too icy for footprints to show up with any regularity. His pursuers would not see that he had left the trail.

They were coming. He could hear them now, moving fast with boots pounding and fabric whiffing and weapons clinking and lungs pumping like bellows. They would not think that he had gone to ground here, for the thicket was very small and looked like a dead end, and they would assume—correctly—that he would not want to risk letting them get ahead and cut off his escape route. An assumption that was correct, needless to say, only in the absence of knowledge about the existence of the alternate trail. Despite the agonizing pain of his shattered knuckles, Vlado smiled and flexed his good hand around the butt of the small-caliber Walther pistol with which he had murdered Bozidar Yagovac.

He kept low, peering out between the pine boughs—and then suddenly there was Merritt, less than ten feet away, sprinting grim-faced down the trail with his harness jangling and his Sten gun clutched loosely in front of him. On his heels was the big American sergeant, Bristow, looking twice the size of the average Partisan and moving with the feral grace of a catamount, his Thompson held one-handed to cover the path ahead.

Then, several yards behind, came Cernović, his face dark with fury. Involuntarily Vlado ducked a little lower. And behind him, Quisp, the inexplicable Englishman who seemed to make a habit out of showing up when he was least expected. Vlado had only encountered him previously on two occasions, and hadn't enjoyed either; the man made him nervous.

And then they were past him, moving out the far end of the thicket and on down Zlostup. It would be many minutes, perhaps even an hour or more, before they realized their mistake. By then he would be far over the crags to the southwest and moving across the snowfields toward Mount Zpoda.

Idiots. Vlado smiled again, got to his feet, and turned to walk up the hidden trail.

There was a harsh metallic clack-*clack* as Sylvia pulled back the bolt of her Schmeisser.

"Stay where you are," she said, her voice low and very steady.

Vlado stayed.

She was sitting cross-legged on a large boulder about ten feet farther up the trail, very erect, with her spine straight and shoulders back. Her head was back, as well, small chin in the air, and her mouth was set, unsmiling. The eyes beneath the mottled gray rabbit fur of her winter hat were so heavy lidded as to appear almost closed. Almost. And once again, despite the fact that her arms, shoulders, and throat—all as pale as ivory—were bare and her torso was covered only by her worn-out men's undershirt, she appeared not to feel the bitter cold. The barrel of the machine pistol she held with easy familiarity wavered not a fraction of an inch.

"Drop the pistol in the snow, Vlado," Sylvia said.

Vlado obeyed, then swallowed and licked his lips. "Syl. How long have you been there?"

"Ten minutes. A long time." Sylvia's flat expression did not change. "Long enough to see you run into Commander Cernović and that Quisp fellow. Long enough to see you fire at the British major and the American sergeant to fool everyone into shooting at each other while you sneaked away. Long enough to

see you duck off the trail onto this little side path and
hide—as I knew you would."

Vlado's mouth twisted into a pained grin. "No one
ever accused you of being dim, Syl. I didn't know you
knew about this hidden trail." He glanced anxiously
over his shoulder at the far end of the thicket.

"They'll be back soon enough," Sylvia said. She
paused, then added, "Tell me what you did, Vlado."

"I . . . what do you mean?" Vlado reached inside
the lapel of his coat with his good hand, but froze as
Sylvia jerked up the machine pistol and squinted at
him through its ring sight. "Wait, wait . . . just getting
a cigarette." He withdrew a tarnished brass 20-
millimeter shell casing with a small wooden plug in
the end—many Partisans used such shell casings to
keep their little hoards of tobacco dry—removed the
plug, and shook out a black-and-gold Richterhaus.
Clamping the filter between his lips, which were
trembling slightly, he smiled, shook another cigarette
partway out of the casing, and held it out to Sylvia.
"You like these, Syl. Have one."

Sylvia lowered the Schmeisser and stared at him
in silence.

Vlado took a step forward, continuing to smile.
"Oh, come on, now. You weren't so particular about
taking my cigarettes the night we slept together in the
mine. Remember?"

Sylvia nodded. "I remember. That was a month ago.
I was cold and lonely that night. And I also remember
asking you how you suddenly acquired such fine cigarettes when everyone else was smoking dried weeds
wrapped in old newspaper." She blinked slowly.
"Where *did* you get them, Vlado?"

Vlado took another step forward, fumbling for his
lighter with his good hand. "I told you: I took them off
the body of an SS officer we killed during an ambush."

"Yes. One cigarette case full. Maybe a dozen cigarettes. They're lasting you a long time."

"Well, these are the last of them. I gave you five

or six, Syl. Remember?" Vlado smiled again, edging closer as he lit his own cigarette. "That was a good night, wasn't it? Worth a half-dozen fine cigarettes."

Sylvia's eyes widened a fraction of an inch. "Are you suggesting that you bought me for the night for six cigarettes?"

Vlado shook his head quickly. "No, of course not. I . . . but it was a good night, don't you think?"

"I told you," Sylvia said, "I was cold and lonely. I needed someone. You happened to be there."

"And you haven't let me near you since then—for nearly a month, as you said."

"I haven't been cold and lonely since then," Sylvia told him, "which is nothing to do with you, incidentally, so don't flatter yourself. As for your cigarettes, I smoked my last one this morning, after saving it for the past two weeks." She raised the Schmeisser again slightly. "That's close enough. Stop sidling toward me."

Vlado kept his feet still, looking hurt. "Syl—"

"Move toward me again and I'll kill you where you stand. On the other hand"—a flicker of a smile lifted the corners of her mouth—"tell me what I want to know and perhaps I'll let you go, for old times' sake." The smile ebbed away as quickly as it had come. "That's more than Cernović will do for you when he returns, I'll guarantee."

Vlado paled at the thought. "What . . . what do you want to know, Syl?"

"I want to know what you did. All of it. And you'd better hurry up, because when Cernović and Merritt get back, I won't be able to stop them from killing you."

Vlado plucked the cigarette from his mouth and exhaled shakily, looking trapped. "Syl—"

"Talk," Sylvia said. "That's the only way you're getting by me and on up this trail before the others return."

"All right!" Vlado jammed the cigarette back into

his mouth. "All right. I made contact about seven weeks ago with an SS officer named Haak. Hauptsturm-fuehrer Ulrich Haak. I agreed to give him information about the Second Proletaran Brigade's operations in the Majevica Mountains until early summer."

Sylvia's eyes were almost closed again. "For what? Cigarettes?"

Vlado shook his head. "No, no. The cigarettes are his, naturally—he's from a rich family and has them custom made in Germany—but they're just a tidbit from our meetings. I've been contacting him during my solo patrols, feeding him information about Partisan movements. . . ." Vlado's voice faltered, and he looked at Sylvia with a sickly expression.

"And what do you get for this betrayal?" Sylvia asked quietly.

Vlado drew a breath. "By spring, the Germans expect to have driven us out of the Majevicas. That's their schedule, anyway. All Germans are fanatical about schedules, like human machines. Haak wants me to continue to provide him with information until June. Then, at that time, I will be given safe passage through German lines and transported to Berlin, where I will be decorated in secret as a hero of the Third Reich, commissioned as an officer in the Wehrmacht, and given a permanent state pension in addition to my army salary. I will spend the rest of the war out of the line of fire, building a new life as a military bureaucrat in the regime that is going to control all of Europe for the next thousand years."

He paused, put his cigarette to his lips, and gazed at Sylvia with empty eyes. And then, like many a man who has sold his soul irredeemably to the devil only to realize in hindsight, to his utter horror, what he has lost, he surrendered to an overwhelming compulsion to keep talking. "I killed Bozi Yagovac, you know. Shot him in the back during the Storch attack a few days ago. It was all prearranged. I was having trouble getting away on solo patrols to contact Haak—people were becoming very paranoid and suspicious, what with all the successful Jagdkommando ambushes and rumors of an SOE team jumping into the Majevicas to join us for some undisclosed operation. So I encouraged Yagovac to harass the retreating Jagdkommado unit that had nearly grabbed Merritt and his men off the drop zone all the way back to the Zpoda Gorge area, where the Storches would attack them at dawn. I would make sure that Yagovac—a combat leader very troublesome to the Nazis—was killed in the assault, and then place a map on his body pinpointing the exact location of the Soujak Mine. Haak would have no trouble finding it; all he had to do was return to the site of the Storch ambush with an adequate force for protection and locate the biggest corpse there. The map would be inside Bozi's shirt, and there was also a statement confirming Tito's presence inside the mine. No one would suspect me, because I would be long gone—still with the Second Brigade. I could continue to provide information to Haak for the foreseeable future, as long as we were creative and cautious about communicating with each other." Vlado paused again to draw on his cigarette. His hand was shaking. "Aren't you wondering why I'm telling you all this, Syl?"

Sylvia's expression did not change. "Confession."

"Eh?"

"Confession. You want me to forgive you."

Vlado looked at Sylvia uncertainly. Then his dark, furtive eyes filled, and he looked away. "I think you may be right."

"I'm no priest," Sylvia said, "and the dead comrades you betrayed are the ones whose forgiveness you need."

Vlado said nothing, but drew on his cigarette.

"You killed Sergeant D'Amato and tried to kill Sergeant Bristow," Sylvia went on. "You knew in advance that a landslide had carried away part of Zlostup and that Merritt's team would be held up trying to get around it. You waited for just the right moment."

"I was going for the German lines," Vlado said hollowly. "I couldn't very well let Merritt blow up the Zpoda Skyway Bridge. Haak would never trust me again if I let that happen right under his nose."

"Of course."

Vlado glanced fearfully over his shoulder at the main trail again. "Syl. I've answered your questions. Merritt and Cernović may be back at any moment. Now I have a question for you."

Sylvia tilted her head back, listening.

"Why don't you come with me?" Vlado suggested. "You know I have feelings for you. Come with me and let's get out of this hellish war together. You know what it is to live well in a great European city. Come with me and leave Yugoslavia to the damned Partisans and Chetniks and Ustashe and Muslims and Nazis and British and Americans and all the rest of them. There's nothing for you here but bitter memories and death."

Sylvia slid off the rock to a standing postion and smiled openly for the first time. "I thought you'd never ask," she said.

The cigarette slipped from between Vlado's fingers and dropped into the snow. "So you'll . . . you'll come with me?"

"I didn't say that."

Vlado's hopeful smile faltered, and he spread his arms in a gesture of confusion. "Wha-what? But you just said—"

Sylvia's eyes narrowed. "I said I thought you'd never ask. And that's all I said."

"But . . . but . . . you're coming with me, aren't you?"

"No," Sylvia declared.

Vlado's arms dropped to his sides, and his expression became ugly. His dark eyes flickered to the Walther pistol lying in the snow at his feet.

"What are you doing?" he growled.

"Giving you my answer, traitor," Sylvia said. "And my answer is no." She turned her head slightly to the side, keeping her hooded eyes on Vlado. "Did you hear that, Captain Throckmorton?"

There was a gentle rustle of pine needles, and Throckmorton stepped out from behind a nearby tree, looking at Vlado over the sights of his Webley revolver. "Yaas, my dear," he drawled, "I heard it. In fact, I've heard it all."

Vlado stared at the British captain in shock, his mouth falling open. Then he turned back to Sylvia. "You . . . you knew he was there. . . ."

"I saw him as he came down the trail five minutes ago," Sylvia said. "And he saw me see him." She looked over at Throckmorton, and a hint of a real smile appeared on her lips. "Captain Throckmorton, as it turns out, is a highly intelligent man—despite his being an English aristocrat. He realized right away that I wanted him to hear what you had to say to me."

Vlado was beginning to shake. "But . . . if you were never going to . . . to come with me, why this long, drawn-out—"

"Because Major Merritt and his men suspect that I may be a traitor just like you," Sylvia told him. "I've known it since we reached the avalanche this morning. I don't know exactly why, but I could feel it, and it was obvious. The major had everyone watching me. He *ordered* Sergeant Weiss to hold me on the far side of the gap in Zlostup when you made your break." She paused and looked at Throckmorton again. "How *is* the sergeant's head, by the way?"

Throckmorton, his gun arm fully extended, didn't take his eyes off Vlado. "A bit bloody, I'm afraid, but I saw him on his feet soon after you whacked him. He's a strapping young lad; I imagine he'll shake it off."

Sylvia returned her gaze to Vlado. "And are you satisfied, then, Captain, that I am not disloyal like this . . . creature?"

Throckmorton nodded. "More than satisfied, my dear."

"Then will you excuse us for a moment?" Sylvia hefted the Schmeisser, the sinewy muscles in her strong, pale arms flexing.

Throckmorton paused before answering, then lowered his Webley and stepped back. "Certainly. If you're sure . . ."

"I'll be fine," Sylvia said. She half turned and motioned with the machine pistol up the little side trail. "Walk up there, Vlado, ahead of me."

"Syl—" Vlado pleaded, his voice cracking.

"Walk."

Merritt was moving at a fast trot back along Zlostup when he caught sight of Throckmorton sitting on a boulder at the edge of the trail in the little copse of evergreens, smoking a cigarette.

"Duncan!" he called out, raising his Sten gun in greeting. Immediately behind him, looking flushed, tired, and angry, were Bristow, Cernović, and Quisp. Throckmorton waved a hand and got to his feet.

"Gotten enough exercise for the day, gentlemen?" he inquired.

Merritt jogged up to him and halted, breathing hard. "This is no time for humor, Duncan," he panted. "Vlado's escaped, and we haven't seen Sylvia, either. We have a major problem."

A sudden burst of machine-gun fire shattered the stillness of the little copse. Merritt, Bristow, Cernović, and Quisp all dropped instinctively onto their bellies in the snow and jerked up their weapons. Throckmorton alone remained standing, unperturbed.

"No, we don't," he said, looking calmly off into the trees and drawing on his cigarette.

Bristow rolled onto his side and glared up at him. "You got a death wish, Captain?" he growled.

The slender Englishman glanced down and cocked

an omniscient eyebrow. "You don't know the half of it."

Merritt rose to one knee with his Sten leveled at his hip, searching the trees behind Throckmorton. "What's going on, Duncan?" he demanded.

Throckmorton flicked the butt of his cigarette into the snow and turned around. "You don't have to concern yourself with Vlado anymore," he said. "Or Sylvia, for that matter."

Cernović exchanged glances with Merritt and got to his feet. The expression on his face would have sent a wild boar running for cover. "Where is Vlado?" he asked Throckmorton, his voice hoarse with suppressed rage.

"Why don't you ask Sylvia when she comes back?" the slender captain replied. "She'll just be a minute."

Cernović stared at him, then abruptly turned aside and walked into the trees in the approximate direction of the little side trail. In a moment he had found the path and was beginning to stride up it when Sylvia appeared, heading down into the copse. She was carrying her Schmeisser slung over her shoulder and a bundle under one arm.

"Comrade Commander," she said, nodding as she went by him.

Cernović eyed her as she passed, then turned and ran up the side trail, disappearing behind the trees.

Sylvia walked into the small knot of men and sat down on the boulder Throckmorton had just vacated. Then she set the olive drab bundle she carried on the ground and began to unlace the black ballet-style slippers she favored for rock climbing, ignoring the tall soldiers hovering over her. Bristow examined her briefly, a scowl of distrust on his face. She was so pale that in the shade of the copse, her skin appeared almost blue.

Throckmorton pointed up the side trail. "Vlado ducked in here," he told Merritt and the others. "Apparently this little path leads up to the crags, and from there on up toward Mount Zpoda. You ran right by him—which is understandable since you can't really see the second trail. I'd have missed it myself if my wind was as good as yours. He thought he had us snookered, old boy, and he would have, too, if not for Sylvia."

Throckmorton glanced down at the pale girl, who was unlacing her second ballet slipper. "She wasn't fooled. Back at the avalanche site, we thought she was scrambling up the cliff to get away from us, like Vlado, but all she was doing was taking a fast route across the top of the crags to cut him off here. She knew about this little trail, you see."

Merritt looked down at her. "I nearly shot you off that cliff," he said.

Sylvia looked coolly up at him and batted her heavy lids. "But you didn't."

The corner of Merritt's mouth twitched upward, and Throckmorton went on. "By the time I got to this little thicket, you and the others were long gone ahead and I could hear voices through the trees. So I cocked the old Webley and sneaked along the trail like a proper footpad, keeping low. There was Vlado with his back to me, and Sylvia holding him at gunpoint. He was talking a blue streak. Sylvia caught my eye but didn't react, so I put two and two together and managed to skulk on up to where I could hear what was being said." He glanced down at Sylvia again. "What I heard explained everything. Vlado was the traitor, no doubt about it. And the only reason he didn't give us the slip is this petite Amazon sitting here." He let out the English blueblood's short, dry laugh. "By God, she's a cool one, I can tell you."

There was a crunching of snow as Cernović came back down the side trail. His livid expression had eased into mere grimness. He was carrying Vlado's Mauser rifle as well as his own carbine.

"Are you satisfied?" Throckmorton asked him as he stepped back onto the main trail.

Cernović's mouth worked for a second or two in silence. Then he suddenly dropped his carbine, seized Vlado's rifle by the barrel with both hands, and swung it like an ax into the trunk of the nearest tree. The wooden stock of the Mauser splintered at the hand grip. Cernović smashed it twice more into the tree, pieces flying, and then flung the ruined weapon through the snow-laden branches and down the slope. He stood there for a moment, arms by his sides and shoulders heaving, exhaling clouds of condensation into the frigid air, and then turned to face Merritt.

"I am sorry one of my men failed you," he said. "If not for his treachery, Sergeant D'Amato would not be dead."

"And quite possibly not Sergeant Hurst," Throckmorton added, "from what I've just heard. Not to mention Bozidar Yagovac and probably quite a few others."

Cernović looked at him briefly, then nodded. "I want to hear everything Vlado Kusić said," he muttered, "but for now, it is sufficient that he has been found out and executed." He looked down at Sylvia. "You shot him in the face," he said. "Good. It warms my heart to know he saw it coming."

Sylvia picked up the olive drab bundle at her feet and shook it out. It was Vlado's combat jacket. She glanced up at Cernović as she slid one pale arm into a sleeve. "Why ruin a perfectly good coat?" she commented. "Or waste a good pair of boots?" She slid her feet, now covered by heavy wool socks, into Vlado's rag-wrapped size-eleven shoepacks. "They're too big, but they'll get me back to my own. I'm not walking through snow and ice along Zlostup for a kilometer or more in climbing slippers."

She got to her feet and picked up her machine pistol. "Shall we go, Comrade Commander?"

Cernović looked at Merritt. "You have, regrettably, taken casualties, Major, but your mission is still secure. And I have new information that makes its success even more vital—that is why I have been trying to catch up to you for the past day. But I will leave it to you to answer Comrade Kozo's question. Shall we go on, or shall we abort?"

Merritt's eyes roved over the men, and came to settle on Bristow. "I can speak for the British, Commander Cernović: myself, Captain Throckmorton, Sergeants Stirling and Weiss—we will carry on. But Sergeant Bristow is an American—under my command, but still an American. He has just lost a comrade in Sergeant D'Amato. I feel I should let him speak for himself." He paused and met Bristow's eyes. "What about it, Sergeant? This mission has been, as you put it, 'snakebit from the git-go.' I don't want a man at my side or watching my back who'd rather be somewhere else. Do you want to see it through?"

The big Texan held Merritt's gaze unwaveringly for a several seconds, then grunted and looked off into the trees. "Hell, yeah, Major—I'll take the whole ride. I'll do it for Frank, like Stirling's doin' it for Hurst. That ain't the only reason—I'll do it 'cause I was sent here to do it, too, and I follow orders when they're given to me—but I'll play the game through the bottom of the ninth for Frank D'Amato." Bristow paused as his throat constricted slightly, and he swallowed to clear it. "He was a professional. He wouldn't want it any other way."

Merritt nodded. "Thank you, Sergeant." He turned back to Cernović. "There you have it, Commander. It's still on, and we're all going."

"Good," Cernović said. "Good. Then I have much to tell you as we walk. And time is of the essence. . . ."

He and Merritt moved off along the main trail in the direction of the avalanche gap, the Partisan commander speaking rapidly in low tones. One by one, the others followed.

" 'O God of battles!' " Quisp recited abruptly, " 'steel thy soldiers' hearts; possess them not with fear; take from them now the sense of reckoning, if the opposed numbers pluck their hearts from them.' "

Bristow blinked and looked sideways at him, practically for the first time. "Who the hell is that?" he growled to Sylvia, meaning Quisp himself.

"Shakespeare," Quisp said, before she could reply.

Part Two

"History will be kind to me,
for I intend to write it."

—Winston Churchill

Chapter
Twelve

The exiled Grand Mufti of Jerusalem was not a happy man. The lecture to which Hauptsturmfuehrers Juttner and Neurath were being subjected, in a gaseous bubble of affronted dignity, had been dragging on for more than an hour. And Haj Amin al-Husseini, true to form as both fundamentalist cleric and reactionary politician, was showing no signs of tiring. Both Juttner and Neurath were reaching the end of their capacity to nod sympathetically and look interested as the mufti paced up and down the length of his private rail car—rocket-shattered windows now boarded over and glass fragments swept up—and holding forth on the negligent criminality of the indignities he was being forced to endure. As usual, Mustapha Snagi loitered silently off to one side as the car, its undercarriage slightly damaged in the Typhoon attack, chattered and shook down the track ahead of the King Tiger train's lead locomotive. The constant vibration was enough to rattle one's fillings and generate a throbbing headache.

"Never before have I been treated with such blatant

disrespect by a senior military officer!" al-Hussein
fumed, prowling along the carpet with one hand be
hind his back and the other upraised, index finger wav
ing. "This SS colonel—Kronstadt—has exhibited i
total lack of consideration for both my personal safet
and the crucial mission I have agreed to undertake a
a special favor to the Fuehrer!"

Neurath remained as animated as a death mask, bu
Juttner couldn't help drawing a silent sigh and rollin
his eyes as the mufti stalked past. The circumstance
under which Haj Amin al-Husseini had agreed to tou
the SS Division Handschar in Yugoslavia were wel
known to him. "Special favor" indeed . . . more like
bartering one's thumb out of the screw before the
bone was crushed.

However, one man's discomfiture was anothe
man's opportunity—particularly, in this case, if Neu
rath happened to be out of earshot. Juttner rose casu
ally to his feet and walked over to the dining table
where a broad-bottomed carafe of good red wine hac
been placed. There were also three crystal goblet
wrapped in white linen napkins and laid on their sides
Juttner picked up one of them, poured it a third full
and swirled the wine against the sides of the glass
Then he turned smoothly on the heel of his jackboot
inhaled the wine's bouquet, and took a sip.

"Whatever the Italians' shortcomings as combatant
in this particular war," he said, rolling the wine on hi
tongue, "they haven't lost their knack for turning ou
an excellent Chianti."

"And that's about all they're good for," Neuratl
declared. He was desperate to forestall the mufti's in
terminable rant, or he would never have deigned tc
engage Juttner in conversation. "Digging in the dir
and stomping grapes with their bare feet. Just anothe
race of mud people, barely higher on the evolutionar
scale than Slavs or Africans." He gave a snort of dis
gust through his thin nose. "I mean, really—look a
the stubby, pithecanthropoid physiology of most o

ıem, how low to the ground . . . and the coarseness
f their skull structure . . ."

"How very phrenological of you to note that," Jutt-
er said, beaming down at Neurath with his most en-
aging smile. "The party scientists would be proud."

Neurath blinked up at him, unsure whether he was
eing complimented or insulted. That was the trouble
ith this damned Juttner, with his easy charm and
azor wit—you never knew. *He* didn't, anyway.

But at least the cursed Grand Mufti had shut his
ap, however temporarily. *Keep the conversation
oing,* Neurath thought; the subject changed.

"Yes," he said, regaining steam, "a race of mud
armers, grape stompers, and common laborers. But
oldiers? Don't make me laugh. Look at the hash they
aade in Ethiopia, Libya, and on their own ground in
icily. We even had to bail them out of their predica-
ıent right here in Croatia when they were about to
ose control of the situation, the damned incompe-
ents!" Neurath snorted again. "Believe me, it was a
ig mistake for us to ally ourselves with Mussolini. He
ıay be a great leader, but his people are racially unfit
ɔ be soldiers. The blood of the warrior does not flow
hrough their veins."

"Oh, I'm sure you're right, undoubtedly," Juttner
aid, sipping wine, "although I can think of a few peo-
le who just might—perhaps—take exception to your
ssertions."

Neurath, of course, was too belligerent, too indoctri-
ated, too self-absorbed, and too stupid to avoid the
rap.

"Who?" he demanded.

"Well . . . Julius Caesar, Scipio Africanus, Pompey
he Great, Marcus Vipsanius Agrippa, and every le-
ionary, prefect, centurion, and tribune in the armies
f the Roman Empire, for example . . ."

Neurath paled and clamped his lips together.

"You *have* heard of the Roman Empire?" Juttner
ent on. "Yes? No?"

Neurath got to his feet. His expression was n▪ pleasant. "I was referring to the present-day Italia soldier," he said tightly. "You know that."

Juttner blinked innocently. "Were you, Hauptsturm fuehrer? I thought we were discussing the blood ▪ the warrior and through whose veins it flows." H▪ sipped his wine. "I was merely playing devil advocate—offering an alternative point of view."

Neurath opened his mouth to retort, but in his su▪ pressed rage only a choking sound came out.

Juttner leaned in, lowering his voice so that th▪ mufti could not hear, although the cleric was no▪ seated at the far end of the car and appeared to b▪ lost in thought. "But supermen of the Reich lik▪ yourself—you're not really very interested in altern▪ tive points of view, are you?" He smiled pleasantly i▪ Neurath's face.

The Gestapo man's left cheek developed a persi▪ tent tic, but still he managed to keep himself i▪ check—barely. "Your choice of words is disturbin▪ Hauptsturmfuehrer Juttner," he snarled throug▪ clenched teeth, "to the point of being treasonou▪ I find your random disrespect for the sacred phil▪ sophies of National Socialism both offensive an▪ subversive—all the more so because you are an office▪ in the SS."

"Oh, come now," Juttner replied, pulling back wit▪ a guileless grin. "Loosen up a bit, Julius, before yo▪ burst a seam."

A blue vein was now throbbing in Neurath's templ▪ Juttner noted it with satisfaction; he had been workin▪ on both tic and vein since the beginning of the trip.

"Once again, I have had enough of you, Hauptsturm fuehrer," Neurath said. "I will retire to my berth, an▪ I warn you: provoke me any further and you will fin▪ out that I am quite capable of dealing with insolen▪ peers on a one-to-one basis."

Juttner sipped his wine. "How terrifying."

The vein in Neurath's temple squirmed like a f▪

blue worm, and the tic in his cheek doubled in frequency. "I will file a full report on your conduct with both the Gestapo and SS at my earliest convenience," he said, brushing past Juttner and heading for his quarters, "and I will make sure that a copy reaches Reichsfuehrer Himmler, as well."

"That's one of the most annoying things about the glorious Third Reich," Juttner muttered, half under his breath. "Everyone's always *telling on* everyone else—like nasty little schoolchildren competing for the best spot in a barbed-wire sandbox."

Neurath stopped halfway across the car and whirled. "What did you say?" he hissed.

"I said, I like this tasty little wine and that it's the best of an otherwise bad lot," Juttner replied. He lifted the glass and smiled. "*Prosit*, Hauptsturmfuehrer."

Neurath snarled unintelligibly and stalked past Mustapha Snagi to the door of his quarters, which he opened and, upon entering, shut with a subdued bang.

Juttner felt warm inside. A tic, a blue vein in the temple, and yet another indignant exit complete with slammed quarters door. Things were going well.

He refilled his wine glass, extracted one of his thin black cigars from its case, and strolled toward the front of the luxury car. The Grand Mufti of Jerusalem, seated in a velvet-upholstered chair near the forward door to the exterior end platform, looked up as he approached.

"Your colleague seems disagreeable," al-Husseini said. "He is a competent enough security officer, but I find his sour demeanor quite wearing in these close quarters we must share."

Juttner smiled. "An irritant you should not have to put up with, Your Excellency, along with all these other inconveniences. I will speak to him about it."

"Another thing," the mufti said. "According to the schedule provided by that reptile Kronstadt, this train will stop once more to take on water for the locomo-

tive boilers, at a town called Bljak. I want you to
speak to him for me. I insist on being transported to
Belgrade in the company of my armed escort by over
land vehicle. I have been consulting the map, and
there is a serviceable road from Bljak to Belgrade
Since the train must stop, anyway, Kronstadt has no
grounds to refuse me. You will convey this demand
to him on my behalf."

Juttner had been expecting this. He dipped his head
and clicked his heels together. "Of course, Your Ex
cellency. I will do my utmost to make him realize that
he must honor your insistence on this matter." He
paused. "However, I do see one problem that may be
insoluble." He paused again as the mufti looked up
sharply. "Vehicles, Your Excellency. With respect, we
do not have vehicles available that are adequate for
the task of transporting you and an armed contingent
of forty SS troopers from this rail line to Belgrade
and we are unlikely to find them by chance in Bljak.'

"That is why you must radio ahead and comman
deer the necessary vehicles from the nearest German
military ground force," al-Husseini told him. "You
see, I have thought it out. You have been using the
radio room in this car to provide security updates on
our progress periodically throughout this journey
Now you will use it to see that the vehicles required
to conduct me safely to Belgrade are waiting at the
station in Bljak when this train arrives."

Juttner hesitated, opening his mouth to speak. "You
may go," the mufti said, waving a hand.

Juttner closed his mouth, bowed his head, and
clicked his heels again. "At once, Your Excellency."

He turned and walked down the car toward the narrow passage that led to the berths and staterooms
The tiny radio room was at the very rear of the car,
the last door before the exit to the back-end platform
There was a yellow glow as Juttner entered and
switched on the light, then a dimming in the passageway and a quiet click as he shut the door behind him.

The Grand Mufti had picked up a book and begun to read when the radio room door opened again after only a few minutes and Juttner reemerged. He made his way forward through the luxury compartment, past the dozing Snagi, and halted in front of al-Husseini with the requisite nod of the head and click of the heels.

"My apologies, Your Excellency," he said. "Some unfortunate news: the radio has been damaged beyond repair. It occurred during the Typhoon attack, apparently; a small piece of rocket shrapnel penetrated the back of the set. The internal workings are completely smashed. It was an oversight on my part not to have checked it sooner."

Al-Husseini's mouth began to work, the color rising to his cheeks.

"However," Juttner continued smoothly, "I intend to walk back past the locomotives and coal cars, using the external catwalks, and locate Standartenfuehrer Kronstadt. I will request that he permit me to use the tank train's communications room for a routine security transmission. He has no reason to refuse me this courtesy. After I have made contact with the local occupation forces and have the necessary vehicles on their way to Bljak, I will inform the Standartenfuehrer of our intent to leave the train and proceed to Belgrade by road. With the logistics of our transportation to Belgrade already in place, he will have no objection to our departure, since he cannot then be accused of simply abandoning you in a potentially hazardous area."

The mufti sniffed. "I have the distinct impression that not only will he not object," he said, "he will be nothing less than overjoyed."

"That may well be the case, Your Excellency," Juttner affirmed, "but the essential point is, we will be off the train and on our way to the relative safety of Belgrade. And in all fairness to Standartenfuehrer Kronstadt, he has his own problems and priorities. I know

the type well: he is a front-line soldier, rather bulli⸗
and mechanistic in his thinking, and is ill prepared ⸗
handle the complex and sophisticated needs of a pe⸗
son of your eminence." The handsome SS office⸗
flashed his irresistable grin. "We will leave him to h⸗
Tiger tanks, where he is happy."

The mufti nodded, looking more pleased. "Th⸗
course of action will be satisfactory."

"Very good, Your Excellency," Juttner said. "No⸗
with your permission, I must go and make arrang⸗
ments with Standartenfuehrer Kronstadt to use h⸗
radio room. It may take some time to establish con⸗
munications with the nearest motorized Germa⸗
ground force, and I must get started."

Al-Husseini waved a dismissive hand. "On yo⸗
way, Hauptsturmfuehrer."

"Thank you, Your Excellency." Juttner bowe⸗
clicked his heels, and strode toward the rear of th⸗
luxury compartment, collecting his knee-length blac⸗
leather coat and SS officer's peaked cap as he went⸗

A blast of frigid air greeted him as he exited th⸗
mufti's private car and stepped out onto the met⸗
grating of the rear-end platform. He shrugged on h⸗
leather coat and, turning the collar up and tugging h⸗
cap down over his brows, crossed the shaking, swayin⸗
catwalk between the private car and the followin⸗
caboose.

The caboose was empty but for a lone civilian rai⸗
wayman snoring in one of the side bunks. A bottle ⸗
cheap schnapps, nearly empty, was tucked under h⸗
arm. A pot of coffee, still steaming, sat on the kero⸗
sene stove of the small galley. Juttner located a mu⸗
wiped the grime out of it with a dish towel, an⸗
poured coffee into it. The brew was as black as crank⸗
case oil and about as tasty, but the night was bitter⸗
cold and it was a long walk back—a dozen cars a⸗
least—to Kronstadt's quarters and the radio room.

He went out onto the rear-end platform of the ca⸗
boose and paused, looking at the huge front end ⸗

e Tiger train's lead locomotive. The noise was eafening—a cacophony of clattering ties, screeching wheels, pounding pistons, and hissing pipes. The vibration of the immense steam-driven power plant rattled the chassis of the caboose under Juttner's feet, giving im the uneasy sense that he could be shaken off the metal grating at any moment. From beneath the driving wheels of the locomotive, a cascade of sparks crackled out into the night as the train began to negotiate a long, gradual turn to the left.

There was a five-foot gap between the narrow service catwalk that ran around the locomotive and the end platform of the caboose. Juttner considered for a moment, then gulped his coffee and pitched the mug out into the darkness. Taking a careful stance, he waited for the train's motion to subside for a second or two, then leapt across the gap.

The metal grating of the catwalk was icy; his jack-boots slipped and he nearly fell, but managed to catch himself by the catwalk railing and avoid tumbling down onto the tracks. He looked down at the dark blur of rushing cross ties and breathed a short sigh of relief. Too close. That would be a stupid way to die in a shooting war—fall off a moving train and get cut in half by its wheels.

He made his way back along the side of the locomotive's massive iron boiler to the engineer's cab. There were two Waffen-SS troopers armed with machine pistols inside it, along with the engineer and his stoker. The steel floor of the cab was scattered with coal fragments and dust, and the door of the boiler-furnace had been left open, white-orange flames roaring inside, to offset the brutal chill of the winter windblast.

Juttner tapped the engineer on the shoulder. The jowly, unshaven civilian, dressed in greasy work coveralls and swathed in scarves, turned and looked at him in annoyance, the stub of a dead cigar jammed into the corner of his mouth. Juttner leaned in close.

"How many engines on the front of the train?" he

yelled into the engineer's ear. "Was it four or five
And how far back to the commander's car?"

"Five engines on the front," the heavyset enginee
yelled back. "Three more spread out over the lengt
of the train. You only have to walk the outer catwall
on these four back here, though, because there aren
any more between the last engine and Kronstadt
car."

"How many cars back from the last engine?"

"Seven, I think, Herr Hauptsturmfuehrer. Four an
munition cars, two bunk cars for troops, and one ant
aircraft gun car. The next one should be Kronstadt'
Nothing but flatcars full of Tiger tanks behind that.

"*Standartenfuehrer* Kronstadt to you!" Juttner shoute(
hardening his expression. The engineer's eyes widene
and he straightened out of his slouch. The two S
troopers glanced at each other and stiffened their ow
posture. Juttner turned on his heel, regarded ther
with cold approval, and proceeded onto the servic
catwalk around the lead locomotive's coal car.

Damned Nazis, the engineer thought, slouching ove
the locomotive's controls again and breathing a sig
of relief.

Ten feet along the catwalk Juttner smiled to himsel
It never hurt to play the diehard SS fanatic with th
lower orders when the opportunity presented itself. I
reinforced his reputation on the brewhouse-and
barracks grapevine as an officer not to be trifled with
and favorable gossip was good security in the Thir
Reich. Someone was always sneaking around behin(
your back, looking for scurrilous rumors with whic
to discredit you.

By the time he reached the fifth locomotive, afte
ten fairly nerve-wracking minutes of clambering alon
icy, swaying steel catwalks in a bone-chilling wind
blast, his leather-gloved fingers were numb and he wa
all but certain he would lose his ears and tip of hi
nose to frostbite. After taking an extra minute to pu
a scare into the engineer, who had been dozing on th(

oor of the cab near the open boiler-furnace door, he
alked around the last coal car and entered the first
f the four ammunition cars. It was packed from floor
o ceiling with ordnance for the King Tigers: 88-
illimeter cannon shells and heavy machine-gun am-
unition, primarily. A narrow walkway had been left
own its center. Juttner wasted little time moving
rough it and the other three cars; with the train's
onstant swaying, the possibility of having an ammuni-
on crate shift and drop on one's head seemed im-
inent.

The bunk cars housing the Waffen-SS support
oops for the King Tigers were jam-packed with
eeping men, the bunks themselves closely spaced and
acked five high in four rows down the length of each
ar. No one was awake. Multiple snorers competed
ith the clattering rhythms of the train, and here and
ere a man noisily passed gas in his sleep. Despite the
old draftiness of the cars, the atmosphere within them
as redolent of human wind. Juttner exited the second
unk car with his eyes tearing and his gloved hand
ver his mouth and nose. Then he remembered: the
oldiers' last meal had been pork sausage and cabbage
oup. Horrors.

He bundled up once more to walk the length of
he open antiaircraft gun car, casually returning the
traight-arm salutes of the unfortunate troopers man-
ing the two sandbagged 40-millimeter pedestal can-
on that were mounted at either end. Then he crossed
he last catwalk and entered the warm vestibule of
Kronstadt's car, closing the door behind him.

Kronstadt was sitting behind a plain steel desk,
oing over some papers, lamplight glinting off his
teel-rimmed glasses and a cigarette in a slim black
older between his fingers trickling smoke up toward
he ceiling. He looked up as Juttner approached; the
atter whipped his cap off and under his arm in one
otion and gave a smart Nazi salute with a click of
is heels.

"So?" Kronstadt said, flipping up his cigarette har
to return the salute.

"Pardon me for disturbing you at this late hou
Herr Standartenfuehrer," Juttner said. "I have
request."

Kronstadt looked back down at his papers wearil
"What?"

"As one of two personal security officers assigne
to His Excellency the Grand Mufti of Jerusalem
Juttner went on, "my duties include the periodic tran
mission of security checks and progress reports bac
to SS central headquarters, for the attention of Reich
fuehrer Himmler himself."

At the mention of Himmler's name, Kronstadt
eyes flicked up. "I'm hearing a lot about reports
the Reichsfuehrer these past few hours," he remarke
"first from that odious partner of yours, Neurath, an
now from you."

Juttner smiled. "A different issue in my case, sir,
assure you. Merely routine—a cautionary procedu
to track the mufti's safe progress through Yugoslavi
I fully understand and appreciate your military prior
ties and responsibilities, and have no wish to interfe
with them now or later."

Kronstadt relaxed slightly. "What is it you need?
he asked, drawing on his cigarette.

"Simply the use of your radio room, Herr Standa
tenfuehrer," Juttner replied. "A staggered series
coded transmissions, for which I must then wait f
reception confirmation. It can take an hour or tw
sometimes, to send and receive the proper sequences.

"What's wrong with your own radio? You mu
have one in the mufti's private car, eh?"

"Destroyed by a piece of shrapnel, sir," Juttner e
plained. "I only just discovered it."

"Well," Kronstadt said, waving his cigarette like
man who wanted to get back to his reading, "the radi
room is at the back of this car. My communication

officer has retired for the night, and no one's using it. Take what time you need."

"Thank you, Herr Standartenfuehrer," Juttner said. "I will try to get it done as quickly as possible." He got his heels together and snapped off another straight-arm salute. *"Seig heil!"*

"Ja, ja," Kronstadt muttered without enthusiasm, cocking his cigarette hand. *"Seig heil."*

Juttner executed a sharp parade turn to the left and strode toward the rear of the car. The door to the radio room was latched open and the overhead light was on. Juttner entered, shut the door, and switched on a desk lamp near the radio set before turning off the overhead light.

The radio was on, the tubes already warm. Juttner draped his coat over the end of the room's small day cot and put his black SS cap with its death's-head insignia down on the radio desk. Then he sat down in front of the radio set, donned a pair of headphones, and began to dial in a high-frequency wavelength.

Pushing aside the microphone in front of him, he checked the connections on the Morse key next to the set. Then, very rapidly, he began to transmit a complex Morse signal, the locked fingers of his right hand vibrating on the sending key with machinelike precision, in one of the most closely guarded codes in Europe: the top-secret cipher used solely for internal memoranda by the Abwehr.

He was done in less than three minutes. Slipping off the headphones and replacing the key next to the set, he spun the frequency dial off the wavelength he'd selected and pushed his chair back. Propping his jackboots up on the desk and crossing his legs, he settled back and took the thin black cigar he hadn't smoked in the mufti's presence from his breast pocket. He lit it, inhaled luxuriously, and blew a long stream of smoke across the room, a smile playing on his lips.

After smoking half the cigar, he butted it out in a metal ashtray and turned off the desk lamp. Then he crossed his hands over his stomach, tipped his head forward, closed his eyes, and went to sleep.

Chapter
Thirteen

Merritt's small team of commandos and Partisans
had walked all day after returning to the avalanche
te and lifting the remaining two mules and all the
quipment across the gap in the trail. They had contin-
ed along Zlostup until two hours before dusk, wind-
g their way up the southern wall of a gorge that
came ever more breathtaking in its depth and over-
l scale, as well as increasingly difficult to traverse;
e trail was badly snowed in and extremely narrow—
ss than three feet wide in some places. The mules
lked as they lumbered forward through snowdrifts
eper than the trail was wide, pack loads scraping
ainst the cliff to the left, and wide, frightened eyes
the dizzying drop mere inches to the right.

Periodically Merritt had halted the group, conceal-
g them temporarily behind a convenient outcropping
rock, and gone on ahead to scan the next section
trail with binoculars, as well as the ridges on the
r side of the Zpoda Gorge. As they approached the
ad of the gorge, the antiaircraft gun emplacements

positioned at regular intervals on the northern ridg
tops were markedly closer. The chance of being spo
ted was very real.

Finally, with the sun about to drop behind t
mountains to the west and plunge the eastern Maje
cas into shadow, Merritt and Cernović, leading t
team, had rounded a sharp turn in the trail and fou
themselves staring at a spectacular, panoramic view
the head wall of the Zpoda Gorge.

It was truly an awesome sight. The head of t
gorge widened into a steep-sided geologic bowl p
haps two miles in diameter from rim to rim and thir
five hundred feet deep to the bottom of the heav
forested valley floor. The head wall itself was a ma
sive sheer cliff of gray granite—an anomaly in the p
marily limestone Majevicas—that plummeted nea
two thousand feet from the top of its thick overhan
ing cap to the broken rock and gravel of the tal
slope at its foot. A natural fault in the otherwise fe
tureless granite bisected the cliff horizontally ju
above midpoint along its entire quarter-mile width.

It was along this precarious route that the ancie
hunter's trail Zlostup ran, on a rocky pathway bare
wide enough for a man to walk on without constant
bumping one shoulder on the head wall. Mules ha
to be side loaded—a highly dangerous practice—an
shepherded along; there was no room for them to pa
otherwise. On many previous occasions, a hunte
pack animal had panicked on the terrifyingly narro
head wall section of Zlostup, shied and bucked, on
to be toppled off its hooves by the uneven weight
its load and pulled into the yawning maw of the gorg
The talus slope far below was littered with the bon
of men and animals that had lost their footing.

  Zlostup followed the horizontal crack all the way
the northern side of the gorge, eventually switc
backing its way up and over the rim. Four hundre
feet above the crack, embedded in the vertical granit
were the mortar-and-steel footings of the Zpoda Sk

ty Bridge's main support girders. The bridge itself
rved around the width of the head wall, tucked in
neath the impregnable overhanging layer of cap
ck. The tunnels at opposing ends of the bridge
ped across the chasm at each other like small,
rk mouths.

Merritt had declared a halt and backed the team
d animals up to a natural alcove in the rock, con-
aled from view by the turn in the trail and the dying
ht. The final approach and assault on the Zpoda
yway Bridge would be a night operation; during
ylight hours anyone on the head wall section of
ostup was clearly visible to the enemy troops man-
ng the antiaircraft gun emplacements on the upper
rth rim, and to the garrison in the old stone chalet
ar the far end of the north tunnel.

The team members had waited in the chill shadow
the the alcove until a half hour after sunset, then
wly and cautiously worked their way around the
uthern wall of the gorge and onto the head wall.

Now, in the small hours just after midnight, Merritt
d his comrades were halted two-thirds of the way
ross the great cliff, unloading ordnance and equip-
ent from nervous mules on a pathway less than a
rd wide. Directly overhead were two of the girder
otings for the bridge's support members. Four hun-
ed feet of vertical granite gleamed in the moonlight
tween the footings and the little knot of soldiers
rking silently and feverishly on Zlostup.

"Put the first six crates of explosive into these
ches," Merritt said in loud whisper. "We're not
ing to get all four footings rigged and wired before
wn, and we don't want the boxes seen when daylight
mes. We're going to have to lie low for one more
y, then rig the last one or two footings after dark.
nd keep your voices down; even quiet sounds travel
long way when they bounce off this cliff face."

"Why four, Major?" Cernović puffed, maneuvering
crate into a shallow crack in the head wall. "It seems

risky, chancing a second night of climbing. If you g
two footings mined, would that not be adequate
bring down the bridge and whatever train may
on it?"

"Our SOE engineers say no, Commander," Merr
replied. He pulled a heavy coil of climbing rope o
the back of the lead mule and laid it on the pathw
against the cliff. "They tell us that with the quality
construction in the Zpoda Skyway Bridge, a minimu
of four consecutive support girders have to be d
placed in order to ensure that a span of sufficient si
falls away. Otherwise, the bridge may not drop at all
even with a train passing over it—or if it does, lo
only a small section that would be too easy to repair

Černović looked at him in the darkness. "We ne
this bridge down and as many of those King Tigers
possible at the bottom of the gorge."

"That," Merritt said, smiling grimly as he unload
more equipment, "is the general idea." He look
over his shoulder. "Stirling."

"Sir." The British sergeant was manhandling a cra
of explosives into a niche in the rock, and did
pause.

"When we get done with the equipment, string
the mules with breakaway cord and lead them alo
the rest of the trail to the northern rim. Find son
place to hide them—and us—for the next fiftee
hours. Captain Throckmorton will accompany you."

"Sir," Stirling said, finishing with his crate. He bac
tracked along the ledge to the third mule, carefull
sidestepping the other team members, and graspe
its halter.

"Watch them ornery critters don't nudge you o
into thin air," Bristow muttered to him as he led th
mule forward. "They got a bad attitude for son
reason."

Stirling grinned as he passed. "Thanks, mate."

"Don't mention it."

Stirling tied the third mule to the second with a six-
ot length of thin manila twine, then did the same
th the second and the first. Throckmorton pushed a
ool of detonator cord into a rock niche already full
explosives and straightened up, his face slick with
eat despite the cold.

"What's the idea of the thin cord?" he asked. "Why
t just use their regular lead ropes?"

"Hedging our bets, sir," Stirling replied. "We need
string the mules up to lead them down the trail
gether. If one animal slips and falls with the other
o tied to it with heavy ropes, we lose all three. This
y, if one falls, the cord breaks and we only lose
e one."

"I really should read up on this mule-skinning busi-
ss," Throckmorton mused. "Perhaps in another
e."

Merritt sidled along the cliff wall toward Stirling
d Throckmorton. "All right, Duncan," he said.
Have you got everything you need?"

Throckmorton slapped a large weatherproof suit-
se that was one of the few items the lead mule still
rried. "Kit and kaboodle right here, old man," he
plied. He smiled at Merritt. Merritt returned it and
e two men locked eyes and stood for a long moment
silence. Stirling saw something pass between them
at was more than the expected "good luck" or
ood hunting." It looked very much like "good-bye."

Merritt held out his hand. "Fair winds, old friend,"
said.

Throckmorton took the hand and shook it. "And
e same to you, Walter. Until we meet again."

"Aye. Maybe I'll see you in an hour or two over
the gorge rim."

"Maybe," Throckmorton replied. "I might go in
er rather than sooner."

Stirling saw Merritt's jaw tighten and then Throck-
orton turned, let out a deep breath, and clapped his

hands to his chest. "Ahhh! Lovely night, what?"
declared, beaming at Stirling. "Well, then, shall v
go, Sergeant?"

"Yes, sir."

Stirling let Throckmorton move ahead, then tugge
the first mule's lead and set off after him. As he d
he sent a puzzled look over his shoulder at Merri
The tall major was standing very still, leaning agair
the cliff and watching Throckmorton depart, an e
pression on his face that could only be described
haunted. Then he noticed Stirling looking at hi
smiled quickly and nodded, and turned away.

"What was that about?" Cernović asked hi
"What does that mean, 'fair winds'?"

Merritt pulled a climbing harness from a duffel ba
"It's something sailors say to each other," he said. '
means something like 'good luck,' I suppose."

"Captain Throckmorton is a sailor?" Cernov
inquired.

"Yes. A very good one. A racing yachtsman who
sailed all over the Mediterranean and Atlantic. A
over the Adriatic, too, before the war—from Tries
to Dubrovnik to the heel of Italy."

"You sound as if you know him well."

"I do. We go back to the early 'thirties, and tl
1936 British Olympic team. We've been friends f
many years."

Cernović grunted, helping pull out a heavy coil
climbing rope. "Not much salt water in the Majevi
Mountains. He's a long way from the sea here."

Merritt glanced once more at the little mule tra
moving off into the darkness along Zlostup. "Yes
he said. "He is."

Cernović was silent for a moment, then changed tl
subject: "This message I was asked to give yo
through Professor Quisp, along with the update on tl
King Tiger train's schedule . . . it's obviously son
kind of code, eh?"

Merritt finished knotting two ropes together. "You mean the reference to gamecock?"

"I believe the exact phrasing was 'gamecock in the field.' " Cernović's eyes searched Merritt's face. "If that message has anything to do with the interests of the Partisan Army of Yugoslavia, I'd like to know about it."

"I understand, Commander," Merritt said, stepping into a webbed climbing harness and tugging it up around his hips. "The fact is, it doesn't concern you or your people at all. It has to do with extraction options for my team once this job is done."

Cernović spread his hands. "Say no more, Major. I was just inquiring."

"There's never any harm in asking," Merritt replied, cinching up his harness.

"All right. I'm at your disposal. What do you need?"

The British major began to shed his heavy outer coat, revealing a tight-fitting black turtleneck sweater underneath. "Well," he said, "I need *her*." He pointed at Sylvia.

"Hssst!" Cernović caught the girl's attention and beckoned. "Sylvia! Come here."

"I say," Quisp declared, stepping past Cernović and Merritt on the narrow ledge, "will you be needing my assistance in whatever deviltry you have planned for the next four hours, Major?"

Merritt looked at him. "Not especially, Professor Quisp. Three of us will be climbing the rock face, and Commander Cernović and Sergeant Weiss will be down here on the trail, rigging explosives for us to haul up. You're not under my command, though I appreciate your assistance thus far. Perhaps you should go after Captain Throckmorton and Sergeant Stirling and help them locate a convenient place to hide somewhere on that forested rim."

"Capital!" Quisp enthused at low volume. "Simply

super! I never was particularly fond of playing th
baby roc in the eyrie, anyway. Off I go, then! Ta-ta!

He executed a little jig step and trotted off nortl
ward along the unnervingly narrow path, hummin
to himself.

"That's one strange sonofabitch," Bristow muttere
watching him go.

"A common enough type of Englishman," Merri
said, "as Miss Kozo will no doubt confirm." H
glanced at her, and the corner of his mouth twitche
upward.

She gave him a slow smile. "I'm beginning t
change my opinion of eccentric English aristocrats,
she said. "Some of them, like Captain Throckmorto
and Professor Quisp, are surprisingly effective."

"They're the reason the map of the world is thre
quarters red," Merritt said. "Eccentric wanderers lik
those two built the British Empire. They're the reaso
you can pull into a port in the South Pacific and orde
a gin and tonic in English from an aboriginal ba
tender who used to be a headhunter."

"Did anyone ever ask the headhunter how he fe
about it?" Sylvia commented.

"Touché," Merritt said. "But this ledge isn't th
place to have a philosophy discussion. Sergeant Bri
tow, are we rigged and ready?"

"Ready, Major," Bristow answered, tugging on h
own hip harness. "I don't know a quiet way to ban
in pitons, though."

"That's where our secret weapon comes in." Merri
rested his steady eyes on Sylvia. "Have you got ar
other long climb in you? If you establish a line to tha
first footing, we won't need to hammer in a singl
piton. We can just ascend the rope."

Sylvia looked up. "It's a long way, but I can clim
it. What I can't do is pull the weight of four hundre
feet of dangling rope with me. Two hundred, ye
Not four."

"We'll use manila twine instead," Merritt sai

Once you're at the footing you can pull the main rope up after you."

"Fine." Sylvia began to shrug off her coat. "Tie it on when I yank twice on the manila."

"I want you to do something else for me this time, though," Merritt told her.

Sylvia blinked her hooded eyes at him.

"I want you to keep your trousers and a sweater on, or at least pull them up after you. We'll be up here for hours and you'll freeze without them."

"No, I won't. I don't get cold when I climb."

Merritt shook his head. "I insist."

Sylvia stuck out her lower lip and glanced at Cerović. The Partisan commander shrugged. She looked back at Merritt. "Alright. I'll pull them up after me. I don't wear heavy clothing when I have to do a long ascent."

Merritt nodded. "Good enough." He tipped his head back and peered upward. The vertical expanse of the cliff face soared upward for what seemed to be a mile, disappearing into the night sky. The footings of the first two bridge supports were tiny, indistinct lumps in the pale moonlight. "Try for this one directly overhead first," he said to Sylvia, pointing. "It looks like there are a couple of small surface cracks running toward it. That may help you."

Sylvia stepped up beside him and put her hands flat on the rock face. "They will. I saw them."

"Frankly, I don't see how you're going to use them without pitons—they get so thin after about fifty feet that I don't think even you can get a fingertip into them."

"You let me worry about that, Major."

Merritt glanced down at her. She was clad in her familiar white undershirt, black shorts, black slippers, and fur hat. This time, however, she wore a climbing harness around her hips and upper thighs. It was much lighter and more minimal in design than Merritt's and Bristow's, consisting of only a few straps of canvas

webbing. There was a large carabiner hooked into
reinforced loop on the hip belt, and from it swung
curious selection of round objects ranging in size from
a cue ball to a pea. Each was suspended by its ow
twelve-inch loop of thin, strong wire and small individ
ual carabiner.

Merritt's brow furrowed. "What are those?" he asked

Sylvia blinked her hooded eyes at him and smiled
"My nuts, Major," she said, and hoisted herself up th
cliff by her fingertips and toes. In ten seconds she wa
twenty feet overhead, trailing the thin manila transfe
cord behind her.

Bristow edged over beside Merritt. "What the hell'
she just say?" he asked in a gravelly whisper.

Merritt shook his head. "You wouldn't believe m
if I told you, Sergeant." He squinted upward and ble
out a slow breath. "Stand by. If she makes it, we'r
next."

"Yessir," Bristow muttered, watching the girl's un
canny, spiderlike progress. "Crazy broad . . ."

The hunting chalet at the north end of the Zpod
Skyway Bridge's two-hundred-yard-long northern ap
proach tunnel had been in existence far longer tha
the bridge itself, and was much more than a simpl
mountain cabin. Built in the early 1800s by the des
potic Serbian ruler Milos Obrenović as a gift to hi
border ally, the despotic Bulgarian baron Janos Barbo
the chalet was, in fact, a small stone fortress—a grea
house built in the shape of a U with attached gues
quarters, staff barracks, and supply buildings. The en
tire structure was enclosed by a rectangular stone wa
twenty feet in height and ten thick, with a two-ma
guardhouse at each of its four corners.

Both Milos Obrenović and Janos Barbo had no
lacked for enemies who would have delighted in th
opportunity to flay them alive, and dared not even g
hunting in their own lands—separately or together–
without a full contingent of escort troops and a secur

ronghold to which they could retreat at night. Hence
e creation of Barbo House—110 years before the
ying of the railway line up the forbidding Majevica
othills toward Mount Zpoda, and the subsequent
nstruction of the Skyway Bridge across the Zpoda
orge head wall.

Barbo House was currently the forward headquar-
rs for the SS Division Handschar, under the com-
and of Standartenfuehrer Egon Zweig, and was
rrisoned by a full company of battle-hardened Bos-
an Muslim troops. These same troops also provided
curity for the northern and southern ends of the
poda Skyway Bridge, constantly patrolling the asso-
ated tracks, sidings, tunnels, and approaches. From
arbo House, the balance of the division was spread
t east and west in a thin line of advance along the
rthern rim of the Zpoda Gorge and the western
oulder of Mount Zpoda, respectively.

And there the SS Division Handschar had been
alled—much to the disgust and frustration of Stand-
tenfuehrer Zweig—for going on eight weeks now.
h, there had been assaults and ambushes, probes and
netrations, mostly by Jagdkommando units under
rd-charging officers like Ulrich Haak, but on the
hole the division's formerly impressive progress
ross the flat river plain approaches to the Majevica
ountains had been lost to nearly impassable alpine
rrain, overstretched and inadequate supply lines,
rsistent harrassing attacks by Partisan guerillas, and
solutely brutal winter weather. It was like Stalingrad
1943 all over again, when the icy breath of Mother
ussia had frozen General Paulus's proud Sixth Army
place to die by inches. Zweig could see a similar
te threatening the SS Division Handschar now: lack
forward momentum was killing morale, and some
his less-than-enthusiastic Muslim troops were begin-
ng to desert. The trend both outraged and unnerved
m. But at least he wasn't an indecisive ditherer like
aulus. At least he knew what he was doing.

Zweig looked up from his huge oaken desk in t
middle of Barbo House's spacious common room. T
Serbian state railway had formerly maintained the o
hunting chalet as staff accommodation for personn
servicing the Zpoda Skyway Bridge, but since t
Nazi-assisted establishment of the greatly enlarge
puppet state of Croatia,[1] which had swallowed near
all of Serbia, the remote structure had fallen into n
glect. The deterioration was not too far advanced
yet, but there was a general shabbiness—a smell
mold and dry rot—that permeated the great wood
beams and once elegant furnishings of the place.

A fire burned in the massive stone hearth at o
end of the room, sending shadows dancing over t
three tiers of mounted game heads that lined all fo
walls. Zweig gazed at them—red stag, European e
brown bear, wild boar, black alpine goat—the oran
firelight dancing in their mad glass eyes. Barbaric tr
phies of a distant, long-forgotten glory, dark and rat
with age, moldering away the years in anonymous is
lation on a remote mountaintop. There was somethi
about the eyes when the firelight was in them—a sta
ing, accusatory quality—that Zweig found vague
chilling. He'd always disliked the killing of animals.

Abruptly he looked back down at the pape
stacked in front of him and took a cigarette from
silver box on one corner of his desk. If those doze
of eyes continued to watch him as he worked, follo
him as he walked through the room, he'd have
have the heads removed. Particularly if the SS Divis
Handschar was going to continue to be held up he
for any length of time. He lit the cigarette with a go
lighter, took off his glasses, and rubbed the bridge
his nose between his thumb and forefinger.

And now, with everything else he had to wor
about, there was this damned mufti showing up—rig
here, for pity's sake. More bloody nonsense. He ha
the solution for declining morale among the Musli
rank and file: decimation. Line them up and shoot or

t of every ten, then see how quickly the remaining
ne could rediscover their loyalty and motivation.
e Romans had had the right idea two thousand
ars ago when they invented the practice.

Distractions, distractions. Between the unreliable
pply lines, the miserable winter weather, and now
e pending arrival of Haj Amin al-Husseini—who
uld undoubtedly require much fussing over—it
uld be a miracle if he could plan a way to jump-
rt Handschar's advance and get it back on schedule
fore spring. SS and Wehrmacht commanders had
en relieved, and some of them shot, for less.

The loud click of a side door opening startled him,
d he glanced across the room in annoyance. The
uslim staff sergeant who had drawn night watch at
s aide's desk was standing there, gray SS field fez
cked on his head.

"Excuse me, Herr Standartenfuehrer."

"What is it?" Zweig snapped. His persistent insom-
a was making him permanently bad tempered.

"Haupsturmfuehrer Haak has returned from the
ld with most of his men," the substitute aide said.
le wishes to report, since the Standartenfuehrer is
vake and in his office."

Zweig scowled at the floor and drew on his ciga-
tte. Might as well. Sleeping was out of the question.
end him in, Scharfuehrer."

"*Jawohl*, Herr Standartenfuehrer."

The aide disappeared, and a few seconds later Ul-
ch Haak entered the room through the same door,
earing Fallschirmjager winter white camouflage and
scruffy four-day growth of beard. He pushed the
or shut with a snow-encrusted jump boot, removed
s battered death's-head fez, and came to attention,
ocking his heels together in a pool of meltwater.

"*Heil Hitler,*" he said, extending his arm in the
azi salute.

Zweig returned it casually and looked him up and
wn. "Stand at ease, Haak," he said, gesturing with

his cigarette. "Well . . . what do you have for me‘
take it your much-ballyhooed Jagdkommando pa
chutists were able to achieve some tangible succes:
in the past hundred hours or so? Particularly sinc(
stuck my neck out in authorizing this pet operation
yours and convinced Luftwaffe command to provi
the transport aircraft you requested."

Haak's tired eyes flickered off to the side. "De
nitely, Herr Standartenfuehrer. We took the Partisa
by surprise at the Soujak Mine, as per my informan
information, and harassed them all the way out
the valley."

Zweig walked slowly around his desk and ashed I
cigarette in a carved stone tray. "I see. Why did y
not destroy them in said valley?"

Once again Haak's eyes shifted. "It was not possit
to cut off their escape, Herr Standartenfuehrer—th
were too quick. But we killed a great many as th
fled, shooting from both sides of the gorge, and th
linked up with our ground Jagdkommando forces a
harassed them all the way to the Ugljevik Pass, whe
they finally retreated up into the high plate
country."

"So you flushed them from one stronghold to a
other, but did not destroy this sizeable contingent
the Second Proletarian Brigade."

"As I said," Haak replied, "we killed a great many."

"How many? Give me a number."

"Impossible, Herr Standartenfuehrer," the grimy (
ficer said. "It was a running battle, through snowf
and rough, heavily treed terrain. It stretched out ov
twenty miles and nearly three days by the time v
were done. There are bodies strewn from Soujak
Ugljevik; bodies covered by snow, bodies down i
vines and in frozen streams. I can't give you even
close guess as to how many there are."

"Then give me a percentage, man. A battlefield es
mate of their percentage losses."

Haak sighed, his jaw flexing. "Maybe . . . ten per-ent," he said.

Zweig sat down and looked up at him. "Ten per-ent? Not exactly a decimation, is it?"

"Actually that's exactly what it is, sir." Haak re-lied, his tone just short of retort.

Zweig's face reddened. He'd just been thinking of ecimation and the word had popped back into his ead. Unfortunately his mouth had been running a ttle faster than his brain and he'd used the term de-criptively instead of literally. But, of course, a 10 per-ent death rate was precisely the definition of decimation, nd Haak—damn his impudence—was smart enough o have caught the mistake. And if there was one thing tandartenfuehrer Egon Zweig's Prussian tempera-ent couldn't tolerate, it was being caught with his oot in his mouth by a subordinate.

"Hold your tongue, Hauptsturmfuehrer!" he arked. Haak didn't come to attention, but did fix his yes straight ahead. Zweig let his blood settle, then ent on with what he hoped was some semblance of is former composure: "What about Tito? He was upposed to be in the mine, wasn't he? That was the uicy carrot that sold your operation to the Luftwaffe."

Haak cleared his throat. "I myself led an assault eam into the mine, Herr Standartenfuehrer," he said. We pursued a small group of Partisan officers and oldiers deep into its inner passages, engaging in an ngoing firefight as we went. I am sure I spotted Tito t one point. When the Partisans saw that we had hem trapped, they set off pre-laid explosives and rought a large section of the mine down on them-elves and some of my men, unfortunately. The rest f us got out and sealed up the mine entrance with emolition charges, just to make certain no one who night be left alive could escape."

"So Tito is dead?" Zweig inquired, leaning forward vith genuine interest.

"I am sure I saw him in the mine, sir," Haak re
plied.

Zweig's eyes narrowed and he settled back. "Ho
sure are you?"

Haak looked down at him. "Would you like it e:
pressed as a percentage, sir?"

Zweig, just beginning to inhale from his cigarett
emitted a short strangling sound.

"Ninety-nine percent sure, Herr Standarter
fuehrer," Haak followed up smoothly, before his supe
rior could speak. "I am ninety-nine percent sure th;
Tito is dead inside the Soujak Mine."

"That—that is news of . . . extreme importance,
Zweig said, dismissing Haak's sarcasm in favor of tr;
ing to suppress a cough. "Why did you not radio
in, Haak? The loss of Tito will change the nature (
the entire Balkan campaign."

"Because ninety-nine percent is not one hundre
percent, sir," Haak told him, "and before I coul
make an irrefutable claim to have killed Yugoslavi;
premier Communist insurgent, I would have to see h
body—or at least observe his army undeniably withot
his leadership for several months."

Zweig wiped his lips with his fingers and butted h
cigarette in the stone ashtray. "Where is the Secon
Proletarian Brigade now?"

"Somewhere southeast of here in the Ugljevik Pl;
teau region," Haak said. "At least forty miles away
I estimate."

"Where *exactly*?"

Haak let out a long breath. "Again, it is impossib
to say, Herr Standartenfuehrer," he replied. "They ar
maneuvering in the high country, and bad weather i
setting in again. We will have heavy snowfall for th
next seventy-two hours. Reconnaissance flights will b
grounded. We will not be able to track their move
ments from the air."

Zweig chewed his thin lower lip. "The bad weathe

ould limit Partisan mobility as well as our own,"
e mused.

"I wouldn't count on it, sir," Haak said. "Their abil-
y to execute forced marches in the worst conditions
becoming legendary."

"I am thinking of sending a large-scale penetration
the southwest," Zweig declared, spreading his fin-
ers on a small map on his desk. "Perhaps engage the
artisans after they have been starving in the higher
titudes for a day or two more."

Haak had gotten used to Zweig's limited capacity
or making sound tactical decisions under less-than-
erfect circumstances. The man, despite his rank, sim-
ly wasn't that gifted a planner—a rather major flaw
a division commander. He tended to forget things.

"Herr Standartenfuehrer," Haak said, "there are
ther Partisan battalions and regiments opposing our
orces to the southwest and beyond. We cannot just
ase blindly after this one part of the Second Prole-
rian Brigade and leave a large gap in our line. We
eate two unprotected flanks that way."

This was something Haak had not gotten used to:
nding himself—a mere captain—in the position of
aving to correct his division commander, a full colo-
el in the Waffen-SS, and having that commander
uite obviously fish for further input, as if he really
ad no idea of how to proceed himself.

Not exactly confidence inspiring, this Standarten-
ehrer Zweig. A competent staff officer who should
ever have been made a field commander. Exactly like
e mediocre Paulus, whose lack of imagination and
ggression had killed the Sixth Army at Stalingrad in
arly '43 . . .

If there was one thing Ulrich Haak did not lack, it
as aggression. He was a hands-on combat leader—
omeone who put himself repeatedly at the broken
nd of the bottle—and the first to suffer, along with
is men, if the decisions that sent him into harm's way

were unsound. And he was getting tired of propping
up Zweig, offering good idea after good idea only to
have the inexpert division commander reserve all the
credit for these ideas for himself, as if they'd been his
alone. Why, the man had even shot off the tip of his
own left little finger a month ago, cleaning his service
pistol. Idiotic. Haak had been watching the slow-
healing stub with its crusty brown scab waver uncertainly over topographic maps for the past two
weeks. . . . Rather disgusting . . . why couldn't the
damned fellow wear a glove or a bandage or
something? . . .

"Haak, have you heard a thing I've just said?"
Zweig was looking at him impatiently, his glasses back
on his face.

"*Jawohl*, Herr Standartenfuehrer," Haak declared.
"Every word."

"Good. Then you agree that we should delay any
further attempts to pursue the Second Proletarian Brigade or advance our main line until after the next
bout of inclement weather has passed."

Haak smiled slightly. "That would be my recom-
mendation, sir. We should hold the line and let the
Partisans exhaust themselves running around in blizzards if they so choose." Bismarck's Beard—hadn't he
just said as much two minutes ago? How he hated
having to repeat the obvious.

"Herr Standartenfuehrer," he said, "my men and I
have just completed nearly four days in the field with
no hot food and next to no sleep. If there is nothing
more I can do for you at this time, I would like to
see to them and get cleaned up myself."

Zweig, looking down at his desk, didn't answer right
away. Rather distractedly he ran his right hand
through his limp blond hair and continued to float his
left, with its revolting partially amputated little finger,
over the topo map. Haak's eyes flickered over the
man's gaunt, weedy face, and he wondered for the
umpteenth time how such an unimpressive creature

d attained the rank of full colonel in the SS by—
hat?—his midthirties. Certainly not more.

Well, he was ten years younger than Zweig, and
tended to be a general in the same time frame. So
e damned to him.

"Herr Standartenfuehrer," he said again.

Zweig looked up suddenly as if startled and cleared
s throat. "*Ahem.* Yes, well, Haak—I've made my
ecision. We'll hold our current position and suspend
ay further offensive operations until the bad weather
ears."

Haak closed his eyes for a moment. By Lucifer, one
ould almost hear the rusty gears grinding in the
ool's head.

"There is one good thing about this weather,"
weig remarked, reaching for another cigarette.
There is a large shipment of King Tigers arriving by
ain approximately twenty hours from now. If the
ils don't become blocked by snowslides, the bliz-
rds should keep the Partisans from attempting to
botage it between Bljak and here."

"King Tigers?" Haak echoed, blinking. "Up in
ese mountains?"

"Yes," Zweig said, sitting down and lighting his cig-
rette. "Apparently they are a new variant specially
esigned for use in mountainous regions. Their de-
loyment here is highly classified, which is why you
aven't heard about it until just now."

Haak blinked again, his mind racing. "How many
ing Tigers?" he asked.

"Oh, fifty or so, I think."

Haak felt his heart leap in his chest. "*Fifty* Tiger
nks?" he said. "Here at Mount Zpoda?"

"That's right, Haak. To be deployed in concert with
andschar, at some point."

At some point? The myriad tactical possibilities
ame to Haak in a flood. The things that could be
chieved with the support of that many specialized
attle tanks—it boggled the mind! And on the eve of

their arrival, here was Zweig, chewing his cud ov
some ill-conceived notion to send troops hither ar
thither without a comprehensive strategy that includ
the use of this deadly new asset. It was enough
make one weep.

Suddenly Haak was very tired. There would I
much to do in only a few hours, and he needed re
to clear his mind for the task of making sure th
Zweig did not end up concocting some ridiculous ne
plan that was doomed to disaster. He mustered h
strength and drew himself stiffly to attention.

"This is welcome news, Herr Standartenfuehrer
he said. "The arrival of these tanks will give us
decisive advantage in our next thrust against th
Partisans."

"Yes, it will," Zweig agreed. "And that's not a
that's arriving. The Grand Mufti of Jerusalem is c
that train. He is coming to tour the division and boc
morale. So we will have a visiting dignitary to de
with, as well. I expect you to help out with securit
Haak."

The Grand Mufti of Jerusalem? Good God, wl
not the Archbishop of Canterbury? Things were mo
ing from the unexpected to the absurd. Who had tin
to nursemaid some unctuous caliph in a war zone-
least of all combat specialist Ulrich Haak?

It was all too exhausting. He would deal with it
the morning.

"Will that be all, Herr Standartenfuehrer?" Haa
declared.

"For the time being," Zweig said. "You're di
missed."

Haak knocked his heels and raised his arm. "He
Hitler."

Zweig tipped back his cigarette hand. "Ja. Goc
night."

"Good night, sir."

Haak executed a right turn and made for the doc
exhaling one long, weary breath the entire way.

Chapter Fourteen

They really were nuts. Standard, high-quality, forged-steel, octagonal nuts meant for securing machine bolts or any other type of threaded bar. But Sylvia Lozo had invented an ingenious new use for them.

Merritt, an extra coil of heavy rope slung diagonally across his chest, was hanging from a sliding prusik[1] hitch two hundred feet above Zlostup, at the midpoint of the rope Sylvia had secured to the closest support footing of the Zpoda Skyway Bridge. This was where the girl, climbing freely without pitons and trailing the thin manila transfer line behind her, had first paused in her remarkable solo ascent.

Far below on the trail, Merritt and Bristow and the others had been unable to see what she was clinging to. It looked like nothing at all, and as it turned out, that was almost exactly what it was. Without any apparent support, Sylvia had used the transfer line to pull up four hundred feet of stout rope, tied it to her harness, then continued to climb the sheer cliff to the

bridge footing, dragging half the rope after her in o
great drooping bight.

Now dangling at the spot where Sylvia had pause
Merritt took a moment to rest and inspect the mini
cule rigging that had secured her to the nearly featur
less head wall. A single nut, not more than a half in
in diameter and with a short length of ultrathin a
craft cable looped through it, had been inserted in
a thin crack in the rock and carefully seated until t
nut itself was lodged behind a portion of the cra
that was only a quarter inch wide, with the wire lo
and its attached carabiner protruding. This tir
fragile-looking arrangement, carabiner clipped into t
front of Sylvia's harness, had been the only thing su
porting her as she hauled up the climbing rope. M
ritt grasped the wire and pulled. To haul a half-in
steel nut through a quarter-inch crack in solid grani
was a physical impossibility, and the wire itself w
extremely strong and unlikely to fail. Merritt w
astounded by the simple ingenuity of it: a reuseal
anchor, noiselessly and instantaneously installed, th
would not give way unless actively dislodged, a
which could be used to attach oneself to even t
smallest crack.

Sylvia had knotted the middle of the rope into t
carabiner. Above his head, at intervals of perha
twenty feet, Merritt could see where she had insert
other nut-and-wire combinations into the crack ar
then run the rope through the carabiners. More ing
nuity: if she lost her hold on the cliff, the ro
attached to her harness would snap tight after she
dropped past the highest carabiner, and arrest her fa
An involuntary smile crossed Merritt's face. So t
invincible Sylvia the Great took a few precautions no
and again after all.

Smart. Smart to think of it, and smart to actual
do it. There were plenty of ways to get killed in
world war without taking a preventable nosedive c
a sheer cliff. With another short length of line, Merr

ed a second prusik hitch around the main ascent rope
bove the carabiner knot, let it take his weight, untied
he first prusik, and then released the main rope from
he carabiner. The initial crack anchor wasn't needed
ow, but they might be able to use Sylvia's device
gain higher up, moving between bridge footings. He
iggled the nut free, pulled it out of the rock, and
lipped its carabiner to his own harness. Then once
gain he began to climb, hoisting himself up the main
ope and sliding the prusik hitch as he went.

It began to snow very lightly, the tiny flakes floating
n the moonlight. Merritt looked up at the bridge and
he dark sky above it. It was difficult to tell what kind
f weather was moving in, but the stars were no longer
isible to the north so there had to be cloud cover in
hat direction. He hoped that heavy snowfall would
old off until they got the bridge mined—twenty-four
ours or so. After that, a blizzard might well help
heir escape.

As he climbed, Merritt removed each successive nut
e came to, clipping it onto his harness. By the time he
eached the massive concrete footing with its equally
massive steel support girder, he'd collected six nuts of
arying diameters. Sylvia, sitting cross-legged at the
ery edge of the footing with her forearms resting on
er knees, looked down heavy lidded at Merritt as he
auled himself up the last few feet of rope.

"Are you quite comfortable?" he panted, grasping
he edge of the footing.

"Yes, quite," she replied.

Merritt heaved himself up another foot. "Don't
vaste energy lending me a hand," he grunted.

"I climbed up here by myself," Sylvia told him. "So
an you."

"Huh!" Merritt grimaced, shaking his head, and
vith one more effort heaved himself over the back of
he footing where it joined the cliff. He lay there for
moment, trying to catch his breath.

"You may be stronger than I am," Sylvia com-

mented, looking off into the dark vastness of th
Zpoda Gorge, "but you've also got to haul all tha
heavy muscle up the cliff, big man." She turned he
head and regarded him over one shoulder. "Ever
thing is relative in climbing, Major. Pound for poun
I'm actually stronger than you."

"I believe it," Merritt panted, still lying on his bac
with his chest heaving in and out. "By the way, I hav
your nuts." He patted the collection of wires and car
biners on his hip.

"I see. I was wondering if you were going to figur
out that you should bring them with you. Thank you.

Merritt sat up, his breathing returning to norma
and pulled over his head the coil of rope he'd bee
carrying. "It's an ingenious way to secure yourself t
the cliff. How did you come up with it?"

Sylvia shrugged her bare shoulders. "Just commo
sense. If you climb enough and look at all the differer
kinds of cracks and crevices in cliffs, rock faces, an
even buildings, it becomes obvious that somethin
much lighter and easier to use than a piton can usuall
be placed in them as a kind of support. I though
about it for a while—the materials were already avai
able. We'd used sailboat carabiners and airplan
control-cable wire as rigging accessories in the famil
trapeze act. The nuts were my idea—it just came t
me in a flash one day. I put the wires and carabiner
on the nuts and tried climbing with them.

"They worked like a charm. You can pull yourse
past an otherwise unclimbable spot with one of then
You can leave them in the rock behind you and ru
a belayer's rope through them if you think you mig
fall on a difficult stretch ahead. You may think m
reckless, Major, but I know what I can climb and wha
I cannot. I don't have a death wish. I'll protect myse
with a belay rope if I think it's necessary." She smile
and went on. "If you have a consistently thin crac
that you can't get a finger in, you can even sling on
unit to each wrist and climb by alternately placing an

ulling each nut in succession." She turned her head
nd pointed toward the next footing over, some sixty
:et away. "Which is what we may have to do to move
) the next support girder. The rock is really smooth
:re—nothing to hang on to. All there is is that very
iin horizontal crack. My smallest nuts should work
1 it."

"If they don't, we'll have to risk quietly tapping in
few pitons," Merritt said. "We have to get over to
iat footing and eventually the two beyond it." He
ot up on one knee. "By the way, Miss Kozo, I'm
npressed. You are one very sharp woman."

"Yes, I know, " Sylvia replied. "And you may call
ie Sylvia, Major, if you think it wouldn't rupture your
nglish propriety."

Merritt smiled. "All right then, Sylvia." He moved
) the edge of the concrete pad and peered down.
ristow was ninety feet below, working his way up
ie primary rope with another large coil of line looped
iagonally over his shoulder and across his chest. He
aused and looked up, his barely visible face shiny
'ith sweat, his lips moving in what Merritt supposed
'as a characteristic string of muttered curses.

"Come on," Merritt called, as loudly as he dared,
'aving him on. The big American sergeant put his
ead down and resumed his dogged hand-over-hand
scent. Merritt watched him for a few seconds, rueing
ie time it was taking Bristow—and had taken him—
) reach the footing. But four hundred vertical feet
'as a long way.

He turned and surveyed the second footing. Like
ie one on which he was kneeling, it was a massive
lock of steel-reinforced concrete embedded in the
ock face with a hundred-foot steel girder extending
p and out from it at an angle perhaps five degrees off
ead vertical and tying into the bridge spans overhead.
here was indeed a thin split in the rock that seemed
) run the entire distance between the footings.

"Sylvia," Merritt said, "can you take this other rope

over to that second upright while we're waiting fo
Sergeant Bristow? We need to pick up the pace."

The lithe Partisan uncoiled to her feet from he
cross-legged position and rubbed her upper arms wit
her hands. "About time," she said. "I was almos
starting to feel a chill." She stepped behind the sup
port girder and picked up one end of the rope Merri
had laid on the concrete pad.

"I tied your clothes to the first crate of explosives.
Merritt said, "since you apparently forgot about then
We'll pull them up for you." He glanced down at Bris
tow again—still with sixty feet to go—and grasped th
second rope, as well. "You don't have any objectio
to me belaying you across that gap, do you?"

"Sylvia," Sylvia said.

Merritt smiled briefly. "Sylvia."

"Not in the slightest, Major." She held out he
hand. "My nuts, please."

"Oh—right you are." Merritt unclipped and hande
them to her one by one.

"Thank you."

Turning toward the second footing, Sylvia flexed he
fingers, shook out her arms, and stepped off the con
crete pad onto the cliff. She worked her way alon
the crack for no more than ten feet, with Merritt pay
ing out rope, before stopping.

"I can't even get a fingertip into this crack for th
next twenty feet," she called back softly, "and ther
are no toeholds, either. I'll have to alternate with m
two smallest nuts."

"Be careful," Merritt said, because what else wa
there to say? He checked the short safety tether he'
looped around the girder and tied into his harnes
and firmed his grip on the rope that was wrappe
around his shoulder blades in a body belay. A gust o
tiny snowflakes whirled up into his face; he shook h
head and blinked them away.

"Jeezus . . . *Christ*," Bristow gasped, getting on

m over the edge of the concrete pad. "Felt like . . .
was . . . climbin' to the . . . goddamn moon . . ."

Merritt stooped to help him, taking one hand off
s belay rope. "Here. Grab hold."

As his hand closed over Bristow's, there was a sud-
en sharp popping sound. The belay rope snapped
ut around Merritt's upper back, yanking him side-
ays. If not for Bristow's weight counterbalancing
m, he would have been snatched right off his feet
the limits of his safety tether. He staggered, let go
Bristow as the big sergeant was pulled onto the top
the pad, and seized the belay rope with both hands.
he safety tether came up tight as his feet skidded to
e very edge of the concrete and he teetered there,
ught between the tether and the tension of the rope
ound his shoulder blades.

He willed his rope-burned hands to stay closed and
anced at the horizontal crack. Sylvia was gone. But
ere was a single nut in place approximately fifteen
et out. The belay rope was as tight as a guitar string
rough its carabiner, quivering, and ran straight down
om there. Merritt looked down as Bristow scrambled
his feet and grabbed the rope to assist him.

Twenty feet down, Sylvia was sitting calmly in her
arness, her slippered feet planted against the cliff,
oking up at him.

"The nut I had my weight on ripped out," she said,
olding up a tiny wire unit by its carabiner. "I thought
at might happen, so I put a solid one in behind me
id clipped the rope to it." She half smiled. "See how
works? If you fall, you don't fall as far, and you
on't swing. It's easier on the belayer, too."

"Thank God for that," Merritt breathed.

"Easier, she says," Bristow muttered, leaning back
the rope. "She should be on this end." He coughed
id spat. "You okay, Major?"

"Barely, but yes," Merritt replied. "Really took me
f guard."

"You should have been watching," Sylvia sai
overhearing him. "You're the belayer. And yo
should have had both hands on my rope."

"I'll try to improve," Merritt retorted.

"Are you two going to pull me up so I can try agai
or leave me here to die of boredom?"

"God*damn*," Bristow growled, incredulous. "Let
just cut the sonofabitchin' rope."

"Ready, Sergeant?" Merritt said. "Together, now . .

The two men hauled, hoisting Sylvia until she wa
back at the nut that supported her.

"Stop," she said, and began to work her way alor
the crack again, going hand over hand with a pair
small nuts and her toes smeared against the vertic
rock.

Merritt stepped around behind the support gird
and braced himself against it, watching Sylvia an
feeding her slack from a secure belaying positio
"I've got her now, Sergeant," he said. "Go ahead an
drop your third line to Cernović and Weiss. Start hau
ing the explosives up here."

"Yessir," Bristow replied. He pulled the coil of rop
he'd brought with him off his shoulder and began
tie one end of it to the base of the girder.

Merritt turned his wrist up and looked at his watc
"Zero three hundred hours," he said. "Maybe an hou
and a half of true darkness left. We have to have a
least two of these supports mined and be off Zlostu
by zero four thirty hours at the latest." He glanced a
Bristow before returning his attention to Sylvia, wh
was now approaching the halfway point of her traver
to the second footing.

"I hear you, Major," the big sergeant said, liftir
the heavy coil of rope. "Pedal to the metal all the wa
We'll make it." He swung the coil once and heaved
out into space. The loops separated cleanly as it fe
Two seconds later the rope snapped taut alongside th
concrete pad.

Bristow peered over the edge, squinting. "Kind

rk to see all the way down there," he muttered,
nd this little bit of snow fallin' don't help, but
ey've got it. It didn't get hung up nowheres."

"Good," Merritt said. "We need at least two crates
r girder, Sergeant. Haul until you're tired and then
'll switch out."

"Yessir," Bristow replied.

"Hsst!" The sound came from the trail behind.
Stirling whirled, dropping to one knee and bringing
s rifle up to his shoulder. Throckmorton, pistol in
nd, sidestepped quickly behind one of the stunted,
ow-laden evergreen trees in the dense thicket they
d been penetrating since leading the mules off
lostup below the northern bridge tunnel. The pack
imals nickered uneasily and shied, reacting to the
o British commandos' sudden movements.

"God save the king," came the loud whisper a sec-
d time. "It is I—Quisp."

Stirling and Throckmorton exhaled and lowered
eir weapons as the professor emerged from the dark
oom behind the little mule train, his Schmeisser at
e ready. He raised a finger to his lips as he ap-
oached, the whites of his manic eyes gleaming, and
e three men knelt together in the snow, heads close.

"There is a two-man patrol moving parallel to us
a larger path just thirty yards through those trees,"
uisp whispered, his voice barely audible. "Handschar
. Watching the side approach to the tunnel, I
resay."

Stirling glanced at Throckmorton and nodded.
We've already seen a single sentry walking the top
the tunnel and another two-man patrol at the gorge
m. It's a bloody miracle they didn't spot us." He
ked his dry lips. "I think we should get off even
is secondary trail, head down around these steep
ck formations"—he indicated a series of ten- and
enty-foot miniature crags that stepped down
rough the trees and drifts to their right—"and try

to find some kind of overhang or cave to shelter i
One of us can go back later to lead Major Merritt ar
the others in before dawn."

"What-ho—I'll do that!" Quisp whispered instantl
"A Zulu leopard soldier can't hold a candle to n
when it comes to stalking, d'ye see? I'm a ghost, I t
you—a veritable will-o'-the-wisp! Quisp the Wisp,
it were . . ."

"Fine, fine—we've got it, old man," Throckmort
cut in, patting the air impatiently. "Right, now, le
find cover, as the sergeant says."

"Spot on, old boot! And Quisp shall lead the wa
my merry men, whilst you deal with the beasties, wha
'Hark! The shrill trumpet sounds, to horse, away! N
soul's in arms, and eager for the fray!' Cibber, th
one, don't you know? 'Course you do . . ."

Despite his lunatic persiflage, Quisp's voice nev
rose above the same low whisper. He was up and stri
ing ahead through the deep snow before Throckmo
ton could say another word. Stirling caught h
captain's eye and they exchanged an exasperate
shake of the head before getting to their feet and lea
ing the mules on, watching and listening for signs
the enemy, with senses heightened by tension almo
to the point of pain. A generous dusting of snowflak
whirled around them as they left the tiny trail ar
began to descend the short, steep slope alongside tl
nearest rock outcropping. It was beginning to sno
in earnest.

"The snowfall should help mask our tracks, sir
Stirling muttered quietly. "Make them harder for
patrol to see. And we'll make sure we keep to tl
trees and off the trails when we have to move." F
stepped down around a large section of fractured ro
and coaxed the lead mule down with tugs on its halte
"Watch the footing right here—it's a bit treacherous

"Right," Throckmorton replied, stepping down ar
to the side. "Lead on. I'll make sure the other tw
mules follow properly." He paused. "By the way,

pose if we turned the beastly creatures loose, since
don't need them anymore, they'd just head for the
arest human noises in search of food and shelter,
? Meaning that German garrison over there."

Stirling nodded. "Almost certainly, sir. Especially in
s weather. And I can't think of a better signal that
nething's afoot than three Partisan pack mules sud-
nly showing up at the SS Division Handschar's front
te. The animals have to be secured, out of sight."

"I thought as much," Throckmorton grumbled,
shing on the third mule's mangy flank as it stepped
wn past him. "Hello—here's the mad professor
ain. . . ."

Quisp had backtracked into view at the very bottom
the forty-five-foot combination crag. He gestured
phatically as Stirling and Throckmorton worked
eir way down the last third of the broken incline.

"Eureka! I have it!" he hissed. "Come, gentlemen,
me. An accommodation worthy of the most discern-
; Neanderthal, and not a mountain troll in sight to
ntest our residency! 'Seek, and ye shall find!'—Saint
atthew, by the Gay Lord Grimsby!"

"Bloody hell," Stirling muttered to Throckmorton
der his breath. "His nonsense is getting to me, sir.
es he think we're walking through the bloody
obe Theatre?"

"I really don't quite know what he thinks, Ser-
ant," Throckmorton replied, "but let's see what
's found."

They followed Quisp for a hundred yards through
ep snow around the base of the crag, finally coming
a narrow split in the rock behind several scrubby
ergreens. It was half drifted in and just barely wide
ough for a mule to get through. Quisp turned, hand
hip, and gestured with the barrel of his Schmeisser.
"Behold the gates of the underworld!" he declared.
've been inside. A damned cozy place, if you ask
e—demons and gremlins and hobgoblins notwith-
nding."

"Christ," Stirling growled, stalking past him.
bulldozed through the snow and into the narr
entrance.

The crevice widened rapidly, until Stirling could
longer feel both walls with his outstretched arms
was absolutely dead black fifteen paces in, and he f₁
bled inside his coat for his Zippo. There was a meta
clink as he opened and fired the lighter.

He was standing in a rectangular cave some twe
by twenty by ten feet high, apparently formed by na
ral fracturing and slippage of the parent rock; th
was no evidence of erosion by water, nor was th
any dampness present—frozen or otherwise. The c
floor was flat, dry stone and quite devoid of dirt
rubble.

Cautiously Stirling walked forward, holding
Zippo up in front of him. At the far end of the ca
there was evidence of fire building—black soot on
rear wall and a crumbled pile of charred wood, as ₁
as what looked like broken fragments of anir
bone—but it did not appear to be recent. Most lik
a hunter, someone who knew the terrain well, st
ping in to shelter for the night. And how long a₁
Ten, twenty, a hundred years? Stirling walked to
rear of the cave and squatted on his haunches, pok
through the ash and char with his index finger.
German wrappers or cans, no cigarette butts, no w
or beer-bottle shards—none of the evidence that s
diers from time immemorial have always left in
wake of their passing.

Stirling rose to his feet. No, this cave had not be
used in a very long time.

And it would do.

"Come on, boy, hurry," Cernović said, dragging ₁
other crate of explosives along Zlostup's narrow le₁
toward Weiss. The young sergeant was lashing B₁
tow's dangling haul rope around the crate already
his feet, working feverishly. The snow, which had be

ht and dustlike all night, was now coming down in
avy flakes and starting to drive into the Zpoda
orge head wall as the wind picked up. Weiss's black
ol balaclava, folded back off his flushed face, was
ked with snow, as were his eyebrows and sparse,
e-day growth of beard.

"I'm hurrying, Commander," he panted. "This is
umber seven. That one you have there makes eight—
o crates per support." He wiped snow out of his
es, stood up, and squinted up into the darkness.
Damned snow . . . can you see them up there?"

Cernović, peering up, as well, with his hands
ielding his eyes, shook his head. "No. But if things
on't start moving faster we're all going to see them
those bridge footings very soon—all of us including
e SS. It will be light in less than forty minutes."

Weiss yanked three times on the rope. It went tight
mediately and the crate was lifted into the air,
mping along the cliff as it rose. "Maybe the snow
ll keep it dark a bit longer," he said, looking out at
e black skies to the north. "Buy us another half
ur."

"Possibly," Cernović replied. "At any rate, we're
ot staying here to get shot off this ledge in broad
aylight, if those three don't come down in time."

Weiss frowned at him through the falling snow.
You'd leave them out here?"

The Partisan commander shrugged. "Don't look at
e like that, boy. I wouldn't be abandoning them—
ey'd be doing it to themselves. I'm not throwing my
e away, or yours, for that matter, for no reason.
lajor Merritt has a choice: get down here while it's
ill dark so we can all get to cover together, or don't.
e knows that."

Weiss looked back up at the swirling gloom over-
ead. "I just don't like the thought of having to leave
ithout them."

Cernović shrugged again. "Like I said, it's out of
ur hands. . . . And I don't intend to die before I

have to." He was quiet for a moment. "Dying i
terribly easy thing to do in Yugoslavia right now, S
geant Weiss. You'd do well to remember that."

Weiss opened his mouth and then shut it again. C
nović was only telling the truth.

"Rope!" the Partisan commander hissed, stepp
quickly to one side. Bristow's haul line came slapp
down the rock face again and hung there, vibratin

Weiss picked up the slack as Cernović hoisted c
end of the last crate and dragged it over to the ro

"All right, boy," he said, and his gravelly voice v
not unkind, "tie."

Sylvia Kozo had put on all the clothing Merritt h
passed her—pants and heavy British army sweate
and was working her way along a convenient series
two-inch horizontal ridges in the cliff face toward
bridge's third support footing. The snow was com
thick and fast now, and before every placement of l
bare fingers on a new hold she was forced to scc
the buildup off the rock to avoid slipping. Her to
only occasionally found purchase, and skidded off
snow-slick granite more often than not.

With all her weight continually supported by l
arms, she was getting very tired, and her fingers we
running with blood from torn nails and rock cuts. A
there was no crack on this route in which to place
safety nut; the belay rope hung down in a large lo
from her waist back up to Bristow at the second fo
ing. He dared not keep any lateral tension on the ro
for fear of hindering her forward progress, or wor
pulling her off the cliff.

She looked ahead. Only another fifteen feet to
forward. Forty-five feet to go back. Easy decision. I
spite her trembling arms and numb, bleeding finge
she was confident. She'd made short work of ledg
only a quarter the width of these many times before
although admittedly not at four in the morning in
snowstorm. But there was no doubt that she wou

ake it . . . that she would not fall . . . none
aatsoever . . .

She fell. There was no reason for it, no justifiable
cuse. No granite flaking away under her fingers or
y patch sabotaging her grip. Her strength, for the
st time in her life, simply failed her. One second she
as clinging to the rock, her arms shaking and her
agers hooked onto the little ledge like claws, and the
xt her fingers had opened and she was tumbling
ackward into a rushing, snowflake-filled blackness.
comprehensible. The breath came out of her in a
ent scream—and then the belay rope went taut and
atched at the waist belt of her harness.

What little air was still in her lungs was forced out
a gasp as she bounced on the end of the line and
rung in a great arc under the second footing, frigid
r whistling past her ears and snow whipping horizon-
lly into her face. She tried to breathe, but her wind
as gone, her solar plexus paralyzed. She twisted help-
ssly at the end of the rope as she reached the top
the arc . . . dropped back . . .

She hit the wall on the backswing, slamming into it
ith her left shoulder and hip. A glancing blow, but
painful one. Still trying to get a breath, she seized
e rope with one hand and pulled herself upright.

The rock face loomed again, and this time her in-
incts took over. She flipped around to a sitting posi-
on and hit the granite with the soles of her feet,
sorbing the shock with her legs. Two more swings
d she managed to halt herself seventy-five feet
low the second footing. She sat in her harness, feet
ainst the cliff, clinging to the rope with both hands
d sobbing in partial breaths of air.

On top of the second footing, Merritt was now be-
de Bristow, helping him take the strain of the taut
lay. He grasped the upright girder with one gloved
nd and leaned out, trying to see.

"At least she's still on the end of the rope," he said.
What happened?"

Bristow shook his head, grimacing as he held
share of Sylvia's weight. "I dunno, Major. I was lo
in' right at her. She just came off the rock—boon
like that. Fell so damn far I almost couldn't hold he
He glanced at Merritt. "Good thing she don't we
no more'n a plucked chicken."

"I didn't see it. I was still bringing that last cr
across from the first footing on the transfer line."

"Goddamn, Major—I think she hit pretty ha
down there."

"All right. Let's pull her up. One, two, three . .

The two big men heaved, getting about three f
at a time. It was nearly four minutes before the snc
caked top of Sylvia's rabbit-fur hat appeared at
bottom of the footing.

Merritt dropped to one knee. "Sylvia," he cal
softly. "Are you all right?"

She tipped her head back and looked up at hi
hugging the rope. Her eyes were quite wide and s
was shaking uncontrollably. She did not speak.

"Get her up here," Merritt said to Bristow. "Sh
frozen, and I don't mean from the cold."

"Shit," the big sergeant said. "Just what we ne
Okay, Major . . . heave."

They hauled the girl up the final ten feet and lift
her onto the top of the concrete pad. She kicked ba
from the edge and sat huddled against the steel gird
still hugging the rope with both bloodied hands. S
was staring out into the darkness, shivering.

Merritt and Bristow glanced at each other. Mer
moved forward, knelt, and put his hands on h
trembling shoulders.

"Sylvia," he said gently. "You're alright nc
You're alright."

Without warning, she leaned into him and buri
her face in his chest. A single wracking sob escap
her, and she let go of the belay rope to clutch t
sleeve of his sweater.

"I'm cold," she whispered, pulling herself closer. "I'm . . . so . . . cold."

Perplexed, Merritt drew her in and rubbed her shoulders and back. "Sylvia. It's alright. You just slipped. The rope caught you." He glanced at Bristow again. The big sergeant was grim faced, and tapped his wristwatch. "Sylvia," Merritt said again. "Sylvia. Come on. We have to finish and get down before daylight."

Her response was to shake even harder and press her face into his sternum.

"We've got to get her off of here," Merritt said. He locked eyes with Bristow. "Cole. You have to finish running detonator cord to the two sets of charges we've placed while I try to lower her down to Cerović and Weiss. Pile snow on the set charges to camouflage them—the snowfall should do the rest. These other four crates . . . they're too small to see from the antiaircraft gun emplacements on the north rim of the gorge, but if some sentry happens to look down off the bridge—"

"I was thinkin' about that, Major," Bristow interrupted, "and I had an idea: I thought I'd tie two crates together with about twenty feet of line between 'em and lower 'em on opposite sides of this big concrete block. They'll hang down under it, close to the cliff, and be hard to spot. Snow'll cover 'em a bit, too. I'll do the same with the last two crates, 'cept make the connectin' line a little shorter. They'll lie flat alongside the cliff, like the other ones. We can pull 'em up when we come back tonight to finish the job."

"Do it," Merritt said. "Then finish running the det cord, and let's get out of here."

"Yessir." Bristow turned and began to peel off arm lengths of rope from one of the spare coils.

Merritt put a hand on the back of Sylvia's neck and squeezed gently. "Sylvia. Sylvia. You have to move. I have to lower you down to the trail. Now, Sylvia . . . there's no more time. . . . Come on. . . ."

*   *   *

Cernović stamped his feet, hands in the pockets his greatcoat. "We'll wait five more minutes," he sa "Then we're leaving."

"I wish we could see through this blasted snow Weiss grumbled, looking up. "I wonder if they're some kind of trouble."

"Well, they're not in the worst kind of trouble th can get into on a sheer cliff," Cernović remarked, "I cause we haven't seen any of them come plummeti past us."

"Gallows humor, Commander," Weiss said. "They– He frowned, shifting his gaze slightly to the left. "W a minute. . . . What's that?"

He slid past Cernović and began to work his w quickly southward along the snow-choked trail, stari up with both hands on the head wall.

Cernović followed, squinting up into the snowflak

"It's the girl!" Weiss said. "She's being lower from the second footing! Come on!"

Cernović's expression hardened as he caught sig of her, a small, huddled form bumping slowly dov the rock face. "Get a hand on her, Weiss," he raspe "There's something wrong. . . ."

Chapter
Fifteen

nexcusable! Inconceivable!" the Grand Mufti of Jerusalem ranted. "You guaranteed me, Juttner, that
would be off this train at the town of Bljak and
ading for Belgrade in a land convoy!"

Al-Husseini grabbed the back of an armchair to
eady himself as the private car continued to rattle
the rails on a steep incline, swaying. Outside the
arded-up windows, the blizzard buffetted the train
th increasing force.

"With all due respect, Your Excellency," Juttner
plied, "I guaranteed no such thing. I merely stated
at I would do my best to accommodate Your Excel-
ncy's wishes. It cannot be helped that there were no
ehrmacht or SS units near Bljak that could spare
hicles adequate for your journey to Belgrade, nor
n it be helped that I was unable to make contact
th any German units at all until just before the train
lled into Bljak to take on water. You must under-
and, Your Excellency, that there is a war on, and
litary forces may not always be exactly where we

271

expect them to be—nor able to render spur-of-t
moment assistance."

"Do not lecture me, Hauptsturmfuehrer!"
Husseini raged. "You will not lecture *me* on li
realities!"

Juttner waved a languid hand. "Perish the thou;
Your Exellency," he said mildly. "I certainly did
mean to give offense—"

"Well, you have! You have given offense! I
offended!"

"Your Excellency—"

"I am offended by your inappropriate manner
speaking *and* I am offended that my simple requ
for safe conduct to Belgrade has been disregarde
The mufti was now a deep shade of purple. "I
offended by the callous attitude of Standartenfueh
Kronstadt! I am offended by Hauptsturmfuehrer N
rath's persistent surliness and the transparent acrim
between the two of you! *I am offended, Hauptstur
fuehrer Juttner!*"

"A veritable bounty of offenses," Juttner mutte;
casually, looking off to one side.

"What?"

"A regrettable sequence of events, I said, Your I
cellency," the elegant SS officer replied, raising
voice again. "I can only hope to make amends or
we reach the field headquarters of the SS Divisi
Handschar at the Zpoda Skyway Bridge." He smi
ruefully, with a sympathetic cast to his eyes. "For t!
is surely where we are going to end up now."

"But it is not what I wanted!" the Grand Mt
opined, throwing a hand up into the air in disbeli
"I specifically stated that I do not want to be expos
to the hazards of a front-line position! I was to cond
lectures for visiting imams from a safe zone—such
Belgrade!"

"That is what you told the Fuehrer?" Juttner inquir
knowing full well it wasn't.

"Yes, of course," al-Husseini snapped indignantly.
And who are you to question me?"

Juttner raised a palm. "Your pardon, Your Excel-
ncy. I was merely inquiring into the original details
your plan to tour Handschar, to which I was not
ivy."

"Where is Neurath?" the mufti demanded. "I have
ot seen him since discovering your turpitude at Bljak.
e must account for his part in this deluge of
angling."

"In his room, I believe," Juttner said, extracting a
gar from its case.

"Snagi!" al-Husseini declared, clasping his hands
hind his back and pacing hunchbacked up the car-
t. "Get Hauptsturmfuehrer Neurath out of his
om. And bring me a tonic at once!"

The silent Macedonian, who had been standing at
e end of the dining table with his arms folded, imme-
ately walked across the car, entered the room-access
ssageway, and rapped on Neurath's door.

The door clicked open an inch. Neurath's blue eye
ared out.

"His Excellency wishes to see you," Mustapha Snagi
uttered. He turned and left.

Neurath closed the door. His trousers, which he had
st pulled on, were still open at the front. He but-
ned them up. A trickle of sweat ran down the center
f his bare chest, and as he reached for his shirt, he
ked the naked girl lying on the tangled sheets of his
unk with a cold stare.

"No noise," he said in Serbo-Croatian. "I will keep
ou for a few days, and if you cooperate, I may send
ou back to Bljak with some money in your pocket.
erhaps some vouchers for food, yes?" His pale face
visted. "But if you do not obey me, you will be given
o the regular soldiers—or worse. I am Gestapo. . . .
nd you know what that means, don't you?"

The girl, her long, dark hair matted around her

shoulders, pulled up a rumpled sheet to cover hers
She appeared to be in shock.

"Don't you, little one?" Neurath hissed sudder
leaning forward.

The girl's eyes darted to his and she let out a we
yelp, hugging the sheet. "Ye . . . yes, sir,"
whispered.

Neurath straightened and began to put on his u
form shirt. "Good. Very good. Now wash yourself
the sink and keep absolutely quiet until I return.
not open the door for anyone who knocks, and do
speak if they call. Do you understand me?"

"Yes . . . yes. I-I understand, sir. . . ."

"Wish we could make a goddamn fire," Brist
grumbled, squatting down and prying the lid off
small tin of bully beef. He gestured at the half-do
guttering candle stubs that had been set up on
cave floor in a two-foot circle. "Them little basta
don't throw much heat."

Stirling passed him another olive green tin. "He
mate. Warm that bully up with this. It goes down e
ier if you melt the grease and soften the bone chip
He grinned.

"Hey, thanks," Bristow said, taking it. "What is it

"Jellied fuel. Our version of what you Yanks c
canned heat or Sterno."

Bristow nodded and set the bully beef down to op
the second can. "Thanks, Colin."

"Let's be careful with food smells," Merritt sa
pulling a steel cup and spoon from a packsack.
was sitting against a boulder on the opposite side
the candle circle. "Don't burn anything or boil ar
thing but water. It's not very likely to attract attentic
but we're close to the garrison and some of those
trols may have dogs."

Bristow flicked open his Zippo and lit the purp
gel inside the can. "Don't worry, Major. I'm j
gonna take the frost off this dog food before I e

" He shivered momentarily inside his combat jacket.
Brrr! It's goddamn cold in here. Good thing we
ought them three mules in, too. They'll warm the
ace up some."

"It's colder out there," Weiss remarked, chewing on
K-ration bar. "And it sounds like the wind's pick-
g up."

"It definitely is," Cernović said. He was seated be-
een Weiss and Merritt on a canvas groundsheet.
And it's snowing hard. But that's a good thing. It
ll cover our tracks and hopefully the explosives on
e bridge footings."

"Sentries aren't as observant and patrols aren't as
tive in blizzards," Merritt said. "If we didn't have
 climb back up that head wall to place those other
o sets of charges and finish stringing the detonator
rd, the snowstorm would be nothing but a good
ing for us." He glanced over at Bristow. "It's going
 be tough, whether it stops snowing by nightfall or
t."

Stirling cleared his throat. "Sir, do you want me to
me along this time? I haven't climbed yet."

Merritt shook his head. "No, Sergeant. Bristow and
 will handle it. I have something else in mind for
u." He looked around the cave at his companions.
n fact, this is the point at which some of us split off
d concentrate on tasks other than blowing up the
poda Skyway Bridge."

Everyone seated within the flickering candlelight
used and looked up. "How's that?" Weiss inquired.

"I'm dividing the team," Merritt said. "Most nota-
y, Captain Throckmorton and Sergeant Stirling will
 leaving later this morning, after they get a few
urs' sleep. The rest of us will concentrate on the
ining of the bridge. Our latest information, provided
 Commander Cernović"—Merritt nodded in the
artisan's direction—"indicates that a military train
aded with King Tiger tanks will arrive at the fortified
alet near the north tunnel sometime around mid-

night, and attempt to cross the bridge to Mount Zpc
soon after."

"King Tigers?" Bristow said. "That what you a
the commander here were whisperin' about all
way along Zlostup?"

"Yes," Merritt said. "Intelligence update. Instead
just blowing the bridge, we now want to blow
bridge with the train on it. So timing suddenly
comes a factor."

"And a variable," Cernović added.

Merritt nodded again. "And a variable. We have
be ready to set off the charges whenever the tr.
moves out onto that bridge."

"I don't like Tiger tanks," Bristow muttered.
person can get seriously killed messin' with Ti
tanks."

"That's why they're going to the bottom of
gorge along with the bridge," Merritt said, "wh
they can't do any harm. If we have our way, that
He paused. "Which brings me to Professor Quisp.

The wild-eyed Englishman was squatting quietly
a little shelf of rock behind Weiss and Cerno
"What-ho?" he declared.

"I have a job for you, if you'd like to continue he
ing us," Merritt said. "I want to know exactly wh
that train arrives, especially if we happen to be up
the cliff when it does. It shouldn't be here that ear
but we'll chance blowing just the two supports we
already got mined if we're caught short of time. A
way, I need a train lookout."

"Capital! Splendid!" Quisp enthused, leaping to
feet. "I'm your man. Approach with stealth and mo
tor the buggers, eh? Well, let me tell you, Major-
Zulu leopard soldier—"

"—can't hold a candle to Professor Quisp when
comes to stalking," Stirling cut in, looking sideways
the demonstrative academic. "He gets around pre
quietly, Major. I can vouch for it."

"So I've noticed," Merritt said. "Anyway, I do

ant to count on the chance that the train may sound
s whistle as it reaches the chalet. A lot of military
ains don't use their whistles. I want to know when
's coming, preferably while it's still down below the
st ridgeline, about half an hour away."

"I know the very thing, old fellow," Quisp declared.
A gamekeeper's cabin on that ridge, some distance
om the tracks. It's abandoned, with the roof partly
ived in, and I doubt if the Huns use it for anything
r have anyone stationed near it. It's about two miles
orth of here and a quarter mile east of the rail line.
othing around it but scrub forest. From there I can
oot the train while it's still a long way down the
rade."

"How will you signal us if you see it?" Merritt
ked.

"There's the rub," Quisp said. "Can't chance a flare,
in't fire a series of shots without arousing suspicion.
ll just have to hoof it back to the gorge rim if the
ain manifests itself, what? Tell you myself, won't I?
es, I will."

"You can cover two miles through heavy snow that
ast? Without getting caught?"

Quisp rolled his crazed eyes. "You haven't been
stening, dear boy. A Zulu leopard soldier has nothing
n—"

"Of course, Professor," Merritt interrupted, smiling.
I forgot. Very well. I'll leave the spotting of the train
) you."

"Marvelous!" Quisp pronounced, hopping down off
ie ledge and slinging his Schmeisser over his shoul-
er. "Well, I'm off!" He strode across the cave toward
ie narrow entrance passage, pulling his hood up over
is head. Two seconds later he was gone.

"No quotations this time," Stirling commented.
Thank the Lord for small blessings."

"Here," Bristow said, holding out a steaming tin.
Have some hot bully beef. Warm you up."

"Appreciate it, mate."

A sound halfway between a sigh and a moan car
from the darkness at the rear of the cave, followed
a rustling of cloth.

"I'd better have a look at her before we continue
Merritt said, starting to rise.

"Don't bother," Sylvia said, her voice quiet b
steady. She walked into the flickering candlelight b
tween Bristow and Stirling, her hands in the pock
of the baggy greatcoat she was wearing. There was
slight hitch in her usual gliding step.

She squatted down on her haunches and gazed
the candles from beneath her hooded lids, her sm
mouth fixed in a frown.

"How are you feeling?" Merritt asked.

"Foolish," Sylvia replied.

Bristow scraped the bottom of his bully-beef
with his spoon. "What for?" he asked. "Not getti
killed?"

The small frown turned into a small smile. "Partly
she said. "But mostly for overextending myself, fallin
and then losing my nerve on the head wall."

Merritt waved a hand. "Understandable. You we
exhausted, trying to climb in impossible conditions.
could have happened to anyone."

Sylvia looked at him. "But it happened to *me*," s
said. She looked back at the candles. "A thing li
that does not happen to me."

"Well, it won't again," Merritt said, putting a t
bag into a cup of hot water. "Sergeant Bristow and
will finish setting the charges tonight. You'll stay
lookout with Commander Cernović and Sergea
Weiss at the Zlostup trailhead, below the tunnel."

She kept looking into the candle flame. "You dor
trust me on the rock anymore."

"I didn't say that," Merritt countered. "You did t
hardest part: you made that free-climbing ascent fro
Zlostup to the first footing and established the ma
rope. You got us across to the second footing usi
that tiny horizontal crack, which looks to be the mo

fficult of the three traverses between bridge sup-
orts. Sergeant Bristow and I can handle the rest. We
ansferred the main ascent rope to the second footing
d left it hanging there, so we can climb back up
thout any trouble."

"How will you get across to the third and fourth
otings?"

"If we can't free-climb the traverses like you, we'll
e a few pitons," Merritt said.

"The Nazis might hear you," Sylvia pointed out. "I
n do it without a sound."

Merritt looked at her for a long moment.

"No," he said finally.

"Why?"

"Because you've done enough. Bristow and I will
ish mining the bridge supports."

"You're afraid I'll freeze," Sylvia said. "Lose my
erve on the rock again."

Merritt pulled the tea bag out of the cup of hot
ater and tossed it into the corner of the cave. "I
on't think that would happen," he replied quietly,
ut I can't take the chance."

Sylvia drew a deep breath. "I won't freeze. I won't.
/hat happened to me has passed, Major. And I can
imb that rock better than either you or Sergeant
ristow."

Merritt shook his head and sipped carefully at the
m of his steaming cup. "No."

Sylvia grimaced and turned to look directly at him
nce more. "If you start pounding pitons into that
iff, you and Sergeant Bristow run the risk of alerting
e Germans," she said. "You may be shot off the
ead wall, and the explosives discovered. The entire
ission, all this effort, would be a waste—along with
e lives of your Sergeant Hurst and Sergeant
'Amato." Her eyes shifted to Stirling and Bristow
nd back to Merritt again. "And besides, no En-
lishman tells me what to do and when to do it! I—"

"You are wrong, Miss Kozo," Merritt cut in, setting

his cup down. "In this case, an Englishman—me—telling you what to do. . . . And you will do exac that. You will not climb that head wall again. Perio

"You are—"

"In command here!" Merritt's voice was stee "And I have a mission to accomplish. That missi takes precedence over your desire to indulge in so kind of dramatic atonement for your paralysis on t cliff. This operation is not a stage upon which you c flog your immaturity and self-absorption, Miss Ko You can engineer your personal catharsis on your o time. Right now, you will do as you're told. You v obey orders like any other soldier—if that is tr what you consider yourself to be."

Sylvia blinked at him, then looked at Cernović. T swarthy Partisan commander was lying back on o elbow, chewing slowly on a ration bar. He return Sylvia's glance without expression, then looked across the cave and continued to eat.

Abruptly she got to her feet and stomped off ir the darkness. The action was very much like that a spoiled child—a fact that was not lost on any of t men sitting around the circle of candles. Sylvia Ko could not have proven Merritt's curt assessment of h any better if she'd done it on paper. There was a lig thump as she threw herself down on her makesh pallet of tarpaulins at the rear of the cave.

"I say, gentlemen—how do I look?"

Throckmorton emerged from a dark corner whe he'd been rummaging for the past forty minutes. Br tow, Stirling, Weiss, and Cernović stared. He w dressed in the field uniform of an officer of the Division Handschar, complete with swastika-an scimitar emblem on the collar and death's-head insi nia on the gray fez cocked on top of his head.

Merritt smiled over his tea. "You look like a rig old goose-stepper," he said. "Handschar style."

Throckmorton adjusted the fez slightly. "Than awfully, old bean," he drawled. "I wouldn't want

ve come all this way and not pass muster." He
ughed suddenly, turned his head, and spat into the
rkness. "Ugh."

Bristow was cleaning his fingernails with his jump
ife. "So, Major . . . since we've waded this far up
e creek together, what is it with that cough of yours?
ou've been spittin' up like a lunger since we first
et in Scotland. If I was any kind of a sawbones, I'd
y you had yourself a whoppin' case of the con-
mption."

Throckmorton wiped his lips on the back of his
nd. "And you'd be wrong, Sergeant," he said. He
cked eyes with Merritt for a moment. "I do not have
berculosis. I have wet pneumonia that has been slow
go away, that's all."

Bristow looked up at him and slid his jump knife
ck into its boot scabbard. "If you say so, Captain."
e refrained from asking why a sick man would have
en sent on a dangerous, physically demanding mis-
on in an occupied country at all.

Merritt got to his feet. "I'm glad you were still here
hen we got off the cliff, Duncan. But it really is
ing to be good-bye this time, isn't it?"

" 'Fraid so, old man." Throckmorton grinned sud-
enly. "The game's on now, and no mistake." He
anced down. "Sergeant Stirling."

"Sir."

"Over in that suitcase you'll find the field uniform
f an SS private first class, coincidentally just your
ze. Please put it on, and make sure you keep your
irt and stripes on underneath it. That way, if you're
aptured, there's at least a small chance you won't be
xecuted on the spot for not wearing your own
niform."

Stirling hesitated for only a second. "That's a cold
omfort, sir," he said, "but I'll take a small chance
ver no chance at all." As he headed for the rear of
e cave, unbuttoning his combat jacket, he let out a
ry chuckle. "This mission's getting more interesting

all the time. From British sergeant to Nazi Sturmm
in one fell swoop—complete with uniform switch."

"I'll fill you in as we make our way toward [
garrison," Throckmorton said. "In the meantime, y
need to collect your complete kit, and wrap that [
field in strip cloth from muzzle to butt plate so
doesn't look like anything but a Mauser. We'll be le;
ing in about two hours."

"Yes, sir."

Merritt put a hand on Throckmorton's should
"Get that two hours' sleep, Duncan. I'll wake y
when it's time to leave."

"All right, old man."

Merritt returned to his boulder and sat down w
his back to it. Pulling his collar up and his black l
laclava down over his ears and neck, he crossed l
arms and stretched-out legs, settled back, and clos
his eyes. Bristow and Cernović, taking their cue fr¢
him like the experienced hands they were, rolled o\
on their backs and likewise tried for some slee
Throckmorton and Stirling were rustling quie¹
through clothing and equipment. Sylvia was dead
lent in the darkness at the rear of the cave, and Qui
was gone. The mules nickered softly, herding togeth
for warmth. Outside the wind whined and moan¢
past the cliff—a lonely, primordial sound. A few str
snowflakes floated into the cave through the e
trance passage.

Weiss spoke: "Major."

"Mmf . . . what is it?"

"What's going on, sir? What are we doing?"

There was a pause before Merritt answered. "Wh
you're doing, Sergeant, is supporting the demoliti¢
of the Zpoda Skyway Bridge, hopefully with the Ki
Tiger train on it. You're with me—as are Command
Cernović, Sergeant Bristow, and Miss Kozo. Capta
Throckmorton has a separate task to accomplish, f
which he can use the assistance of Sergeant Stirlin
The original mission always had two parts—one

ich was my priority, and the other Captain Throck-
orton's. None of you needed to know that until now,
you weren't told."

Weiss's voice was very quiet. "What exactly *is* Cap-
in Throckmorton's objective, sir?"

Merritt sighed, and settled himself more comfort-
ly against the boulder. "You still don't need to
ow that, Sergeant Weiss," he said.

It was snowing hard in London, too, the wet, heavy
akes of southern England drifting down to accumu-
te six inches deep on the windowsills of the Prime
inister's residence. Seated at the great desk in his
udy, Churchill poured more sherry into a cut-crystal
ass and pushed it across the polished walnut top.

"Have another, Martin," he said in his rumble of a
ice. "I think the present circumstances justify it."

The elegant, white-haired industrialist seated oppo-
e Churchill ceded a slight smile. "Well, I don't often
dulge in refills, Winston. You know that. Even during
rictly social engagements I usually end up watering
e potted plants on the sly with them."

"No wonder my ficus trees are looking sickly,"
hurchill remarked. "And I thought it was the
eather." The two men exchanged a brief laugh.
Come now, Martin," the Prime Minister said, tapping
e glass. "On occasion it's good for the nerves."

The white-haired man picked up the glass and
pped it forward. "Your health, Winston," he said.

"And yours."

The two old friends drank. Martin Judson held his
ass thoughtfully in his lap as Churchill selected a
gar from the box on his desk and proceeded to clip
e end of it with a sterling silver cutter.

"Stop worrying," he growled, without looking up.

Judson shifted in his chair. "When was the last
mmunication?"

"Twelve hours ago. Nothing since."

"The train must be well up into the Majevicas by

now." He took a small sip of sherry. "When do y
think we might hear something?"

"Menzies' people have received no further messa
from Berlin as yet," Churchill said. "Unfortunate
it's just a wait-and-see proposition, Martin. That's
I can say, and you know it."

"Yes, I do," Judson replied. "That's the trouble

Churchill lit the cigar and drew on it until the e
was glowing like a miniature furnace. A great p
of aromatic smoke began to collect in the air ab
the desk.

"It's going to be fine," he said. "With him it alw.
is, because he's always smarter than everyc
around him."

Judson looked at the Prime Minister, then out
frost-etched windows at the falling snow. "How ma
incredibly smart people have we lost in the past s
eral years because the infinitely more stupid peop
surrounding them finally managed to put two and t
together and not get five, Winston?"

Churchill harrumphed and drew on his cigar, frov
ing. "Have some more sherry, Martin," he said.

Chapter Sixteen

Ready, Sergeant?" Throckmorton muttered through the scarf covering most of his face.

"As ready as I'll ever be, sir," Stirling answered.

"Then let's go."

Throckmorton stepped out from the behind the scrub trees at the edge of the rail bed and made his way quickly—but not too quickly—up onto the train tracks. Stirling followed, a bulky figure in white hooded anorak, German helmet, and scarved face, rucksack on his back and cloth-wrapped rifle slung over one shoulder. Throckmorton, too, wore the German winter camouflage parka, but with his head almost completely wrapped in scarves, leaving only a slit for his eyes. Under the coat's white hood, he also wore an officer's Bergmütze mountain cap.

The snow was still falling very heavily, and although it was now close to noon, the dense overcast of the blizzard kept the daylight muted almost to a twilight level. Up ahead, perhaps two hundred yards away, Throckmorton could just make out the looming gray

mass of the fortified chalet, and below it to the l
the dark arched entrance of the northern bridge t
nel. Coming up on the right side of the main line
a switching signal for the small siding that paralle
the primary tracks and dead-ended in front of the c
let. The dim figures of at least a dozen soldiers, sin
and in pairs, were moving in the area between
chalet and tunnel entrance.

Throckmorton and Stirling walked together do
the tracks, keeping to the cross ties between the ra
Stirling staying a pace or two behind his captain. Th
moved purposefully but unhurriedly, like soldiers f
lowing routine. There was a pair of what seemed
be sentries hanging on the left bank of the prim
rail line, across from the walled chalet's main gate.
avoid them, Throckmorton veered unobtrusively
the right, following the siding tracks.

He saw the sentries' body language change as th
noticed him, saw them stiffen and orient toward
two new arrivals. He did not alter his stride as
approached, and trusted that Stirling would do the sa
Indifferent confidence was the key. However, if th
were challenged, asked for a password, things co
get a bit sticky. . . .

As he drew near, the two sentries came to attenti
and gave him the Nazi salute. He returned it casua
and strode on past without giving them a second lo
He could hear Stirling's boots crunching in the d
snow behind him. Two seconds went by. Five secon
Ten. But no verbal challenge came. Throckmorton
out a long breath through his scarf and started
the short incline between the siding tracks and
chalet gate.

The gate was a twelve-foot-high archway in t
twenty-foot stone wall. Its massive wooden doors we
pulled back, and a sentry stood to one side of the e
trance. Both Throckmorton and Stirling noted the sa
bagged machine-gun positions next to each of the t

orner guardhouses in view atop the wall, and the
aired guards manning them.

The sentry at the gate seemed, unfortunately, to be
ttentive to his duties, despite being obviously very
old. He stepped forward, shivering, as Throckmorton
nd Stirling approached, his Schmeisser slung across
ne front of his snow-powdered greatcoat, his free
and moving up in a halt gesture. . . .

"My God, man," Throckmorton said in perfect Ger-
an, "haven't you had the hot soup ration yet? You
ook half frozen."

The Muslim trooper, who had learned the command
anguage of the SS only in the past year during divi-
on training in France, and then only partly, lowered
is hand. "Your pardon, Herr—?" His eyes roved
uickly over Throckmorton's clothing, searching for
n insignia of rank.

"Sturmbannfuehrer," Throckmorton filled in for
im. "Sturmbannfuehrer Mendel. Carrying intelli-
ence updates from the western flank to Standarten-
uehrer Zweig."

The Muslim private licked his lips. Throckmorton
ould see him thinking: *An SS major—and an SS
najor entrusted with intelligence reports for the divi-
ion commander.*

"Answer me, Schütze," Throckmorton demanded,
a a tone that was neither hostile nor friendly. "Have
ou or have you not had the hot soup ration today?"

"Er . . . *nein*, Herr Sturmbannfuehrer . . ."

Throckmorton shook his head in disgust. "Ridicu-
ous," he said. He turned and looked at Stirling.
Even the first pair of sentries who challenged us this
norning had their ration, didn't they, Suljak?"

Stirling nodded. "*Jawohl*, Herr Sturmbannfuehrer,"
e grunted through his scarf.

"And the second pair and the pair after that,"
'hrockmorton went on, turning back to the sentry.
'And yet the cooks forget the man at their very gate."

He eyed the Muslim private sympathetically. "W
this won't do. Suljak: I want a double ration of
soup and a half ration of bread—hot bread, w
butter—brought to this man immediately after we
port to Standartenfuehrer Zweig's office. See to it.

"*Jawohl,* Herr Sturmbannfuehrer," Stirling grunt
again.

"Um—" the sentry began.

Throckmorton clapped a gloved hand onto the p
vate's shoulder and squeezed good-naturedly. "Damn
inefficiency. The fools in their warm kitchens ke
forgetting that an army marches on its stomach. We
if that doesn't include the good soldier faithfu
standing guard in a blizzard, who does it includ
Eh?" He clapped the shoulder again, making the se
try stagger sideways a step.

"Er—" the soldier said.

"Your name, trooper, so I can mention your go
conduct to Standartenfuehrer Zweig."

"Ah—Fikret Pandža, Herr Sturmbannfuehrer. Schüt
Fikret Pandža."

Throckmorton stepped back and regarded the se
try approvingly. "Very good, Schütze Pandža," he d
clared. "Very good indeed. Carry on!" He stood the
plainly waiting for a salute.

The sentry got his heels together and snapped
arm out. "*Jawohl,* Herr Sturmbannfuehrer!"

Throckmorton flipped his hand back, turned brisk
and stalked through the gate toward the cha
greathouse, with Stirling close behind.

"Sergeant Weiss," Merritt said. "Wake up."

Weiss pushed himself up to a sitting position, yaw
ing. He rubbed his eyes and looked around him. T
candles had burned down to stubs; only four of t
original six were still alight. The cave was as dark a
cold as ever, except that now it also stank of mu
dung. Cernović was still sleeping nearby, flat on h
back in his heavy winter coat with his arms folde

cross his chest, as was Bristow. The big American
ergeant was snoring gently in a rumbling baritone.

The young commando looked over his shoulder
>ward the rear of the cave. Sylvia, wrapped in layers
f winter clothing and a canvas groundsheet, was an
ndistinct lump in the meager glow of the candles.
'loser to the mules were several rucksacks of gear
nd the suitcase that had contained the German uni-
>rms worn by Throckmorton and Stirling.

Merritt was sitting on his boulder, waiting, a weath-
rproof document folder in one hand. He was looking
nto the darkness without expression.

Weiss eased onto one knee, stiff from lying on the
old stone of the cave floor. "You want me, Major?"
e whispered.

"I do," Merritt replied. "Come here."

Weiss did so, squatting in front of Merritt and
tretching his aching back. "Yes, sir." He glanced
round the cave again. "Captain Throckmorton and
ergeant Stirling—they've left already?"

"An hour ago," Merritt said. "They're no longer
our concern."

Weiss looked at him. Merritt's voice held the same
teely edge that earlier had stopped Sylvia Kozo in
er tracks.

"Yes, sir," he said quietly.

There was a pause. Merritt gazed down at the docu-
nent folder in his hand. For a brief second, Weiss had
he impression that the man was gathering himself.
'hen Merritt spoke:

"You're familiar with the Grand Mufti of Jerusa-
em, Haj Amin al-Husseini?"

Weiss's eyes widened. The name was anathema to
member of the Jewish Brigade.

Merritt waited.

"I know who he is," Weiss said.

"Good. Do you know what he looks like?"

"I have a vague idea."

Merritt opened the document folder and extracted

a five-by-seven-inch black-and-white photograph. "H
looks like this," he said, holding out the picture.

Weiss took it, leaned down, and picked up the st
of one of the candles. He examined the photo by t
light of the guttering flame. Merritt watched hi
closely. The young sergeant's face seemed to conto
as he surveyed the mufti's neatly barbered featur
Muslim cleric's headdress, and robe.

Weiss lowered the photograph. "Why are you sho
ing me this?" he asked tightly.

"That individual," Merritt said, "is one of the wor
enemies the Jewish people have got. He is a N
collaborator who advocates the extermination of t
Jews in Europe so that they cannot emigrate or I
transported to Palestine. He is responsible for the r
cruiting of thousands of Muslims into Heinrich Himn
ler's SS Division Handschar."

Weiss looked down at the photograph again, the
handed it back. "I know this," he muttered. "Wh
does it have to do with—"

"Sometime tonight," Merritt said, "the train v
have come to destroy along with the Zpoda Skyw
Bridge will arrive at that chalet over there. The Gran
Mufti of Jerusalem will be on it."

Weiss was dead silent.

"He was to give a series of inspirational lectures
the imams in charge of the spiritual welfare and m
rale of the Muslim soldiers in Handschar. He hope
to do this from the safety of Belgrade—or at lea
some point well behind the front lines." Merri
paused. "Chance and circumstance have redirecte
him here."

Merritt did not look at Weiss as he extracted a se
ond photograph from the document folder. Then l
raised his eyes and fixed the young sergeant with
penetrating gaze.

"Just a few weeks ago," he said, "the mufti was tl
target of an assassination attempt in Berlin. It wa

ery nearly successful. His bodyguards, however, were ole to intervene and kill the assassin."

Weiss swallowed as Merritt went on:

"The assassin was a young Jew, a member of the ewish Agency out of Cairo and, at the time, an active OE cooperative. He had been deeply under cover in ne heart of Berlin, in disguise, for nearly four months. Vaiting for a chance to kill the Grand Mufti of Jerusa-m. He gave his life trying to accomplish this.

"His name was Aaron Weiss. He was your brother." Merritt held out the second photograph.

"This is what they did to him."

The stark image of the young man who had tried o assassinate Haj Amin al-Husseini outside the Hotel irgenplatz was truly horrible. He was pictured from ead to midthigh, naked, on some kind of metal slab. Iis well-muscled body was black with numerous bullet oles, slash wounds, and contusions. His dark hair was frayed mat, his once handsome face bloated and dis-orted in death, the jaw broken. His eyes appeared to ave been punctured by a knife blade or spike. His bdomen had been laid open, the intestines visible. His enitals were half gone, mutilated and partly torn away.

Merritt got up and walked slowly toward the ruck-acks at the rear of the cave.

From Sergeant David Weiss, hunched over the pho-ograph holding the stub of a flickering candle, there ame a muffled choking sound.

Merritt picked up Throckmorton's suitcase and, tak-ng his time, carried it back to the boulder on which e'd been sitting. He set it down in front of Weiss.

"In here you'll find one more SS field uniform," e said, "complete with full white winter camouflage norak and trousers. You will also find one .45 caliber)e Lisle fully silenced short carbine, painted white, vith sixty rounds of ammunition. There is a cloth car-ying sheath for it, as well, which makes it look a ommon German artillery spotting scope.

"You speak fluent German and adequate Serb
Croatian. You are a crack shot. Before the King Tig
train crosses the bridge, the mufti's private car w
almost certainly be moved onto a short siding in fro
of the chalet and uncoupled, as it is his mobile ba
of operations and there is no reason to expose it—
him—to the fighting front. He will be received by t
division commander, which means that at some poi
he will have to leave the car." Merritt let a beat pa
"A man with your abilities should be able to find
way to get close enough."

Through the hot tears stinging his eyes, through t
grief that threatened to close his throat, and throu
the fierce rage rising in him like a flood, Weiss cou
hear, echoing in his head with haunting clarity, t
words of General Sir Colin McVean Gubbins:

*Anyone in our business can find himself in the po.
tion of having to use lies or manipulation, even w
respect to allies, to achieve an immediate goal. Cou
you respect the higher motive, even if it was done
you?*

"This was . . . all set up . . . in advance," Wei
croaked. "You must have had this picture of . . . m
brother . . . before we left Bari." He let the photogra\
slip from his hand. "Where's . . . where's his body?"

Merritt shook his head. "It was in Berlin when th
picture was taken. By now it will have been di
posed of."

"How did you get hold of that . . . that phot
graph?"

Merritt suddenly became aware that Cernović ar
Bristow were both wide awake and watching the e
change intently. He ignored Weiss's last question.

"You have an opportunity to finish your brother
mission and avenge him at the same time," he sai
"by killing the man most responsible for his deat
You also have an opportunity to rid the Jewish peop
of one of their worst enemies."

Weiss hung his head. "You set me up," he repeate

'You . . . Gubbins . . . whoever provided you with
that picture from Berlin . . . all of you."

"The mufti was going to be in Yugoslavia at the
time of Operation Handschar," Merritt said. "His
presence in the country was a bonus that couldn't be
ignored. The only thing we didn't know was exactly
where he'd be—Belgrade, Zagreb, or closer to the
front."

"So you attached a Jewish commando who didn't
know he had a dead brother to your team," Weiss
filled in, regaining partial control of himself, "knowing
that if you unleashed him somewhere near the mufti
after telling him about his brother, there wouldn't be
any chance he wouldn't take—anything he wouldn't
risk—in order to hunt him down. Like cutting a cannon loose on a rolling deck to see what it hits."

Merritt's face was impassive. "You don't have to
go," he said simply.

Weiss looked at the suitcase. Then he got to his
feet, picked it up by the handle, and carried it over
to his groundsheet.

"Of course I do," he said, setting the suitcase down.
"And you know it. You've always known it—even
when I didn't."

He knelt in front of the suitcase and opened it, and
said nothing more.

Standartenfuehrer Egon Zweig had just pulled on
his black leather gloves and was reaching for his winter coat when he sensed the door opening behind him.
Irritated, he took the coat from its hanger and began
to brush the lint off, without bothering to turn around.
Feder, his regular aide, hadn't announced any visitors,
and he was about to take his daily constitutional: a
walk down the north tunnel and back.

"Who are you and what do you want?" he demanded snappishly. "You don't enter my office without first identifying yourself to my aide and being
announced."

"Your pardon, Herr Standartenfuehrer," a muffle
voice said. "Your aide is not at his desk. Perhaps h
has stepped out."

Zweig's irritability flared. "What? Impossible." H
turned on his heel. "He had better be at his . .
desk . . . " His voice trailed off. Standing in the midd
of the chalet common room were two tall men in win
ter camouflage—one obviously an officer, since h
wore the Bergmütze under his anorak hood. The
faces were completely obscured by scarves, and bot
were caked with snow from head to foot.

There was something intimidating about then
something predatory in their poise, that had mad
Zweig lapse into involuntary silence. They were Jag
kommando, he decided. Most of them had that unse
tling, latent lethality.

"I'm busy," Zweig said, walking forward and stand
ing behind his desk. He folded his coat over his arm
"I also don't like to repeat myself: who are you an
what do you want?"

The officer pushed back his hood and began to ur
wrap the first of the two scarves that covered his fac
"My name is Zwilling," he said, "and I have a que
tion for you."

Zweig was appalled by the man's effrontery. H
could feel the the flush rising to his cheeks. "Rank
damn you!" he barked.

The officer continued to unwrap his scarves. "Star
dartenfuehrer," he said.

Zweig gaped. "Wh-what?"

"Standartenfuehrer, Herr Standartenfuehrer."

The other soldier moved slowly off to one side.

Zweig came around the desk. "What is this non
sense?" he exclaimed, clenching a fist. "You are insub
ordinate! You—"

He stopped in his tracks as the last scarf fell awa
from the officer's face. His eyes widened and his jav
went slack.

'hrockmorton grinned at him. "My question is,
ndartenfuehrer Zweig: would you like to retire?"
It—it can't . . . *be*!" Zweig whispered, staring.
ou . . . you're . . ." His eyes remained fixed on
ockmorton as the British captain began to circle
.

'Unbelievably handsome?" Throckmorton drawled
English.

weig sucked in breath for a yell—and in one light-
g motion, Stirling snapped a wire garotte down
r his head and around his neck. The German com-
nder's eyes popped and his tongue bulged from his
uth. Stirling crossed his powerful forearms, cinch-
the garotte, spun 180 degrees, and leaned forward.
eig's booted feet came off the floor. Stirling carried
, back to back, across the room to a small walk-
closet. Throckmorton opened the door. Stirling
pped inside, with Zweig still thrashing energetically.
only sound was a low, horrific gurgling.

Throckmorton was about to follow when a knock
the main entrance of the office stopped him. He
lded to Stirling and hurriedly shut the closet door.
ossing the room, he began to shed his winter
thing.

'Yes?" he called out. "Speak, but do not enter. I
busy."

There was silence outside the door, then a voice:
'It is Hauptsturmfuehrer Haak, sir. I—"

'Can you not announce yourself through Feder,
uptsturmfuehrer?" Five minutes earlier, in the pro-
s of eliminating Zweig's aide, Throckmorton had
ted the nameplate on the outer desk. "These sud-
n interruptions are most distracting." He bundled
: winter camouflage anorak and tucked it behind a
ng cabinet. His gloves and undercoat he threw onto
orner armchair.

'Untersturmfuehrer Feder is not here, Herr Stand-
enfuehrer," Haak said.

There was a rattling thump and the closet
jumped on its hinges as something—probably a b
ing boot—walloped it from the inside. Throckmo
cast an anxious glance that way as he hurried ac
the common room to Zweig's desk, smoothing
blond hair into place with the palm of his hand.
dropped into the commander's oak swivel chair
picked up a sheaf of reports just as Haak's v
came again:

"Is there something wrong, Herr Standar
fuehrer?" The main office door unlatched and sw
open a couple of inches. "Herr Standartenfuehre

"Come in if you must, Haak," Throckmorton ca
swiveling the chair so that his back was to the d
He pulled a small Walther pistol from his unif
pocket, tucked it between his legs, and began sor
through the reports.

There was a creak of hinges and a clicking of j
boots as Haak entered and proceeded across the c
mon room. Throckmorton gave him time to co
within what sounded like ten feet of the desk and t
swung around to face him.

Haak looked at his commanding officer, came
attention with a curt smile and a click of his he
and snapped off a Nazi salute.

"Heil Hitler!" he said.

Throckmorton nodded and flipped his hand ba
"Heil Hitler," he echoed. He glanced back dowr
his reports. "Where is Feder, Haak?"

The SS Hauptsturmfuehrer stood easy and s
Throckmorton a puzzled look. "I have no idea wh
your aide is, sir."

"Don't be impertinent, Haak," Throckmorton :
idly. "I was merely wondering if you happened
know." He peered up at the combat officer. Haak
a big man, rangy and tough looking, with a tr
Aryan hawk face.

Haak was looking back at him. "Do you feel

t, sir? You seem rather pale, and your voice—
—it sounds odd."

Another damned cold," Throckmorton said,
ghing for effect. "It started coming on last night.
survive, I suppose." Noticing the carved box on
corner of the desk, he reached over, opened it,
extracted a cigarette. "Cigarette, Haak? Help
rself."

Haak was taken aback. It was the first time in their
re two-year association that Standartenfuehrer
on Zweig had offered him anything. His brow fur-
ing, he stepped forward and selected a cigarette.
aank you, sir. I've run out of my own."

Don't mention it," Throckmorton said, sliding a
of wooden matches across the desktop at the same
e as he transferred the Walther to an open desk
wer and pushed it shut. "Now, what can I do for
?"

*What in the name of Odin has infected Zweig's brain
morning,* Haak wondered as he lit the cigarette.
e commander was positively amiable—not to men-
n relaxed. Even if he did look a little unwell.

'Er . . . I thought we would discuss possible scenar-
for utilizing the King Tigers in conjunction with
ndschar, Herr Standartenfuehrer," Haak said,
nce their arrival is imminent."

'Ah, yes. Well, why don't we?" Throckmorton
od up, still holding the sheaf of reports in his left
nd. He dropped them on the desk, put that hand in
pocket, and cleared a space on the desktop with
right. "Damned mess. Here we are—a decent top-
aphic map of Mount Zpoda, with our positions
wn on it." He pointed at the markings clearly rep-
enting Handschar's deployment, his unlit cigarette
ated between his second and third fingers. "Any
gestions you have would be welcome."

Baffled but pleased, Haak stepped around to the
e of the desk and perused the map. "Well, sir," he

said, "I'm concerned primarily about our right fl
since the Second Proletarian Brigade has repositi
itself somewhere west of the Ugljevik Pass. The po
tial exists for it to continue to move west across
alpine plateau south of Mount Zpoda, then nort
link up with other Partisan battalions and regim
currently opposing us here"—Haak tapped his i
finger on the map—"here, and here. It's possible
their combined forces could drive forward and sp
in half at the mountain, with the Zpoda Gorge ma
it impossible for our left flank to sweep around
Partisan salient and attack it from the side
behind."

Throckmorton nodded. "I see," he mused, ge
into the spirit of the thing. "We should reinforce
right quadrant by advancing south along the wes
shoulder of Mount Zpoda, and deploying perha
quarter of the Tiger tanks to hold positions the
mobile artillery, if you will—while the bulk of
tanks and infantry assault units from, say, the Twe
eighth SS Regiment push forward in an arc that
lows the mid-level elevations. Oh, and I would sug
that elements of the Twenty-nineth—perhaps Ba
ions Three and Four—be moved into the slot and I
in reserve in case the Partisans launch a serious co
terattack from the northwest."

Haak blinked in astonishment. What had happe
to Zweig? Not only had the Standartenfuehrer de
oped a personality overnight, he had also appare
turned from a dull-minded tin soldier who co
barely read a map into a shrewd military tactician v
an appreciation of terrain. Security of the position
rently held by the Twenty-eighth SS Regiment
critical, the lynchpin of the Mount Zpoda defen
strategy. If the Twenty-eighth SS was ordered to
vance, other forces would have to be shifted to t
its place. . . . And Zweig had understood that insti
ively. Absolutely stupefying.

"That is a very good point, Herr Standar

hrer," Haak followed up, checking the map again.
'e should indeed have reserves available to protect
neck of our own salient." There was a scratching
nd as the division commander fired a match to light
cigarette.

'I'm glad you agree, Haak," Throckmorton said,
king out the match and exhaling smoke. "And I
nk the majority of the tanks should be deployed
: the tines of a fork along these three descending
ges." He leaned forward slightly and pointed.
ere, here, and here. They will give fire support to
infantry units sweeping the valleys in between. Do
1 concur with that assessment?"

There was no answer.

'Haak?"

Throckmorton looked up and straight into the muz-
of a Luger pistol. On the other side of the weapon,
uptsturmfuehrer Ulrich Haak's face, completely
ained of color, was working in confusion.

'Don't move," he blurted, taking a step backward
:h his gun arm fully extended. "Whoever you are."

Chapter
Seventeen

Throckmorton brought his cigarette to his lips drew on it, one eyebrow raised. "What do you th you're doing, Hauptsturmfuehrer?" he deman turning to face Haak.

"I told you not to move," Haak hissed. His pro nent Adam's apple moved up and down as he sy lowed. Throckmorton's split-second assessment that the man's reactions were generated by al rather than fear—he was obviously too seasone combat soldier to be unnerved for very long.

"Now see here, Haak," he said, stepping forwa "this has gone far enough."

The German officer moved back. "One more ste he snarled, "and you're dead."

Throckmorton spread his open hands, palms ward. "Alright, alright."

"You are not Standartenfuehrer Zweig," H declared.

Throckmorton smiled and raised his cigarette to

again. "You're delusional, Hauptsturmfuehrer
ık," he said. "The strain of too much combat, per-
s. Of course I am Egon Zweig."

ʃaak wagged the Luger. "Then explain to me," he
ɔrted, "how it is that the little finger of your left
ɹd, which was accidentally shot off a month ago,
somehow grown back overnight."

ʃhrockmorton's expression remained a pleasant
ık as he blew out a long stream of smoke.

No answer, Standartenfuehrer?" Haak said. He
ɔ breathing hard, focused on Throckmorton. "In-
ʃible. Subtle differences in appearance, but nothing
ɔpeak of. Noticeable differences in personality, abil-
and intellect, but in the context of the astounding
ɔsical resemblance—dismissable. I would have been
ɔpletely fooled if not for the finger." He paused,
ɔking his head. "Unless you are an unknown twin
ɔther, you are a true doppelganger. An unrelated
ɹr-perfect double of Egon Zweig."

ʹWell, old man," Throckmorton said in English, cal-
ɔating that the well-spoken German would likely un-
ɔstand it and several other languages, "not so near
ɔfect as you might imagine. My natural hair color is
ɔwn, not blond, and my nose was once not as thin
Herr Zweig's. Fortunately, however, I had access
ɔsuch things as peroxide and surgery."

ʹYou're British," Haak replied. "I might have
ɔwn. SOE, I expect."

ʹA captain, actually. Like you."

ʹRemarkable," Haak said. "Congratulations. Your
ɔrman is excellent."

ʹWhy, thanks awfully, old fellow," Throckmorton
ɔnowledged. He thought fleetingly of the Walther
ɔthe lower desk drawer.

ʹBut, Captain," Haak went on, making the mistake
ɔstarting to enjoy his own cleverness, "you are very
ɔiously in the wrong uniform. You are impersonating
ɔ SS division commander. That makes you a spy.

And spies are shot." He smiled. "After they are ⌐
tioned by our intelligence services . . . ra
extensively."

Throckmorton drew on his cigarette again. "
don't say."

Haak's eyes narrowed, and the smile left his
"I would hardly be flippant if I were in your positi
he growled. "Now, then, before I march you ou
here: where is Standartenfuehrer Zweig? What ⌐
you done with him?"

Too arrogant, Throckmorton thought. *Too*
absorbed. You should have called in a squad of sol
three minutes ago.

"He's around," he said.

Haak stepped forward and placed the muzzle of
Luger against Throckmorton's forehead. *"Where?*

Throckmorton cleared his throat. "The closet.
one over there underneath the Russian boar."

Haak stepped back and glanced up quickly at
huge black trophy head with its curling tusks and
sane glass eyes. He gestured with the pistol. "V
over to the closet—carefully."

Throckmorton eyed him, took one last draw on
cigarette, and butted it in the desk ashtray. The
began to saunter slowly across the room. Haak
lowed, keeping his gun arm at full extension with
Luger aimed at the back of Throckmorton's head

"Stop," the German ordered.

Throckmorton strolled to a halt in front of
closet and began to turn around, habitually putting
left hand into his pants pocket.

"Keep facing the closet door," Haak said, "
keep your hands out of your pockets."

Throckmorton shrugged, removed his hand,
turned the other way.

"Open that door," Haak told him, moving up u
he was less than six feet behind the British capt
"And stay in the doorway until I tell you to mov

Throckmorton put his hand on the latch and opened the door, pulling it outward. Haak cocked his head to one side, then the other, trying to see past him. As instructed, Throckmorton remained in place.

"Step aside," Haak growled.

Throckmorton took one long step to the left, revealing the interior of the closet. Egon Zweig was sitting up against the back wall, legs outstretched and hands in his lap, head lolling onto one shoulder. His face was the color of a boiled beet, his tongue protruding from his mouth. His bulging eyes, bright but lifeless, stared out through the doorway in mute shock.

Haak's own eyes fastened onto Zweig's in an uncontrollable reflex.

In that moment of distraction, Stirling dodged out from behind the right-hand doorjamb and shot Hauptsturmfuehrer Ulrich Haak through the left eye with a silenced .22 caliber Hi-Standard automatic pistol.

Chuff.

Haak's gun arm sagged, his knees buckled, and he collapsed onto his back on the floor without a uttering a sound. Blood pooled in his left eye socket; the other stared straight up at the ceiling, as inanimate as the dozens of glass eyes staring down from the walls.

"Excellent marksmanship, Sergeant," Throckmorton commented. "A very clean kill."

"Thank you, sir," Stirling breathed, tucking the automatic with its long silencer back inside his jacket. "Into the closet with him?"

"Most definitely." Throckmorton took one of Haak's boots, Stirling the other, and together they dragged the dead German through the closet doorway.

"We're getting a bit of a body count in the vicinity of this office," Throckmorton said. "That aide, Feder—we'll need to move him in here, as well. Other personnel have too much access to the outer closet, even if it is locked."

"We'll see to it, sir," Stirling replied. "But no rush,

I think. We can make sure the coast is clear. He
Feder's nicely tucked away in that trash can for th
moment."

Throckmorton nodded. "Agreed. Now, I want
look at my dear departed doppelganger here. I wasn
quite doppelganger enough, apparently." He stoope
lifted Zweig's left hand, and pulled the glove off i
"Damnation. He *is* missing half the little finger.
fresh wound. Certainly a dead bloody giveaway if yc
happened to be in daily contact with the man, eh?
He dropped the hand back into the corpse's lap, co
lected Zweig's left and right gloves, and stood up. "N
way we could have known about this back in Englan
so soon after it happened. We're lucky, Stirling, b
we won't press our luck. Strip the fellow down an
let's check him for any more unknown anomalie
Who knows? Maybe he's recently had a toe shot o
as well."

"Yes, sir."

As Stirling began to undo the buttons of Zweig
coat, Throckmorton pulled on the dead Standarte
fuehrer's fine black leather gloves. "Mmm. Ki
leather," he muttered. "Very nice—and a perfect fi
too. Good thing, because I guess I'll be wearing th
left one pretty continuously from now on."

"You could always wrap the finger with a bandag
sir," Stirling said, peeling Zweig's coat off. "Claim it
slow to heal."

"True," Throckmorton returned, "but I rather lik
the affectation of black leather." He held up his le
hand and flexed the fingers inside the glove. "There
something so fundamentally . . . *German* about i
Don't you think, Stirling?"

"Whatever you say, Captain," the commando se
geant replied. "Whatever you say."

Throckmorton exited the closet and walked over t
the commander's desk, taking a good look out the wir
dows as he did. Everything seemed normal outsid
there was no indication that anyone had noticed any

ing amiss. There were a few soldiers moving here and
ere through the continous snowfall, but that was it.

On top of Zweig's desk was an appointment ledger.
hrockmorton took another cigarette from the box, lit
, and began to browse through the last few pages of
e book, stopping at the current date. There were no
ntries.

"Huh," Throckmorton grunted. "Lazy bastard."

When he returned to the closet, Stirling had Zweig's
ody stripped to its underwear. "Nothing else, sir,"
e reported. "No scars, no abnormalities—everything
here it should be, right down to his wedding tackle."

"Fine, Sergeant,'" Throckmorton said. "Tuck the
ugger into a corner along with Haak and let's lock
em up."

Stirling dragged the bodies into one end of the
loset, shoved a large trunk in front of them, and
epped out into the common room. Throckmorton
cked the door with the old-style key that protruded
om the latch and put it into his pocket.

"Alright, Sergeant," he said, "except for moving
eder, we're done. I can handle my end now. Are you
lear on your part in this thing from here on out?"

Stirling nodded. "You've explained it perfectly, sir.
illed in all the blanks."

"I'm sorry about Hurst," Throckmorton said, meet-
g his eyes.

"Yes, sir," Stirling replied. "I appreciate that, sir."

Throckmorton looked out the window at the falling
now. "You've picked your spot?"

"Yes, sir. That tall pine on the rise just above the
orth tunnel. I get a clear view over to the German
ositions on the gorge rim where the tunnel connects
o the bridge."

"And you have all your gear? White camouflage
hroud, rifle silencer, and such?"

Stirling nodded again. "Yes, sir. If it all goes to hell,
'll be up there doing as much damage to the SS as I
an, for as long as I can."

"Very good, then. But remember: only in supp‹ of the team blowing the bridge, if they're discover‹ Otherwise, sit tight and then slip away once the brid' is gone. If you can link up with some of the othe‹ fine, but try to get back to the Partisans." Throckm‹ ton turned away suddenly, put his fist to his mou‹ and coughed violently for several seconds. He stepp‹ to the desk, leaned down, and spat red into the was‹ paper basket beside it.

Stirling waited for him to collect himself befo‹ speaking. "Well, sir, I think maybe we'd better tra‹ fer Feder's body, if there's no one around. I shou‹ get moving."

"Fine," Throckmorton said, looking flushed. "Le‹ see to it, shall we?"

"But first, sir, I'd like to shake your hand."

"Eh?" Throckmorton finished wiping his lips on t‹ back of his glove and raised a skeptical eyebrow.

"I said I'd like to shake your hand, Captain Throc‹ morton," Stirling said quietly. "That's all."

"Why . . . certainly, Sergeant," Throckmort‹ replied.

He put his hand out and the two men shook s‹ emnly.

"You're a brave man, sir," Stirling said. "I ju‹ wanted to tell you that."

Throckmorton looked at him and smiled his cynic‹ half-smile. "It's easy to be brave when you have r‹ choice, Sergeant. But thank you. Thank you indeed‹

"Yes, sir," Stirling said. "You're welcome." F‹ looked down at the floor for a moment, then over ‹ the office door. "Well, then—time to move th‹ Feder bloke."

Quisp had been running for twenty minutes throu‹ thigh-deep snow when he finally reached the small s‹ ries of granite inclines that concealed the cave. F‹ rolled and tumbled the forty-five feet down to the cli‹ base, mindless of the snow-covered rocks he crashe‹

to, and floundered through the drifts toward the en-
ance crevice. His lungs were all but frozen solid from
cking in frigid air by the time he staggered into the
ve and collapsed to the floor in a spent heap.

"*The train!*" he gasped. "*The train . . . . it's
ming . . . maybe ten minutes . . . from the
alet . . . now . . .*"

Merritt leapt to his feet and looked at his watch.
Bloody hell!" he exclaimed. "The damned thing's not
pposed to be here until after midnight!" He cut his
yes at Cernović. "How did it make up so much
me?"

The Partisan commander shrugged as he scrambled
p and collected his small packsack and Mauser car-
ine. "I don't know, Major," he said. "Maybe your
telligence services underestimated the train's speed—
r overestimated the delay caused by the Typhoon
ttack."

"That's pretty goddamn obvious," Bristow growled,
inging up his Thompson.

Cernović shot him a hard look. "I reported the last
formation we received from British intelligence to
ou word for word, Major."

"I believe you, Commander," Merritt said. "I be-
eve you. But it's only thirteen hundred hours right
ow—the middle of the day. We can't climb that cliff
om Zlostup without the cover of night—we'll be
potted from that first antiaircraft battery along the
im. Unless the train stays on this side of the gorge
ntil after dark, we're going to have to try blowing
he bridge with just the two supports mined as it
oes across."

"But *you* said SOE's *own engineers* said that would
ot be enough to guarantee the collapse of the spans!"
Cernović exclaimed in frustration. "*Žplūgk!* To have
ome so far and risk complete failure . . . ." He
nashed his teeth and spat. "Major. Those King Tigers
ust not make it across the bridge to be deployed
gainst my people on the slopes of Mount Zpoda. The

Majevicas are the Partisans' last stronghold in cent
Yugoslavia. We cannot allow ourselves to be push
back into Montenegro and Albania."

"Then you'd better hope we planted enough plas
explosive on those first two supports, Command
Cernović," Merritt retorted, starting for the cave e
trance, carrying his Sten and demolition rucksa
"Sergeant Bristow! Bring the detonators and the re
of the det cord! Professor Quisp"—he glanced do
at the prostrate eccentric as he passed by—"I assu
you're going to come back to life at some point. Wh
you do, feel free to rouse Miss Kozo, who is appa
ently either indisposed or uninterested, and lend
what reinforcement you can at the gorge rim."

"Wh-where is . . . that young sergeant . . . Weiss
Quisp gasped.

"Gone," Merritt called over his shoulder. "Forg
him." He began to run as he entered the cave's e
trance passage. "Come on, Bristow!"

The American sergeant hurried out of the cav
swinging two half-empty rucksacks over the sar
shoulder, with Cernović right behind him. Merritt w
already churning up the steep slope beside the cra
digging into the snow with his free hand and drivi
with his legs. Through the dense curtain of falli
snow—from very far off, it seemed—came the fai
drawn-out scream of a train whistle.

By the time Bristow and Cernović reached the to
of the crag, gasping for breath, Merritt was already
hundred yards through the trees, following the litt
footpath that descended gradually to the gorge ri
below the northern tunnel and just above the sho
climb down to Zlostup. He paused in the deep sno
and turned, beckoning urgently. Bristow and Cernov
steeled themselves and plowed toward him, trying
recover their wind as they went.

Merritt had started down the trail again before
noticed that he had been running along in another s

f relatively fresh tracks; they were only partly filled
y falling snow. He twisted around as Bristow and
´ernović caught up, patting the air with his hand.

"Keep a sharp eye out!" he whispered. "And no
oise. There are new tracks on this trail—probably a
ïerman patrol. Maybe only one man, maybe two."

They continued on down the path in a tight, single-
le group, no one speaking, dark gray phantom figures
ïoving rapidly through the stunted trees and whirling
ïow. They were traveling too fast to be truly careful,
ïnd each man knew it. At any moment they expected
ɔ encounter the enemy in some form—a lone scout,
 two-man patrol, or even a full Jagdkommando squad
ɔnducting a precautionary sweep of the area prior to
he arrival of the approaching train.

Merritt plunged on through the drifts as the vast
ray emptiness of the Zpoda Gorge appeared through
he trees. The snowfall had lightened somewhat; he
ould just make out the entire head wall through the
ʌlizzard's gray veil, the Zpoda Skyway Bridge curving
ɪn a dark arc across the top of the granite face beneath
he huge, overhanging rock cap.

The throaty scream of the train whistle pierced the
ʌir again, reverberating off the cliffs and crags. It was
ïuch closer this time. Merritt willed his aching legs
ɔ carry him even faster. Up ahead, through the snow-
ʌaden evergreens, he caught a glimpse of the stone-
vork that formed the foundation of the north
unnel. . . . The horizontal steel girders of the bridge
ɪtself where it joined the tunnel's southern exit . . .
he sheer drop down the granite face beneath it . . .
ʌnd a sandbagged machine-gun nest—

Merritt dove to his left, toward the very rim of the
ʒorge, and belly-flopped into deep snow. He could feel
ɔme part of Bristow's body strike his boot and hear
he sergeant grunt as he duplicated the maneuver im-
ïediately behind him. A third light thump in the snow
ʌnd Cernović was down, too.

Merritt kept his head low as Bristow wormed
beside him on his left. A few seconds later Cernovic
swarthy Gypsy face appeared to his right.

"Machine-gun nest," Merritt whispered, pointing
gloved finger. "Right above the climb down
Zlostup. It's level with the train tracks, just to the si
of the tunnel. About a hundred yards ahead. See it"

"Goddammit," Bristow muttered. "That wasn
there yesterday."

"They must have just put it there this morning
Merritt replied, pulling a small set of powerful binoc
lars from his rucksack. He focused through the tree
"Probably a precaution to defend the approaches
the bridge as the train goes across."

"Do you think they know about Zlostup?" Cernov
asked. "Maybe they've set up to sweep it clear if the
see anyone on it."

"I don't think so," Merritt said. "They could fir
down the four hundred vertical feet to Zlostup, b
they're not oriented in that direction. They've got th
gun angled more toward the woods, as if they thin
any attack might come from the trees." He passed t
binoculars to Bristow. "I imagine they want to sto
sappers with charges from getting to the souther
mouth of the tunnel and the first bridge span. I don
think they're worried too much about the main sup
ports and footings way down the cliff. They probab
don't consider them accessible."

"MG-42 with a two-man team," Bristow growle
squinting through the binoculars at the nest. "No
body's runnin' into that chopper and livin' to tell th
tale."

"Nobody's going to, Sergeant," Merritt whispere
He glanced at Cernović. "We can crawl over the ri
about twenty yards ahead, climb down below the edg
where we can't be seen, and traverse through the bro
ken rock to the head of Zlostup where we left th
end of the detonator cord we laid out along the trail.

Merritt was interrupted by a series of thumping an

king sounds from the direction of the chalet, ac-
panied by blasts of what was obviously high-
sure steam being vented.

They're uncoupling the mufti's private car, I ex-
t," he muttered. "Leaving it on the siding." He
ked back at Cernović. "Anyway, we put a short
e-delay fuse on the end of the det cord and activate
nce we see the train moving onto the bridge. Then
get the hell out of here."

ernović grimaced. "But, Major, again—we do not
e enough supports mined! What if the bridge
sn't fall? What if only one span collapses and
ee-quarters of the Tiger tanks make it to Mount
oda? We have to set more charges!"

"You tell me how," Merritt shot back in frustration.
d take any chance if I thought we might succeed,
: in broad daylight there's no way to backtrack
ng Zlostup without being—"

"Holy shit, Major," Bristow grunted, focusing the
oculars on the head wall. "You're not going to be-
ve this. . . ."

Theobald Quisp had lain on the stone floor of the
e for nearly twenty minutes, praying that his lungs
uld eventually defrost and permit him to breathe
operly once more. Finally, when the raw, burning
ins had stopped lancing through his chest with every
aalation, when his heart had slowed from a crazed
radiddle to a brisk, steady thump, he got laboriously
his feet and began to stagger toward the rear of
: cave. *From a purely physical standpoint,* he
ught, *it's bloody terrible to get old.*

He dropped to one knee beside Sylvia Kozo's
undsheet-swaddled form and tapped her gently on
: shoulder. "Wake up, my dear," he sighed.
here's work to be done, don't you know? 'Course
u do!"

When the young woman didn't move, he tapped
ain, a little harder.

"Come now, little one," he coaxed. " 'Stiffen
sinews, summon up the blood . . . and once more ▪
the breech'—to play fast and loose with the invic
verse of the Bard, damn me! We have compan
who need support, do we not? Yes, we do!"

There was still no sign of movement. Tired and
asperated, Quisp clapped a hand down and sh
hard.

"Miss Kozo!" he barked. "Arise, I say!"

The carefully arranged bundle of coats and tar
lins fell apart beneath the groundsheet that cove
them. Quisp swept the canvas to one side, probed
loose pile for a second or two, then sat back on
heels and peered quickly around the cave.

But Sylvia Kozo was gone.

"Jeezus H. Christ," Bristow muttered, squin
through the binoculars. "It's her. It's that crazy P
san broad."

"What?" The same astonished exclamation esca
Merritt and Cernović in unison. "Where?" Me
added quickly.

"On the goddamn bridge," Bristow said. '
rather . . . *under it.*" He handed the binoculars b
to the British major. "About halfway between the
and second vertical support members."

Merritt focused, searching. Then he saw her. "Je
bloody Christ," he muttered.

"That's about what I said," Bristow grunted.

"I can't make her out," Cernović said. "Still
much snow falling, I think."

"That's good," Merritt returned. "Maybe the G
mans in that antiaircraft battery back behind us wo
be able to see her, either. Or in this machine-gun ▪
up ahead."

"I don't think anybody's gonna be able to see
from the tracks or the tunnel area," Bristow put
"as long as she stays up under those girders."

"What exactly is she doing?" Cernović pressed.

Merritt passed him the binoculars. "You have to it to believe it, Commander. Look carefully: right underneath the second span."

Černović raised the glasses to his eyes. At first, ough a thin gauze of falling snow, he could see y the massive gray-black girders, rivets, gussets, and bler plates that made up the steel skeleton of the dge. He focused and concentrated. Then a movent caught his eye.

ylvia Kozo, clad in her familiar black shorts, old dershirt, black slippers, and rabbit-fur hat, was making her way steadily along the span—hanging upside wn from the outermost horizontal support girder. e was clinging to the lower flange of the huge steel eam with hands and heels. Her only concession to freezing climate and her own torn fingers, apparly, had been a pair of dark gloves. She was wearing small, light climbing harness, and from it swung collection of wired nuts and carabiners. A large l of rope was draped over her shoulder and across chest like a bandolier.

"What the hell's she thinkin'?" Bristow rumbled. "hat's she gonna do up there—start takin' apart s and bolts? She ain't got no charges with her."

"I'll tell you what she's going to do," Merritt said. "he's going to tie off that rope at the third vertical pport and rappel down to the footing. Then she's ng to try to finish mining the third and fourth dge footings before the train starts to cross."

Bristow looked at him. "But how's she gonna do t?" he exclaimed in a hoarse whisper. "I left the t two sets of charges tied together in pairs and ped over the number two footin'. That little gal n't tote them four boxes across a hundred and enty feet of cliff by herself. Then she's gotta place m right and run the det cord to string 'em all tother! How many trips back and forth is that, even she can carry the charges? Six? Eight? She's gonna t spotted, Major!"

Merritt chewed his lower lip for a moment i
lence. Then he made up his mind. "She's got sc
thing figured out," he said, "or she wouldn't be tl
As far as her being spotted, we might be able to
vent that." He turned onto his side and looked I
the way they had come. "The only SS with a g
view of the cliff and bridge supports are manning
first antiaircraft gun emplacement." He caught I
tow's eye. "Sergeant, do you think you can c
house up there without attracting any attention?"

Bristow nodded with a hard smile. "That's wh
do, Major. It's what Frank D'Amato did, too. Be
he'll be watchin' my back."

"Do you have the necessary tools?"

The big sergeant patted his chest. "Silenced
Standard right here, sir," he growled. "Stiletto in
boot. That's all I need."

"Right," Merritt said. "Go. Be careful, but hu
Commander Cernović and I will work our way d
to where we can monitor the girl's progress and
the fuse on this end of the det cord. Work your
back as soon as you can. . . . If you can."

Bristow nodded once more and began to squ
backward through the snow, keeping low. "Rem
ber," Merritt called softly, "it's about not raising
alarm. No noise, Sergeant."

"Yessir." Bristow worked his way over a little
out of sight of the machine-gun nest, then got to
feet and hustled back up the rim trail.

"All right," Merritt breathed. "We've got to m
too, Commander. Are you ready?"

"Yes," Cernović replied. He was silent for a
ment. "I'd hate to see anything happen to Sylvia.

"So would I," Merritt told him. "But she's ta
matters into her own hands. All we can do is try
best to give her support. And Commander"—Me
turned and looked at him directly—"just so you kn
if that train pulls out onto that bridge, I'm wai

l the last possible moment and then I'm firing
se charges—no matter where Sylvia Kozo is."

le crawled forward through the snow and low ever-
:ns, leaving Cernović staring darkly after him, his
muscles working.

Žplūgk!" the Partisan commander swore, and
an crawling along in Merritt's track.

Chapter Eighteen

Sergeant David Weiss had crossed the tracks sev[eral] hundred yards north of the tunnel and siding, u[nder] cover of the incessant snowfall, and worked his [way] around to the northwest corner of the chalet c[om-] pound, keeping to the trees. There he had foun[d a] perfect spot: a thirty-foot-high granite crag with a s[hal-] low ledge just beneath its overhanging crest. The le[dge] was concealed by drifted snow and just large eno[ugh] to accommodate a man lying at full length.

The ledge was about ten feet higher than the s[tone] wall enclosing the compound, and offered a clear v[iew] down into the inner quadrangle. The linear dista[nce] from the ledge to the sentry box on the northw[est] corner of the wall was approximately 100 feet—q[uite] close—and another 250 feet to the front door of [the] chalet great house, for a total of 350 feet. The v[iew] from the great house door to the arched main g[ate] was unrestricted. By a stroke of good luck, the [two] sandbagged machine-gun positions on the wall w[ere] located beside the southeast and southwest corner s[...]

boxes—oriented, understandably enough, toward
Partisan forces to the south. Single sentries paced
ly back and forth on the north wall—one for each
he two remaining corner boxes—trying to keep
m.

the dense trees immediately below and to the
of the ledge, there was an old wooden shack—
aps once used for the hanging of game meat—
was on the verge of collapse from the weight of
snow that had accumulated on its roof. The win-
s were broken out of it, and through one of them
ss could see the shack's dark, dirty interior. It was
than fifty feet away, looking down at a forty-five-
ree angle. There was no evidence that it was cur-
ly being used for anything.

e settled back into the deepest recess of the rock
ty, taking care not to disturb the drifted snow in
t of him. Well shielded from the wind and insu-
d by the high-quality German white-camouflage
rak and pants he had put on over his regular win-
combat clothing, he felt almost warm. That was
d, because he had no idea how long he would have
ie within the confines of the ledge without mov-
Waiting.

he .45-caliber De Lisle silenced carbine was an
sual weapon, specifically designed by the SOE for
covert removal of sentries. It was basically a
dard-issue Lee Enfield infantry rifle, cut down
il virtually only the stock remained. It had been
hambered for the subsonic .45-caliber pistol round,
its new nine-inch barrel was encased along its en-
abbreviated length by a two-inch-diameter si-
cer. It made for a strange, clumsy-looking
apon—like a rifle stock with a foot-long section of
k black pipe grafted to it—but in the hands of
ert commando marksmen like David Weiss, the De
le had proven to be deadly accurate at up to 250
ds and, as a result of its below-the-speed-of-sound
munition and huge silencer, completely noiseless.

Using the utmost care, Weiss cut a deep, na
groove with the edge of his hand through the v
shaped snowdrift that concealed his vantage po
just enough to accept the long, fat silencer of th
Lisle and allow him an unhindered view of the
between the compound's main entrance and the
house. Then he settled the odd rifle into position
suring that its muzzle did not protrude beyond
front of the drift, and got himself as comfortab
possible.

With typical efficiency, the Germans had p
high-powered lights around the compound, V
noted; some on poles, others mounted on the
pound wall and the eaves of the chalet buildings.
was good. He had no doubt that they'd be lit
dark, and if the gamecock didn't make the trek
tween his private rail car and what was clearly
division headquarters office in the great house be
then, he'd nevertheless be easy to see in the gla
the floodlights.

These had been Merritt's final words to him as
departed the cave:

"The gamecock you're hunting now has the v
turban of a Muslim cleric, Weiss. Remember that
a white turban. He won't be seen without it. It'
badge of office."

Gamecock. The same bird General Gubbins ha
casually referred to during the interview at SOE h
quarters in London.

Weiss stared grimly over the sights of the De L
He'd been waltzed into position like a puppet
strings. And *oh* how the puppet masters loved t
game.

Hauptsturmfuehrer Matthias Juttner tucked
wool scarf a little tighter around his neck and tu
up the collar of his black leather greatcoat. His
stung from the cold, but his peaked SS cap loc
less elegant when it was combined with earmuff

he like, and it was important to make a solid first impression on the Handschar rank and file. Latent intimidation always made doors easier to open—and easier to walk through.

He stepped down from the forward-end platform of the mufti's private car and backed away from it a few paces, his jackboots crunching in the snow. The rolling stock that made up al-Husseini's original train—SS escort bunk car, antiaircraft flatcar, private coach, and caboose—was now parked on the siding directly in front of the main chalet compound gate and had just been uncoupled from the lead locomotive of the King Tiger train. The big engine was now some two hundred yards away, backing the train up onto the main line again in preparation to cross the Zpoda Skyway Bridge. True to his word, Standartenfuehrer Kronstadt was wasting no time in dispensing with the inconvenient Grand Mufti of Jerusalem and his entourage and proceeding to his priority destination on the slopes of Mount Zpoda.

Snowflakes were catching on Juttner's eyelashes; he blinked them away, then pulled his coat cuff back and glanced at his watch. Midafternoon. Both the Tiger train and the Grand Mufti were at Barbo House at least ten hours earlier than anticipated. The hard-driving Kronstadt had let no grass grow under his feet in Bljak and spared no coal in getting the train up the Majevica foothills.

Well . . . time to announce al-Husseini to the commander of the Muslim SS Division Handschar. The mufti might as well start moving about in the fresh air instead of hibernating in his private car. Juttner smacked his leather-gloved hands together, turned, and began to stride purposefully up the short, snow-packed incline toward the chalet compound gate.

Pushing the raggedly dressed girl ahead of him with a hand clamped on the back of her neck, Hauptsturm-fuehrer Julius Neurath descended the steps of the pri-

vate car's rear-end platform, his long coat flappi
around his jackboots, and began to march up the si
ing next to the caboose. A couple of Muslim troope
loitering nearby took notice, but quickly turned awa
What a well-connected Aryan dressed in what looke
ominously like Gestapo plainclothes did was his bus
ness, and his alone.

With a few surreptitious glances over his shoulde
Neurath hurried the girl past the caboose and up th
tracks about seventy-five yards. Then he redirecte
her toward the wooded area just north of the chal
compound. Very soon they were off the rail bed an
moving into the trees, all but hidden by the fallir
snow.

Neurath was in his usual foul mood, made eve
worse by the incessant carping of the mufti and Jut
ner's relentless sly mockery. He needed release. Tru
release. And at the same time, he needed to take o
the trash. It wouldn't do to be caught with this litt
Jewess—for that is what he had decided she was—i
his quarters, and besides, she whimpered too muck
Like right now. Her terrified sniveling was getting o
his nerves. One more day, he knew, and he would b
thoroughly bored with her.

Better to do it now while he was still intereste
enough to draw some pleasure from the act.

"Do my eyes deceive me," Handschar antiaircra
gunner Muhammed Korkut said to the Scharfuehre
beside him, "or is that something swinging from th
bridge?"

"What?" The Scharfuehrer, whose name wa
Turku, stepped past the 40-millimeter automatic car
non and squinted across the gun emplacement's to
row of sandbags. "How, by the Beard of the Grea
Bey, can you see all the way to the cliff through thi
cursed snow?"

"I'm telling you, Scharfuehrer Turku, I caught
glimpse of something. Something swinging like a pen

ulum around the base of the . . . one, two . . . the
third upright support from the north. Look! There it
is again! It swung to the base of the fourth support
and stopped there!"

"Korkut," the Scharfuehrer said, his dark face twisting into a scowl, "I warned you several days ago that I
would no longer tolerate you sneaking that putrid
Lebanese hashish into your cigarette tobacco."

The Bosnian Muslim gunner whirled. "Let's get this
straight between us, Turku," he snarled. "Now that
you've been promoted to Scharfuehrer, you can come
and go as you please—spend as much time as you
like hanging around the soup wagon near the officer's
outpost down behind the ridge. But we're stuck up
here in this isolated shit hole, freezing our balls off,
day in and day out." The other two enlisted men in
the emplacement, seated on planks next to the sandbag walls, giggled. "What's it to you if we share a
little something to take the edge off the cold? Eh?"

"If I catch you again," Turku said, "it's punishment
detail for you."

"Bah!" Korkut jerked his head around and squinted
at the head wall again. "There's something there, I
tell you. . . . Something strange . . ."

The Scharfuehrer sighed. He liked his new noncom-
missioned rank, but didn't like the dissention—the
resentment—it had caused in the two weeks since his
promotion. "Very well, Korkut," he said. "Let's have
another look. Mahmet! Glasses!"

One of the enlisted men got slowly to his feet and
picked up a set of Zeiss binoculars. "Here you are,
Scharfuehrer," he said, bringing them over. Turku
took the glasses; the soldier moved back against the
sandbags to join his friend in a standing stretch,
yawning.

"There, see?" Korkut said, leaning forward and
pointing. "A line of some kind hanging down from
the bridge. I can just barely see it."

"By Shaitan, you're right!" Turku exclaimed. "And

there's somebody moving around on the base of t
fourth upright. Mahmet," he said without turni
around, "ring up division headquarters. Find out
there is some kind of work being done on ropes u
derneath the north spans of the Zpoda Skyw
Bridge."

"Do you see any workers on the bridge itself
Korkut demanded.

"No," the Scharfuehrer replied, "just the one pe
son." He stared a few seconds longer, then lower
the binoculars. "Mahmet! Are you going to ring hea
quarters or not?"

He looked behind him in irritation. Mahmet and I
friend were crumpled on top of each other in the fr
zen mud at the base of the sandbag wall.

"Korkut!" Scharfuehrer Turku blurted, reaching f
his sidearm. The Muslim gunner spun around, alarm
by the urgency in the sergeant's voice.

Chuff.

Turku's chin snapped down onto his chest and I
pitched forward on his face.

Muhammed Korkut's final yell was cut off before
left his throat by the fourth .22-caliber slug from tl
silenced automatic, which tore through his larynx fro
behind, just to the left of his spinal column. He gu
gled once, half turning and reaching for his collar, a
Bristow, who'd been lurking on the outside of tl
sandbag wall, finished him off with a fifth shot to h
left temple. The gunner dropped like a stone on tc
of Turku.

Glancing around quickly, Bristow scrambled ov
the sandbags and crouched down inside the emplac
ment, out of sight. After checking that all four SS me
were truly dead, he picked up the Zeiss glasses tl
Scharfuehrer had dropped and cautiously focuse
them on the head wall, keeping low.

He was just in time to see, through the veil of falli
snow, a tiny figure in black shorts and a white unde

irt swing on the end of a long thread from the fourth
the third bridge support footing.

Once again, Sylvia Kozo was working too hard to
el the bitter cold that enveloped her partly clad
ody. Having secured the rope to the underside of the
idge span just behind the third vertical support
rder, she'd rappelled down the one hundred feet to
e footing, concealed from view by the girder itself.
e hadn't lingered long; in a great, looping arc, run-
ng across the rock face on the end of the rope, she'd
vung over to the second footing.

Then the manual labor had begun. One by one,
e'd hauled the four dangling boxes of explosives up
to the concrete pad and taken them—tied to her
arness two at a time—back to the third footing. Then
e'd planted two of the boxes on the base of the
ird support girder as she'd seen Bristow and Merritt
o on the first and second, and carried the remaining
vo boxes over to the fourth footing.

By the time all the charges were placed, her arms
nd legs were trembling and she was gasping for
reath. It had taken a total of five great swings, fully
xposed to any watching eyes on the gorge rim, to
ansfer the explosives from the second to the third
nd fourth footings. The falling snow provided some
over, no doubt, reducing long-distance visibility, but
was still broad daylight. That she hadn't been spot-
ed, she concluded, was nothing short of a miracle.

The only thing left to do was swing back to the
econd footing once more and collect the long coil of
etonator cord Bristow had left there. Run it across
e cliff to the third and fourth supports, tie it into
e charges, and the task was done. The far end of the
etonator cord was lying on the Zlostup trail head just
elow the rim of the gorge. All Merritt or one of his
en had to do was attach a short fuse and detonator
it and wait for the train to cross.

Sylvia took a deep breath, tensed, and lunged
yet again into empty space on the end of the ro
swinging toward the third footing.

"Standartenfuehrer Zweig insists that you come
the chalet great house immediately," Juttner told
Grand Mufti. "Word of your arrival has spread, a
the imams and Muslim troops are anxious to see y
The Standartenfuehrer also wishes me to convey
you that he cannot ensure your security while y
remain aboard your private car, and that you sho
enter the compound without delay."

Al-Husseini remained hunched in his favorite ar
chair. "No," he said, his eyes furtive, nervous. "I sh
remain here until the locomotives return to take
back down to the flatlands. Zweig can no more gu
antee that there are no Partisan sharpshooters near
in this front-line area than I can turn lead into gol
He fluttered his fingers in a cranky, dismissive gestu
"That is my final word on it."

Mustapha Snagi, leaning against the wall with le
crossed and arms folded, stirred and crossed his le
the other way.

"Your Excellency," Juttner said, "the very purpo
for which you have come to Yugoslavia, as per t
Fuehrer's wishes, is right outside this door. The m
of the SS Division Handschar know you are here a
long to catch even a glimpse of you. What it wou
mean to their morale . . ."

"I will conduct a rotating series of lectures for v
iting Handschar imams from the safety of Belgrade
the mufti declared, "which was always my intent.
will not expose myself to these front-line conditions
Then his frightened eyes narrowed and Juttner cou
see his mind working. "But you are correct. Perha
the men stationed here should at least see their spi
tual leader firsthand as he visits the division comman
er's office. . . ."

It had just occurred to al-Husseini that it was in h

est interest to ensure that at least some of the Mus-
m troops in Handschar be able to corroborate the
ct that he had been at the front in person. . . . In
ase his movements became an issue with Hitler at
ome later date.

"Yes," he mused, stroking his beard with two fin-
ers. "I think that the good Muslim soldiers of
Iandschar's headquarters garrison deserve to see the
rand Mufti of Jerusalem in their midst, even from
distance. . . ."

The long, loud scream of a steam whistle jolted
veryone's nerves. The King Tiger train was on the
ove. Out of idle exasperation with the mufti and his
wn natural interest, Juttner stepped over to one of
he private car's boarded-up windows and peered out
hrough a crack between planks, looking toward the
ain tracks and the wooded area beyond. Through
he whirling snow, something caught his attention on
he far side of the rail bed, just at the edge of the
rees.

Abruptly he backed away and headed for the front
oor of the car.

"Your pardon, Your Excellency," he said quickly.
I must attend to something."

And then, to the Grand Mufti's considerable plea-
ure, he strode through the forward exit and disap-
eared.

"Snagi," al-Husseini commanded, "come here."

Sylvia made one final outward swing to the fourth
ooting, the blue-and-red detonator cord tied into her
arness and trailing behind her. Once on top of the
oncrete pad, she pulled the slack out of it, wrapped
t three times around the plastic explosive inside the
irst crate, then did the same with the second, making
ertain in both cases that the cord was well buried in
he waxy compound.

A last swing back and she was on the third footing,
he rope hanging straight down from the bridge span

overhead. As she summoned her remaining streng
and prepared to climb, the muted blast of the tra
whistle sounded again, echoing through the gray em
tiness of the Zpoda Gorge.

She had considered rappelling down to Zlostup a
rejoining Merritt's team that way, but the new
placed German machine-gun nest above the trailhe
made using the trail impossible. Anyone approachi
on Zlostup from the south, coming off the head wa
would be spotted. It was climb up to the bridge a
crawl along its underside back the way she had com
or nothing. And there was no time to waste, becau
from the sound of the steam whistle, the train cou
emerge from the tunnel and move out onto the brid
at any moment. Sylvia had not the slightest doubt th
Merritt or any one of his men would blow the brid
at the crucial moment, regardless of whether or n
she was in the clear. So, for that matter, would Con
rade Cernović.

And so would she, if their positions were reverse
The destruction of not just the Zpoda Skyway Bridg
but the Zpoda Skyway Bridge *and* the King Tig
train, was that vital. It was worth however many liv
it took to do it.

But, truth admitted, one did not stop trying to liv
Not even if, with failing hands and trembling arms,
simple hundred-foot climb up a rope looked more lik
a thousand.

Sylvia wiped the palms of her blood-soaked glove
on her black shorts, flexed her fingers around the rop
gritted her teeth, and began to climb.

Juttner bounded over the main tracks ahead of th
oncoming locomotive and trotted toward the thre
gray figures he'd spotted emerging from the trees. Th
King Tiger train was still some distance away, movin
slowly forward. There were constant intermitte
blasts of steam as the engineers on each of the eigl
locomotives checked boiler pressures for the upcom

run across the bridge and up the shoulder of
unt Zpoda.

he SS Hauptsturmfuehrer glanced left and right as
hurried along, his black leather greatcoat flapping
inst his jackboots. There were few other soldiers
und, and most of them had congregated in the vi-
ty of the tunnel entrance and the approach to the
et compound. As had been the case all day, the
ng snow was a ubiquitous gray shroud that ob-
ed both detail and motion.

e held up a hand as he approached the three men.
o were helmeted Handschar SS troopers, bundled
or patrol. The third man, who was stumbling along
ween them, wore a British military issue olive drab
et and battle harness. His head was bare and he
eared to be half dazed, disoriented. A trickle of
od ran down the side of his face from an ugly gash
is temple.

Halt!" Juttner ordered, moving in close. "What do
have here?"

eeing the immaculate SS uniform with its peaked
th's-head cap and captain's insignia, the two Mus-
troopers drew themselves up straight but did not
ate, opting instead to keep their machine pistols
ned on the man between them. "A prisoner, Herr
uptsturmfuehrer," one of them said. "He was
ving through the trees near the gorge rim, only
ew hundred yards from the tunnel. Sturmmann
ahimović"—he indicated the other trooper—
pped out from behind a tree and struck him on
head with his weapon when he walked past." The
t man unslung a Sten gun from his shoulder and
d it up. "He was carrying this."

Does he say who he is?" Juttner asked, peering at
man's unshaven face.

He claims to be a Muslim deserter from the Parti-
Army," the trooper said. "He claims his name is
ejman Hafiz and that he wishes to join the SS Divi-
1 Handschar." The soldier scowled. "But he is well

equipped for a deserter, do you not think? This
British weapon."

"The British and Americans drop their wea
and equipment to the Partisans all the time," Ju
remarked. "His clothing and gear tell us only th:
is not in the German military. More likely he
Partisan scout, lurking around to see if there i
easy way to disrupt operations at the bridge. You!
demanded in Serbo-Croatian, addressing the prisc
"You do not look like a Muslim to me. And yo
not have the look of a deserter. You are a Par
spy, aren't you?"

"Ugh—" the man grunted, his eyelids flutterin

Juttner slapped him hard across the mouth wit
gloved hand. The prisoner's head jerked up and b
but he did not cry out. "Silence!" Juttner bar
"Don't even attempt to lie to me!" He looked at
of the SS troopers in turn. "We want information
this fellow. We will escort him to Standartenfue
Zweig's office immediately. Bring him along qui
and say nothing to anyone as we go. I do not wis
raise an unnecessary alarm while the Grand Mu
present. Do both of you understand me?"

The two SS troopers stiffened again and nod
"*Jawohl,* Herr Hauptsturmfuehrer," they choruse

"Very well. Bring him."

Juttner spun on his heel and stalked back the
he had come, eyeing the soldiers around the tu
entrance and compound gate. Behind him, the
troopers thumped their fists into the prisoner's b
driving him forward, and followed.

The four men marched briskly down the si
tracks, the prisoner stumbling occasionally betw
the two SS troopers, and past the Grand Mufti's
vate car. Juttner led them up the incline to the c
pound gate, pushing a bow wave of Nazi officious
that parted the Muslim troopers, loitering in his p
like the Red Sea before Moses. He did not even d
to look at Schütze Fikret Pandža, who was still

rd duty at the gate, wondering when his double
on of hot soup and buttered bread would arrive.

he prisoner was hustled through the archway and
oss the compound to the front of the chalet great
se. Juttner mounted the stone steps to the large
ibule and opened the front door.

Inside with him!" he ordered, drawing his Luger.
waited as the two troopers shoved the weaving
tive through the doorway, then followed, closing
door behind him.

hey were in the deserted outer office of Zweig's
e, Feder. Juttner walked past the aide's desk and
cked on the door to the division commander's
er sanctum, the greathouse trophy-and-common
m.

Who is it?" a voice shouted.

Your pardon, Standartenfuehrer Zweig," Juttner
ed. "It is Hauptsturmfuehrer Juttner again. I only
spoke to you about receiving the Grand Mufti."

Juttner?" the voice said. "Enter."

he SS Hauptsturmfuehrer pushed open the door
grunted over his shoulder, "Bring the prisoner."
He marched across the spacious common room and
pped three paces from Zweig's desk with a sharp
k of his heels and a Nazi salute. *"Heil Hitler!"* he
ped out. Behind him, the two Muslim troopers
ne to a halt, jostling the prisoner between them.

hrockmorton rose out of his chair, removing the
ding glasses with which he had been perusing daily
orts, and flipped his hand back. *"Heil Hitler."* His
s roved over the two troopers and their captive.
hat's the meaning of this intrusion, Juttner?" he
nanded.

This man claims to be a Partisan deserter, Herr
ndartenfuehrer," Juttner explained. "A Muslim—
so he says. He was captured by these two excellent
opers while they were on patrol near the gorge rim.
states that he wishes to join the SS Division
ndschar."

"Indeed?" Throckmorton peered at the wob▮ captive. "What is your name, Partisan?"

"Sulejman Hafiz," Major Walter Merritt said.

"Huh!" Throckmorton drew back and exam▮ Merritt from head to toe. "He doesn't look like n▮ of a Muslim to me," he said. "Take him out ▮ shoot him."

As the two SS troopers grinned and seized M▮ by the upper arms, Juttner raised a gloved finger. ▮ cuse me, sir, but shouldn't we interrogate him ▮ I'm sure that with a little . . . motivation . . . he c▮ be convinced to tell us everything he knows abou▮ lastest Partisan troop movements. That is, unles▮ truly *is* a deserter who wishes to join Handschar▮ which case he should be only too happy to brin▮ up to date."

Throckmorton scratched his chin and nodded. "▮ have a point, Juttner, you have a point." He rega▮ each of the two troopers in turn. "An excellent jo▮ picking up this specimen, for which you will bot▮ commended," he said. "Hauptsturmfuehrer Jut▮ and I will have a word with him. You are dismis▮ Oh, and in light of the Grand Mufti's presence h▮ you will not speak of this capture to anyone for ▮ time being, not even your fellow soldiers. That ▮ direct order. Do you understand?"

"*Jawohl,* Herr Standartenfuehrer."

"*Jawohl,* Herr Standartenfuehrer."

"Good," Throckmorton said. "You may go."

The Muslim troopers saluted and departed, clo▮ the door behind them. Merritt was left standing ▮ puddle of melting snow, his left eye swollen pa▮ shut from the bloody smash on his temple and br▮

Throckmorton sat back down behind his desk▮ Juttner turned to face the British major. Me▮ locked eyes with the SS Hauptsturmfuehrer. Then▮ mouth twisted into a pained smile.

"Well, Matthew," he said in English, "do you t▮

safe for me to sit down for a moment now—before
l down?"

It's fine with me, Walter," Juttner replied in kind,
t perhaps you'd better ask Duncan. After all, it's
office."

Chapter Nineteen

"The train," Merritt said to Throckmorton. "It's early. We've only got the bridge supports p■ mined." He winced, stiffening in the armchair as ■ner dabbed at the open wound on his temple wi■ disinfectant swab. "It's building steam to move ■ the bridge as we speak, isn't it? Can you stop it? ■ us some more time?"

Throckmorton shrugged helplessly. "On what ■ text? That train's movements are the responsibilit■ the tank unit commander charged with getting ■ King Tigers to Mount Zpoda. I have no plausible ■ cuse for stopping it."

"Kronstadt," Juttner said. "His name is Krons■ SS Standartenfuehrer. And he's not the type to ■ up for anyone without an ironclad reason."

"The only way I could delay the train," Throckr■ ton said, "would be to declare the bridge unsa■ which would result in an inspection and the disco■ of the explosives. It would defeat the whole blo■ purpose. . . ." His voice trailed off in frustration. "■

all have our separate missions, Walter. You know
. You know we're bound by the Prime Minister's
rity Directives. We daren't jeopardize my position
:, or Matthew's vital placement. There is only so
:h we can do right now, or all our plans for the
re—and all the unforseen opportunities that may
e our way—will be lost."

You have to get me out of here now," Merritt
, rising unsteadily to his feet. "The bridge is partly
ed to blow. It may be completely rigged by now,
all I know. I have Cernović positioned at the
stup trailhead, ready to ignite the fuse on the main
1 detonator when the train's lead engines pass the
rth vertical support."

How could it be completely rigged?" Throckmor-
asked. "Who did it in broad daylight?"

Sylvia," Merritt replied. "She must have slipped
of the cave when I was dozing. Took it on herself.
climbed out on the underside of the bridge spans
rappelled down to the footings to place the rest
the explosives. She may or not have finished. I
n't see. I had to try to divert those two damned
tries when they suddenly came through the trees
r the rim where Cernović and I were hiding. We
e too close to a new machine-gun nest—any com-
tion would have alerted the crew manning it. So I
1 to draw the sentries back into the woods, away
n Cernović and the machine gun."

So you diverted their attention by allowing one of
m to bash you in the head with a machine pistol?"
tner remarked, taping gauze over Merritt's temple.
Merritt sent him a dry glance. "That wasn't my orig-
l idea," he said, "but that's the way it worked out.
d incidentally, you didn't have to cuff me so hard
oss the mouth out there on the railroad tracks."

For benefit of those two SS troopers, old boy,"
tner replied, clapping him on the upper arm. "Real-
counts in this business, as you know perfectly
l."

"Of course." Merritt looked from Throckmort
Juttner and back again. "I have to get out of h
he reiterated. "I know you can't help me without j
ardizing your own separate missions, but I have t
to the bridge and do what I can."

"There is a conveniently dead Jagdkomm;
Hauptsturmfuehrer dressed in SS winter combat c
ing in that closet over there," Throckmorton
pointing. "He's behind the chest at the far end, a
with Zweig and his aide. He's about your size.
don't you try on his things, wrap your face up,
out the back window like Stirling did, and strol
through the front gate. You should be able to
into the trees again without too much trouble an
down to Zlostup."

"What choice do I have?" Merritt muttered,
rying toward the closet door.

"I'll help him," Juttner said to Throckmo
"You'd better stay at your desk, eh?"

"Yes." Throckmorton let out a short sigh as Ju
moved after Merritt. "Do you know what just
curred to me?"

"I haven't the foggiest," Juttner said over
shoulder.

"I was just thinking," Throckmorton went on, "
it's been an awfully long time since we three had
and bangers and mash in Picadilly together. A
time since school days at Oxford."

Juttner managed a smile before he ducked into
closet after Merritt. "A long time, Duncan," he
"And awfully far away."

Quisp watched from the trees as a stocky ma
middle height, wearing a fine winter overcoat, t
scarf over his nose and mouth, and a strange, we
shaped white turban on his head descended the forv
steps of the luxury passenger railcar on the siding
hurried, in the company of several uniformed
bodyguards, toward the chalet gate. To most Eur

s, the turban would have been an anonymous curi-
ity; nothing more. But the culturally astute Quisp
cognized it for what it was: the headgear of a senior
uslim cleric.

Interesting . . . but not more interesting than the
ct that the luxury car that had just disgorged the
ric was sitting on slightly inclined rails—rails that
clined to the south and declined to the north. The
r's manual brakes and those of the caboose, bunk
r, and antiaircraft flatcar to which it was coupled
re all that prevented it from rolling back down the
ding the way it had come.

Again . . . interesting. A possibility with potential.
uisp just adored possibilities with potential. Galileo
d Leonardo would have been lost without them.

And here was something else interesting: the mas-
e, oncoming bulk of the King Tiger train, five great
ack locomotives huffing and screeching and steam-
g, tank-laden flatcars stretching down the track bend them as far as the eye could see. Quisp could
el the ground vibrate through the snow as the train
mbled up abreast of him at five miles per hour.
eading for the tunnel to the bridge.

The snowfall, which had lightened but never ceased
roughout the day, was becoming heavier again, fur-
er reducing visibility and obscuring detail. Soldiers
ould soon be only vague gray shapes at more than
ty yards.

Slowly Quisp rose to his full height behind a conve-
ent evergreen, watching the King Tiger train rumble
d clank by at its snail's pace. He shifted his Schmeis-
r to the crook of his elbow and dug into his pocket
r a piece of dried beef he'd been saving.

A little snack, a little more train watching, and then
would be time for a stroll.

Weiss had first caught the movement out of the cor-
er of his eye.

A pinch-faced Aryan type with the plainclothes look

of a Gestapo officer had come through the trees n
the dilapidated little shack below and to his left. Str
bling along in front of him through knee-deep sn
her long black hair flyaway and her ragged c
clutched around her, was a teenaged girl. She
being driven forward by the scruff of her neck,
she was absolutely terrified.

Weiss had been unable to look away as the Germ
noticing the shack, had dragged the girl inside it
thrown her down on the filthy floor. She'd tried
crawl away, but he'd kicked her to a wall and hove
over her, opening his coat and unbuckling the belt
his trousers.

Weiss had little doubt what was about to happ
next. He could hear the German snarling at the
above her quiet sobbing.

He refocused his attention down the barrel of
De Lisle. The fate of one more refugee was none
his business. He would not give away his position,
risk missing a clear shot at the Grand Mufti of Jeru
lem, for the sake of one Yugoslav girl. Thousand:
not millions of rapes had already occurred in Eur
throughout the course of the war and there would
thousands if not millions more before it was done.

His people needed deliverance from a mor
enemy, and his brother needed to be avenged. T
was all that mattered.

He flinched as the girl let out a little shriek.

Then, through the veil of falling snow, he saw wh
he had been waiting for. Coming through the co
pound gate at a brisk walk, waving and nodding
the sentries and soldiers of the SS Division Handscha
some of whom bowed their heads and clasped th
hands in deference—was the Grand Mufti of Jeru
lem, Haj Amin al-Husseini, his white turban disti
tive even in the deteriorating visibility. He slowed
pace as he passed a knot of troopers between the gr
house and the gateway arch, his SS guards shado
ing him.

Weiss rested his right cheekbone on the De Lisle's
oden stock and sighted in on the white-turbaned
ure. The snow was an irritant, but he could still see
t well enough to make the shot, and the light wind
s not a factor.

Below and to his left, the girl shrieked again. The
und was so despairing that Weiss lifted his cheek
m the stock and turned his head to look.

The girl was on her back and the German was on
of her, still clad in his heavy trench coat. His pants
re loose around his ankles, and his hips were mov-
; in a frantic rhythm. His hands were locked around
r thin throat.

He was strangling her.

Weiss's eyes darted back to his target and he reset-
d his cheekbone on the carbine's stock. The mufti
s in front of the great house now, moving toward
 vestibule. Some of the Handschar troopers were
lking beside him, bowing their heads repeatedly.

Weiss's finger tightened on the trigger. He would
t try for a head shot at this distance, in this visibility.
stead he would aim at the center of body mass, con-
ntrating on the chest region, and the massive .45-
liber slug would do the rest. Few people survived
 tremendous impact of the round originally de-
ned for the American Colt 1911 automatic pistol, if
ey were hit in the thorax or abdomen.

The girl was trying to scream, but only a thin, gur-
ng sound reached Weiss's ears. The German was
eezing and grunting like a pig.

The Grand Mufti of Jerusalem mounted the steps
 the great house vestibule, waving to the soldiers on
 compound wall.

Weiss focused every shred of his concentration on
 center point of the black coat below the white
rban, and began to squeeze the De Lisle's trigger.

The German's frenzied grunting was reaching a cre-
endo. From the girl there was no sound.

The Grand Mufti faced the north and spread his

arms to the watching soldiers. Behind the scarf
protected his face from the bitter cold, he was aln
certainly smiling. The thick snowflakes whirled
way and that, pushed by random puffs of wind.

The piercing scream of a steam whistle cut the
Weiss fired.

The train was coming.

Sylvia could hear it. Its rumbling and clanking
squealing reverberated out of the tunnel mo
Under her bloody hands, the outer girder from wl
she was hanging began to vibrate. On impulse,
swung over to the inside of the span next to the r
face, stood up cautiously on the inner girder's lo
flange, and peered over the steel-grating catwalk
ran alongside the rails.

She was hoping to see the train coming through
tunnel. Instead she saw multiple flashlights swing
back and forth in the tunnel's dark mouth. It was q
apparent what was happening: SS troopers were w;
ing the rails ahead of the train, checking them for ;
indications of structural failure or sabotage. Someon
probably the tank group's commander—was tak
no chances.

Sylvia had little doubt that the SS would inspect
bridge, too—its spans, supports, and footings—bef
waving the train on. Unless they could be distract

The lead flashlights were almost out of the tun
She pulled herself up onto the catwalk and began
run back toward the center of the bridge, parti;
concealed by the interlocking steel beams that forn
the upper strength members of the individual span

Bristow, still in the antiaircraft gun emplacem
high up along the gorge rim, refocused his Zeiss bin
ulars, tracking the girl as she ran back to the sout'

"What the hell's she doin'?" he muttered under
breath. "Crazy broad . . ."

The clanking and squealing of the train, interspei

steam blasts, echoed off the head wall and through
gorge. Bristow shifted the binoculars to the right.
could just make out the north end of the tunnel
ough the falling snow and treetops, and the tank-
rying flatcars of the King Tiger train filing slowly
) it. Any moment now the lead locomotive would
erge from the tunnel's south end and move onto
bridge.

He trained the binoculars lower, below the rim of
gorge to the Zlostup trailhead. Cernović was still
uched there, a dim shape in the snow behind a
nted evergreen, staying below the line of sight of
men in the new machine-gun nest. Of Merritt
re was no sign, and had not been for nearly half
hour. Bristow had no idea where he'd gotten to. He
fted the binoculars to the bridge's support footings.
The explosives were in place, thanks to the girl.
istow chewed the unlit Camel in his mouth. You
d to give her credit: that was one tough little broad.

He glanced over his shoulder as the shifting wind
aned through the trees near the gun emplacement
a few seconds. Still no sign of anyone. There was
ne kind of temporary field outpost about a quar-
mile down a shallow ravine behind his position, but
one seemed to be in a big hurry to leave it.

Good, he thought. *Everybody stay right where
·y're at for another five or ten minutes.*

He lit the Camel with his Zippo and squinted
·ough the glasses toward the south end of the tunnel
ain, looking for the train.

Two small columns of SS troopers, one on either
·e of the tracks, were emerging from the tunnel
)uth and proceeding onto the bridge. The men were
·ll spaced, perhaps ten feet apart, and were walking
th weapons loosely at the ready, looking this way
d that. The lead SS trooper in each column began
glance down over his side of the bridge, as well.

"Shit," Bristow breathed. He jerked the binoculars
the left, searching.

· Sylvia Kozo was in the middle of the bridge
tween the third and fourth vertical supports. She
walking back toward the SS men in plain sight, d
the center of the tracks.

Back at the tunnel mouth, the massive front en
the lead locomotive nosed into view, keeping
with the flanking infantry columns.

For a moment, the lead SS man on the outer
side of the bridge, a veteran Scharfuehrer na
Vogel, thought he was seeing things. Through
flurrying snow up ahead, in the center of the rail
there appeared to be a scantily clad girl. A scar
clad girl in very abbreviated shorts, an undershir
bulky fur hat, and gloves . . . standing at rigid at
tion, giving the Nazi straight-arm salute. Vogel blin
and looked again—but the apparition was still th

He was so surprised that he didn't think to stop
train. Rather, he stepped over to the edge of the
hand rail and began to trot forward, sending a
order across the tracks to his counterpart at the h
of the second column:

"Bauer! With me!"

The other SS man picked up the pace, falling
beside him along the opposite rail, and the two
them jogged down the track toward the lone fig
standing in the middle of the bridge. Several ot
troopers, catching sight of the girl, began to hu
along behind them.

The train kept moving forward, slowly gather
speed.

Cernović had lost sight of Sylvia when she'd clim
out of the bridge's underpinning girders and up o
the rail bed. All he could see now from his posit
several hundred feet below on the Zlostup trailh
was Tiger tank after Tiger tank sliding out of the t
nel and onto the bridge, with a thin column
capable-looking SS troops moving alongside it.

rtisan commander hunched closer to his evergreen
e, fingering the igniter of the fuse he'd attached to
end of the main detonator cord. If one of those
men on the bridge took a good look down . . .

But they weren't looking down. Most of them
med to be looking forward. . . . And a few were
ginning to trot, as if something ahead on the bridge
d caught their attention.

Černović put Sylvia out of his mind and began to
unt the seconds until the lead locomotive would
ch the fourth vertical bridge support.

Sylvia backed slowly off the center of the track, still
lding the Nazi salute, as the SS men approached at
: run. Behind them, the huge black shape of the
ng Tiger train's lead locomotive loomed larger with
ch passing second, gaining speed. She backed be-
een the upright girders of the bridge's superstruc-
e, until she was against the catwalk railing next to
: bare granite of the Zpoda Gorge head wall.

The SS Scharfuehrer in the lead slowed to a walk
d ran his eyes up and down her, taking in the pale,
nder figure with its youthful shapeliness, the com-
ctely inadequate garb covering—or rather, not
vering—it, and the stiffly held Nazi salute. Then he
gan to laugh, and stepped through the girders to
nfront what appeared to be a very attractive young
ugoslav mental patient.

"Where have you sprung from, pretty one?" he de-
anded in Serbo-Croatian, eyeing the firm breasts be-
ath the filthy undershirt. A knot of SS troops began
gather behind him, most of them grinning in bewil-
red amusement. The lead locomotive of the train
ew near, then clanked on past.

"*Seig Heil, mein Fuehrer!*" Sylvia shouted at the
p of her lungs, stiffening her straight-arm salute and
apping her shoulders back until her breasts strained
her undershirt.

Scharfuehrer Vogel raised an eyebrow, still chuck-

ling. "What the devil do you make of this, Baue
he said out of the side of his mouth.

"I couldn't tell you," Bauer responded, "but s
not supposed to be on this bridge."

From the soldiers gathered behind, the comme
began to flow thick and fast over the metallic cla
of the passing King Tiger train:

"Is she crazy?"

"Why isn't she cold? She should be freezing."

"She is cold. Look at them pointing."

"I don't like it. What's she doing here? Where
she come from?"

"Maybe she likes schnapps. Would you like a dr
to warm you, fraulein?"

"Herr Scharfuehrer, don't you think we should
her to shelter? I volunteer to be in charge of gett
her to shelter."

"No, I volunteer for that duty. . . ."

"No, I do!"

The fifth locomotive of the front five chugged p
The bridge shook with the weight of the tons of s
passing over it.

Come on, Sylvia prayed silently, staring out i
space as if demented. *Come on . . .*

"Forgive me, girl," Cernović whispered, and pul
the igniter.

He clambered away over the steep, snow-cove
rocks below the gorge rim, trying to traverse bene
the sight line of the soldiers manning the machine-g
nest just above him. He managed to cover about f
feet before the fuse burned down and the detona
went off.

SNAP.

The detonator fired the det cord that led to
bridge charges. A fraction of a second later, the cor
nothing more than an elongated version of the sa
material that made up the bulk explosives—vapori
along thirty feet of Zlostup.

CRACK!

And there it stopped.

Cernović whirled, staring at the trail in confusion. Then he saw it: the reason the entire cord had not detonated all the way back to the charges on the bridge supports. A small rockfall—an unlikely, chance occurrence—had, by the worst luck imaginable, cut the cord at some point during the day.

Cernović stared up at the bridge. The King Tiger train was more than halfway across now, its five lead locomotives on the far side of the fourth vertical support. Everything was perfect—except for the faulty det cord.

Voices were coming from above the gorge rim, alerted by the explosion of the detonator and the short length of cord. Cernović didn't even stop to think. There was no time.

He leaped down toward the trailhead, bounding from rock to rock. In his coat pocket were two more sealed detonators. The little rockfall that hid the cut end of the det cord was less than ten running strides away. To find the end and attach another detonator would take no time at all. And this time, it would work. It had to.

They could not fail when they had come so far and were so close.

He dashed down Zlostup, vaulted over the little rock pile, and dug frantically in the snow with both hands. Where was it? Where—

There.

Yanking the cord out of the rocks, he pulled a detonator from his pocket and began to affix it to the cut end, fumbling in his hurry. His fingers felt like rubber balls. . . . *Žplūgk!* . . . *clumsy oaf* . . .

Done, by God.

The rogue-Gypsy grin creased Cernović's swarthy face once more as his fingers touched the igniter.

Brrraaaaaaaaaaaaaaaaaaaaaap!

The savage hail of bullets from the MG-42 in the

machine-gun nest on the gorge rim hammered
Cernović's chest, driving him back off the rock
The unignited detonator dropped into the snow as
body spasmed and shook in a frenzied final dance
the edge of Zlostup.

And then Anton Cernović fell, tumbling like a d
ragged sacrifice into the empty gloom of the Zp
Gorge.

Merritt broke into a run as he heard the buzz
chatter of the MG-42. So did every soldier in the vi
ity of the siding and the chalet gate. The last fla
of King Tigers was just disappearing into the ne
end of the tunnel, followed by the inevitable cabo
As the tail-end car entered the tunnel, several do
SS troopers swarmed across the main rail line
down toward the machine-gun nest overlooking
gorge.

Merritt, bundled up in Ulrich Haak's Hauptsturm
fuehrer's uniform, slowed and hung back when
machine gun did not fire again. He'd heard the cr
of the misfiring det cord, but hadn't been sure w
it was. Now, with a dozen SS clustering around
machine-gun nest and pointing down toward Zlost
he knew with dreadful certainty that the courage
Partisan commander Anton Cernović was gone.

Equally dreadful was the knowledge that the Zp
Skyway Bridge had not been blown, the King Ti
train was well on its way across the head wall, a
there was absolutely nothing he could do about it.
did not even know what had gone wrong—whet
the detonators or the det cord or the charges the
selves had malfunctioned. Something had explod
but what? Whatever it was, it had not taken the fo
ings out from under the bridge.

He could only watch in helpless desperation as
King Tiger train chugged around the long curve
neath the overhanging rock cap, heading for the saf
of the southern tunnel.

*   *   *

Did you hear something?" one of the SS troopers ind Scharfuehrer Vogel shouted to a comrade. nding as they were in the narrow gap between the sing train and the solid rock face of the head wall, clanking and screeching of metal on metal was ost deafening. "Something like firing."

he other trooper was still gazing hungrily at Sylvia zo's breasts. "What? No. Who can hear a damn ig with all that racket going on?"

'Listen to me, girl," Vogel called, leaning in toward via. "You're going to have to come with us."

ylvia responded with a pirouette into a ballerina's nce. *"Jawohl, mein Fuehrer!"* she shouted. "But y after we dance!"

Iow long can I keep this up? she thought.

'The woman's a lunatic," Bauer said into Vogel's . "We're going to have to drag her off the bridge."

Vogel nodded, then noticed the carabiners and ed nuts swinging at Sylvia's hip. Curious, he nted at them. "What are those, pretty one?"

At a loss for anything better to do, Sylvia pirouetted in. "My nuts, *mein Fuehrer!"* she shouted at the of her lungs.

'Your what?"

'Nuts!" Sylvia yelled. *"Nuts, nuts, nuts!"*

'Truly unhinged," Bauer growled to Vogel. "I've d about enough of this."

'Wait," Vogel said. He didn't often encounter dis- ctions this entertaining. "What are your . . . nuts . . . , girl?"

'For climbing!" Sylvia bellowed. "Watch me! atch me!"

She turned, hopped up on the catwalk railing, and ipt across the four-foot gap onto the nearly feature- s granite of the head wall. There was a collective sp from the soldiers, followed by a series of clamations.

Sylvia unclipped a tiny nut and inserted it into a

small crack. "See?" she shouted, swinging from it ‍a monkey. "See what my nuts are for?"

Vogel started to smile, then realized that he coul‍ lay a hand on the girl while she was clinging to ‍cliff. His expression reorganized into a frown. "‍down from there," he ordered over the rumblin; ‍the train. "Right now."

At that instant, nearly a mile away on the u; ‍north rim of the Zpoda Gorge, Sergeant Cole Bris‍ depressed the firing triggers of the 40-millimeter ¿ ‍aircraft cannon he'd aimed at the gorge head wall ‍walked a long burst of incendiary shells across ‍rock and into the explosive charges on the brid‍ second vertical support footing.

Chapter
Twenty

e first white-hot incendiary shell from Bristow's
olley to hit the paired charges on the second bridge
ting detonated them. They exploded as one with a
nderous *CRACK* that caromed through the gorge
m head wall to peak to precipice. A fraction of a
ond later, the long runs of det cord connecting the
er three sets of charges on footings one, three, and
r vaporized simultaneously, detonating the re-
ining explosives. The rapid-fire blasts sounded like
riplet rolling off a titanic snare drum:
RACKCRACKCRACK!

he powerful explosions shattered the concrete
dge footings and sheared through the thick steel of
vertical support girders as if it was so much tinfoil.
eir primary bracing gone, the bridge spans beneath
overhanging rock cap sagged.

Vogel and his men were still looking up at Sylvia
en the bridge suddenly tilted twenty degrees away
m the head wall in a screeching of metal and a
pping of rivets. The violent vibrations shook Sylvia's

slippered feet off their tenuous purchase on the g
ite and she swung free, suspended by one hand
the tiny nut she'd jammed into the thin crack. T
were shrieks of alarm as some of the SS troopers
back through the superstructure girders toward
rumbling wheels on the train tracks.

For a few brief seconds, the bridge held. Then,
a horrible grating screech of tearing metal and
CLANG-BANG-CRACK of buckling joints and s
ping gussets and failing rock anchors, the entire n
ern two-thirds of the Zpoda Skyway Bridge brok
the head wall and dropped into the yawning de
of its namesake gorge—carrying with it the last tw
cars of the King Tiger train.

Sylvia twisted in the air on the single wire
stared down goggle-eyed as the steel superstruc
surrounding her . . . and the great tank-laden t
caged within it . . . simply fell away. It dropped sl
at first, then faster and faster, the huge interloc
spans twisting and undulating as they shrank
something resembling a child's toy. . . .

And then it struck the talus slope at the foot of
head wall, tons of iron and steel crashing into boul
and gravel and snow in a great boiling eruptio
white and gray and black and smoke and flame.
shattered girders tumbled down the steep incline
the dense trees at the bottom of the gorge; in
same avalanche of broken metal rolled the batte
black carcasses of dozens of King Tiger tanks, n
with their turrets and long guns wrenched off, s
with ruptured fuel tanks spewing fire.

Bristow was watching openmouthed from the g
ner's seat of the 40-millimeter antiaircraft cannon
had literally triggered the whole sequence of dest
tion. And it was not over yet. The weight of the fal
flatcars had yanked the front third of the train b
ward, the steel wheels of its five lead locomot
screaming and throwing sparks. The coupling at
rear of the fifth locomotive's coal car then failed, le

the engines to drive forward again, suddenly re-
ed of tons of load. As Bristow continued to watch,
the detached cars—ammunition boxcars, SS bar-
s cars, Kronstadt's headquarters car—were pulled
uccession off the remaining section of bridge like
links of a chain dropping off the edge of a table.

last of the forty-eight King Tigers tumbled into
mangled forest at the bottom of the Zpoda Gorge
illowing clouds of kicked-up snow.

Damn!" Bristow muttered, as the booming echoes
he cataclysm died away.

le slid off the gunner's seat of the 40-millimeter,
ed his Thompson and the Zeiss binoculars, vaulted
r the sandbag wall of the emplacement, and ran
the trees. But before he lost sight of the head wall,
stopped to focus on the spot beneath the rock cap
rhang where, just before he'd fired at the explo-
s, he'd seen Sylvia Kozo climb into view above
passing train. He searched and squinted. . . . And
n grinned.

he was still there.

lerritt, in the company of a dozen other soldiers
'd run up the rim trail to get a better look at the
ckage of the Zpoda Skyway Bridge and the King
er train, could also see Sylvia clinging to the head
l under the rock cap. She was inconspicuous, high
in the deepening shadow beneath the overhang,
the late-afternoon light was waning quickly. No
else appeared to have noticed her; they were all
ring down.

lerritt turned and walked, then ran, back down the
trail. At the dead end of the rail siding onto which
four cars of the Grand Mufti's private train had
n shunted there was a lineman's utility shack. Mer-
kicked open the door and found what he was look-
for: rope. Hundreds of feet of heavy-duty manila
d for block-and-tackle rigging in various types of
dge service.

It would be dark in an hour. Merritt glanced
riedly around. Most of the SS had run to the g
rim, but there were still a few near the tu
entrance.

"*Achtung!*" he shouted in German, pointing a
finger. "You and you! Get over here right now!'

The two Handschar troopers glanced at each o
then jogged back through the falling snow to
Merritt.

"*Jawohl*, Herr Hauptsturmfuehrer!" the first
panted. "The bridge . . . it—"

"I know all about the bridge, idiot!" M
snapped. "We have a man trapped on the cliff ben
the overhang, several hundred yards out. Pick up
rope—that coil and that coil—and follow me. W
going out on the rock cap ridge to save him!"

Once again the soldiers glanced at each other.
top of the rock cap was a broken, knife-edged a
barely safe for a mountain goat to walk on, which
why the Zpoda Skyway Bridge had been constru
beneath it in the first place. It was hazardous in
best of conditions, never mind a snowstorm in
dark.

"Get moving, curse you!" Merritt barked. "Th
a direct order!"

They moved. Between the two of them, they hoi
the big coils of rope over their shoulders and, wor
together, waddled clumsily after Merritt as he
them up the steep, broken incline above the tun
Two hundred backbreaking vertical feet later,
were trudging out onto the rock cap, gasping
breath, urged on by their clearly sadistic Hauptstu
fuehrer.

The Hauptsturmfuehrer was over the edge of
rock cap the instant the first rope was secured
flung off the edge, rappelling downward with the
ond coil lashed to his back, mountaineer style, t
somehow swinging under the overhang and worl
his way in to the head wall. He hadn't even both

take off his gun belt and sidearm, but the two SS
roopers weren't about to argue the point with him.
he man was clearly one of those overzealous Nazi
iehards—a person with whom it was a good idea not
o get into conflict.

It was more than an hour later, and well into dusk,
hen the two troopers finally became impatient
nough to pull the rappelling rope back up from be-
eath the overhang—only to realize that the hard-
riving Hauptsturmfuehrer was no longer attached
o it.

David Weiss was running through the trees, plowing
hrough the deep snow as fast as his tired legs would
arry him. He was heading northeast, away from the
halet compound, on a diagonal course that would
ventually intersect the main rail line. Behind him,
eing virtually dragged along by one hand, was the
irl who'd been assaulted and nearly murdered in the
ilapidated shack. She was in a state of shock, and
nly Weiss's constant admonitions to keep moving
ept her staggering forward in his tracks.

Gestapo Hauptsturmfuehrer Julius Neurath was
ying on his back on the dirt floor of the shack with
is trench coat open and his trousers bunched around
is ankles. He was staring up at the musty, sagging
afters of the derelict structure's collapsing roof. The
45-caliber slug meant for the Grand Mufti of Jerusa-
em had punched a large hole in the center of his
orehead and turned the back of his skull into a crim-
on mush.

Weiss had swung the De Lisle back toward the
nufti after the girl's final pitiable moans and her mur-
lerer's obscene grunting had stung him, at the last
econd, into shifting his aim. But al-Husseini had al-
eady turned and started through the door of the great
iouse. And then the sentry on the northwest corner
if the compound wall had spotted him. Weiss had shot
iim off the wall as he'd yelled a challenge, then bolted

out from beneath the ledge and down the rocky slo
to the shack.

The girl had been nearly catatonic, trembling a
staring with her mass of tangled dark hair falling ov
her tear-stained face, but somehow Weiss had gott
her to her feet and out the door as German a
Serbo-Croatian shouts echoed down from the co
pound walls. He'd been running for his life and he
when a series of what could have been either thunde
claps or explosions had boomed through the gau
black trees and undulating snowdrifts. The bridg
One could only hope.

He had no idea where he was going—only that if th
could get onto the rail bed far enough away from t
chalet garrison, they could travel more quickly on
shoulder. The snow was not as deep beside the track

"Come on, girl!" he panted in Serbo-Croatia
"You have to keep moving! Quickly, now!"

"I . . . can't," the girl sobbed. She sank to her kne
in the snow and tilted her head back, tears streami
down her young face. "I . . . want . . . to . . . die . .

Weiss looked back through the trees in desperatio
then dropped to one knee in front of the girl and too
her head in his hands. "Look at me," he said.

Her flooding eyes opened and fixed on his.

"What is your name?" Weiss asked.

"M-Magda," the girl replied.

Weiss nodded. "Listen to me, Magda. My name
David. And I want you to live. I want you to kee
going."

The girl's dark, lovely eyes remained fastened c
his, full of pain.

"Will you do that for me?" he prompted. "We don
have much time."

She nodded. "I'll . . . I'll try."

"Good. That's all a person can do." He got to h
feet, helping the girl up at the same time. "No
let's go."

They ran on through the snowbound forest, until

st the trees thinned and an open corridor appeared
their right.

"The main rail line," Weiss panted. "It's starting to
t dark. We'll follow the tracks for a while. It'll be
sier to walk along the . . ."

His voice trailed off as the rumbling of steel wheels
ught his ear. He ducked low, pulling the girl down
ith him, and swung up the De Lisle. Through the
ees to the south, movement caught his eye. The rum-
ing grew louder.

The caboose and private car of the Grand Mufti's
ain slid into view, rolling northward down the
ightly declining tracks, powered by nothing but grav-
y and momentum. Sitting on the roof of the private
r with a Schmeisser across his knees, atop the fly-
heel that controlled the brakes, was Professor Theo-
ald Quisp.

On the private car's rearward-end platform, looking
ack up the tracks toward the chalet, was Sergeant
olin Stirling, his long Enfield sniper rifle resting on
e platform's handrail. Beside him was Sergeant Cole
ristow, his Thompson submachine gun cradled in his
rms. A cigarette dangled from his mouth.

Magda let out a terrified whimper, but Weiss jerked
er to her feet and began to run toward the free-
olling cars, pulling her along at his heels.

"Run, Magda!" he blurted over his shoulder. "Run
ist once more! If we can catch those cars, we're free
nd clear!" He raised the De Lisle above his head as
ey floundered out of the trees. *"Hey!"* he yelled in
nglish. "Stirling! Bristow! Quisp! Don't shoot! It's
e, Weiss!" He plowed forward through the snow,
ragging the girl along with all his remaining strength.

The two sergeants started at the sound of his voice,
ringing their weapons around, then lowered them as
ey identified him. Stirling stepped down on the plat-
rm boarding stairs, holding out a hand. Bristow
limbed the roof ladder and yelled to Quisp: "Put a
ttle brake on, Professor! That's Weiss over there!"

Quisp got up and spun the braking flywheel
Weiss and Magda cleared the deep snow and dash
down the edge of the rail bed through the flurry
snow in pursuit of the caboose and private car. The
was a squeal as the brake linings tightened on t
wheel drums, slowing the cars just enough to all
them to catch up.

As Sergeant David Weiss lifted the exhausted g
into Colin Stirling's strong arms, he was struck out
the blue by a sudden pang of regret. It was a reg
he would carry with him the rest of his life.

To the end of his days he would never be able
forgive himself for failing to kill the man most respo
sible for the death and mutilation of his brother.

There was chaos in the aide's office adjoining Star
artenfuehrer Egon Zweig's inner chambers. Har
schar SS officers and noncoms of every rank betwe
Scharfuehrer and Sturmbannfuehrer were crowd
into the small space, spilling through the doorway in
the common room, pushing and jostling and shouti
reports and requests at the slender blond divisi
commander who was standing calmly in front of I
desk, smoking. He was nodding at everyone at t
same time, his brow furrowed in apparent concern,
the information came thick and fast.

"Sabotage, Herr Standartenfuehrer! The Zpo
Skyway Bridge has been completely destroyed! A Pa
tisan was shot and killed below the gorge rim ju
before the explosions! There may be more sabotei
still about!"

"Sir! The north-ridge outpost reports that all me
bers of the gun crew assigned to antiaircraft emplac
ment number four—that was the position seen firi
at the bridge just prior to the detonations—have be
found dead! Executed with single shots to the head

"The Grand Mufti's private coach, Herr Standarte
fuehrer! Someone has uncoupled it and its caboo

om the escorting gun car and allowed it to roll back
wn the main track! It is not in sight, sir!"

Throckmorton homed in on that one. "And why
sn't someone watching it? Why do I post sentries
d run patrols if not to secure the immediate area?"

The youthful lieutenant who'd spoken shrank visibly
being singled out. "Everyone was . . . distracted by
e collapse of the bridge, sir."

"Bah!" Throckmorton declared. "Dereliction of
ty. Put yourself on report, Untersturmfuehrer."

As the cacophony continued Hauptsturmfuehrer
atthias Juttner unobtrusively slid along the wall of
e common room and out the connecting doorway
to the aide's office. The Grand Mufti of Jerusalem
as sitting quietly in a chair at one end of the room,
tting the frenetic activity rage around him. He was
ill wearing his winter coat, the collar turned up, and
ill had his thick wool scarf wrapped around his
outh and nose. Only his keen eyes showed in the
t between the top of the scarf and the bottom edge
 his white turban.

Juttner was on the verge of making the decision,
nce the assassin attached to Merritt's team had been
able to get the mufti in his sights, to talk al-Husseini
to a back room where he could quickly and quietly
it his throat. It violated his Priority Directive from
hurchill, but he had come to the conclusion that the
enefit was worth the risk of discovery. The free world
ould be much better off without the Grand Mufti of
rusalem constantly plotting against it and abetting
e Nazi regime.

He put a hand on the mufti's shoulder and leaned
own. "Your Excellency," he called over the noise.

Al-Husseini looked up at him.

"Your Excellency," Juttner said, removing his hand
d giving a little bow. "Perhaps we should get out
f here. Go to one of the back rooms until the com-
otion dies down. You should stay inside where it is

safe until the situation has been properly analyzed a
the area secured, but there is no need for you to
subjected to this uproar."

The mufti blinked at him, reached up, and pul
down his scarf.

Juttner stared.

"I think I stay here," Mustapha Snagi growled
his broken German.

Back in the common room Throckmorton was s
standing against the front of his desk, gazing up at
mad glass eyes of the mounted game heads as they
turn gazed down at the madness seething bene
them.

"Standartenfuehrer Zweig! We estimate that the c
struction of the bridge and train has just cost us
excess of four hundred men—tank crews, SS suppo
ing infantry, and various Handschar personnel!"

"Herr Standartenfuehrer—the commander of t
King Tiger tank group, Standartenfuehrer Kronsta
has been killed along with all his men! His tanks ha
all been completely destroyed! Not one is left!"

"Herr Standartenfuehrer! There is enemy activity
the north wall of the chalet compound. One sen
has already been killed—others claim that Partisan
filtrators are active in the trees as close as fifty yard

Throckmorton almost smiled as he finished his cig
rette. It was music to the ears. As sweet as
Brahms lullabye.

"Sir! This is critical! A report has just come in of
coordinated series of Partisan attacks against t
Twenty-eighth SS Regiment on the northeaste
shoulder of Mount Zpoda! The attacking forces a
pear to be made up primarily of elements of the Se
ond Proletarian Brigade! Fighting is intensifying, sir

Again Throckmorton almost smiled. *Tito.* He
made it across the Ugljevik Plateau and linked up wi
other Partisan units for a diversionary attack agai
the Handschar main line of advance, as Cernov
had promised.

Well, they didn't need a diversion anymore—the
ridge was down and the Tiger train with it. But there
was certainly another opportunity here. . . .

You're on, Duncan, he thought. *Time to tread the
boards and chew the scenery.*

He looked at the anxious Hauptsturmfuehrer who'd
hammered out the last report. "Communicate this
order at once to the commander of the Twenty-eighth
Regiment," he said. "Pull back to the northwest
without delay. Take no further casualties. Disengage
the enemy and retreat into the Bulvar Valley immedi-
ately to regroup."

The Hauptsturmfuehrer looked aghast. "But . . .
but—Herr Standartenfuehrer," he protested. "That
will allow the Partisans to break through—"

"Do not second-guess my direct orders!" Throck-
morton shouted, purpling nicely. "The Twenty-eighth
SS will withdraw, regroup, and counterattack at my
discretion!"

"But, sir," the Hauptsturmfuehrer soldiered on
bravely, "should I at least . . . relay your *additional*
orders to move the third and fourth battalions of the
Twenty-ninth SS Regiment into the gap? Sir?"

Triumph was spreading through Captain Duncan
Throckmorton like warm wine. He lit another ciga-
rette, gazed beneficently down at the stupefied young
officer, and cleared his throat.

"No," he said.

Chapter
Twenty-one

By the time word of a pair of runaway train cars—caboose followed by a passenger coach—reach each successive repair station and gunnery unit alo the Zpoda Gorge main line, the cars had already rur bled past. . . . A result of some kind of inexplicab inefficiency in communications from the Barbo Hou field headquarters of the SS Division Handscha which had lost the rolling stock in the first place. was well after dawn when the coach and caboos which had been rolling backward down the line night with brakes tightened just enough to prevent tl wheels from jumping the track, finally slid out betwee the lowest foothills of the Majevica Mountains an onto the frozen, marshy flatlands beyond.

The coach and caboose squealed slowly to a halt gravity finally relinquished its grip. The cars sat on tl rails in the middle of an empty winter landscape, bur brake linings smoking, for ten minutes before the tw self-powered jitterbugs that had been chasing the ru aways down the slopes for nearly fifteen miles final

ht up. Each small service trolley contained, in ad-
n to a railroad lineman, half a squad of SS troops,
:d to the teeth.

ie Obersturmfuehrer in charge of the squad leapt
of the lead jitterbug as the lineman braked it
ity feet behind the passenger coach. Luger drawn,
an along the snow-covered rail bed, waving his
on.

'ake the right side, Scharfuehrer!" he shouted.
d I want men up at the front of the caboose!
ll enter and clear the cars from both ends at the
: time!"

'awohl, Herr Obersturmfuehrer!" the sergeant
:ed. "Kruger! Buschhagen! At the other end of
caboose. *Schnell!*"

he fifteen SS troops fanned out around the cars,
hine pistols pointing up at the board-covered win-
s of the coach and caboose.

Careful, careful!" the lieutenant instructed, brac-
himself at the boarding stairs of the coach's end
form. He glanced down the sides of the cars,
:king the positions of his men, then nodded to the
neisser-bearing trooper opposite him. "Ready? . . .
!"

.t both ends of the caboose and coach, SS troopers
;ed up the platforms and through the doors. There
e shouts—but no shooting—as the assault person-
communicated with each other and then linked up
de the cars.

'he coach and caboose were empty. If there had
r been anyone riding in them during their lengthy
down from Mount Zpoda, they were long gone
/.

'he Obersturmfuehrer holstered his pistol and
ked slowly through the luxurious interior of the
'ate car, taking in the velvet armchairs, polished
ıogany, and lush carpets. He paused beside the
ng table, pulled the stopper from a cut-glass de-
ter that sat in a specially made nook, and sniffed it.

"Chianti," he muttered. "Good, too." He lifte
decanter. There wasn't much left. Pity.

He passed the decanter to his Scharfuehrer. "
Emil. Have a drink."

The noncom smiled as he took it. "Thank you
ersturmfuehrer Dietrich."

Dietrich's roving gaze settled on a teacup jan
into a crumpled cloth napkin in the center of the
It had been used as an ashtray. There were
crushed cigarette butts in it. On a whim he p
them out and examined them. Then his eyes wid
the tiny logos both read CAMEL.

The muted clang of a cooking pot sounded thr
the open door of the luxury car's small, narrow g
Every man in the compartment flinched and s
up his weapon. Obersturmfuehrer Dietrich yanke
Luger from its holster again and dodged behin
the jamb of the galley doorway. Cautiously he pe
around the corner, pistol brandished.

Empty.

"Nobody there," he whispered, turning his l
"Maybe just something shifting—"

There was another dull clang, followed by a
tained rattling.

The SS troopers crowded up behind their lieuter
machine pistols ready. Dietrich crouched low to a
them to fire over his head if need be, then sprang
the galley onto one knee, searching down the b.
of his Luger for a target.

The elongated little kitchen was truly empty.
the sliding metal door of the storage cabinet ben
the food-preparation countertop was vibrating. It
been jammed shut by a heavy crate of canned
that had fallen over and become wedged against

"Emil," Dietrich said to his sergeant again, this
waving him forward with his pistol. He took up a
tion just to one side of the cabinet door as the Sc
fuehrer stepped past him and gripped the crate
one big hand.

eady?" Dietrich mouthed, aiming carefully.
."

e Scharfuehrer jerked the crate loose. The door
ack with a bang.

etrich stared.

e man in the sights of his Luger was curled up
fetal position, his long robes bunched around his
. He was covered in baking flour, apparently from
k that had burst next to him. His reddish-blond
d and thinning gray hair were caked with it, and
yes, blinking painfully in the sudden light, were
y and red. He focused on the SS Obersturm-
rer, then asked in a cracked, plaintive voice:
re they . . . are they gone yet?"

etrich glanced up at his sergeant, then back down
e cramped figure jammed in with the cooking pots
dry goods. "Who the hell are you?" he demanded.
Vho am I? *Who am I?*" the well-floured cabinet
bitant responded, his energy if not his dignity ap-
ntly returning. "I am Haj Amin al-Husseini—*the
ld Mufti of Jerusalem!*"

ietrich looked at his sergeant again, then pursed
ips in irritation and glared down at the stowaway.
Of course you are," he growled. "And I'm the
in the moon." He waved the Luger. "Now get
of there."

Chapter Twenty-two

"A remarkable achievement," Wild Bill Don
said, swirling the cognac in his glass. "R
quite unbelieveable that it went as well as it did.
raised the snifter toward Winston Churchill and S
art Menzies, who sat opposite him in the Prime M
ter's 10 Downing Street study. "Here's to Oper.
Handschar."

"Here's to the men who pulled it off, Gene
Martin Judson appended, lifting his small glas
sherry, "and the woman."

Donovan, ever the American gentleman, turne
nodded courteously in Judson's direction. "Of co
To them. To all of them."

The four power brokers drank, and afterwar
in silence for a long moment. With practiced ri
Churchill cut and lit one of his trademark cigars.

"So that's your boy, Martin," Donovan said to Ju
"SS Hauptsturmfuehrer Matthias Juttner is actually .

362

Matthew Judson," the elegant industrialist filled in.
only son."

onovan shook his head, smiling. "How the Sam
did you get him into the SS," he asked, "much
placed so highly? He's right in the wolves' den,
God's sake—rubbing shoulders with Kaltenbrun-
and Schellenberg and even Himmler himself. I
he even sat in on piano at a few dinner parties
n that animal Heydrich—may he rot in hell—got
ncontrollable urge to show off his violin skills to
ptive audience."

According to Canaris, he did indeed," Judson re-
d. "Matthew always had a nice touch for both
h and American jazz. In his teens he used to sit
hours, trying to replicate the phrasings of a rather
eputable New Orleans bordello musician by the
e of Jelly Roll Morton—much to my dismay, I'm
sorry to say. I felt he should be spending more
studying business management fundamentals,
e he was going to work for me at my offices in
nich after completing his studies at Oxford."

And that's where he first met Merritt and
ockmorton?"

Yes. They were together at Oxford from 1928 to
1. Inseparable. Young and handsome and smart
athletic and . . . *rich*, of course. The cream of the
lish upper class, denied nothing by their proud
ents. Perhaps, I remember fearing at the time,
rindulgently so." Judson smiled a bit sadly. "Their
rs used to refer to them, with considerable lack of
ginality, as the Three Musketeers."

onovan, his instincts flawless as usual, promptly
e up with the perfect comment: "I would say your
rs have proven groundless, Martin—with regard not
to your son, but all three of these exceptional
n."

udson inclined his impeccable head. "Thank you,
neral."

'Bill, please," Donovan said.

"Of course—Bill." Judson sipped sherry
crossed his legs. "You asked how Matthew can
be a member of the SS. It's quite simple. He
been working for me since 1932 in a rather anony
capacity as an industrial salesman, learning the
ness he would one day inherit from the ground up
was based in Munich, but traveled extensively thr
Germany and the rest of Europe, servicing and se
up new accounts. His language skills—particular
German—became first-rate. After Hitler and his
gang pulled off what was effectively a coup in 19
group of us—Winston, Stewart, myself, and a
others—were quite certain we could see the wr
on the wall, though we could never convince that
varicating milksop Chamberlain[1] to hold a hard
against the so-called Fuehrer and his political th
For a moment the perpetually composed English
tleman looked almost angry.

"Matthew was approached with the idea of infil
ing the SS in its formative stages by becoming a w
recruit—a long-term commitment, though no one
any idea exactly *how* long. I suppose I should
realized that he would jump at the chance to take
in some kind of cloak-and-dagger adventure; he
only twenty-four at the time and quite bored with
life of an industrial salesman–cum–privileged hei
was a simple matter for MI-6 to create a new ide
for him and provide forged documents of the hig
quality—birth certificate and such—that identified
irrefutably as one Matthias Juttner, scion of a
established family of German brewers from sout
Bavaria. My long-standing business connections in
around Munich helped in this regard."

"So he's been a bona fide member of the SS s
1934?" Donovan said. "That's *ten years.*" He pau
"And in that time he's attained the rank of cap
and positioned himself next to the most powerful
ple in the SS hierarchy. Amazing. That would m
him—"

"One of the most important Allied agents in Europe," Churchill grunted, puffing on his cigar. "He's situated himself perfectly, right on the periphery of the Nazi inner circle, remaining inconspicuous by keeping his head low and turning down promotion after promotion. A high-ranking officer—a lieutenant colonel, full colonel, or general, for example—has duties and responsibilities that limit his movements; a lowly captain can go anywhere . . . particularly if that captain has the social and political skills—the intellectual *dexterity*—of Matthew Judson."

"You wouldn't want a man like this compromised by allowing him to take unnecessary risks," Donovan remarked. "He's far too valuable right where he is, feeding information out and disinformation back in."

"Exactly," Menzies said, "which is where the Prime Minister's concept of Priority Directives comes in. A Priority Directive is a standing order to an operative who occupies a covert position of extreme importance. He is not to risk discovery under any circumstances. He is to limit the chances he takes in order to preserve his position. This means, for example, that even though Matthew Judson, as Matthias Juttner, passes within arms' reach of many notables in the Nazi regime on a regular basis, he cannot actually reach out and assassinate any of them—not even Hitler himself. The damage he is able to do by orchestrating events and passing information far exceeds the value of removing a single man, regardless of who he is."

"So he's still well placed," Donovan said, "despite the debacle with the Grand Mufti."

Menzies and Churchill and Judson exchanged amused glances. "An embarassing episode from which Haj Amin al-Husseini's prestige within the Third Reich may never recover," Menzies commented. "But the redoubtable Hauptsturmfuehrer Matthias Juttner has managed to deflect all blame for the fiasco onto a degenerate, and *dead*, Gestapo agent named Julius Neurath, and a belligerent, and also dead, SS Standar-

tenfuehrer named Wilhelm Kronstadt, the command
of the King Tiger tank group."

"It's too bad Weiss wasn't able to take the Gran
Mufti out," Donovan said. He looked at Churchill an
Menzies. "You didn't tell Joe Haskell and me abo
that part of the operation during our meeting a mont
or so ago."

"Well, that was something we threw in at the la
minute," Menzies explained, "once we heard throug
Juttner and Canaris that the mufti was heading fo
Yugoslavia after the failed assassination attempt b
Aaron Weiss in Berlin. The main objective of Opera
tion Handschar was to get the bridge blown an
Throckmorton positioned. Merritt was instructed t
turn Weiss loose against the mufti with the appro
priate amount of—shall we say, *motivation*?—at th
most opportune moment. It almost worked. The assa
sination of al-Husseini would have been a nice bonus.

"One can't have everything," Churchill growled, ex
haling smoke, "although one can try."

"I suppose," Donovan said. "But now—the personne
involved. I know we have Bristow and Stirling bac
They made their way to Slovenia in the north and man
aged to make contact with the OSS mission workin
with Partisan groups up there. They were flown out b
Blenheim bomber to Sicily. But what about Weiss?"

"No word," Menzies told him. "According to Bris
tow and Stirling, he and the girl, Magda, left the rol
ing cars in the lower foothills of the Majevicas withou
explanation, only shaking hands and saying good-bye
They jumped on a slow corner just before dawn an
disappeared into the trees."

Donovan was silent for a moment. "Do you thin
Weiss was annoyed that you used his brother's deat
to manipulate him into taking a shot at the Gran
Mufti of Jerusalem?" he asked.

Menzies's face was a pleasant mask. "He may have
been a touch put out."

Churchill filled in the slightly charged void that fol

by changing the subject: "Merritt and that ex-
inary young Yugoslav woman Sylvia Kozo made
n off the head wall of the Zpoda Gorge. They
l until dark, then used the rope Merritt had
ht, Sylvia's climbing nuts, and their own incredi-
ountaineering skills to descend to Zlostup. Then
etraced their steps along that ancient hunter's
ll the way back to the grove where Sylvia had
ted the traitor Vlado. They scavenged the re-
ng clothes from his body—Merritt had been
g his with Sylvia, and they were both close to
ng—then took the ascending side path to the
a snowfields. Two days later they rendezvoused
rear-guard elements of Tito's Second Proletar-
rigade.

ajor Merritt was flown out to Bari five days later,
ylvia Kozo elected to go with him, with Tito's
ng. They're in London at this very moment, hav-
late dinner, I expect." Churchill beamed around
gar, the broad grin creasing his bulldog face. "By
ge," he declared, his shrewd eyes twinkling, "if
's one thing I like as well as a fine adventure
it's a fine romance."

suppose MI-6 and SOE aren't done with them
Donovan surmised. "They're valuable assets. So
ling."

) is Bristow," Menzies pointed out.

ou can't have him," Donovan retorted good-
redly. "He now belongs exclusively to me, as a
me member of OSS."

nzies chuckled. "Touché, General," he said.
I you're right: we'll find a use for Major Merritt
Miss Kozo again soon enough. But for the time
, we'll leave them alone."

's a shame about Cernović," Judson said quietly.
to mention Hurst and your other man, Bill—
ant D'Amato."

novan nodded. "A shame. But they helped get
b done."

" 'Favored are the warriors who fall in tł
fight,' " Churchill recited, " 'for they shall dw‹
ever in the undying glow of their own glory.
drew on his cigar. "A quote from my favorite

"I like that," Donovan said. "Who is it?"

Churchill blew out smoke and smiled. "Me.'

Donovan returned the smile and sipped ⊂
"Speaking of quotes," he said. "What abo‹
Quisp fellow? He seems more than a little us
odd. Where is he?"

"Still in Yugoslavia," Menzies replied. He
his fingers. "We don't know exactly where. I
Bristow and Stirling moving in the right dir
traveled with them for a day and a half, the
adieu and split off. He's back in his beloved Maj
making trouble for the Germans and their a
expect. I imagine we'll hear from him in som‹
or another eventually. . . . We always do."

Donovan drained his snifter, savored the ⊂
and held up his glass. "Do you mind, Mr. Prime
ter?" he said to Churchill. "I really feel that
time I've heard the full story of Captain L
Throckmorton, I'll need a fully charged glass."

Churchill, always delighted to accommodate
low drinker, got out of his chair to proffer the ⊂
decanter. "Allow me, General Donovan."

"Thank you, sir," Donovan said. Churchill p
a generous splash of the premium brandy into h‹
ter, and both men reseated themselves.

Martin Judson began, "Duncan Throckmor
from one of the great landowning families in
western England, a dynasty with holdings on
sides of the Scottish border. He's the second ș
his generation. He was a tremendous sportsman
teens and early twenties—a sailor, skier, and
shot with rifle and especially pistol. He was ⊂
'thirty-six British Olympic team with Walt Merri‹
won a silver medal in pistol shooting.

"But his great love was acting. He underst

ivier at the Royal Shakespeare Company and per-
med in productions all over Britain. His Hamlet
s one of the best I've ever seen. A true natural,
d with such a genuine interest in portraying *charac-*
that he did not become particularly famous: he was
chameleonlike that you couldn't put your finger on
n. He had no desire to be a star, per se.

"Like many young men of his age and class, he was
cruited into MI-6, and from there into SOE. His
lls as an actor, as well as his education and ability
handle a pistol, made him an ideal covert agent."

"Not unlike his old friend Matthew Judson,"
urchill rumbled. "They both share the same poise,
e same damn-your-eyes confidence that enables
em to function convincingly in the company of some
the most dangerous villains in Europe."

Judson smiled appreciatively at Churchill before
ntinuing: "Duncan Throckmorton had already been
half a dozen missions into occupied Europe—two
th Walt Merritt—when we received an intelligence
port on the composition of Reichsfuehrer Himmler's
est creation, the all-Muslim SS Division Handschar,
ich was just completing its formative training in
ance. In that report were photographs of Hand-
har's commanding officer and his staff. It was Gen-
al Gubbins, I believe, who was first struck by the
canny resemblance between Egon Zweig and Dun-
n Throckmorton.

"We dug up everything we could on Herr Zweig—
mily photos, school pictures, military portraits and
ld shots. We even obtained some invaluable film
otage of him reviewing the newly trained Muslim
oops of Handschar—courtesy of SS Hauptsturm-
ehrer Matthias Juttner and his Berlin connections."

"Useful, that Juttner, isn't he?" Donovan remarked.
Judson smiled his appreciation. "It became clear to
that Duncan Throckmorton was indeed a virtual
uble of Egon Zweig—what is referred to in German
a doppelganger. Oh, there were a few subtle differ-

ences in hair color and the bone structure of
face—particularly the nose—but those were easily ⟨
rected by surgery."

"Throckmorton had no problem with that?" Do⟨
van inquired. "Having his face surgically altered⟨
resemble another man?"

Judson glanced over at Churchill and Menzies. ⟨
silent exchange between the three Englishmen was ⟨
ticeably sober.

"No," Judson said. "Duncan didn't mind."

Donovan shrugged. "I mean, having to spend ⟨
rest of your life with a face other than your ow⟨
surgically modified so that you can eliminate and t⟨
impersonate someone you don't particularly adm⟨
Not many people would do it."

"The rest of his life," Menzies echoed. "He kr⟨
that when he agreed to go under the knife."

"He's a tremendously dedicated soldier," Dono⟨
said, raising his snifter to his lips. "I admire him.'⟨

"Yes," Menzies commented. "Quite."

"The idea to actually replace Zweig was Duncan⟨
Judson said. "We'd been trying to think of some v⟨
to exploit the resemblance, perhaps by having him ⟨
personate Zweig here and there, temporarily, to ⟨
tain certain kinds of intelligence or use his autho⟨
as a Standartenfuehrer to enable saboteurs to acc⟨
this or that target. Duncan volunteered to have s⟨
gery so that the resemblance would be perfect, a⟨
then take Zweig's place at the head of the SS Di⟨
sion Handschar."

"Amazing," Donovan said. "For how long?"

"Indefinitely," Menzies said.

Donovan looked at him. "What do you mean, ⟨
definitely? How and when are you going to pull h⟨
out?"

"We're not going to pull him out," Menzies said⟨

"I don't understand," Donovan persisted. "W⟨
he's doing right now, effectively mismanaging Ha⟨
schar on purpose, is very dangerous. Sooner or la⟨

s going to be called to account for it—for getting
e of Himmler's pet SS divisions raked over the
ls. And when he does he'll probably either be
ged or shot."

'It's Duncan Throckmorton's decision," Menzies
lared. "He can request an extraction any time he
oses." He paused. "But none of us think he will."

Donovan was about to ask why not when Churchill
rrumphed and exhaled a long cloud of cigar smoke.
amn fine work he's been doing, too, these past sev-
l weeks," he growled. "The day after the Zpoda
yway Bridge and the King Tiger train were de-
oyed, Tito's Partisans broke through a gap in the
ndschar lines on the western shoulder of Mount
oda. They trapped the Twenty-eighth SS Regiment
the Bulvar Valley—which is something of a box
yon, to use one of your American Old West meta-
ors, General Donovan—and shot it to pieces. The
venty-ninth SS Regiment lost its third and fourth
ttalions due to poor tactical deployment. Essentially
SS Division Handschar took two black eyes, a bro-
n nose, and a bloody lip at the hands of Captain
ncan Throckmorton, alias Standartenfuehrer Egon
veig."

"The Handschar advance across the Majevica
ountains has been stalled decisively," Menzies said,
nd the division's ability to prosecute further cam-
igns in Yugoslavia severely curtailed." His smile was
rd. "If the SS leadership thought they had a morale
oblem with the Muslim rank and file before, it was
thing compared to the one they're having now.
ere are more Bosnian Muslim troopers shedding
eir uniforms and heading for home in the dead of
ght these days than there ever were."

"Incredible," Donovan said. "But that's our busi-
ss, isn't it? Engineering the incredible."

"Oh yes," Churchill remarked dryly, "we're incredi-
e, all right." He raised his cognac glass. "Here's to
, damn it."

Everyone toasted and drank.

"Who," Donovan inquired mildly, setting his sni
down, "is the Black Lyre?"

Churchill's sharp eyes flicked over to Menzies
Judson.

"Let me guess," the OSS general continued. "J
ner?"

The three Englishmen were silent.

"Canaris?"

No answer.

"Someone I'm not aware of, then," Donovan s
shrugging. "I thought all of us in OSS, SOE, and I
6 trusted each other. We're in this fight together.
Aren't we?"

Churchill harrumphed again, then began to cut
end of another cigar. "Point well taken, General D
ovan," he said. He stuck the cigar between his I
fired it up, and settled back with his cognac gl
"Admiral Wilhelm Canaris, as you well know, is
head of Abwehr. He is also an old-school Gern
patriot who despises the Nazis—in particular Hi
and Himmler. For years now he has been trying
effect political change in Germany while retaining
position of power within the regime—not an easy tr
when you're dealing with Nazis. But he has mana
this delicate balancing act successfully so far

"Canaris is also the head of the Schwarze Kap
Do you know the translation?"

"'Black Orchestra,'" Donovan replied with
hesitation.

Churchill nodded through a fog of cigar smo
"Correct, General. The Black Orchestra. It is a co
name for the high-level German opposition to Hit
and the Nazi regime. The Black Orchestra includes
its membership some of the most important men
Germany. Under Canaris's leadership, they have be
trying and continue to try to destabilize the Nazi
gime without having the country they love colla
with it into a smoking ruin."

"They'd better hurry up," Donovan remarked.

"Yes, they had," Churchill went on. "But with re-ect to the Black Lyre: that is a code name we came with to identify specific communications between ttner, Canaris, and the men in this office. A conspir-y ring within a larger conspiracy ring, if you like. e Black Lyre is an instrument that plays in the ack Orchestra—and we are all part of it."

"Evocative," Donovan said. "I like the name."

"It's apropos, isn't it?" Churchill replied. "Look at General Donovan. What do we do? We deceive, : manipulate, we mislead, we connive. We prowl like ieves and strike without warning out of the darkness. e endeavor to create confusion and misdirection at ery turn. We set up puppets and dance them across e stage, and for this we use friend and foe alike, if will further our aims.

"In wartime, Truth is so precious that She should ways be attended by a bodyguard of lies. With that our premise, every last one of us, out of necessity, a black liar."

Donovan smiled slowly. "A black liar. By God, Mr. ime Minister, I do believe I am. *Mea culpa*, and no cuse submitted." He raised his snifter. "And your mark about Truth needing to be attended by a body-uard of lies—a memorable turn of phrase. You ould use it in one of your speeches."

Churchill raised his own glass. "Why, thank you, eneral," he said in his bulldog growl of a voice. "I believe I shall."

Epilogue

You could smell summer in the air, even in the gr
inner courtyard of a gray-walled prison. And ov
head, feathery white clouds were scudding acros:
clear blue sky. . . . The kind of fast-moving clo
that were harbingers of fair winds and fine sailing
the Adriatic Sea south of Trieste.

It had been nearly a month since the Allied invasi
of Normandy. The Americans, British, and Canadi:
had secured their beachheads, moved inland, and w
battling their way through France with multiple sup
lines pumping munitions, machinery, and fuel to th
spearhead units in a ceaseless flow. Not even Romn
could stop them now.

The SS Hauptsturmfuehrer was reading somethir
Something to do with charges. Throckmorton cau;
fragments of it, though he wasn't really paying attenti

". . . Treasonous incompetence . . . criminal in
sponsibility . . ."

He coughed wetly—it was truly painful now
turned his head, and spat on the gray flagstones
the courtyard.

". . . Betrayal of trust . . . failure to follow esta
lished tactical doctrines . . ."

Throckmorton put a cigarette into his mouth a

ly lit it with a wooden match. His prized jeweled
hill he'd given to Walter Merritt months earlier.
. . Resulting in the virtual nullification of the SS
sion Handschar as an effective fighting force . . ."
e inhaled the cigarette smoke deeply. Funny that
dn't hurt his chest the way coughing or panting
It was still a pleasant enough diversion, even if it
probably contributed to the terminal lung cancer
been diagnosed with a year earlier. Thank God
adn't had to walk over any more mountains dur-
his four-month tenure as division commander of
dschar. A Standartenfuehrer always got to ride,
when he was retreating.
here was a loud CLACK-*CLACK* of Mauser
bolts.
hrockmorton drew on his cigarette again, looking
t the clouds riding the wind far overhead. It had
a a good life, if a short one. And he was lucky:
many men were given the opportunity to choose
r own exit, and accomplish something meaningful
he process.
e coughed again, grimaced, and spat, tasting
od. Yes, it had been a good life. But now it was
to go.
aptain Duncan Throckmorton flicked his cigarette
y, clasped his hands behind his back, and picked
perfect cloud to watch sail across the sky.
Ie was thinking again of the sea off Trieste.

What's that?"
Iagda jumped down off the sun-warmed rock of
little outcropping, ducked behind a stunted olive
, and dropped to her haunches with coltish energy
ront of David Weiss, who was sitting in the grass,
hing water from a canteen on his sun-bronzed face,
The Bosporus," he said. "It's a narrow strait that's
t of the waterway connecting the Mediterranean
Black Seas. Istanbul is at the southwestern end
t." He held out the canteen. "Here. Drink some."

Magda shook her head, her mane of dark hair
ing around her shoulders. "I'm not thirsty."

"You soon will be. Drink."

The girl stuck out her lower lip, then took the
teen and tipped it up. *She is nearly as brown a*
bark of the tree I'm sitting beside, Weiss tho
Months of moving slowly through mountainous c
try, living off the land and avoiding settlements
soldiers of every kind—for in Nazi-controlled Mad
nia and Greece and Bulgaria they were invar
hostile—had made both of them lean and fit, an
most feral in their survival instincts.

"Do we have to cross it?" Magda asked, her
eyes flashing. She tossed him the canteen and sh
the strap of the Schmeisser machine pistol she ca
over one shoulder. She'd flourished on the long
ney despite its many privations, turned from fr
ened child into confident, capable young wo
Weiss had noticed this happening and felt justifi
taking some credit for it.

"Yes, Magda," he said. "We have to cross it.
we have to get through the rest of Turkey—past
kara, Tarsus, and Antioch—to reach Syria."

"Are there Germans in Turkey?" Magda inqu
looking deeply into his eyes, as she always did.

"There are Germans everywhere," Weiss gru
leaning back on one elbow. "Including Turkey."

"Mmm. Well, we'll have to be careful." *She do*
sound too concerned, Weiss thought.

She moved up beside him and rolled onto her
in the grass. "Do you know what day it is today"

Weiss put a hand over his eyes to block the
"No idea. How about Wednesday?"

Magda dug her elbow into his ribs, giggling. "St
man. It's my birthday."

Weiss removed his hand from his eyes and loo
at her. "Really?"

"Really."

"How old are you?"

e propped herself up on one arm, letting the ma-
pistol slide to the ground. "You have to guess,"
said mischievously, tickling his jaw with a piece
'ass.

slapped the grass away and scratched his face.
en," he said.

e pulled his hair. "No! Guess again."

Jmm . . . eight, then."

agda lunged onto his chest, forcing him back into
grass and pinning him there. He let her, laughing.
'm sixteen today," she said, smiling down at him.
e smiled back. "Happy birthday, Magda," he
ed.

e looked at him for a long moment, then sat back
looked out toward the strait of blue water in the
'distance.

What do we do after we get to Syria?" she asked.
We go through it," Weiss told her, sitting up and
hing loose grass off his collar.

s it far? Through Turkey, I mean."

Yes. Very far."

That's all right," Magda said. She thought for a
nent. "And Syria? Is it far, too?"

avid Weiss looked at her and nodded. "Very far,
gda. A long way."

But then we're in Palestine?"

e nodded again, this time with an encouraging
e. "Then we're in Palestine."

he smiled back, her strong white teeth gleaming in
tanned face. Then she rocked onto one knee,
ed up her Schmeisser, and got to her feet.

We'll make it, won't we, David?" she said. It
n't really a question.

avid Weiss picked up his own machine pistol, the
teen, and the small rucksack he always carried, and
ted himself to his feet beside her.

Yes, Magda," he said. "We will."

Postscript

"The bomb did not go off, Colonel. The trigg
mechanism failed."

"Thank God for sloppy workmanship." The I.
Defense Force colonel adjusted the Glock automa
its holster on her hip and looked again at the s
Palestinian boy sitting on the steel bench in the ho
cell of the Tel Aviv police substation. "What's tha
got on under his shirt?" she demanded.

"Some kind of medieval chain-mail vest, believe
not," the young IDF sergeant said. "A museum
really." He patted the homemade bomb belt laid
on the table next to him. "We noticed it after
stripped the explosives off him. I thought I'd lea
on so you could have a look."

The colonel walked over to the boy and gently tu
down his shirt. "It's chain mail, all right. And very
Her eyes narrowed as she looked at the boy's back.
is interesting: there are three holes in the back of it.
bullet holes. See where the links are torn?"

The sergeant moved up on the boy's opposite side
examined the holes. "You're right, Colonel. M
bullets—although I suppose, from the age of the thing,
could just as easily have been made by spears or lance

"Mmm." The stern, handsome woman stood b

d her arms, and gazed into the child's eyes. "Pal-
ian ID card?"

"es," the sergeant said, holding up the little rectan-
f plastic. "This is Jamal Amin Snagi, resident of
allah."

low old?"

leven."

ie colonel shook her head. "God."

e sighed, pulled up a chair, reversed it, and sat
n facing the boy. "Jamal."

ie boy glanced fearfully at her, taking in the olive
military fatigues, the hard lines of the face beneath
ray-streaked black hair, and the strong brown fore-
s that were folded on the back of the chair.

Vho sent you to blow yourself up on the bus?"

ie boy was too young and frightened not to answer.
grandfather Mustapha," he stammered.

ie young sergeant scribbled in his notebook.

Did he give you the bomb?" the woman went on.
d he help you put it on?"

Y-yes," the boy said. "Grandfather Mustapha
. . . some other men . . ."

Who were they?" the IDF sergeant barked, step-
forward.

he boy cowered back on the table, clamping his lips
ther. The colonel shot the sergeant a quick glare
raised a hand to make him back off. Then she
ed until the boy had stopped trembling before
king to him again.

Jamal. Do you know why your grandfather and
. . . friends . . . told you to blow up the bus full of
cent Israelis?"

he boy nodded, his wide dark eyes flicking from
to side. "Y-yes."

Why?"

Be-because!" the child blurted. "Grandfather Mus-
a says that all Jews hate all Muslims, and we are
slims, and we should not allow . . . allow people
hate us to—to tell us where . . . and how . . .

we can live in—in our own land. . . ." His ou
trailed off.

The IDF colonel sighed quietly again, then l
toward the boy. "Jamal. Do you want to know
thing interesting?" The boy looked at her withou
swering, but nodded. "My name is Magda Weis.
father, David, was a Jew. But my mother, Magd.
whom I was named, was a Muslim orphan girl
Yugoslavia. Her full name was Magda Noor Ma
tović. She was adopted and raised by an old Se
couple who took her in out of kindness after her
ents died. The old couple were Christians."

The IDF colonel paused. It was a lot of inform
for a frightened eleven-year-old to absorb.

But the Palestinian boy was intelligent, and surp
her with his comment: "So . . . you are . . . b.
Muslim and a Jew?"

Colonel Magda Weiss nodded. "Yes, I am.
and half."

Jamal's smooth young brow furrowed. "But
wear the uniform of a soldier of Israel."

"I live with my father's people," she explained.
inside, I am still half Jewish and half Muslim."

Jamal considered this, chewing his lip, then sai
think that would be very confusing."

Magda Weiss brushed a hank of salt-and-pepper
off her forehead and smiled. "Sometimes it is."

She sat in silence, gazing at Jamal Amin Snagi.
in turn, gazed back at her, reexamining her tanned
hard but kind, and sinewy forearms and militar
tigues and the big automatic pistol holstered on her
After a few minutes he spoke again:

"We can talk some more, if you'd like."

Magda lifted an eyebrow. "Oh? You don't min
Jamal shook his head. "No. I like talking to yo
Magda drew a deep breath, resettled herself or
chair, and smiled once more at the Palestinian bo

"I think that's a good idea, Jamal," she
"Let's talk."

"In wartime, Truth is so precious that She should always be attended by a bodyguard of lies."

—Winston Churchill
Teheran Conference, World War II

Notes

Chapter 1

1. This is a short extract, slightly modified for clarity, from an actual letter written by Palestinian Arab leader Haj Amin al-Husseini, the Grand Mufti of Jerusalem, to Adolph Hitler, leader of Nazi Germany, on January 20, 1941. For the complete, unaltered text of this historical document, see appendix B of Zvi Elpeleg's *The Grand Mufti: Haj Amin Al-Hussaini, Founder of the Palestinian National Movement* (London: Frank Cass & Co. Ltd., 1993).

2. Italy surrendered to the Allies in September 1943, barely six weeks after dictator Benito Mussolini had been removed from power by his own Fascist party. Under the new premier, Marshall Pietro Badoglio, Italy declared war on Germany—its former Axis partner—in October 1943. In response, German military forces proceeded to occupy the country, seizing Rome and other key cities.

3. Abwehr was the military intelligence branch of the regular German army, the Wehrmacht. Although controlled by Germany's political leadership, Hitler and his Nazi Party, the Wehrmacht was not a Nazi entity. The SS and its constituent intelligence and security branches, the SD and Gestapo, on the other hand, were entirely Nazi creations, devoted to the Fuehrer and the party rather than to the German nation as a whole.

4. This is a direct quote attributed to al-Husseini. (*Elpeleg.*)

Chapter 2

Special Operations Executive, or SOE, was the Brit-
espionage and sabotage organization authorized by
irchill and given by him the famous directive, "Set
ope ablaze." It was headed by General Sir Colin
Vean Gubbins. Its American counterpart was the Of-
of Strategic Services, or OSS—the WWII precursor
the CIA—headed by General William "Wild Bill"
iovan.

Jedburgh teams were joint American-British-French
imando units trained in clandestine warfare and in-
ded for insertion by parachute into occupied France
advance of the D-day invasion, where their mission
ild be to link up with the French Resistance and dis-
t the German military infrastructure in every way
sible.

Chapter 3

static line is a length of heavy webbing used to auto-
tically deploy a parachute. One end is attached to the
end of the packed parachute canopy, the other to an
hor point inside the aircraft. As the jumper or cargo
kage falls away from the aircraft, the static line pulls
canopy out of the pack tray, then breaks free as the
achute begins to fill with air.

Chapter 6

rman paratrooper.

e German invasion of the British-held island of Crete
the eastern Mediterranean Sea, in May 1941, was the
t large airborne operation of World War II. Deployed
d supplied entirely by air, a force of nearly twenty
iusand Fallschirmjager and glider troops were able to
est control of Crete from twenty-seven thousand Brit-
troops, mostly tough Australians and New Zealanders,
o initially fought the invaders to a standstill. Lack of
ective resupply eventually handicapped the British, and
y were forced to withdraw from the island. But the

victory cost the Germans dearly: sixteen thousa
were killed or wounded, and two hundred out
hundred transport aircraft were lost. Hitler was
palled by the casualty figures that he prohibited
operations in the future. It was the last major
airborne troops by Germany during World War

3. Literally, "assault rifle." The Sturmgewehr w
world's first true assault rifle, and the source of th
All well-known assault rifles of the last half of the
eth century—the AK-47, the M-16, the Galil—a
descendants of the Sturmgewehr.

Chapter 9

1. Dr. Ivan Ribar was a distinguished Yugoslav inte
and politician who became a key member of the C
nist Partisans during World War II. Both his so
Lola Ribar and Jurica Ribar, were Partisan comn
who were killed while fighting the Nazi invaders.
revered as heroes of the long and successful Y
Communist resistance to the Third Reich and its

Chapter 10

1. A Tyrolean traverse is a horizontal rope stretched
over a gap, to which climbers and equipment ca
be secured by carabiner or block and pulled acros

Chapter 13

1. The enlarged Kingdom of Croatia, originally forme
the help of the invading Axis Italians under Mu
was ruled by one of the most murderous racists in
pean history, Ante Pavelić. Pavelić was the leader
Ustashe—a band of Croatian fascists whose goal
eliminate the Serbian minority in Croatia, along
its Jews and Gypsies. Perversely, the Ustashe h
qualms about murdering Muslims as well, even
both Croatian Catholics and Muslims served in
(racially and ethnically separate) German combat

Chapter 14

A prusik hitch is a method of securing a thin line to a thicker one with a knot that binds when tightened and slides when loosened, enabling a climber to ascend a vertical rope without supporting his/her weight by main strength alone.

Chapter 22

Pre-WWII British Prime Minister Neville Chamberlain has gone down in history, perhaps not quite fairly, as the man who was soft on Hitler during Germany's ever increasing aggression in the late 1930s. Famously, he favored a policy of appeasement rather than confrontation, which enabled the Nazi dictator to retain newly annexed territories such as the Sudetenland and Czechoslovakia and to continue to build the Third Reich's war machine. The then-unpopular Winston Churchill's trenchant comment was that it was utter folly to try to appease a ruthless dictator. He was right.

Waffen-SS/U.S. Army Rank Conversion Chart

Schütze	Private
Sturmmann	Private First Class
Rottenfuehrer	Corporal
Unterscharfuehrer	Sergeant
Scharfuehrer	Staff Sergeant
Hauptscharfuehrer	Master Sergeant
Stabsscharfuehrer	Sergeant Major
Untersturmfuehrer	Second Lieutenant
Obersturmfuehrer	First Lieutenant
Hauptsturmfuehrer	Captain
Sturmbannfuehrer	Major
Obersturmbannfuehrer	Lieutenant Colonel
Standartenfuehrer	Colonel
Brigadefuehrer	Brigadier General
Gruppenfuehrer	Major General
Obergruppenfuehrer	Lieutenant General
Oberst-Gruppenfuehrer	General
Reichsfuehrer-SS	(No equivalent; title reserved for SS head Heinrich Himmler)

Military action from
JOHN MANNOCK

"John Mannock gives readers a compelling and
stereotype-breaking story...With a
combination of action, war, love and betrayal."
—*Soundings*

IRON COFFIN
0-451-21140-5
Far below the surface.
Far from the Fatherland.
And too close to the enemy for comfort.

THE SEN-TOKU RAID
0-451-21440-4
Underwater Demolition Team operative
Lieutenant Charlton Randall and his crew must
destroy a sea base of subs aimed at
Washington, D.C.—or die trying.

Available wherever books are sold or at
penguin.com

s114

Ø SIGNET

"Brilliant...breathless high adventure...by the mo
romantic of all the top thriller writers!" —*Time*

#1 International Bestselle
KEN FOLLETT

"Follett goes down with the ease and impact of
a well-prepared martini." —*New York Times*

Available wherever books are sold or at
penguin.com

S439/Fo